Edward Cre__y,

The Imperial and Colonial Constitutions
of the Britannic Empire

Edward Creasy

The Imperial and Colonial Constitutions of the Britannic Empire

Reprint of the original.

1st Edition 2023 | ISBN: 978-3-36815-026-6

Verlag (Publisher): Outlook Verlag GmbH, Zeilweg 44, 60439 Frankfurt, Deutschland
Vertretungsberechtigt (Authorized to represent): E. Roepke, Zeilweg 44, 60439 Frankfurt, Deutschland
Druck (Print): Books on Demand GmbH, In de Tarpen 42, 22848 Norderstedt, Deutschland

THE CONSTITUTIONS

OF

THE BRITANNIC EMPIRE.

LONDON: PRINTED BY
SPOTTISWOODE AND CO., NEW-STREET SQUARE
AND PARLIAMENT STREET

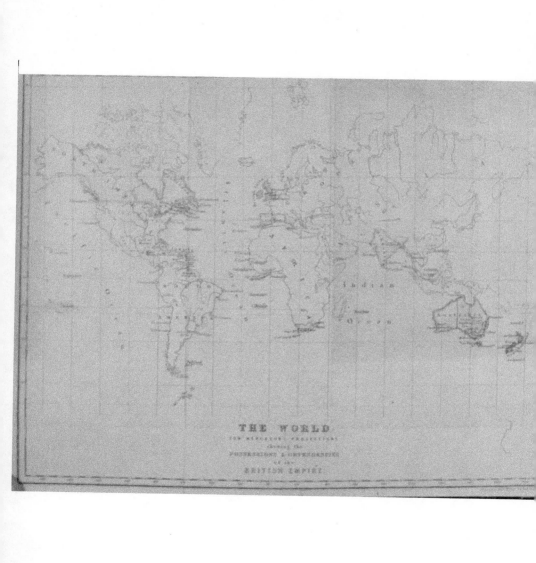

THE WORLD
(ON MERCATOR PROJECTION)
showing the
POSSESSIONS & DEPENDENCIES
of the
BRITISH EMPIRE

THE

IMPERIAL AND COLONIAL CONSTITUTIONS

OF

THE BRITANNIC EMPIRE,

INCLUDING INDIAN INSTITUTIONS.

BY

SIR EDWARD CREASY, M.A.

AUTHOR OF 'THE RISE AND PROGRESS OF THE ENGLISH CONSTITUTION,'
'THE HISTORY OF ENGLAND,' ETC.

' May He, who hath built up this Britannic Empire
to a glorious and enviable height, with all her
daughter lands about her, stay us in this felicity!'

MILTON.

LONDON:

LONGMANS, GREEN, AND CO.

1872.

DEDICATED BY THE AUTHOR

TO

SIR HERCULES ROBINSON, K.C.M.G.

IN RESPECT FOR HIS STATESMANSHIP

AND

GRATITUDE FOR HIS FRIENDSHIP.

PREFACE.

In 1853 I published a little book on 'The Rise and Progress of the English Constitution,' which received an indulgent share of public favour, and is still, I believe, much used in education. It dealt with English affairs only; but it was my intention to complete it as a Manual of the Constitutions of the Britannic Empire, by adding notices of Scottish and of Anglo-Irish institutions, and of the successive Unions of England with Scotland, and of Great Britain with Ireland. I knew also that such a Manual ought to comprise notices of the institutions of our Colonies and of India; and that it ought to explain the operations of Imperial rule over the dominions of Her Britannic Majesty which lie beyond the British Isles. I accumulated from time to time materials for this purpose. My change of abode, from England to Ceylon, in 1860, delayed the execution of this and other projects; but a long residence in an important colony, which is much

connected with India, has caused me to examine
Colonial and Indian affairs with increased attention ;
and has, I hope, improved my judgment of them.

The two first chapters of the present volume
deal with the British Constitution, that is to say,
with our home Constitution after the Unions of
1707 and 1800. Explanatory accounts are given
of the Scottish and of the Anglo-Irish systems of
government before those periods respectively. I
have completed the account of the Imperial Parliament in the Home Department up to the present
time, by a brief statement of the chief provisions
of the Reform Bill of 1867.

The rest of the book is devoted to the institutions
of the great mass of our Empire, which is unrepresented in the Imperial Parliament, to the institutions
of the Colonies and to those of India, and to the
manner in which the authority of the Crown and
of Parliament is exercised over them.

This book is far from pretending to the ambitious
character of a history of the growth of our Colonial
and Indian Empire ; but I found it necessary to
sketch the means by which the principal provinces
of our transmarine dominions were acquired, and
also how some were lost.

Some Maps are inserted in this volume ; and the careful student will probably find them the most useful parts of it. By continually referring to them, and by frequently copying them, he will get the main features of the geography of our Empire mapped upon his brain ; and he will then acquire historical. statistical, and political knowledge respecting each part of that Empire with ease, perspicacity, and retentiveness. Otherwise he may experience the truth of the remarks of the old Greek historian Polybius, in the thirty-seventh section of his third book, that 'when the student has no geographical knowledge of the places mentioned, a talk about places is to him as if his would-be informant spoke in an unknown tongue, or uttered mere gibberish.'

E. S. CREASY.

LAKE COTTAGE, COLOMBO:
December 6, 1871.

CONTENTS.

CHAPTER III.

CHAPTER IV.

CHAPTER V.

CHAPTER VIII.

DIRECTIONS TO THE BINDER.

IMPERIAL AND COLONIAL CONSTITUTIONS

OF THE

BRITANNIC EMPIRE.

———+———

CHAPTER I.

Distinction between the British Constitution and the Constitution of the British Empire—Different Functions of the Imperial Parliament —Its far-reaching Supremacy—Sense in which the word 'Parliament' is used—Variety of Colonial Constitutions—Crown Colonies and Crown Dominions—Parliament supreme over these also—Extent of British Transmarine Empire—Population—Variety of Races and Creeds—Practical Interest of Englishmen in the Condition of India and the Colonies—Knowledge of the British Constitution should be gained before studying the Constitution of the British Empire and Colonial Constitutions—British Constitution that of the United Kingdom—Need of superadding to Knowledge of the English Constitution a Knowledge of the Unions with Scotland and Ireland and their Effects—General Plan of the Work.

EVERY ENGLISHMAN ought not only to know the principles of the Constitution of his country, but also to know the principles of 'the Constitution of the British Empire as distinguished from the Constitution of Britain.' These last words are the words of Burke. They will be found in his great speech on American taxation, which was delivered by him on

B

April 19, 1774. No one has ever pointed out more forcibly than Burke did in a few sentences of that speech, the difference between the functions of our Parliament in respect of the government of the Kingdom of Great Britain, and the functions of the same Parliament in respect of those colonies which possess local representative Legislatures. Burke says : 'The Parliament of Great Britain sits at the head of her extensive empire in two capacities: one is the local Legislature of this island, providing for all things at home immediately, and by no other instrument than the executive power ; the other, and I think her nobler capacity, is what I call her Imperial character, in which, as from the throne of heaven, she superintends all the several inferior Legislatures, and guides and controls them all, without annihilating any.'

This imperial paramount authority of the British Parliament extends over *all* the transmarine dominions of the British Crown ; not only over the colonies which have representative Legislatures, such as the old American colonies, of which Burke was speaking, but also over the very extensive regions, where no such representative assemblies have been established. The Imperial Parliament is supreme over all. It may be useful to premise that the word '*Parliament*' is used here, not in the sense, which it often bears in constitutional histories and treatises when limitations on royal authority are discussed. The word '*Parliament*,' in such cases, frequently means the two Houses of Lords and Commons as contradistinguished from the Crown. But in the complete and correct sense of the word (in which it will be used throughout in this treatise when the authority of the Imperial Parliament is spoken of) '*Parliament*' means a Parliament composed of King, Lords and Commons. The co-operation of the Sovereign in parliamentary proceedings with regard to the colonies and other transmarine regions of the Britannic Empire is as essential (save as to parliamentary impeachment) as that of either of the Houses.

There are many great differences and variations with regard to the amount of local self-government as to legislation, as to taxation, and other matters, which the colonies and other transmarine portions of the British Empire respectively possess. These will be pointed out and explained in a subsequent part of this treatise. But it may be well at once to remark that much of the British Empire consists of colonies called Crown Colonies, and of other dominions obtained by cession or conquest, which are considered to be dominions of the Crown. The King or Queen of England for the time being ordinarily rules all these by virtue of his or her regal prerogative and authority. But still this royal prerogative authority of the Crown is subordinate to the authority of Parliament. The Crown, in its government of each Crown colony, of each Indian province, and of other transmarine Crown dominions, must follow and conform to such statutes, if any, as the Imperial Parliament of King, Lords, and Commons has made on the subject.[1]   And the governors and other officers, whom the Crown appoints in any part of the Empire, are liable to parliamentary impeachment for misconduct in their office.   The case is similar with regard to the supreme and final administration of justice in lawsuits and other judicial matters arising in the colonial and other transmarine courts.   It is the settled prerogative of the Crown to receive appeals in all these cases.   The form of the appeal is to the Queen in Council.   It is by her Majesty that the order is given for the confirmation, or reversal, or modification of the proceedings in the court below.   But the order is made on the advice of the Judicial Committee of the Privy Council, and . Parliament has prescribed how that Committee shall be constituted.[2]

[1] See Lord Mansfield's judgment in Campbell v. Hall; Cowper's 'Reports,' 204; and vol. xx. 'State Trials,' p. 304. See Forsyth's 'Cases on Constitutional Law,' p. 21; and Bowyer's 'Constitutional Law,' p. 46.

[2] Statutes 3 and 4 William IV., cxliii. There are other statutes as to this Court and its functions.   See Bowyer's 'Constitutional Law,' p. 127; Forsyth's 'Cases on Constitutional Law,' ch. xi.; and the notes, which are peculiarly valuable. The cases there cited of

I have already alluded to the variety of the colonial and other transmarine members of the British Empire. The vastness of their aggregate territorial amount will be better judged of by a glance at the map than by any elaborate statistical description. It is sufficient to quote here the estimate made by a writer of excellent authority,[1] that 'the colonies and dependencies of Great Britain embrace about one third of the surface of the globe, and nearly a fourth of its population.' Among the hundred and seventy millions of our fellow-subjects, who inhabit or reside in these regions, may be found members of almost every existent race and almost every known creed.[2]

Over all these myriads, and over all their countries (countries in many cases capable of supporting mani-

Cuvillier v. Aylwin, 2 Knapp 78, and of The Queen v. Alloo Paroo, 3 Moore Ind. App., 488, show very strongly how subordinate the authority of the Crown alone is to the authority of Parliament, i.e., of Crown, Lords, and Commons, combined. The Crown cannot by its mere prerogative abandon its power of receiving an appeal, and thereby deprive a subject of his right to appeal ; but the ' Crown may abandon a prerogative, however high and essential to public justice and valuable to the subject, if it is authorised by statute to abandon it.'

[1] ' Statesman's Year Book ' for 1870, by F. Marten, p. 273.

[2] The Queen of England has been termed the greatest Mahometan Sovereign in the world, meaning that she has more Mahometan subjects than any other Sovereign has. In a similar sense the Queen may be said to be the greatest Brahminist Sovereign in the world, and (with the exception of the Emperor of China) the greatest Buddhist sovereign.

fold myriads more), the Imperial Parliament of the United Kingdom of Great Britain and Ireland is supreme. There can scarcely be, at the present time, an educated Englishman, who has not, or who cannot, if he pleases, acquire a vote in the selection of Members of the Commons House of that Parliament. It is not too much to expect of him that he should qualify himself mentally for such a vote, by the possession of at least general knowledge as to the constitutional condition, not only of his own country in which he dwells, but also of ' her daughter-lands ' (to use the Miltonic phrase), of the colonies and other transmarine British dominions, which the votes and resolutions of the House of Commons may influence so largely for weal or for woe. Another cause which ought to make a fair general knowledge of the political *status* of India and of the colonies widespread among our middle classes, is the increasing practical connection between the population of the home country and the populations of these distant possessions. How few families are there, which have not some member or connection residing in India, or in one of the colonies, and pursuing there some official, or mercantile, or other career. How few families are there, in which appointment, or employment, or speculation in one of those lands is not looked forward to as the means by which one of the rising generation is to get his living. Moreover, a residence in most of these countries by no means implies the same amount of exile and severance from a man's native land, as was the case formerly. Facilities of communication have increased, and are increasing so rapidly, that the Colonist and the Anglo-Indian may now enjoy frequent periods of temporary return to England, besides the hoped-for season of rest (which most cherish in expectation) when the pension shall have been earned, or the competence secured, when the chain of care shall be unwound, when the mind shall lay aside its load, and when the weary wanderer shall repose in his own household in his old home.[1] There are certainly some colonies, in which the proportion of settlers, in the strict sense of the word, is becoming larger; that is, of colonists who regard their new abode as a permanent home, and who design it to be the home of their children and their children's children. But these are precisely the colonies, which have the most liberal representative institutions, and in which constitutional rights are most dearly valued. All causes concur in giving increased interest to the study of the political condition of their populations, and to the study of their political relations with the Imperial Government itself.

No one can hope to understand these things, unless

[1] Oh quid solutis est beatius curis,
Quum mens onus reponit ; ac peregrino
Labore fessi venimus Larem ad nostrum,
Desideratoque acquiescimus lecto ?—*Catullus*.

he has a fair general knowledge of the component parts of the Imperial Parliament, and of the powers and functions of these parts relatively to each other. In other words, before the student begins his scrutiny of Parliament in its Imperial character, he ought to understand it in its character of the Parliament of the United Kingdom of Great Britain and Ireland. He ought to be acquainted with the rise, the progress, and the main principles of the English Constitution, and also of the British Constitution. By which last phrase (though not strictly accurate) is generally understood the Constitution of the United Kingdom of Great Britain and Ireland after the unions of England with Scotland and with Ireland respectively.

I have in another work (of which this is, in some respect, a supplement) treated of the Rise and Progress of the English Constitution. The successive unions of England with Scotland (1707), and of the United Kingdom of England and Scotland with Ireland (1799), made that Constitution the British Constitution, as now it is commonly called, meaning the Constitution of the United Kingdom of Great Britain and Ireland; and the Parliament of this United Kingdom of Great Britain and Ireland is the Imperial Parliament.

The principles of the British Constitution are substantially the same that grew up in England as the principles of the English Constitution. But the composition, as well as the numbers of both our Houses of Parliament, has been affected by the unions; and there are still some distinctions as to political and legal institutions and rights between the respective kingdoms making up the United Kingdom. In order to give a full and clear understanding of the British Constitution and of the Imperial Parliament, it will be useful to begin with a recapitulation of the leading principles of the English Constitution. Next it will be serviceable to sketch the Constitutions of Scotland and Ireland before their respective unions with England, and to observe the main provisions of the compact, by which each union was regulated. We must see to what matters the union extended, and what matters were left unaffected by it. We shall have to consider, also, how far the introduction of the Scottish element influenced the character of the old English Constitution, and how far the introduction of the Irish element influenced the character of the Constitution of the Kingdom of Great Britain. We must finally advert to the important constitutional changes that have been effected during the present century by the Reform Bills of 1832 and 1867–68, and other enactments. We shall then be in a position to comprehend and remember the Imperial Constitution of the United Kingdom itself. We can afterwards proceed to the more enlarged view of this Constitution, as it affects those parts of

the Empire which lie beyond the territorial limits of
the United Kingdom.   In this last part of our work
we must necessarily take a general view of the circumstances, under which these transmarine dominions
have been acquired: and it will be useful to add a
brief notice of the form of local government now
actually existing in each of these dependencies of the
Kingdom of Great Britain and Ireland.   To do all
this in detail would require the writing of many
volumes ; but it may be possible in a few chapters to
prepare a sound and plain first platform of information on the subject, to which each student may from
other stores superadd for himself a more copious and
elaborate treasure-house of knowledge.

CHAPTER II.

Primary Fundamental Principles of the English Constitution—
Royal Prerogatives—Exaggerated under the Tudors and First Stuarts
—Popular Resistance—Close of the Struggle between People and
Crown in 1688—The Bill of Rights—Union with Scotland—Early
Scottish Constitutional History—The Scottish Parliaments—Effects
of the Reformation in Scotland—Terms of the Union—Irish Union
—Early State of the Anglo-Irish and the mere Irish—Irish Parlia-
ments—Poyning's Law—Attempt to introduce Protestantism—Effect
of the Revolution of 1688, and of the Battle of the Boyne—The
Penal Laws—Rising Spirit of Independence in the Anglo-Irish—
Relaxation of the Penal Laws—The Irish Parliament attains its
Independence—Its great Leader, Grattan, advocates Catholic Emancipation—Union of Ireland with Great Britain—Terms of the Union
—The Catholic Emancipation Bill—Effects of the Reforms of 1832
on Scotland and Ireland—Movements for further Reform between
1835 and 1867—New Electoral Laws of 1867 and 1868—Present
State of the Imperial Parliament.

THE main object of this chapter is to see how the
English Constitution became the British Constitution, i.e., the Constitution of the United Kingdom of
Great Britain and Ireland. It may, however, be
useful to preface this by a few sentences reminding
the reader of what the acknowledged great principles
of the English Constitution were before the union
with Scotland in 1707.

Ever since the reign of Edward I. (if not earlier)
certain fundamental principles of the English Constitution had been established. These are:—

1. The government of the country by a hereditary

sovereign, ruling with limited powers, and bound to summon and consult a Parliament for the whole realm, comprising hereditary peers and elective representatives of the Commons.

2. That without the sanction of Parliament no tax of any kind can be imposed, and no law can be made, repealed, or altered.

3. That no man be arbitrarily fined or imprisoned; that no man's property or liberty be impaired; and that no man be in any way punished, except after a lawful trial; and that the regular common law mode of trial is by a jury consisting of a man's equals in the eye of the law.

4. That all subjects, except the actual great peers who sit as such in Parliament, are commoners with equal rights in the eye of the law.[1]

By the time when the Tudor dynasty acquired the throne of England, at the end of the Wars of the Roses (1485), the following constitutional rules, also, had been brought into operation :—

1. The division of the High Court of Parliament into two Houses, one called the House of Lords, consisting of the spiritual peers and of the temporal peers; the other called the House of Commons, consisting of the knights of the shires and of

---

[1] I have discussed these subjects in ' The Rise and Progress of the English Constitution,' chapters xi., xii., and xiii., and in my ' History of England,' vol. i., ch. xiii., pp. 443–175.

the elected citizens and burgesses of the towns that possessed the parliamentary franchise.[1] The Houses were certainly thus divided early in Edward III.'s reign, and probably before the reign of Edward II.

2. That Parliaments ought to be summoned frequently.

3. The right of the Commons to impeach and to bring to trial before the House of Lords the Ministers and servants of the Crown.

4. That no one, who has violated the rights of the subject, can justify himself in our courts by proving that he acted under the authority of the Crown.[2] Another maxim closely connected with this is the maxim that the King can only act through a responsible Minister.

Under these restrictions (and some others, which are partly of too little consequence and partly too much controverted for setting out here) the Crown exercised supreme authority. In other words, the Government was and is a monarchy, though a limited monarchy. The King represented the State, and acted both *for* the State and *as* the State in all that relates to the outer life of the State, that is to say,

---

[1] For the importance of the 'Bicameral System,' see Lieber on 'Civil Liberty and Self-Government,' p. 157.

[2] For the great practical importance of this rule (which was peculiar to England), see Lieber on 'Civil Liberty and Self-Government,' p. 91.

in its dealings with other States. The King made war or peace. The King received and sent ambassadors. The King commanded all the military and naval forces of the State. The King had the dominion over all acquired territories. The King appointed and changed the high officers of state, both judicial and ministerial. No subject could leave the realm against the King's will. The King convened and the King prorogued or dissolved the Parliament. He granted all dignities and honours. He could create peers and add members to the House of Lords. He could grant charters of incorporation for trading and other purposes. He had many other prerogatives, important to enumerate and study when we are specially dealing with the English Constitution, but not indispensable for citation in this portion of our present work.

During the Tudor period (1485–1603), Parliaments were summoned much less regularly, than had been the case under the last ten Plantagenets. It would be going beyond the limits of the present work to discuss how far the liberties of the English nation really retrograded during this time, and the causes of such retrogression. Suffice it to say, that very startling doctrines of high royal prerogatives were often asserted, and sometimes enforced, by the Tudor Sovereigns and their Ministers and courtiers, but by no means universally admitted by the representatives of the people. When the dynasty of the Stuarts succeeded (1603), high-flying theories of the transcendental power of the Crown were put forward still more offensively; but they were encountered by a spirit of resistance that grew fiercer and more determined, until the long struggle between Crown and people, after many alternations, was terminated at the Revolution of 1688. I allude to these topics here (and I only allude to them) because the century before 1688 was the period of the laying the foundations of our American colonial dominion, and the planting the seeds of our Indian empire. The student who examines the charters granted to the early English settlers in America, and to the early English traders in the East, will find it instructive, and indeed essential, to watch the prevalent or conflicting opinions in England, at the date of each grant, as to royal powers with respect to granting transmarine territories and exclusive privileges of settling and of trading, of imposing laws and exacting payments.

Resuming our series of views of the condition of the English Constitution at special epochs, we shall find that soon after the Revolution of 1688 (that is, when the Bill of Rights had been passed in December 1688, and the Act of Settlement in 1701) many more constitutional maxims of the highest importance for the liberty of the subject had been finally established. Foremost among these is the power of

Parliament over the throne, even to changing and determining the line of succession to the throne.[1] Next is the maxim that it is illegal to raise or to keep a standing army within the kingdom in time of peace, unless with consent of Parliament. The Bill of Rights also declared that Parliaments ought to be held frequently, that elections of members of Parliament ought to be free, that there ought to be freedom of speech in Parliament, and that no man should be called in question in any court or place out of Parliament for the part taken by him in the debates or proceedings in Parliament. It declared the subject's right to petition. It ordained that excessive bail ought not to be required, nor excessive fines imposed, nor cruel and unusual punishments inflicted. It abolished the power of the Crown to dispense by regal authority with laws or the execution of laws. The Act of Settlement gave additional safeguards to freedom. One was, that the judges should not be removable at the royal will, but that addresses for their removal from both Houses of Parliament should be requisite.

It was when the English Constitution had been thus matured, and when the long struggle between the Crown and the people had ended, that Scotland

---

[1] This had long before been the doctrine of the best English statesmen. See Sir Thomas More's opinion on it in 2 Froude, p. 270. But the Stuarts and their partisans had introduced the theories of divine right and indefeasible hereditary succession.

was united with England into one kingdom (1707). Both realms had been brought under the same sovereign since the time when James VI. of Scotland became James I. of England; but their Legislatures had been separate, and they had continued to be distinct sovereign states.

The early constitutional history of Scotland before the population of the Lowlands became Anglo-Saxon, is obscure and unimportant. Anglo-Saxons overspread southern Scotland during the seventh, eighth, ninth, and tenth centuries; and institutions resembling those of the Saxons in England became predominant in Scotland, except in the Highlands, where the Celtic tribes of mountaineers preserved their own language and their own wild usages. After the Norman conquest of England, the disputes of the kings and barons in this country caused great numbers of men of the Norman race to migrate into the territories possessed by the Scottish kings. They were welcomed there by the Scottish sovereigns, and received liberal grants of land; so that the Scottish nobility became almost as largely tinged with Norman blood as the nobility of England. Feudalism was established in Scotland, and the Scottish kings, like other feudal kings, had their great councils of Bishops, Abbots, and Barons. The Scots, in imitation, as it seems, of the English, called their great councils 'Parliaments;' and representatives of the boroughs attended the Scottish Parliaments early in the fourteenth century. Representation of the small tenants-in-chief by chosen members of their own body for each sheriffdom, analogous to our knights of the shire, was recognised by a law passed a century later; but the practice seems to have been irregular. None but tenants-in-chief had a voice in these elections.

These Parliaments, presided over by the King, passed laws, and sometimes granted subsidies. They differed from the English Parliaments in two very important matters, besides others of less moment.

1. All the members of a Scottish Parliament, Spiritual Peers, Lay Barons, representatives of the minor tenants-in-chief, and representatives of boroughs, all sat and voted together in a single House.

2. By an usage, which had become established in the fifteenth century, if not earlier, all matters to be laid before the Scottish Parliament were first considered by a small body or committee, called 'The Lords of the Articles.' Without the recommendation of the Lords of the Articles nothing could be submitted to Parliament. The usual or regular course for the appointment of this important body was election by the Parliament; which generally nominated eight spiritual peers, eight lay peers, eight representatives of the boroughs, and eight great

officers of the Crown. But various means[1] were used to give the Crown the virtual appointment of a majority of the Lords of the Articles. Charles I., in 1633, introduced a device which made this certain. It was stopped in 1641, but re-established in 1661, after the Restoration of Charles II. After the Revolution of 1688, the Lords of the Articles were finally abolished.

The Scottish kings, from the time when their country's independence was secured by Bruce, to the time when James VI. of Scotland acquired the English Crown, were engaged in an almost incessant struggle against the overbearing power of their turbulent nobility. The Commons generally sided with the Crown, but they were not of much might; and it was not until the development of the stern spirit of independence, which the Reformation awoke among the Scottish people, that the opinions and feelings of their middle and lower classes became important in determining Scottish legislation and remodelling Scottish institutions.[2]

---

[1] They are detailed in a note of Robertson's ' History of Scotland,' book i. See also Hallam's ' Constitutional History,' vol. iii., ch. xvii.

[2] Mr. Froude has in his tenth volume, p. 456, nobly done justice to the transformation which John Knox, above all others, wrought in the character of the Scottish community. He says of Knox :— ' Ilis was the voice which taught the peasant of the Lothians that he was a free man, the equal in the sight of God with the proudest peer or prelate that had trampled on his forefathers. He it was that

The storm of the strife of religions, which Luther, Calvin, and other Reformers raised in the sixteenth century, was nowhere more violent than in Scotland. It ended in the complete overthrow not only of Roman Catholicism, but of Episcopalianism, so far as regards State connection and State support. There were several alternations of success in the contest. Presbyterianism was established in the interval between the death of James V. (1542) and the return of his daughter Mary Queen of Scots from France to Scotland in 1561. James VI. (the James I. of England) succeeded in reviving Episcopacy to a considerable extent; and Charles I. endeavoured to make the revival more complete. This was checked by the civil wars; but, after the Restoration of the Stuarts, Episcopacy was set up again in Scotland, to fall again at the Revolution of 1688, when Presbyterianism was permanently re-established.

The Union of the two kingdoms had often been projected, and it was at last effected in Queen Anne's reign. Twenty-five Articles of Union were agreed to by the Parliaments of both nations (1706).

In accordance with them, and with Acts passed by the two Parliaments, the kingdoms of England and Scotland became one kingdom, by the name of ' The

raised the poor commons of his country into a stern and rugged people, who might be hard, narrow, superstitious, and fanatical, but who nevertheless were men whom neither king, noble, nor priest could force again to submit to tyranny.'

United Kingdom of Great Britain.' It was ordained that the succession to the monarchy of Great Britain should be the same as was before settled with regard to that of England; that the United Kingdom should have one Parliament; that Scotland should be represented in the Upper House of the United Parliament by sixteen Peers chosen for life by the Scottish nobles from among their own body; that Scotland should be represented in the Commons House of the United Parliament by forty-five members, two-thirds to be elected by the Scottish counties and one-third by the Scottish boroughs; that the Crown should be restrained from creating any more peers of Scotland; that all privileges of trade should belong equally to both nations; that navigation and intercourse between them should be free; that both parts of the United Kingdom should be subject to the same excise duties and to the same customs, export and import; that where England raises two millions by a land-tax Scotland should raise 48,000*l.*, and so, in like proportion; that the maintenance of the Episcopal Church in England and the maintenance of the Presbyterian Church in Scotland shall be for ever observed as fundamental and essential conditions of Union.

Scotland retained her old municipal law, which is very different from English law. The Roman law, to a very great extent, supplies the principles of the law of Scotland.

One very important effect of the Union with Scotland was that it was thenceforth impossible to maintain, with regard to the Imperial realm of Great Britain, either in theory or practice, the principle of complete unity of Church and State. Scotland became one kingdom with England; but the Scottish Church continued to be Presbyterian, and, as such, differed widely from the Anglican Episcopalian Establishment. This remarkable, though partial, recognition of the principle of equality as to political rights among members of the same realm, who differ from one another as to creeds, must have had some effect in promoting a tolerant and liberal spirit in the Legislature, in the tribunals, and in the councils of the Imperial Kingdom as to exempting colonists and settlers abroad from restrictions and disabilities on account of the church or sect, to which they belonged or did not belong. Many of these colonies were themselves very intolerant, each in its own little sphere, as to such matters; but the home Government, in its regulations affecting religion in its transmarine dominions, during the seventeenth and eighteenth centuries, was usually fair and sensible. It has, in fact, generally been in advance of the average standard of public opinion on such matters in Europe for the time being.

We now come to the Union of Ireland with the United Kingdom of Great Britain, and to the introduction of the latest new national element in our Imperial Parliament.

It would be a long and melancholy task to give even a sketch of the constitutional history of Ireland before the Union. The forms of the English Constitution were introduced there soon after the commencement of the conquest of the island by the English; but they were only introduced among the English conquerors and settlers themselves and the Ostmen, the descendants of the old Danish pillagers, who had occupied and inhabited the maritime towns. These, collectively the Anglo-Irish, as it is convenient to term them, were considered to be under the common law of England, and to possess all its rights. The provisions of the Great Charter were extended to Ireland, and copies of it sent over there soon after its grant at Runnymede. The Justiciaries, or the Law.—Deputies of the English kings convened Parliaments in Ireland, to which the prelates and barons, and the knights of shires and burgesses, were summoned, as in England. But the native Irish, with few exceptions, were not considered as within English law, or as entitled to rights such as those of Englishmen. The Anglo-Irish themselves degenerated rapidly from the civilisation which they had brought with them, and in many instances assumed the wild usages and the garb and the language of the Celtic natives. The Tudor sovereigns of England made vigorous, and not wholly unsuccessful attempts to stem the progress of Irish anarchy, and to maintain an orderly, or at least a strong government in the dependent island.   One of the ablest of the English governors in Henry VII.'s reign caused an Irish Parliament to pass a very important statute, called, after him, Poyning's Law (1495).   It redressed many abuses ; but its most important constitutional provision was an enactment that no Parliament should thenceforth be held in Ireland until the statutes, which it was to pass, had been submitted to the King and his Council in England, and had received the royal approval.

After the Reformation, the English Government attempted to force the Anglican Church upon the Irish, who were almost all devoted adherents of the Pope ; and the animosity of religious strife was now added to the old animosity of the natives against their conquerors.   Very many, however, of the Anglo-Irish clung to the old faith, and took part with their Celtic co-religionists against the Protestants.   Rebellions and massacres multiplied, followed by reconquests and merciless retaliations.   When at last James II. made his final efforts to establish Roman Catholicism and despotic rule in his dominions, the great mass of the Irish nation sided with their king ; but the small body of Irish Protestants were his most determined adversaries.   The results of the Revolu-

tion of 1688, and of King William's decisive victory
over James at the Boyne in 1690, were to leave
Ireland in complete subordination to England. A
series of penal laws were passed by William's Parliament, and aggravated by subsequent legislation in
the reigns of Anne and George I., which, beside
other heavy inflictions of penalties, forfeitures, and
disabilities, took from the great majority of the Irish,
as Roman Catholics, almost all political rights of
every kind. The Irish Protestants had the Irish
Parliament to themselves. But they soon began to
chafe against the fetters which the Crown and the
United Parliament of England and Scotland kept
over them; and a struggle for Irish parliamentary
independence began, in which Molyneux and Swift
were, by their writings, the earliest champions on the
Irish, or rather on the Anglo-Irish, side; for nothing
could exceed the scorn which these Protestant Irish
patriots exhibited towards the mere Irish, ' the Papist
multitude,' as they termed the bulk of the nation.
Some relaxations of the English rule were obtained
early in the reign of George III.; and the alarm
caused by the American War and by the formidable
armament of the Irish volunteers, on whom the Government, amid the disasters of that war, had been
obliged to rely for the defence of the island against
French invasion, obtained much ampler concessions
before and during 1782. Complete legislative inde-

pendence was granted to the Irish Parliament. The great leader of the Irish Protestants, in their contest for national independence, was Henry Grattan. He, more wise and more generous than many of his compeers, sought at the same time to deliver his Roman Catholic fellow-countrymen from their political disabilities. He condensed and decided the whole subject in a single sentence, when, in his speech on February 20, 1782, he told the Irish House of Commons, ' The question is, whether we shall be a Protestant settlement or an Irish nation.' In 1793, the parliamentary franchise was given to Roman Catholics ; but they continued for more than thirty years more to be ineligible as members ; nor could peers of that creed take their places in Parliament.

The experience of the working of two independent Legislatures side by side—one in Great Britain, one in Ireland—was by no means favourable, during the period of nearly twenty years for which that system lasted. Other troubles also, unconnected with that system, towards the end of the eighteenth century, afflicted Ireland and alarmed Britain. After the suppression of the rebellion of 1798, it was resolved by the Government that Ireland should be no more a separate realm, but that it should be united with Great Britain, as Scotland had been formerly united with England. This is not the place for comments on the circumstances under which the Union was effected, or for considerations of what might have been the result of the conciliatory measures, by which the statesmen, who projected the Union, designed that measure to be accompanied, but which they were unable to carry.[1] I will proceed at once to set out the main provisions of the Union between Great Britain and Ireland which was completed in 1800.

They are as follows:—

1. 'That on the 1st day of January, 1801, and for ever after, the kingdoms of Great Britain and Ireland shall be united into one kingdom, by the name of the United Kingdom of Great Britain and Ireland.

2. 'That the succession to the Imperial Crown of the said United Kingdom shall continue limited in the same manner as the succession to the Crown of the two kingdoms was before settled, and according to the terms of the Union between England and Scotland.

3. 'That the United Kingdom shall be represented in one and the same Parliament, to be called "The Parliament of the United Kingdom of Great Britain and Ireland."

4. 'That four lords spiritual, by rotation of ses-

---

[1] The student who wishes to make himself acquainted with Irish constitutional history will find benefit from a very careful study of the eighteenth chapter of Hallam's 'Constitutional History,' vol. iii., and by then studying the sixteenth chapter of Sir Erskine May's 'Constitutional History,' vol. ii.

sions,[1] and twenty-eight lords temporal of Ireland, elected for life by the peers of Ireland, shall sit and vote, on the part of Ireland, in the House of Lords; and that one hundred commoners (two for each county, two for Dublin and Cork each, one for the University of Trinity College, and one for each of the thirty-one most considerable cities, towns, and boroughs) be the number to sit and vote, on the part of Ireland, in the House of Commons of the said United Kingdom.' [But by Stat. 2 & 3 William IV., c. 88, s. 11, the number of commoners has been increased to 105.] Irish peers, not being elected to sit in the House of Lords, may be elected members of the Commons' House for any place in Great Britain, in which case they will be considered merely as commoners. The King may create one peerage of Ireland for every three that become extinct; and when the peerage of Ireland shall be reduced to one hundred, a peerage may be created for every one that becomes extinct, so that the peerage of Ireland may be kept up to one hundred, over and above those Irish peers who are also peers of Great Britain or England.

Another article ordained that the Churches of England and Ireland, as then by law established,

---

[1] This provision for Irish bishops sitting in the House of Lords of the Imperial Parliament is now abolished by the Act for the Disestablishment of the Irish Church, 1869.

should be united into one Protestant Episcopal Church, to be called the United Church of England and Ireland. But the late Act of the Imperial Legislature (1869) for the Disestablishment of the Irish Church makes it unnecessary to set out this article more fully.

Other articles of the Union provided :—

'That the subjects of Great Britain and Ireland shall be on the same footing in respect of trade and navigation in all parts and places in the United Kingdom and its dependencies, and in all treaties made by his Majesty with foreign Powers.

'That the laws and courts of the respective kingdoms shall remain as by law established, subject to the regulations of Parliament from time to time; provided, however, that all writs of error and appeals which might have been decided in the respective Houses of Lords of the two kingdoms shall be decided by the House of Lords of the United Kingdom; and provided also, that there shall be an Instance-Court of Admiralty in Ireland, the appeal from which shall be to his Majesty's delegates in the Irish Court of Chancery, and that all existing laws contrary to these articles shall be repealed.'

In 1829, the Act for the Removal of Roman Catholic Disabilities was passed by the Imperial Legislature. This applied to the whole of the United Kingdom, but it specially affected Ireland, where seven-tenths of the population held the Roman Catholic faith. This great liberating statute was followed in three years by the still greater and more important measure for reforming the representative system. I have elsewhere spoken of the operation of the Reform Act of 1832 [1] as it affected England. The changes introduced in Scotland and Ireland were even more extensive, inasmuch as the defects and abuses of the old systems of representation there were far greater than they were in England.[2] By the Scotch Reform Bill of 1832 the number of members for Scotland, which had been fixed at strictly forty-five by the Union in 1707, was raised to fifty-three. Thirty of these were to be county members, and the county electors were to consist of all owners of landed property of 10*l.* a year, and of certain holders of long leases. The electors of the twenty-three city and borough members were to be 10*l.* householders.

In Ireland the right of election in boroughs was given to the 10*l.* householders (extended to 8*l.* householders in 1850), and the county franchise was made more extensive. The number of members for Ireland, which the Union had fixed at a hundred, was raised to a hundred and five.

[1] 'Rise and Progress of the English Constitution,' p. 348.
[2] In 1831 the entire electoral body of Scotland was not more than 4,000. See Sir Erskine May, vol. i., 295. Two-thirds of the Irish members were returned by between fifty and sixty influential patrons. See the same volume, p. 299.

The object of the Parliamentary Reform of 1832 was to give to the middle classes the preponderance in political power. They held it for thirty-five years; and the statute-books of those years bear record how much evil was abolished or mitigated, how vigorous, yet prudent, was the action of enlightened liberality during that period. But the masses of the population, who were still excluded from the franchise, or admitted to it only in small numbers, sought for extension of political rights. Many of the higher and middle ranks co-operated with them. This is not the place for comments on either the motives or the prudence of those who conducted, or of those who opposed the political movements for further reform between 1835 and 1868. My purpose is to set out the actual composition of the Imperial Parliament as it at present exists; and I will therefore proceed at once to point out the changes which were made by the New Electoral Code, as the English Reform Bill of 1867, and the supplementary Bills for Scotland and Ireland which were passed early in 1868, may not unfitly be designated.[1]

The general result of the new measure has been to increase enormously the electoral body. In England and Wales the total number of electors was raised by

[1] These Reform Bills were accompanied by an Act for defining the boundaries of boroughs, and by a very important Act by which election petitions are to be tried by the judges. Property qualifications for members had been abolished in 1858.

it from a little over one million to a little over two
millions.[1] The additions in Scotland and Ireland
may not have been equally large, but they must
have been very considerable.

On coming more to details, we find that in England and Wales the franchise is now given to every
man of full age, and not subject to legal incapacity,
coming within the following classes, and duly registered:—

' 1. In *Boroughs*.—(1) *Householders* having resided
in the same or different dwelling-houses within the
borough for twelve months up to the last day of
July, who have been rated to all poors' rates, and
have paid all such rates due to the preceding 5th of
January. (2) *Lodgers* occupying for the same period
apartments in a dwelling-house of the clear annual
value (unfurnished) of 10*l*. and upwards.

' 2. In *Counties*.—(1) *Freeholders*, *Copyholders*, or
holders on any tenure for any lives, and *Leaseholders*
for a term (or its residue) of sixty years, of the
clear annual value of 6*l*. (2) Tenants of lands or
tenements of the clear annual value of 12*l*., subject
to the same conditions of residence and rating as in
boroughs. (3) These new franchises are in addition
to all existing franchises; but no plurality of votes
is allowed. (4) In places returning three members,

---

[1] See Tabular Statement cited in 'The Statesmen's Year Book,
1870,' p. 203.

each elector can only vote for two, and in the City of London (which returns four) for three.'

By the same Act four boroughs were disfranchised for corruption, and seven for the smallness of their populations. All other boroughs having less than 10,000 inhabitants, and heretofore returning two members, lost one member each, making a total deduction of fifty-two seats.

Seats added.—Boroughs.—Received increase from two members to three *Manchester*, *Liverpool*, *Birmingham*, and *Leeds*. Received increase from one member to two *Merthyr-Tydfil* and *Salford*. Two new Metropolitan boroughs were made, with two members each: one *Hackney*, two *Chelsea* and *Kensington*. Nine new boroughs were created with one member each. Total of new borough seats, nineteen. Net decrease in boroughs, thirty-three seats.

Counties.—Seats added, chiefly by subdivision, each new division having two members, twenty-five seats. The *University of London*, one seat. Net increase in counties and universities, twenty-six seats. The balance of seven seats was transferred to Scotland, leaving England and Wales four hundred and ninety-three members, instead of five hundred.

In Scotland the same rights of voting for borough and for county members were given that had been established for England. Three new seats for Scotch boroughs, two new seats for Scotch counties, and two new seats for Scotch Universities were added. Thus Scotland now has sixty members instead of fifty-three, the number given by the Reform Bill of 1832.

In Ireland the county franchise was left unchanged. In boroughs the household franchise was reduced from 8*l.* to 4*l.* ; and a 10*l.* lodger-franchise similar to the lodger-franchise in English boroughs was established.

One very important new principle has been introduced, though only to a very limited extent, by the new Reform Act. It is the principle of giving minorities in large constituencies *some* share in representation, though of course a far less share than is enjoyed by the majorities. Many schemes for doing this had been suggested by those who thought the principle right, as to which there was and is much difference of opinion. One suggested plan was that of cumulative voting. Another was the plan of compelling each voter to vote for a smaller number of candidates than the total number who are to be returned. This was adopted in the clause of the English Act, which directs that, in places returning three members, each elector can vote for two only ; and in the City of London for three only out of the four members whom that constituency returns. A strong minority, by giving their votes to one candidate, would be enabled in such places to bring in one

member out of the three or out of the four. The
working of this clause will be watched with the
deepest interest.

The aggregate number of the members of the
Commons' House of the Imperial Parliament for
the United Kingdom of Great Britain and Ireland,
according to the new Reform Bill, remains the same
as it was before the Reform Bill of 1832, and as
that Bill had left it. The number is six hundred
and fifty-eight. These six hundred and fifty-eight
exercise more power than any other body of men that
ever existed in any clime and any age. The power
over the Empire and the influence over the world
possessed by the voters who elect them, though less
direct, is proportionally great, and involves heavy
responsibility on its possessors.

CHAPTER III.

Vast Amount of the British Empire unrepresented in the Imperial Parliament—Schemes for Colonial Representation—Main Divisions of our Transmarine Possessions—Classifications of Colonies—Title by Conquest—Title by Occupancy—Mediæval and Modern Theories as to the Rights of Heathen Pre-occupants—Distinction between Crown Colonies and Representative Colonies—Official Classification of Colonies—Colonies with responsible Governments—Geographical Classification—The Three great Masses.

LOOK at the map, and see how small a territorial portion of the British Empire the United Kingdom of Great Britain and Ireland comprises. Yet none but the inhabitants of this United Kingdom send representatives to the Imperial Parliament, which is politically omnipotent over the whole Empire. A very large proportion of the natives of its outlying portions, such as the Asiatics of India and of the adjacent districts, the Hottentots and Kaffirs of the Cape, the aborigines of Australia, the Esquimaux, and the Red Indians of the Hudson Bay territories, may be rightly considered to be unfit for the constitutional functions of electors to the sovereign Legislature. But there are many thousands of the British race settled or resident in our transmarine possessions to whom that observation does not apply. There are many colonies, especially in North America and Australia, in which men of European race form a majority ; men who, as to education and property, are at least on a level with the bulk of the electors in the home country. Almost all philosophical and political enquirers into our institutions, almost all who, like Burke, have felt it to be a duty ' to instruct themselves in everything which relates to our colonies, and also to form some fixed ideas concerning the general policy of the British Empire ;' almost all students of this character have inquired more or less frequently, and more or less vividly, whether it be not possible and desirable to admit the people of the colonies into an interest in the Constitution by giving them representation in the Imperial Parliament. While the thirteen North American colonies, which afterwards became the independent commonwealth of the United States, still formed portions of the British Empire, projects of this nature were very frequently put forward ; but they never found general acceptance from the leading statesmen on either side of the Atlantic. In 1754, when discontent among the American colonists was beginning to create anxiety, Shirley, the British Governor of Massachusetts, proposed to the great colonial leader, Franklin, ' the plan of uniting the colonies more intimately with Great Britain, by allowing them representatives in Parliament.' Franklin discouraged the project, though others of his fellow-colonists regarded it with favour.[1] In 1768, Otis, the most vehement of the early supporters of American rights, strongly advocated ' a general union of the British Empire, in which every part of its wide dominion should be represented under one equal and uniform direction and system of laws.'[2] The Congress at New York opposed this. Their reasons for this opposition may be found in the correspondence between the French Minister Choiseul and his agent in America, who obtained his information chiefly from Franklin. The French Minister was told that the Americans objected to a solution of the difficulties between them and England by admitting deputies from each colony into Parliament as members, because they could not obtain a representation proportionate to their population, and so would be overwhelmed by superior numbers, because the distance made their regular attendance in Parliament impossible, and because they knew its venality and corruption too well to intrust it with their affairs.'[3]

Mr. Grenville, in England, declared his opinion that the colonies ought to be allowed to send members to Parliament.[4] Burke, in his great speech in

---

[1] Bancroft's ' History of the American Revolution,' vol. i., p. 187.

[2] Bancroft, p. 133.

[3] Bancroft, vol. iii., p. 201.

[4] Adam Smith, whom some will consider a higher authority than

the House of Commons on March 22, 1775, spoke of the project as follows: 'You will now perhaps imagine that I am on the point of proposing to you a scheme for a representation of the colonies in Parliament. Perhaps I might be inclined to entertain some such thought; but a great flood stops me in my course. *Opposuit natura*—I cannot remove the eternal barriers of the creation. The thing in that mode I do not know to be possible. As I meddle with no theory, I do not absolutely assert the impracticability of such a representation. But I do not see my way to it, and those who have been more confident have not been more successful.'

Though many expressed opinions favourable to it, no actual attempt was made to introduce colonial representation before the agitation in England of the Reform measure of 1831–32. In the Parliamentary Debates of the first of those years, it is reported that on August 16, 1831, Mr. Hume brought forward a motion that members should be given to the colonies, and that the motion was negatived without a division. Yet the debate in the House of Commons on this subject is of permanent interest, and so is the commentary on it which is to be found in the fourth volume of Alison's 'History of Europe.'[1] It is to

any that have been previously named, considered Colonial Representation to be both practicable and desirable.

[1] P. 344.

be remembered that the proposer of this motion,
Mr. Joseph Hume, was a very advanced Liberal;
and that the historian, who laments the indifference
which the proposal met with, was a very strong
Conservative.   Mr. Hume's proposal was of the most
moderate kind, for all he asked was, that nineteen
members should be given to the whole colonies of
Great Britain, including four for British India, with
its 100,000,000 of inhabitants.   He proposed to give
the Crown colonies eight, Canada three, West Indies
three, and the Channel Islands one.   One member of
politics generally opposed to those of Mr. Hume, who
spoke in the debate (Mr. Keith Douglas), observed that
' the idea of giving due proportion to the commerce
and colonies which had raised this country to its
present pitch of greatness was worthy of the most
attentive consideration.   They were now about to
localise the representation, and in all probability the
various boroughs would in future return gentlemen
resident in their immediate vicinity, so that the class
of persons connected with the colonies who had
hitherto found their way into Parliament, and who
were alone able to give information concerning
colonial matters, would be completely excluded.   In
whatever point of view the great question of our
colonial policy and government came to be considered, it was impossible to doubt that the honour-

able member for Middlesex had done perfectly right in bringing it forward.'

The practical importance to colonies of having some one present in Parliament specially qualified to express their wishes and protect their interests had been proved by a very anomalous institution, which existed long before the Reform Bill, and for certainly some time after it. Whether it has now been quite abandoned I do not know. I mean the practice of the colonies employing members of the English Parliament as their paid agents, 'to solicit the passing of laws, and to transact other public matters for the good of the colony.' Edmund Burke was agent for New York from 1770 to 1775, with a salary of 500*l.* a year. Mr. Roebuck, while a member of the House, was agent for Canada. Other instances are given in the book and pamphlets referred to in the note.[1]

It is probably too late now (even if it were proper in such a treatise as this) to discuss the wisdom of giving representatives in the Imperial Parliament to such colonies as we have considered fit to be trusted with almost entire self-government. The main object of many statesmen of the home country seems to

---

[1] See article 'Colonial Agents' in the 'Standard Political Cyclopædia,' which is believed to have been prepared with the sanction and under the superintendence of Lord Brougham. It is not meant in the least to say that a colonial agent was always an M.P., but he frequently was so; especially in times when colonial politics were matters of importance in Parliament.

be to promote the Euthanasia of all connection
between the Imperial Realm and her dependencies.
Probably, also, colonial statesmen would be jealous as
to receiving the Imperial representation, which might
seem likely to bring with it liability to Imperial
taxation. Yet certainly the main objections raised
by Franklin and by Burke against the Parliamentary
representation of such colonists, as the inhabitants of
the thirteen North American colonies were a century
ago, and as the inhabitants of the dominion of North
America and of the Australian settlements are at
the present time, have ceased to be applicable. The
objection of distance in the present state of navigation has become trifling. The .veto of Nature,
which Burke cited, has been withdrawn, since steam
has bridged the oceans. Our Parliaments are no
longer tainted with the wholesale venality, which unquestionably existed a century ago; and the arrangement of fit numbers of colonial and Indian representatives in the Imperial Parliament would not be
a matter of difficult detail, if the principle were once
ascertained and agreed to. The true principle seems
easy to find, if we call to mind what was done when
Scotland was united to England. Scotland did not
then receive the right of returning a number of
representatives in the Imperial Parliament equal to
the number, which she would have been entitled to,
if the amount of her population relatively to the

population of England had alone been considered. Inasmuch as by the Union she was to contribute a far less sum than England to the Imperial revenue, the number of her representatives was lowered below the number at which the comparative amount of population would have placed it.[1] With respect to the colonies, it is not to be supposed that the rule (now nearly a century old) would be departed from, by which the Imperial Parliament holds itself morally bound not to tax the colonies. The colonies would be admitted to shares in the Imperial Parliament on the understanding that they contributed nothing at all to the Imperial revenue by taxation. The number, therefore, of representatives to which their population would at first seem to entitle them respectively, would be diminished on account of their non-contribution to the Imperial revenues. The smallness of Scotland's contributions to the pecuniary supply of Imperial exigencies reduced her number of representatives in 1707 to less than a twelfth of the number of members of the House of Commons. The entire absence of all such contribution by the colonies would be a just cause for reducing their aggregate number of representatives to a much smaller amount, to an amount that would not inconveniently increase the total number of the House of Commons, but would

[1] See Hallam's 'Constitutional History,' vol. iii., chap. 18, p. 339.

ensure the presence in the Imperial Parliament of men thoroughly acquainted with the affairs and the interests of the colonies, and with the prevalent feelings of each class of their communities. The local representative Legislatures of each colony would still continue to regulate their own local affairs, and to levy and dispose of their own local revenues, as they do at present. These rights are no more incompatible with representation in the Imperial Parliament than the similar rights of Ontario, Nova Scotia, and the other provinces of the Canadian Dominion are inconsistent with representation in the Parliament of the Dominion. The objection that the inhabitants of the United Kingdom would not endure taxation, for which colonial representatives had voted, is, in my belief, visionary, considering the small number suggested of such members. If real, it could easily be removed by a clause forbidding the colonial members to speak or vote in Committees of Ways and Means.

But our business is with things as they are, and not with things as they might have been or may be. We have seen how the Imperial Parliament is composed, and what is the United Kingdom over which that Parliament is the immediate organ of government. We have now to see how the rest of the Britannic Empire is made up, and what interest the populations of the transmarine portions of the Britannic Empire have in the Imperial Constitution.

In seeking to know the condition of the colonies and other dependencies, it is very useful to learn first how we got them, and how we have treated them. A full history of our settlements, conquests, and other acquisitions in America, India, and elsewhere, would far exceed the pre-appointed limits of this volume. Still, a brief and general sketch of how we obtained the principal portions of our transmarine empire may be serviceable. And it is less difficult to arrange this, than would seem likely at first sight, notwithstanding the very great number and variety of our colonies.

If we look at the map, we shall see that there are three great main masses of our dominions beyond the United Kingdom. These are:

1st. Our North American possessions. .

2nd. Our Indian possessions.

3rd. Our Australasian possessions, which include Van Diemen's Land and New Zealand, as well as the various colonised districts of Australia itself.

The student, who knows the leading historical circumstances of our acquisition of each of those great masses of empire, and also the main facts and theories as to our tenure of them, will have accomplished much towards mastering Anglo-colonial history and Anglo-Indian history, and also towards understanding the principles of our government of dependencies. There are other parts of our Empire not included in any of these great masses, which must not be forgotten, especially the West Indian Islands that belong to us, and the Cape Colony. But for the purpose of this volume it will be enough to describe the British West Indies and British South Africa briefly; and, with regard to the numerous smaller colonies, it will be sufficient to mention them, and to state their respective positions, areas, climates, and populations, with the date and mode of the acquisition of each, in a general list of all our colonies, plantations, and dominions of every kind that lie beyond the limits of the United Kingdom. That list will form nearly the last part of this book. Before I come to this part I may often have occasion to mention some of those colonies not included in the American, or the Indian, or in the Australasian division. Such readers of this book as may have hitherto learned little about these places may, when they find them thus mentioned, turn with advantage at once to this list, and gain general information respecting them.

There are some classifications of colonies which may be usefully stated here, though they introduce several topics, which must be more fully considered a little farther on. One is the classification which

Heeren, in his 'Manual of the History of the Political System of Europe and its Colonies,' gives of the colonies generally, which have been founded by Europeans during and after the close of the fifteenth century. He says: 'The term *colony* embraces all the possessions and establishments of Europeans in foreign quarters of the world. They may, however, be divided, according to their object and nature, into four classes. Of these the first is that of *Agricultural Colonies*, whose object is the cultivation of the soil. The colonists, who form them, become landed proprietors, and in process of time become a nation, properly so called. The second is that of *Plantation Colonies*, whose end is the cultivation and supply of certain natural productions of the colony for consumption in Europe. The colonists in these, although possessors of land, are less permanently fixed than those of the former; nor does the smallness of their number permit any approach to a nation. Slavery belongs peculiarly to this kind of colony. The third consists of *Mining Colonies*, whose object is expressed in their name. The colonists of these become naturalised, but, although sometimes extensively spread, they cannot, as mere mining colonies, ever attain to much population. The fourth is of *Trading Colonies*, whose object is a traffic in the natural productions and the native manufactures of the country. These consist at first of nothing more than factories and staples for the convenience of trade; but force or fraud soon enlarges them, and the colonists become conquerors, without, however, losing sight of the original object of their settlement. Though masters of the country, they are too little attached to it to become naturalised.

'These are the chief colonial divisions; and although several of these objects may have been embraced in one colony, we shall find that there is always some feature distinct from, and more important than, the rest, which determines to which it belongs.'[1]

Heeren's first class, that of agricultural colonies (the word ' *agricultural* ' being understood as meaning the occupations of the herdsman and the sheep-farmer, as well as of the tiller of the soil), embraces the great bulk of our North American possessions and all our Australasian. His fourth class, that of trading colonies, where the colonists become conquerors and lords of large territories, applies to our East Indian possessions.

Of Heeren's other two classes, one, the class of mining colonies, is not exemplified in British colonisation. The hope of finding precious metals was a strong inducement to the adventurers who made our early voyages of discovery; but none of the English expeditions to the supposed regions of gold and

---

[1] Heeren on the 'State System of Modern Europe and her Colonies,' p. 23.

silver, resulted in the foundation of a mining colony. And, though in aftertimes the discoveries of gold in parts of Australia and British Columbia, and of diamonds at the Cape, have caused a great influx of Europeans to those regions, there has been no case in which an absolutely, or even a substantially new colony has owed its existence to mining adventurers.

Heeren's other class, his second class of what he calls ' *Plantation* colonies,' requires some observation. It does not seem to be very widely divided from his first class, that of *Agricultural* colonies. In almost all the *Agricultural* colonies the export from the colony to Europe of part of the produce of things cultivated and grown in the colony, forms part of the theory, and part of the practice of the settlement. Nor does there seem to be any broad distinction between settlements where the settlers till the soil or rear herds or flocks, and settlements where the growth of certain plants, such as the tobacco-plant, the sugar-cane, or the coffee-shrub is the main object to which the settlers devote their labours. Both classes are ' cultivators.'

There is, however, in fact, a very great difference between them as to the interest which they take in the lands which they cultivate, and in the probability of new nations being developed from them. This difference is caused by climate. In countries favourable to the health of European settlers, *and to the*

E

health of their children, the cultivating colonist at-
taches himself to the land which he cultivates, and
so do his children after him.   But in countries where
the physique of the European deteriorates under cli-
matic influences, the natural desire of the cultivating
colonist is to realise wealth, or at least a competency
as rapidly as possible, and then to hurry back to
Europe.   He may retain his estate in the colony; he
may send his children there to cultivate and to make
money for a short time, as their father did before
them; but neither he nor they can ever regard such a
colony as their home, or feel anything like patriotism
towards it, except so far as it is a component part of
the great Britannic empire.   Now, all colonies where
the cereals grow copiously, and where flocks and
herds can be bred and reared abundantly, i.e. all
agricultural colonies, are colonies having climates
favourable to Europeans, or, at least, not seriously
injurious to them.   But the colonies, where sugar,
cotton, coffee, and the like are produced, are in
almost all instances places with climates such that
few Europeans can reside in them and retain vigour
of mind and body for many consecutive years; and
their climates are such that European children cannot grow up there in robust health.   Practically,
therefore, Heeren's class of *Plantation* colonies is
    named and correctly named, if we take the
word to mean colonies where the main object of

those who go to them is to plant and rear certain vegetable productions which abound in hot climates only, and which are of great value in European markets.

In this sense of the word we have many *Planta-tion* colonies. Such are our West Indian islands, and Demerara, and Mauritius, and Ceylon; though the latter, when first in our hands, was a mere *trading* colony, and is a trading colony to some extent still. But coffee-planting there has increased rapidly during the last thirty years; and the influx of Europeans who remain there for some years is becoming more and more considerable.

We may employ the term 'Plantation colony' in the sense now described; but it will be useful to warn the student that he will find the phrase 'the Plantations' very laxly and variously employed in old books, in state-papers, and in statutes. It was frequently used as applying to all the British possessions in America, including the West Indies.[1]

---

[1] In the case of Lubbock and Potts, 7 East 449, Lord Ellenborough said :—' The term " Plantations," in its common known signification, is applicable only to colonies abroad, where things are grown, or which were settled principally for the purpose of raising produce, and has never, in fact, been applied to a place like Gibraltar, which is a mere fortress and garrison, incapable of raising produce, but supplied with it from other places. In truth the term *Plantation* in the sense used by the navigation laws has never been applied either in common understanding or in any Acts of Parliament (at least none such could be pointed out when demanded in the course of the argument) to any of the British dominions in Europe; not to

This classification of Heeren's has reference to the purposes for which the various classes of colonists have used the places, which have been the respective scenes of their colonisation. Another division of colonies is sometimes made with reference to the motives, which induced the colonists to leave their home-country. The spirit of commercial enterprise has been one great cause of colonisation; and this has been generally most active in periods marked by numerous and great maritime discoveries. Indeed the two, the spirit of commercial enterprise and the spirit of maritime discovery, have been almost always contemporaneously active, and each has stimulated and maintained the other. Reports came to an European maritime state that distant regions had been found, or would probably be found on search, with fertile soil and other natural advantages, or with a population eager to purchase European commodities, or with the most attractive attribute of all, with abundance of the precious metals. Merchants and others who heard this, would form companies and expeditions to these depôts of new wealth; and, sometimes, the State itself would send out an organised body to occupy

Dunkirk, while that was in our possession, nor at the present day to Jersey, Guernsey, or any of the islands in the Channel.'

Lord Bacon, in his essay on 'Plantations,' uses the word as meaning the planting of colonists in a new country. He speaks of 'the people wherewith you ought to plant,' and of when 'it is time to plant with women as well as with men.' This essay will be referred to in the text, in a subsequent part of the present work.

the newly-discovered regions in the State's name; to establish, it might be, village communities or town communities there, or mere factories for purchase and sale, or for exchange of the products of the new land with the products of Europe. If the European State was old and at all thickly peopled, many individuals, who found it difficult to obtain a competency, or to rise in the social scale at home, would be glad to seek subsistence and the prospect of wealth and elevation in the new country. The State itself might often desire to relieve itself of part of its population by sending them thither. Thus the spirit of emigration, both of voluntary emigration and of emigration under State direction and State patronage, would be called into action. These motives for colonisation are more powerful at some times than at others; but they are permanent, and they always will operate so long as European States are thickly peopled in comparison with habitable transmarine countries, and so long as men wish to gain wealth by temporary residence and industry abroad, even though they do not mean to abandon their old homes entirely. But other and very peculiar motives have created a considerable portion of British colonisation. The leading motive (though not always the sole motive) that caused the first settlers in many of the English North American colonies to leave England, was the desire to escape from ecclesiastical interference at home, and to

set up and practise elsewhere the form of worship
which, and which alone, they considered to be holy
and right. The men who first came as settlers to the
parts of the North.American coast, since called New
England, and who constituted there the five colonies
of Plymouth, Massachusetts, Rhode Island, Connecticut, and Newhaven, were Puritans, who left England
that they might withdraw themselves from the operation of the laws against Nonconformists, and especially from the oppressiveness of the Bishops' Courts
in James I. and Charles I.'s reigns. The permanent
colonisation of Virginia was chiefly effected, and that
of Maryland was entirely effected, by Roman Catholics, who sought to escape the penal laws against
those who professed that creed in England. Pensylvania was founded by and for Quakers, who had been
subjected to cruel persecution in the old country,
and to still worse persecution in New England.[1]

[1] There is much truth, and truth that ought to be remembered,
in the remarks of Mr. Wakefield on the sectarian element in our old
North American colonisation. He thinks indeed that a desire to
live in a place where their own religious usages, and no others, should
be practised, was the main cause that led the Puritans, Quakers,
Roman Catholics, &c., to emigrate from England to the New World.
I cannot concur with him in all his opinions, but I believe that
the sentences which I am about to quote are well founded: ' In
colonising North America, the English seem to have thought more
about religious provisions than anything else. Each settlement was
better known by its religion than by any other mark. Virginia,
notwithstanding the official reception in England of the proposition that its inhabitants had souls to be saved like other people,
was a Church-of-England colony; Maryland was the land of promise for Roman Catholics; Pensylvania for Quakers; the various

Another remarkable feature of English colonisation with reference to the motives which originated it, was the establishment of penal colonies. While England possessed the thirteen colonies in North America, which proclaimed their independence in

settlements of New England for Puritans. Their object was, each body of them respectively, to find a place where its own religion would be the religion of the place; to form a community, the whole of which would be of one religion, or at least to make its own faith the principal religion of the new community. The Puritans went further; within their bounds they would suffer no religion but their own. They emigrated not so much in order to escape from persecution, as in order to be able to persecute. It was not persecution for its own sake that they loved; it was the power of making their religion the religion of their whole community. Being themselves religious in earnest, they disliked the congregation and admixture of differing religions in their settlements, just as now the congregation and admixture of differing religions in schools and colleges is disliked by most religious people of all denominations; they wanted to live, as religious people now send their children to school, in contact with no religion but their own. Penn and Baltimore, indeed, or rather Baltimore and Penn (for the example was set by the Roman Catholic), made religious toleration a fundamental law of their settlements; but whilst they paid this formal tribute of respect to their own history as sufferers from persecution at home, they took care, practically, that Maryland should be an especially Roman Catholic colony, and Pensylvania a colony for Quakers. Therefore, the Roman Catholics of England were attracted to Maryland, the Quakers to Pensylvania. New England attracted its own sect of religious people, and so did Virginia. Altogether, the attraction of these sectarian colonies was very great. The proof is the great number of people of the higher orders who emigrated to those colonies as long as they preserved their sectarianism or religious distinctions. All that colonisation was more or less a religious colonisation; the parts of it that prospered the most were the most religious parts; the prosperity was chiefly occasioned by the respectability of the emigration; and the respectability of the emigration to each colony had a close relation to the force of the religious attraction.'

1776, it had been usual to send thither great numbers of convicted criminals, whose offences were not
considered to merit capital punishment, but to require a severer penalty than imprisonment at home.
This practice had commenced as early as James I.'s
reign. In the year 1619, he commanded that 'a
hundred dissolute persons should be sent to Virginia,
which the Knight Marshal would deliver for that
purpose.' This was directly contrary to the sound
and wise policy which his great statesman, Lord
Bacon, had recommended in his 'Essay on Plantations' as to the kind of persons who ought to be
sent to colonies. Bacon there says, 'It is a shameful
and unblessed thing to take the scum of people, and
wicked and condemned men to be the people whom
you plant.' But transportation was thought to be a
convenient way of ridding the mother country of criminals who were not bad enough for hanging, but were
too bad for keeping in England. The demand for
labour in the colonies was great; and no objection for
a long time was raised there about receiving such cargoes of debased humanity. In George I.'s reign this
mode of punishment was brought into more general
operation than before, by a statute which gave the
English criminal courts a discretionary power to order
that such convicts as were entitled to benefit of clergy
(which then applied, generally speaking, to first convictions for most felonies), should be transported to

the American Plantations. The number of transported convicts increased, until it reached, according to some authorities, the amount of more than a thousand in one year. When the American war broke out, this mode of relieving the English jails was put an end to. The state of the overcrowded English prisons became horrible; and little mitigation was effected by the confinement of some offenders on board of hulks, which was authorised by a statute passed in the sixteenth year of George III. Our statesmen then bethought themselves of using some of the new regions in Australia (or New Holland as it was then named), which Captain Cook had recently explored, for the reception of English convicts. An Act of Parliament was passed in 1784 authorising the King in Council to appoint places beyond the seas, whither convicted criminals might be transported, and where they should be confined and kept at hard labour during the terms for which they were sentenced. In 1787 a body of English troops in charge of a considerable number of convicts arrived in Botany Bay on the eastern side of Australia, and soon afterwards formed a penal settlement in Port Jackson, near which the town of Sydney was slowly built, consisting at first chiefly of barracks for the soldiers, and of workhouses and penal cells for the convicts. This was the beginning of colonisation in Australia.

Other settlements of the same kind were made

there; and the neighbouring island of Tasmania or Van Diemen's Land was used for the same purpose. But, as a free population gradually grew up in those regions, and became continually stronger in numbers and in commercial importance, the contamination caused by the continuous influx of vice and crime from the old country was felt to be a grievance and a wrong. And after many complaints and remonstrances, the system of transportation to colonies has been almost wholly abandoned. Some few are still sent to Western Australia, and large numbers of convicts are employed on the Government works at Bermuda and Gibraltar; but the penal system at those last-mentioned places is very different from the old transportation system.

Some of the transmarine parts of the British Empire have been occupied and retained almost exclusively on account of their value in time of war, though some of these are also of considerable commercial importance, especially as coaling depôts, now that steam-navigation has become so general and so far-reaching. Still the class of places which we now speak of are regarded rather as military posts than as colonies. Such are Gibraltar and Malta in Europe, and Aden at the entrance of the Red Sea.

One group of dependencies of the British Crown cannot be said to have ever been occupied or acquired by the English at all. These are the islands

of Jersey, Guernsey, Alderney and Sark, which are
commonly called by the collective name of 'The
Channel Isles.' The Channel Islands are the first,
in point of antiquity of connection with England,
though nearly the last in point of magnitude, of the
British dominions, which are not included in the
United Kingdom of Great Britain and Ireland. Their
connection with the English Crown came by conquest,
but England was the conquered party. They formed
portions of the Duchy of Normandy; and, as such,
belonged to the old Scandinavian Viking, Rolf the
Ganger, after the French King ceded to him the
northern region of Gaul, formerly called Neustria, and
afterwards Normandy from the men of the north who
conquered it. Rolf's descendants retained the Channel
Islands as his successors in the Dukedom of Normandy, and after they had become Kings of England also. King John, in 1204, lost to the King of
France his Norman territories on the Continent, which
the House of Rolf had held for four centuries; but
the adjacent islands were either never lost, or were
speedily regained by John; and they have remained
united to the Crown of England. They retain their
old feudal laws or *coutume* of Normandy, and have
their own courts, which are independent of the
courts at Westminster; but there is an appeal from
these to the Queen in Council. Their local Assemblies
(called States) have no power to legislate without

the express sanction and authority of the Crown for such new enactment. On the other hand, the States of Jersey have lately asserted that their concurrence is necessary for the validity of any legislation respecting them by the Queen in Council.[1] The Imperial Parliament has unquestionably power to bind the Channel Islands by its Acts, and frequently does so.

The Channel Islands cannot be properly said to have been acquired by us at all. But with regard to the rest of the transmarine dominions of the British Crown, another and a very important classification of our colonies and other dependencies is based on the mode in which they were severally acquired. This to a great extent (but not entirely) regulates their constitutional conditions respectively. I shall have occasion to investigate the subject of these various constitutional rights more fully in a subsequent part of this treatise; but the general classification to which I allude may be usefully stated at once in a general manner. It is to be found in almost all modern writings which deal with the political *status* of the parts of the British Empire which lie beyond the territorial limits of the United Kingdom. Especially Sir George Bowyer, in the fourth chapter of his ' Commentaries on Constitutional Law,' and Mr. Forsyth in the notes to the first chapter of

[1] See Forsyth's ' Constitutional Law,' p. 382.

his 'Cases and Opinions on Constitutional Law,' set out this classification with very learned and valuable comments.

The substance of this classification is as follows: Our colonies and other foreign possessions are divisible into three classes, with reference to the mode by which they were originally acquired and annexed to the Empire.

Those modes are—1st, conquest; 2ndly, cession by treaty; and 3rdly, occupancy.

First, we will speak of those which are acquired by conquest from an enemy.

By the law of nations, not only the property in things movable and immovable, taken in lawful war, is thereby transferred, but the sovereignty over towns, territories, provinces, and states is acquired by their being forcibly taken possession of by a lawful belligerent, and the dominion over them renounced by the person or body in whom it was vested before the conquest.[1]

Secondly, where a colony or other territory is acquired by cession, the title of the new sovereign arises also from the law of nations.[2]

Both in cases of conquest and in cases of cession, it is in the Crown (i.e. in the King acting on his own royal authority) that the dominion over the newly-acquired territory is vested.

[1] Bowyer, p. 43, citing numerous authorities.   [2] Ibid., p. 45.

The articles of capitulation on which a conquered country has surrendered to the British arms (when there has been a capitulation on terms), and the articles of peace, by which an acquired country is ceded, are sacred and inviolable.

So that such capitulations and articles are not violated, the Crown has the sole and absolute power of legislation over a conquered or ceded colony or other territory.

Until the Crown alters the laws, which are in force in such a place at the time of the cession or conquest, those laws continue in force.

The laws in force in a conquered or ceded colony or territory, whether they be the continuing old laws which prevailed before the cession or conquest, or whether they be new laws introduced by the authority of the Crown, equally affect all persons and all property within the limits of the colony or territory. In Lord Mansfield's words, the law and legislative government of every dominion equally affect all persons and all property within the limits thereof; and make the rule of decision for all questions which arise there. Whoever purchases, lives, or sues there, puts himself under the law of the place.

Colonies acquired by conquest or cession, and which are under the rule of the Crown, as just explained, make up what are commonly called the Crown colonies; and British India is a Crown territory, as are several other places, which are not usually called colonies. But (as was pointed out in the first chapter) the authority of the Imperial Parliament, consisting of King, Lords, and Commons, is paramount over the authority of the Crown sole in respect of these places ; and the Crown cannot of its sole authority repeal or contravene any statute of the Imperial Parliament affecting a Crown colony or a Crown territory. And there is another very important constitutional rule to be remembered respecting them. Although the power of the Crown sole over conquered and ceded possessions extends to altering at will their local political constitutions or forms of Government, still if the Crown once grants to a Crown colony or Crown territory the right of having a representative assembly of its own, with power to make laws and raise a revenue, such grant is irrevocable by the Crown sole, though always liable to be revoked or modified by the Imperial Parliament.

By the operation of this rule many colonies and territories which, when they first became parts of the Britannic Empire, were under the Crown sole, have obtained free local constitutions, and have ceased to be subject to the sole prerogative of the reigning king or queen of Great Britain. The colony of the Cape of Good Hope is an example.

A very large proportion of the transmarine British Empire has been gained neither by conquest nor by

cession, but by *occupancy*. The acquisition of title
to lands by occupancy applies strictly to taking
possession of uninhabited and desert places only.
In such cases occupancy gives the best of titles.
Grotius says of this ' Occupancy or the taking possession of that which previously belonged to no one is
the only natural and original mode of acquisition:
that is to say, it is the only mode of acquiring by
the natural law without deriving a title from any
other person.'[1]

Yet neither England nor any other European State
could make out a good title by 'occupancy' to much
transmarine dominion, if this definition were to be
rigidly applied. The cases in which the territories
beyond Europe, now held by Europeans, were quite
' desert and uninhabited' when first visited by Europeans, are rare and exceptional. In the vast majority of instances the European 'occupants' found
native tribes already existing in the countries, which
were new to Europeans, but not new to human
beings. It might have been, and may be fairly
thought, that in cases where large territories were
merely roved over by a few sparse savages, such
countries ought not to be considered as already
' occupied,' and that the European new-comers gained
a true title by occupancy. But in many cases the
natives were in considerable numbers; they were

[1] Grotius, lib. 2, c. iii. sect. iv.

often more or less agricultural; in some cases they
had attained a high degree of peculiar civilisation.
But the interpretation of the law of nations, as between European new-comers and old natives, was
always pronounced by the European, that is by the
stronger side; and the stronger side naturally interpreted according to its own interest. In the
fifteenth and sixteenth centuries statesmen and
churchmen in European Christendom held doctrines,
which got rid of all difficulties in such matters.
Heathens were considered to be beyond the pale of the
law of nations. The Pope, according to some myste-
rious but certainly widely prevalent mediæval theory,
claimed the paramount dominion over all islands, and
over all territories discovered beyond remote seas.
The well-known Bull of Pope Alexander VI., in 1493,
divided between the Portuguese and the Castilian
monarchs all new regions inhabited by heathens then
lately discovered, or about to be discovered, laying
down an imaginary line between the Azores as the
boundary. The rulers of other States did not altogether acquiesce in the titles thus given to the two
favoured nations of Spain and Portugal; and after
the Reformation the English and the Dutch mariners
scoffed, and did more than scoff, at the Pope's pre-
tensions and at the rights of his grantees. Even at
an earlier time our Henry VII. authorised Cabot
to sail under the banner of England towards the east,

F

north, or west, and to take possession, in the name of
King Henry, of all countries discovered by him which
were not occupied by the subjects of any Christian
sovereign. Cabot had express power given him to
trade with the inhabitants, which shows that much
more than the occupation of desert countries was
designed. Not to accumulate instances, the charter
given by Queen Elizabeth to Sir Humphry Gilbert,
whose expedition to Newfoundland will be mentioned
in another chapter, authorised him to take possession
of all remote and barbarous lands, unoccupied by
any Christian prince or people. Prior occupation by
heathens was evidently regarded as conferring no
rights of territorial title at all.

We return now to consider the constitutional position of colonists in a colony, which has been acquired
by occupancy, as contradistinguished from the constitutional status of colonists in a colony or other transmarine territory, that has been acquired by either
conquest or cession.

'When British subjects take possession of a desert
country by public authority (and they cannot, consistently with their allegiance, take possession of a
territory by an independent act of jurisdiction[1]),

[1] Neither can a British subject or any company of British subjects
acquire by compact or by conquest any territory for their private
dominion. All is subject to the British Crown. Thus it is declared
by the Act, 53 Geo. III., c. 105, that the sovereignty of the Crown
over the possessions acquired by the East India Company is *undoubted*.

the whole country becomes vested in the Crown;
and the Crown will assign to particular persons
portions of the land, reserving, as Crown-land, all
that which is not so granted out, and reserving also
a jurisdiction over the whole territory.

' But subjects of the British Crown so forming a
colony or plantation, are entitled to divers privileges
over the inhabitants of colonies acquired by conquest
and cession. " It hath been held," says Blackstone,
" that, if an uninhabited country be discovered and
planted by English subjects, all the English laws
then in being, which are the birthright of every
subject, are immediately there in force. But this
must be understood with very many restrictions.
Such colonists carry with them only so much of
the English law as is applicable to their own situation, and the condition of an infant colony—such,
for instance, as the general rules of inheritance,
and of protection from personal injuries. The artificial refinements and distinctions incident to the
property of a great and commercial people, the laws
of police and revenue (such, especially, as are enforced by penalties), the mode of maintenance for
the established clergy, the jurisdiction of spiritual
courts, and a multitude of other provisions, are
neither necessary nor convenient for them, and therefore are not in force. What shall be admitted,
and what rejected, at what times, and under what

restrictions, must, in case of dispute, be decided, in
the first instance, by their own provincial judicature,
subject to the revision and control of the king in
council; the whole of their constitution being also
liable to be new-modelled and reformed by the general superintending power of the Legislature (i.e. the
Imperial Parliament) in the mother country."'

It is to be observed here, that the colonists carry
with them a right to be governed by the laws in
being at the time of their forming their settlement.
Laws subsequently enacted in Parliament will not
bind them, unless they are specially mentioned
therein.[1]

In a colony of this nature, as well as in all others,
the Crown is invested, by its general prerogative,
with the right of appointing governors and other
officers for the execution of the law and of erecting
courts of justice.[2]

It is, however, to be understood that this prerogative right of the Crown to establish courts extends
only to the establishment of courts which are to
administer English common law, and to proceed
according to English common law. The Crown
cannot create any court to administer any other

---

[1] They are also bound by all Acts which, although they do not
specially mention such colonies, must by reasonable construction
be understood to apply to the whole empire. Such are many portions of the Mercantile Marine Acts.

[2] Bowyer, p. 48.

law without an Act of Parliament.[1] This applies to occupancy-colonies as well as to the United Kingdom.

The Crown can also in occupancy-colonies summon representative assemblies from among the inhabitants for the purposes of local taxation and local legislation.

A recent statute as to the validity of colonial laws (28 & 29 Vict. c. 63) gives a definition of representative legislatures, which may probably be adopted as a definition for other purposes as well as for the immediate objects of that enactment. It defines them to be ' legislative bodies, of which one-half are elected by the inhabitants of the colony.'

In occupancy-colonies the Crown cannot, by virtue of its prerogative, either legislate or impose taxes. But the Imperial Parliament has enabled the Crown to provide by Orders in Council for the government of occupancy-colonies, in which no system of government with a representative legislature has yet been established. This power was first given by the statute 6 Vict. c. 13, as to the new settlements in the Falkland Islands, and on the coast of Africa. The statute empowered Her Majesty to make and establish, by Order in Council, such laws, institutions, ordinances, courts, and officers, as may be necessary for the good government of the settlements, and

---

[1] See the cases cited in ' Forsyth,' p. 186.

to delegate her powers and authorities to resident officers.

This power has been extended by the statute 23 & 25 Vict. c. 121, which, after reciting that divers of Her Majesty's subjects have occupied, or may hereafter occupy, places being possessions of Her Majesty, but in which no Government has been established by authority of Her Majesty, enacts that the provisions of statute 6 & 7 Vict. c. 13, by which the Crown is empowered to establish by Order in Council laws, institutions, and ordinances for the government of Her Majesty's settlements on the coasts of Africa and the Falkland Islands, shall extend to all possessions of Her Majesty not having been acquired by cession or conquest, nor, ' except in virtue of this Act,' being within the jurisdiction of the legislative authority of any of Her Majesty's possessions abroad.

Occupancy-colonies are frequently called *Settled* colonies.

Besides this division of British colonies into Crown colonies, and into colonies with representative institutions (which we may term briefly representative colonies), another class has lately been created of colonies possessing both representative institutions and *responsible government*. The full explanation of this term will be given when we speak of the North American and the Australian colonies. But

I mention it at once because it forms part of the classification of our colonies now adopted by our Government. In the 'Colonial Office List' (officially published by direction of the Secretary of State for the Colonies) the first chapter of the rules and regulations for Her Majesty's Colonial Office deals with the classification of colonies. It commences as follows:—

CLASSIFICATION OF COLONIES.

British colonies may be divided into three classes:—

1. Crown colonies, in which the Crown has the entire control of legislation, while the administration is carried on by public officers under the control of the Home Government.

2. Colonies possessing representative institutions but not responsible government, in which the Crown has no more than a veto on legislation, but the Home Government retains the control of public officers.

3. Colonies possessing representative institutions and responsible government, in which the Crown has only a veto on legislation, and the Home Government has no control over any public officer except the Governor.

A subsequent paragraph gives a further explanation of responsible government. It is as follows:—

'Under responsible government the Executive Councillors are appointed by the Governor alone with reference to the exigencies of representative government, the other public officers by the Governor on the advice of the Executive Council. In no appointments is the concurrence of the Home Government requisite.

'The control of all public departments is thus practically placed in the hands of persons commanding the confidence of a representative legislature.'

I now revert to the geographical classification of our colonies and other dependencies, which I gave in the early part of this chapter. I then pointed out to the student the three great masses of our empire which appear conspicuously upon the map—the North American, the East Indian, and the Australian, or the Australasian, as it is better called, to show that we are speaking of Van Diemen's Land and of New Zealand, as well as of the great continent, formerly called New Holland, but now Australia. The other classifications which we have been considering will not conflict at all confusedly with the geographical one. We shall find that the North American mass, and also the Australasian consist of colonies with local representative assemblies, either by virtue of having been originally settlements made by occupancy, or by virtue of the Crown having granted them representative assemblies. They have also now almost all received the rights of responsible self-government. We shall moreover find that both these masses of our empire are inhabited chiefly by agricultural colonists (according to Heeren's definition), and by men who are permanent settlers, not transitory traders or planters. On the contrary the great Indian mass of our empire has been acquired by cession or by conquest, and not by occupancy. It has no representative local self-government, though the power of the Crown over it is greatly controlled and regulated in many particulars by statutes which the Imperial Parliament has passed respecting India. Again, the Europeans in India, unlike the Europeans in British America or Australasia, are mere temporary residents, never intending to make the Indian territory their permanent home or the home of their children.

As I mentioned before, the Cape colony and its neighbouring territories make a group for separate consideration; and the same is the case with reference to our West Indian possessions.

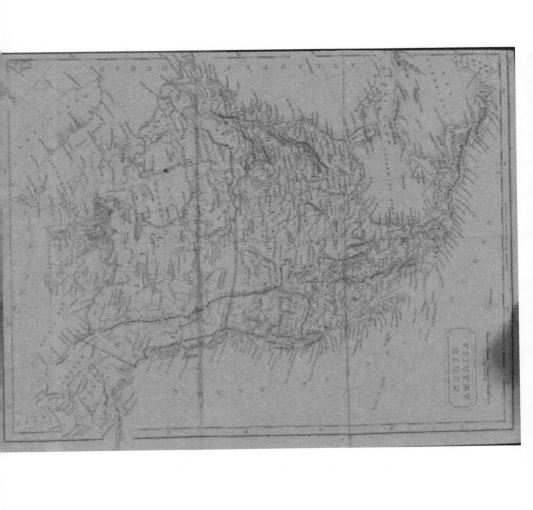

CHAPTER IV.

Our North American Dominions—Newfoundland discovered by
Cabot, partly settled by Sir Humphry Gilbert—Gilbert's Views of
Colonisation—Queen Elizabeth's Charter to Gilbert—His Voyage—
His Death—Subsequent Colonisation of Newfoundland—Subsequent
History, Area, Climate, &c.—Cape Breton, Prince Edward Island,
New Brunswick, Nova Scotia—General Sketch of British Colonisa-
tion in America after the Death of Sir Humphry Gilbert resumed
—Raleigh—Virginia—Hakluyt—King James's Charter—Robertson
—Bacon—Jamestown founded—Martial Law—First Representative
Assembly—Negro Slavery—The New England Colonies—The
Puritans—Maryland—Rhode Island—Connecticut—Newhaven—
New Hampshire—Maine—Treatment of Massachussets by Charles II.
—The Navigation Acts—The Colonial System—New York, New
Jersey, Pensylvania, Delaware—The Hudson's Bay Territory—
The Seven Years' War—Decisive Contest between the French and
the English for Mastery in North America—Wolfe—Conquest of
Canada—The thirteen North American Colonies rise against English
Domination—War of Independence—Establishment of the United
States—Causes of the American War—Taxing Colonies—Distinc-
tion between the Imperial Parliament's legal right and moral right
to tax—The Statute supposed to renounce such Taxation—Lord
Mansfield's Judgment in Campbell v. Hall—Its general Importance
—History of the remaining North American Provinces of our
Empire—Canada, Upper and Lower—Their Constitutions and
Troubles—Increased Action of the Home Government in Colonial
Government—Discontents—New System of Colonial Responsible
Government—Abandonment of the old Commercial System—Lord
Durham's Mission to British North America—Reunion of the
Canadas—Union of other Provinces—Dominion of Canada: its
Constitution—Population—The Hudson's Bay Company—British
Columbia—Climate.

I AM now about to sketch separately the main circumstances of our acquisition of the great North
American mass of our transmarine empire, leaving

for separate sketches the great Indian mass, and the great Australasian mass, besides the Cape, and besides the West Indian possessions. But though I think this, on the whole, the most convenient course to follow, a student who took the North American part and the Indian part together, and worked up these subjects in chronological order, would find the process easy and instructive. The history of the English, as a nation founding colonies and acquiring distant dominion, begins in the reign of Elizabeth. It was in the same reign that the germs of both our American and our Indian empires were planted. The charter, by authority of which Sir Humphry Gilbert occupied part of North America (which we shall speak of in a page or two further on) was granted by Queen Elizabeth in 1575; and in December 1600 the same great Sovereign granted the primary charter to 'the Governor and Company of Merchants in London trading to the East Indies,' which was the origin of our renowned East India Company in after times, and of our present Oriental Empire. It was, indeed, to voyages undertaken with the view of effecting a north-west passage to the Indies and to Cathay (as China was then termed) that the early English discoveries of North American territory and the first English settlements in the New World are due. In the same reigns (of James I. and Charles I.) in which the settlements in

Virginia and New England were formally planted, the East India Company obtained its Firmans from the Mogul Emperors, which allowed them to establish their factories at Surat (1616) and Bengal (1624–1640). In Charles II.'s reign the Dutch settlements in the Hudson were ceded to the English, and added to the Anglo-American possessions; and in the same reign the East India Company obtained the important territorial acquisition of Bombay. Other cases of synchronism in the progress of these two transmarine branches of our empire—the Great Eastern and the Great Western—might be cited. But it is enough to point out that the Seven Years' War (1756–1763) was the great epoch of the gigantic advance of our power in both East and West. Clive's victory at Plassy was won in 1757, and Wolfe's victory at Quebec in 1759.

I have indicated a mode of working up Anglo-American and Anglo-Indian history together, which may be usefully followed, so far as those two branches of our dominions are concerned; but for the purposes of this work I take Anglo-America separately. I shall include in the sketch, which I am about to give of its acquisition, some notice of the thirteen colonies which once formed the fairest portion of our possessions in the Western Hemisphere, but which severed themselves from us nearly a century ago, and have grown into the great commonwealth of the present United States of America. I do so because very much occurred during our acquisition of these colonies, during our retention of them, and during the struggle by which they were dismembered from the Imperial dominion of Britain, that throws valuable light on the theories, which from time to time have prevailed respecting colonisation, and respecting the political connection between colonies and their mother country. But it will be unnecessary for the purposes of the present work to trace, even in the most general manner, the progress of the United States after they had achieved, and after Great Britain had solemnly acknowledged their independence.

Look at the map of North America, to the parts where that continent and its adjacent islands project furthest into the Atlantic. You see there the earliest seats of British colonisation. Newfoundland, which is the northernmost of the habitable regions along the coasts of that ocean, is the first in point of date of the acquired transmarine portions of our Empire. Sebastian Cabot, sailing under the orders of an English king, and with English ships, had visited the island of Newfoundland as early as 1497; and after Cabot's voyage of discovery the British merchants sent fishing fleets more and more frequently and regularly to these regions, for the abundant supplies of cod and other fish that were found there; and the mariners of these ships carried on a slight traffic with the natives of those rugged shores.

More extensive discoveries were made by Frobisher, Hudson, and others; but it was not till 1583 that anything which can be called even the rudiment of a British colony in North America was planted. Even then the project of finding a north-west passage to Cathay was the chief motive of the primary coloniser. This was Sir Humphry Gilbert, one of the bold band of British mariners, who threw such lustre over the Elizabethan era.

He was a native of Devonshire, and half-brother to Sir Walter Raleigh. Like his illustrious kinsman and many more of the chiefs of England's heroic age, he combined the various glories of the scholar, the orator, the author, the sailor, and the soldier. His career in the House of Commons as a statesman was deformed by the taint of excessive adulation of the reigning Queen, and of unconstitutional exaggeration of the royal prerogative over the people's rights. This was a common vice in those days; and it will be found to have existed in a worse degree in Bacon, in Raleigh, and in other greater men than Sir Humphry Gilbert. In other matters of statesmanship he deserves to be ranked high. He was the first to discover and declare the benefit which colonies would bring to England's commerce, and the relief which colonial emigration would bring to the pressure of pauperism on the commonwealth at home. Sir Humphry published, in 1576, his 'Discourse to prove a Passage by the North-West to Cathay and the East Indies.'[1] Part of his scheme was to plant English settlers on the North American coasts along which such an expedition must pass. He says, 'We might inhabite some part of those countreys, and settle there such needy people of our country which now trouble the commonwealth, and, through want here at home, are enforced to commit outrageous offences, whereby they are dayly consumed with the gallows.' 'Also here we shall increase both our ships and mariners without burdening the State, and also have occasion to set poore men's children to learn handicraftes, and thereby to make trifles and such like, which the Indians and those people do so much esteeme; by reason whereof there should be none occasion to have our countrey combred with loiterers, vagabonds, and such like idle persons.'

Two years after this treatise was published, Gilbert obtained from the Queen a charter authorising him to occupy and colonise any parts of the North American continent that were not already in the possession of any of her Majesty's allies.[2] The

---

[1] It will be found in Hakluyt's old collection of 'Voyages,' vol. iii.

[2] The French had made attempts at colonisation on the shores of the St. Lawrence in 1541 and 1542 under Cartier (the discoverer of

charter was to be of perpetual efficacy, on condition
of a plantation by virtue of it being effected within
six years of its date.   Queen Elizabeth granted to
Gilbert as his own for ever all such 'heathen and
barbarous countries as he might discover;' and he
was to exercise over them supreme executive and
legislative dominion.   Somewhat inconsistently, the
charter promised to settlers in the new colony 'The
rights of Englishmen.'   The reservations in favour
of the English Crown were that Gilbert and his successors should do homage to Queen Elizabeth and
her successors, and that they should pay, as tribute,
a fifth part of the gold and silver that the colonised
regions might produce.   Gilbert put to sea in 1579,
but was driven back by stress of weather after losing

Canada in 1534) and under Roberval. Under the directions and by
the influence of Coligni, other expeditions were sent out in 1562 and
1564 to Carolina (so called after Charles IX. of France) and to
Florida. All these ended in the destruction or flight back to
Europe of the colonists. The Spaniards, in 1565, massacred the
French settlers in Florida, who were nearly all Huguenots. The
Spaniards then built the city of St. Augustine in Florida. 'It is by
more than forty years the oldest town in the United States.'—*Bancroft*.

Besides Florida, the Spanish Empire in the New World extended
far into North America, including California and other important
regions, at the time when Elizabeth gave Gilbert his charter. She
had no scruples about permitting and encouraging Drake, Hawkins,
and others, to burn and capture the King of Spain's ships or his
towns along the American coasts; but she was nominally at peace
with him ; and it was thought too much to take permanent possession of his territories and make them part of the dominions of
England in peace time.

one of his best ships. He sailed again in 1583 with a large company of volunteer adventurers, and reached Newfoundland in the month of August. He took formal possession of the territory round the harbour of St. John's, and granted several allotments of land to the intended colonists who were with him. None of these remained in Newfoundland that winter ; but as several of them afterwards returned, and took possession of their allotments under Sir Humphry's grants, it is not without reason that he has been called the father of our North American Empire.

The manner of his death, and the spirit in which he foresaw and encountered danger, deserve recording. It is the same spirit that has animated Englishmen in many a dire extremity on sea and on land, and without which our colonial and eastern empires never could have arisen. In the treatise already mentioned respecting the North-Western passage, Sir Humphry had professed his readiness to lead the expeditions which he recommended. In the concluding words of that treatise he pledged himself ' always to live and to die in this mind; that he is not worthy to live at all, who, for fear or danger of death, shunneth his country's service and his own honour; seeing death is inevitable, and the fame of virtue immortal. Wherefore in this behalf " *Mutare vel timere sperno.*" '

These were brave words; and the truthfulness of him who uttered them was proved by as brave a death. In September, 1583, Sir Humphry Gilbert left St. John's harbour, and sailed southward with three vessels, intending to make further discoveries along the coast of the North American continent. He had gone on board the 'Squirrel,' a little barque of only ten tons, and therefore best adapted for running into bays and up rivers; but in the judgment of his brother mariners 'too small a barque to pass through the ocean sea at that season of the year.' The other ships were larger. One of them soon struck on a rock, and was wrecked; and then Sir Humphry, in the 'Squirrel,' with his sole remaining consort—the 'Hind'—put about and ran for England. The 'Hind' alone reached port. On the 9th of September her crew saw the last of the barque that carried Gilbert. They were close to her during part of the day, both vessels being then in great danger from the heavy seas, especially the 'Squirrel.' The 'Hind' was carried past her a little before nightfall; and the crew of the larger ship plainly saw Gilbert standing abaft with a book in his hand, and heard him call out to his men, 'We are as near to Heaven by sea as by land.' That same night, about twelve o'clock, the lights on board the 'Squirrel' suddenly disappeared, and neither the little barque, nor any of those who manned her, were ever seen more.

Seafaring men of other nations besides the English frequented Newfoundland; and the home Government took little or no heed of it until 1623, when Sir George Calvert, afterwards Lord Baltimore, obtained a charter from James I., under which he formed a colony on the south-eastern part of the island, which he called Avalon. He made his son the Governor. He himself soon afterwards founded the colony of *Maryland*, on the continent. It is remarkable that the colonists led by Lord Baltimore were chiefly Roman Catholics, who left England to avoid the penal laws enacted there against members of that Church, while the Puritans were beginning to emigrate, in order to avoid the laws in England against Nonconformists. Other colonies, consisting principally of Irish, were planted in Newfoundland by Lord Falkland in 1633, and in 1654 by Sir David Kirk. After the Restoration, further colonisation in Newfoundland was discouraged by the Stuarts. William III. judged more wisely of the value of this possession. But the number of French who had settled in Newfoundland was then considerable, and they had a strong post there named Placentia. Louis XIV. claimed the whole island; and it was the scene of many contests in the war which ended in the Peace of Ryswick, in 1697. When war broke out again in 1702, the struggle of the English and French for the rule of Newfoundland recommenced. The

French were most vigorously supported by their own Government, and they conquered nearly all the English stations; but the Treaty of Utrecht in 1713 gave to Great Britain exclusive sovereignty over Newfoundland and the adjacent islands, reserving to the French only some limited rights of fishing.

Newfoundland has always been regarded as a settled colony. Its Representative House of Assembly was established by the Crown in 1832.[1] Some variations in its local government were made by the Imperial Legislature in 1842 and in 1847. Responsible government was established in 1855. It has a Governor appointed by the Crown, an Executive Council of 7 members, a Legislative Council of 15, and a House of Assembly of 30, elected by household suffrage. Newfoundland is certain before long to

[1] The Newfoundland House of Assembly, in 1838, committed one of the inhabitants of the island to prison for contempt of the House, such contempt not having taken place in the face of the House. This led to an action and to a very learned argument, and to a very important decision of the Judicial Committee of the Privy Council. (Kielley v. Carson, reported in Moore's Privy Council Reports, vol. iv., p. 63). It was then determined that a Colonial House of Assembly has not, as the Imperial House of Commons has, the power to arrest and punish for contempt if it is not committed in its presence. Other important questions were discussed in this case. It was treated as settled constitutional law that the Crown can by its prerogative create a Legislative Assembly in a settled colony, subordinate to the Imperial Parliament, but with full power within the limits of the colony for the government of its inhabitants; but it was doubted whether the Crown can by its prerogative bestow on such an assembly a power of committing for contempt, such power not being incidental to it by common law.

become part of the new great North American Confederation, called the Dominion of Canada, the constitutional and political condition of which will be
described in a later portion of this chapter.

The area of Newfoundland is estimated from 40,000
to 60,000 square miles. The probable amount of the
population at present is about 130,000. All or nearly
all of these are Europeans, or of European origin.
The native tribes that once were to be found in the
island have abandoned it, or have become extinct.
A settler from Europe, if of strong habit of body,
may enjoy vigorous health in Newfoundland, and
may reasonably hope to see his children grow up
there in health and strength. The cold in winter is
severe, but not so bitter as in the neighbouring
regions of the North American continent. The vast
Atlantic sea which surrounds Newfoundland tempers
its cold, but gives it an atmosphere which for great
part of the year is humid and foggy. The fisheries
have always been the great sources of the wealth of
Newfoundland. French writers since Louis XIV.'s
time have appreciated this; and Chateaubriand and
others have commented bitterly on the ignorant indifference with which their *Grand Monarque* by the
Treaty of Utrecht parted with the claims of France
to the inexhaustible fisheries of Newfoundland. The
Abbé Raguel[1] says of Newfoundland: ' Other colonies

---

[1] Cited by Mr. Bourne in ' The Story of our Colonies,' p. 75.

have yielded productions only by receiving an equal value in exchange. Newfoundland alone hath drawn from the depths of the waters riches formed wholly by nature, and which furnish subsistence to several countries of both hemispheres. How much time hath elapsed before this parallel hath been made! Of what importance did fish appear when compared with the gold which men went in search of in the Old World? It was long before it was understood that the representation of a thing is not greater than the thing itself, and that a ship filled with cod and a galleon are vessels equally laden with gold. There is even this remarkable difference, that mines can be exhausted, but never fisheries. Gold is not reproductive; the fish are so incessantly.'

The fisheries, and the processes of preparing and curing fish, furnish occupation to nearly all the population of the island for six months of the year, from May to October. Seal-hunting in March and April, when the loosened fields of ice are floating southward from the polar regions gives a lucrative temporary employment to some fifteen thousand of the hardiest and most daring of the islanders. But Newfoundland is capable of supplying large stores of wealth from its own soil, besides those which are gained from the seas around it. Wheat, barley, oats, potatoes, and turnips of the best quality are produced there; and as more and more attention is being continually paid to their cultivation, New-foundland will before long rank high as an agricul-tural colony, besides the pre-eminence as an island of fishermen which it is certain always to retain.

To the south-west of Newfoundland, and on the lower sides of the estuary of the great river St. Lawrence, and of the Gulf of St. Lawrence, we see a group of countries that are marked on the map as British possessions. There are Cape Breton, Prince Edward Island, New Brunswick, and Nova Scotia. I shall have to speak of Lower Canada presently. These four regions, Cape Breton, Prince Edward Island, New Brunswick, and Nova Scotia were all visited by Cabot in his original voyage of discovery to the North American continent in 1497; and the English always claimed title to them by reason of Cabot having taken formal possession of them in the name of the King of England. But the first real attempts at settlement in these regions were made by Frenchmen. The English on more than one occasion destroyed the French settlements and expelled French settlers ; but it was not until the Treaty of Utrecht in 1713, that the islands, since called Prince Edward Island, New Brunswick, and Nova Scotia, were secured to British Sovereignty. Cape Breton was then retained by the French, but was ceded to us by the Treaty of Paris in 1763. It will be more convenient to speak of them presently in connection with the subject of our acquisition of the Canadas. Meanwhile, we will resume our general subject of British colonisation in North America; and we will take it up at the time of the death of Sir Humphry Gilbert in 1583, after he had taken possession of Newfoundland, as described a few pages back.

Gilbert's half-brother, Sir Walter Raleigh, had taken active part in the planning, and in the equipment of Sir Humphry's expedition, though he had not personally accompanied his relative on that calamitous voyage. Undaunted by disaster, Raleigh in the next year (1584) obtained another charter from Queen Elizabeth, under which he designed to found a colony on some favourable part of the North American continent. He sent out two barques, under Captain Amadas and Captain Barlow, to explore the Atlantic coast, and to select a site for the new settlement. They coasted for some distance along the sea-board of the country that is now North Carolina, and chose the island of Roanoke, near the mouth of the inlet now called Albemarle Sound. It was at this place that the first English colony on the continent of America was founded (August 25, 1585). Amadas and Barlow, on their return to England, gave such a glowing account of this part of America, that Queen Elizabeth highly favoured the project for occupying the territory, and she desired

that the new country should be called 'Virginia.'
But the first attempts at settlement there were dis-
astrous failures. The scanty bands of colonists
perished by starvation, or were massacred by the
natives; and when James I. became King of England
(1603) there was not a single Englishman settled on
the American continent. There had, however, been
a voyage made by Captain Gosnold in 1602, which
did much to revive the spirit of colonising enterprise.
Gosnold explored the American shores in higher
latitudes than the spot where Raleigh's unfortunate
colonists had landed and perished. He entered
Massachusetts Bay, sowed wheat on some of its
islands, traded with the neighbouring Indians, and
returned with a remunerative cargo of wood, furs,
and gums.

The effect at home of the favourable report given
by Gosnold of the places, which he had explored, was
aided by the prosperous results of an adventure of
some London merchants, who sent out a ship in
1606, which discovered Long Island, and brought
home a profitable shipload acquired by traffic with
the Indians of Connecticut River and the districts
near it.

Many of the English nobility and gentry, as
well as of the commercial classes, were now eager
to co-operate in new .schemes for planting settlements in America. A clergyman, named Richard

Hakluyt[1] (the collector and editor of the well-known series of narratives of voyages and discoveries made by Englishmen), who had applied himself to the study of geography and navigation, did more than any other to excite and keep alive this spirit. King James was favourably disposed to such speculations, if conducted in a pacific spirit; and he listened graciously to the request addressed to him by an Association that was formed for establishing colonies in America, when they besought him to give to their undertaking the sanction of his kingly authority.

The Association wished for power to occupy in King James's name whatever parts they pleased of the North American coast from Roanoke (where Raleigh's settlers had been placed) indefinitely northward. But the King thought this too great a power to be given to a single company. He therefore divided the vast territory that lies between the thirty-fourth and the forty-fifth degrees of latitude into two nearly equal portions; one of which was to be called the first, or south colony of Virginia, and the other the second or north colony. Each of these was allotted by him to a separate company. He divided the Association into a London Company, formed of members who chiefly resided in the metro-

---

[1] 'Richard Hakluyt, prebendary of Westminster, to whom England is more indebted for its American possessions than to any man of that age.'—Robertson's *History of America*, book ix.

polis, and into a Plymouth Company, formed of the knights, gentlemen, and merchants of the West of England, who were members of the Association. He granted a charter by which the London Company were licensed and empowered 'to make habitations and plantations, and to induce a colony of sundry of the King's people into that part of America commonly called Virginia.' The London Company were to take the lower or southern half of the territories between the thirty-fourth and forty-fifth degrees. The Plymouth Company were to take the upper or northern.

Some of the provisions of this charter are remarkable. The Supreme Government of the colonies founded by virtue of it was to be vested in a Council resident in England. The King was to nominate the members of this Council, and they were to act according to such laws and ordinances as the King should give them under his sign manual. The details of local government were to be regulated by another Council resident in the colony; and the members of this Council also were to hold office by Royal appointment, and were to follow instructions given by the King. After the complete and arbitrary power of the Crown over the colonies had been thus ordained by the charter, clauses followed which now read like mockeries, but were probably considered by James to be quite consistent with the assertion of unlimited Royal prerogative.   To this prerogative all rights of the subject were, in James's opinion, subordinate.

These clauses were copied from the old charters that had been given to Gilbert and to Raleigh. They declared that the settlers in the new plantations should have and enjoy all the privileges of free denizens and natives of England, any law, custom, or usage to the contrary notwithstanding; and the settlers were to hold their lands in America by the freest and least burdensome tenure.   Then came some very remarkable clauses in favour of the new colonists.   All supplies from England that were necessary for the support of the new colonies or for the commerce were to be exported from the mother country to them, duty free, for a term of seven years; and the colonists were to have liberty to trade freely with foreign nations.   All such duties as might be levied in the colony on imports for the first twenty-one years after the settlement were to make a fund for the benefit of the colony.

Robertson, in the valuable chapters on the English discoveries and settlements which he has left us in his unfinished History of America, pauses naturally to comment on the contents of 'this singular charter.'   His observations on the clause, which gave the colonists free trade with foreigners, draw our attention to the contrast between the theories prevalent on such subjects at the time when the learned and accomplished historian was writing, and the antagonistic theories by which the old ones have within our own recollection been superseded. Robertson regards the free-trade article as ' unfavourable to the interests of the parent State ;' inasmuch as ' by the unlimited permission of trade with foreigners the parent State is deprived of that exclusive commerce which has been deemed the chief advantage resulting from the establishment of colonies.' But King James, in giving this unusual commercial liberty to his intended young colony, was probably guided by the advice of a statesman who was far in advance of his own age, and of Robertson's age also, as to political economy. Lord Bacon, in his ' Essay on Plantations ' (already referred to [1]), says, respecting the treatment of young colonies ; ' Let there be freedom from custom till the plantation be of strength; and not only freedom from custom, but *freedom to carry their commodities* where they may *make their best use of them*, except there be some special cause of caution.' [2]

---

[1] P. 52, *supra.*

[2] The experience in colonial matters which we have gained in the last thirty years enables us to appreciate the marvellous amount of strong practical common sense, as well as of enlightened philosophy contained in this little essay, written two centuries and a half ago. The indignant remonstrances raised by the Australian settlers against the transportation system show the truth of Bacon's words, ' that it is a shameful and unblessed thing to take the scum of people and

Three vessels, sent out by the London Company, were caught in a strong southerly gale as they approached the American coast, and were fortunately carried past Roanoke Island, the site of Raleigh's attempted settlements, into the noble bay of the Chesapeake. Their crews gave the names of James's sons to the two capes at the entrance of the gulf, and they still are called Cape Henry and Cape Charles. The adventurers sailed some distance up a river which they named James River, after their Sovereign ; and they saw opening before and round them a country which, in their own words, ' claimed the prerogative over the most pleasant places in the world.' They selected a peninsula about fifty miles from the mouth of the river as the site of their settlement. They named it ' Jamestown.' It still exists under that name; and, though never flourishing or

---

wicked condemned men to be the people with whom you plant.' When we read the instructions that during the last few years have been issued by the Emigration Commissioners as to the classes likely to thrive in our colonies ; on the demand for labourers and mechanics; and the warning that those who are neither capitalists nor ' accustomed to work with their hands' will be doomed ' not only to almost certain disappointment, but also to severe hardship,' we seem to hear the echo of the old statesman's advice given in the same essay to founders of colonies : ' The people wherewith you plant, ought to be gardeners, ploughmen, labourers, smiths, carpenters, joiners, fishermen, fowlers, with some few apothecaries, surgeons, cooks, and bakers.' Much also has occurred in the colonies where gold has been found to show the worth of the essayist's caution— ' Moil not too much under-ground, for the hope of mines is very uncertain, and useth to make the planters lazy in other things.'

populous[1], it is the most ancient of English habitations on the North American continent.

But the Jamestown settlement had many narrow escapes from perishing in infancy like its unfortunate predecessor at Roanoke. The narrative of them is very interesting, but would be out of place here. The enthusiasm of the English nation for colonising did not abate. Fresh subscriptions were poured in, and the shareholders in the London Company of Virginia became a numerous and powerful corporation. They had strong influence at Court, and they obtained from King James an abrogation of the old charter, and the grant of a new one, which vested the supreme power over the colony in a Council in England to be appointed by the shareholders themselves [1609]. This Council was to make such laws as they thought best for the good government of the adventurers and inhabitants in the colony; and they were to nominate a Governor of the colony, who was to carry out their orders there.

It was under a Governor appointed in pursuance of this new charter, that the colony made its first steady advance in the enjoyment of good order

---

[1] Its position was well suited as a post of defence against the attacks of savage nations, but not for permanence as a thriving town. Jefferson's observation on it deserves to be remembered :— 'There are places at which the *laws* have said *there shall be towns*, but *nature* has said *there shall not*.' Cited in 'Macgregor,' vol. ii., p. 136, n.

and prosperity. This was Sir Thomas Dale; and it is remarkable that he administered the country avowedly under *martial law*. The Charter of 1609 had empowered the Governor to exercise martial law in cases of rebellion and mutiny; and, as the reports from the colony described a chronic state of disorder and strife, the treasurer and chief manager of the London Company when Dale was appointed Governor sent out a printed code of martial law, drawn up from the rules of war as acknowledged and practised in the armies of the Low Countries, which were considered (as Robertson says) to be the most rigid military school at that time in Europe.

' This system of government is so violent and arbitrary, that even the Spaniards themselves had not ventured to introduce it into their settlements ; for among them, as soon as a plantation began, and the arts of peace succeeded to the operations of war, the jurisdiction of the civil magistrate was uniformly established. But, however unconstitutional or oppressive this may appear, it was adopted by the advice of Sir Francis Bacon, the most enlightened philosopher, and one of the most eminent lawyers of the age.' [1]

The passage in Lord Bacon's works to which Robertson refers is in that statesman's ' Essay on

---

[1] Robertson's ' History of America,' book ix.

Plantations,' so often alluded to before. Bacon says there: ' For government, let it be in the hands of one, assisted with some counsel; and let them have commission to exercise martial laws, with some limitation.' The necessary limitation was in this case found in the disposition of Sir Thomas Dale himself. All accounts praise his judgment and industry. ' By the vigour which the summary mode of military punishment gave to his administration, he introduced into the colony more perfect order than had ever been established there; and at the same time he tempered his vigour with so much discretion, that no alarm seems to have been given by this formidable innovation.'[1]

But the Virginians soon experienced that it is not in the hands of every governor that the severe simplicity of martial law works as a beneficial despotism. One of Dale's new successors, named Argall, made this arbitrary authority subservient to his avarice and his capricious vindictiveness. He was persuaded with great difficulty to allow to one of the persons, whom he had sentenced summarily to death, the liberty of appealing to the Company in London. Argall's friends in the Council at first had the majority, and voted that ' martial law is the noblest kind of trial, because soldiers and men of the sword are the judges.' But this judgment was soon after-

---

[1] Robertson's ' History of America,' ib.

wards reversed, and resolutions were carried asserting the rights of the colonists to trial by jury.

In 1619 Sir George Yardley, a man of mild and
benevolent character, became governor. He was
aided by a local council authorised by the Company
at home; and in June 1619, Sir George Yardley, by
the advice of this local council, took the important
step of summoning to a Legislative Assembly two
elective representatives of each of the eleven corporations then established in Virginia. This was the
first popular Assembly that ever met in America.
All laws and all measures for the common weal of
the colony were debated in it.   This measure is said
to have given great contentment to the colonists,
and the number of fresh immigrants from Europe
increased rapidly. The majority of the London
Company were men favourable to popular rights;
and by a formal ordinance they gave Virginia a
written free Constitution.

The form of government prescribed for Virginia
was analogous to the English Constitution, and was
the model of the systems which, with some modifications, were afterwards introduced into the various
royal provinces. Its purpose was declared to be
' the greatest comfort and benefit to the people, and
the prevention of injustice, grievances, and oppression.' Its terms are few and simple; a Governor, to
be appointed by the Company; a permanent Council,

likewise to be appointed by the Company; a General Assembly, to be convened yearly, and to consist of the members of the Council, and of two burgesses to be chosen from each of the several plantations by their respective inhabitants. The Assembly might exercise full legislative authority, a negative voice being reserved to the governor; but no law or ordinance would be valid unless ratified by the Company in England. With singular justice and a liberality without example, it was further ordained that, after the government of the colony shall have once ' been framed, no orders of the court in London shall bind the colony, unless they be in like manner ratified by the General Assembly.' The courts of justice were required to conform to the laws and manner of trial used in the realm of England.[1]

It is a melancholy reflection that the establishment of constitutional freedom in British North America was almost contemporaneous with the establishment there of negro slavery. In 1619 a Dutch ship with a cargo of slaves from the Guinea coast anchored off Jamestown. They were purchased by the colonists, and other importations of slave labourers followed. At the present time, when not only has slavery been abolished for nearly forty years throughout the British Empire, but when the great commonwealth sprung from that Empire has at a fearful but not

[1] Bancroft's ' History of the United States,' vol. i., p. 119.

disproportionate cost of strife and suffering, put the accursed thing away from her, it is needless to dwell on this subject, which is one of tenfold more shame to England than to Anglo-America. But the fact of the long existence of a large servile population in Virginia and the neighbouring territories, as well as in our West India Islands, has too deeply affected their political and social history—it still too deeply affects the social and political condition of all those countries—to justify us in passing it over unnoticed. So far as regarded the relations of Virginia and the colonies like her with the mother-country, the oft-observed phenomenon was fully displayed, that bodies of men who, in respect of those below them, are intensified oligarchs, are frequently, in respect of those who try to exercise authority over them, the fiercest and the most determined democrats.[1]

---

[1] Burke's remarks on this are as follows:—'In Virginia and the Carolinas they have a vast multitude of slaves. Where this is the case in any part of the world, those who are free are by far the most proud and jealous of their freedom. Freedom is to them not only an enjoyment, but a kind of rank and privilege. Not seeing there that freedom, as in countries where it is a common blessing and as broad and general as the air, may be united with much abject toil, with great misery, with all the exterior of servitude, liberty looks amongst them like something that is more noble and liberal. I do not mean, Sir, to commend the superior morality of this sentiment, which has at least as much pride as virtue in it; but I cannot alter the nature of man. The fact is so, and these people of the southern colonies are much more strongly, and with a higher and more stubborn spirit, attached to liberty than those to the northward.'— *Speech of March* 22, 1772.

The London Virginia Company was, commercially, a failure. The shareholders got no dividends; yet the shares were still to some extent sought after. The meetings or courts of the Company were numerously attended; and the contest between arbitrary government and popular liberty, which was being waged in Parliament, was carried on in these courts with much more advantage to the popular side. Gondomar, the Spanish ambassador, told King James that 'the Virginia courts were but a seminary to a seditious Parliament.'[1] It was easy to find many irregularities, and many things which were worse than irregularities, in the proceedings of the Company; and in 1625 their patents were cancelled by a judgment of the Court of King's Bench on a *quo warranto* which the King had caused to be brought against them. Meanwhile the Virginian Assembly in the colony passed a law enacting that 'The governor shall not lay any taxes or ympositions upon the colony, their lands or commodities, other way than by the authority of the General Assembly, to be levyed and ymployed as the said Assembly shall appoynt.'[2]

They also showed that they had made an advance in what would be now called Political Economy, far beyond the old nations of Europe, where for centuries legislators had been competing in the

---

[1] Bancroft, p. 141. [2] Ibid., p. 144.

vain endeavour to keep provisions cheap, by fixing a compulsory low rate of prices. The Virginian colonists ordained, 'For the encouragement of men to plant store of corn the price shall not be stinted, but it shall be free for every man to sell it as deare as he can.' [1]

King James, after the quashing of the charter of Virginia, intended (as is believed) to frame by his own kingly wisdom a code of fundamental laws for the colony. He sent out what he meant to be a temporary direction to Sir Thomas Wyatt and the local council in the colony, by which he empowered them to govern 'as fully and as amply as any governor and council resident there at any time within the space of five years now last past.' As Bancroft observes,[2] these model five years were almost exactly the five years during which representative government had been in practice in the colony; and the order operated as a royal sanction and recognition of Virginia's popular Assembly.

King James I. died soon after the issuing of this order; and before he had composed a code of laws, as he had purposed, for Virginia. Charles I. was free from his father's passion for legislation. He let the colonists alone, except so far that he desired

[1] Bancroft.
[2] 'History of United States,' vol. i., p. 146.

to have a right of pre-emption of their tobacco, in order to make money by the monopoly of it in England. The Virginians were eminent for their loyalty, but they clung also to their free institutions. An attempt was made by a small party in 1642 to restore the system of government under the ancient royal patents, but a large majority of them protested against the change, and addressed the King in a remarkable document, in which they maintained the necessity of free trade, saying that 'freedom of trade is the blood and life of a commonwealth.' The modern American historian adds, 'And they defended their preference of self-government through a colonial legislature by a conclusive argument: There is more likelihood that such as are acquainted with the clime and its accidents may, upon better grounds, prescribe our advantages than such as shall sit at the helm in England.' In reply to their urgent petition, the King immediately declared his purpose not to change a form of government in which they 'received so much content and satisfaction.'[1]

The Virginians continued to be loyal subjects of Charles I.; and even after the overthrow of the Crown in England 'Virginia was whole for monarchy, and the last country belonging to England that submitted to obedience of the commonweath.' This

---

[1] Bancroft, vol. i., p. 155.

obedience was compelled by a fleet and army, which
the Parliamentarian Government sent out in 1652.
But a solemn compact was made between the colonists and the Commissioners who had been sent with
the expedition from England. 'It was agreed,
upon the surrender, that the " PEOPLE OF VIRGINIA "
should have all the liberties of the free-born people
of England, that they should intrust their business,
as formerly, to their own grand Assembly, should
remain unquestioned for their past loyalty, and
should have " as free trade as the people of England." No taxes, no customs, might be levied,
except by their own representatives ; no forts
erected, no garrisons maintained, but by their own
consent.' [1]

We have for some time been watching the growth
and progress of the great colony which was originated by one of the two companies created by James I.
in 1606. His London Company founded Virginia.
The other, the Plymouth Company, was intended to
plant colonists northward of the region assigned to
the London Company; and the Plymouth Company
did, in the two first years of its existence, send out
some feeble expeditions, but they accomplished
little. A few trading vessels annually visited the
shores near Cape Cod ; the coasts on either side
were explored, and the region northward of Long

---

[1] Bancroft, p. 170.

Island, as far as Penobscot Bay, became known by
the name of New England. ·

The history of the early Puritans under Elizabeth
and the two first Stuart Kings of England has been
written too often and too ably to justify a fresh narrative of their peculiar tenets, of the causes that
make them obnoxious to the chief authorities in
Church and State, of their sufferings and persecu-
tions without learning mercy, and of the indomitable
conscientiousness and courage (not unmingled with
narrowmindedness and love of singularity) which
sustained them throughout all their trials. These
men became the English of New England. A party
of one of the most advanced sects of the Puritans
had fled from England to Holland. They called
themselves 'Pilgrims.' When they were in Holland
they found themselves ill at ease in a strange
land, with foreign rule and foreign tongue. They
heard of the 'New England' which had been found
beyond the Atlantic seas, and they resolved to seek
a home there, in a region that was English, though
not part of their mother-country herself. They left
Holland in 1620, for Southampton, and thence began
their voyage across the Atlantic in the 'Speedwell,'
a ship of sixty tons, and the 'Mayflower,' of a hundred
and eighty. Some of them soon lost heart, and returned to England in the 'Speedwell.' The more
resolute, a company of forty-one men, who with their

families made up a total of one hundred, continued their course in the ' Mayflower;' and on November 11, 1620, landed in Massachusetts Bay, at a place to which they gave the name of New Plymouth.

Their sufferings and perils, and the holy heroism with which danger, disease, famine, and slaughter were endured by them, are topics not suited for these pages. We are dealing chiefly with Institutional History. They had no royal charter, or ordinance, or instrument of government. But, 'before they landed, the manner in which their government should be constituted was considered; and, as some were observed " not well affected to unity and concord," they formed themselves into a body politic by a solemn voluntary compact:—" In the name of God, Amen. We whose names are underwritten, and loyal subjects of our dread sovereign King James, having undertaken, for the glory of God and advancement of the Christian faith, and honour of our King and country, a voyage to plant the first colony in the northern parts of Virginia, do, by these presents, solemnly and mutually, in the presence of God and one of another, covenant and combine ourselves together into a civil body politic, for our better ordering and preservation, and furtherance of the ends aforesaid; and by virtue thereof to enact, constitute, and frame such just and equal laws, ordinances, acts, constitutions, and offices, from time to

time, as shall be thought most convenient for the
general good of the colony. Unto which we promise all due submission and obedience." '[1]

The Pilgrim Fathers at first endeavoured to follow
the primitive Apostolic system of having all things
in common. But this was soon found to cause
discontent; as the industrious naturally disliked to
work for the idle, and the idle refused to bear a fair
share of toil for the community; so that there was
an aggravation of the general dearth. Allotments of
land to individuals, at first for a season, and soon
afterwards in absolute property, were agreed on, and
were made. After this the little settlement produced
corn enough for its members, and also a surplus,
which they traded in with the neighbouring Indians.
The constitution was a democracy pure and simple.
For eighteen years every male inhabitant was a
member of the Legislature. Finally, the increase and
spread of numbers caused the adoption of the representative system. Still, New Plymouth continued
to be a voluntary association of unchartered freemen, ' held together by the consent [2] of its members

---

[1] Bancroft, vol. i., p. 234.

[2] Robertson's ' History of America,' book x., calls this the 'tacit '
consent of its members. But this is not quite correct as to the
patriarchs of the colony. For them the written agreement which
the Pilgrim Fathers signed in the cabin of the ' Mayflower ' was itself
a written consent, and a primary instrument of self-rule. All new
members of the community must have been held to have *tacitly* con-
sented to it.

to recognise the authority of laws and to submit
to the jurisdiction of magistrates framed and chosen
by themselves.'

These New England men must have possessed in
a very high degree, and all the Anglo-American
settlers must have possessed in a considerable degree
that sentiment, which Mr. Grote, in his ' History of
Greece' has termed ' constitutional morality,' and
which Professor Lieber describes as the spirit of
' institutional liberty.' There must have been frequent differences of opinion in these communities—
differences likely to be vehement and bitter in proportion with the paucity of numbers. Majorities
would have disfranchised and otherwise oppressed
minorities, minorities would have had prompt re-
course to armed opposition, if each party had not
been restrained by a feeling of loyalty to the law
because it *was* the law, and by a feeling of respect
for the rights of others. Unless the great mass of
the citizens are to some extent influenced by these
sentiments, no democratic community can long
exist. No such community could have maintained
itself under the circumstances, which surrounded
the rise and progress of the New England colonies,
unless these sentiments had been almost universally felt very vividly, and acted on very conscientiously.'

¹ See the comments of Mr. Grote in the second volume of ' Plato
and the other Companions of Socrates,' pp. 38 *et seq.*, and 84 *et seq.*

New Plymouth is the first in date, and I think it is the first in interest, of the New England colonies; but it was soon surpassed in population and power by its younger sister Massachusetts. A large and wealthy association of Puritans, or of men with at least strong puritanical inclinations, obtained from King Charles I. (1629) a charter for planting the province of Massachusetts Bay. At first it was prescribed that the legislative powers should be in a council of proprietors at home; but this was soon altered, and the Government was transferred to the

He justly praises the beautiful myth in which Protagoras teaches that men cannot exist in political societies unless they have implanted in them true feelings, justice, and the sense of shame—Δίκη καὶ Αἰίώς. [The last of these words, Αἰδώς, means more than ' sense of shame.' It means self-respect, and a respect also for the feelings of others.] Mr. Grote says in his commentary on this:— ' The very existence of the social union requires that each man should feel a sentiment of duties on his part towards others, and duties on their part towards him; or (in other words) of rights on his part to have his interests considered by others, and rights on their parts to have their interests considered by him. Unless this sentiment of reciprocity—reciprocal duty and right—exists in the bosom of each individual citizen, or at least in the large majority, no social union could subsist. There are doubtless different degrees of the sentiment. Moreover, the rights and duties may be apportioned better or worse, more or less fairly, among the individuals of a society; thus rendering the society more or less estimable and comfortable. But without a certain minimum of the sentiment in each individual bosom, even the worst constituted society could not hold together.' Mr. Grote quotes a striking remark of Professor Bain in his work on the emotions and the will:—' Doubtless, if the sad history of the human race had been preserved in all its details, we should have many examples of tribes that perished from being unequal to the conception of a social system, or to the restraints imposed by it.'

settlers in New England. On this being done, a large number of recruits, many of them men of good property and highly educated, joined the new settle-ment, the chief town of which was at first Salem; but Boston (so named after the English town from the neighbourhood of which many of the Puritan farmers had emigrated), from its superior advantages of maritime position, became soon recognised as the capital of Massachusetts.

The Massachusetts men carried their spirit of bold adventure into their politics. They cared little for the restraints of their charter, by which they were forbidden to make laws or ordinances repugnant to the laws of England, and which, by empowering the governor to administer the oath of supremacy, appeared to make by implication the Anglican Church the established Church of the colony. The Massa-chusetts men set up an anti-Episcopalian Church of their own; and they passed a law by which no man who was not a member of their Church was allowed to exercise the political rights of a freeman in their community. They based their criminal code on, or rather they copied it from, the Mosaic law. Accord-ing to the charter, the votes of those entitled to take part in the government of the colony were to be given personally; but in 1634 the colonists effected 'an innovation which totally altered the nature and constitution of the Government. When a general court was to be held in the year one thousand six hundred and thirty-four, the freemen, instead of attending in person, as the charter prescribed, elected representatives in their different districts, authorising them to appear in their name, with full power to deliberate and decide concerning every point that fell under the cognisance of the general court. Whether this measure was suggested by some designing leaders, or whether they found it prudent to soothe the people by complying with their inclination, is uncertain. The representatives were admitted and considered themselves, in conjunction with the governor and his assistants, as the supreme Legislative Assembly in the colony. In assertion of their own rights they enacted that no law should be passed, no tax should be imposed, and no public officer should be appointed, but in the General Assembly. The pretexts for making this new arrangement were plausible. The number of freemen was greatly increased; many resided at a distance from the places where the supreme courts were held; personal attendance became inconvenient; the form of government in their own country had rendered familiar the idea of delegating their rights and committing the guardianship of their liberties to representatives of their own choice; and the experience of ages had taught them that this important trust might with safety be lodged in their hands. Thus did the

Company of Massachusetts Bay, in less than six years from its incorporation by the King, mature and perfect a scheme which some of its more artful and aspiring leaders seem to have had in view when the association for peopling New England was first formed. The colony must henceforward be considered, not as a corporation whose powers were defined and its mode of procedure regulated by its charter, but as a society which, having acquired or assumed political liberty, had, by its own voluntary deed, adopted a constitution or government framed on the model of that in England.'[1]

These bold politics of the Massachusetts men were watched with eager attention and interest by the opponents of royal prerogative and of prelacy in England. Great numbers crossed the Atlantic, most of whom became permanent settlers in the New World. Some returned to take active part in the scenes of civil strife in England; and among the last class were two men of no little mark, Hugh Peters and the younger Sir Harry Vane. The strength of the current of emigration to New England, and the defiance of kingly prerogative both in state matters and in church matters, which was displayed there, drew at last the angry attention of King Charles. A writ of *quo warranto* was issued against the Corporation of Massachusetts Bay. It was easy to show

---

[1] Robertson's 'History of America,' book x.

breaches of the charter, which was declared accordingly by the Court of King's Bench to have been forfeited.

This would, in all human probability, have been followed by royal edicts for the administration of the colony by a strong government, taking its orders from the Crown, and unfettered by popular assemblies; but the storms of disaffection and civil war broke out in Scotland and England; and the King was soon too much occupied by the serious perils of his throne at home to be able to attend to the coercion of his democratic colonists beyond the Atlantic. The majority of the Long Parliament regarded the New Englanders with fellow-feeling and approbation. The House of Commons in 1642 passed a vote for the exemption of all the people in the plantations in New England from payment of duty on either exports or imports. Cromwell also looked on them favourably. When he conquered Jamaica in 1655, he offered his conquest to the New Englanders on condition that they would leave their settlements in a cold and harsh clime, and migrate to that fertile island. They wisely declined the offer. A love of the land, in which they had now for many years lived in freedom and in gradually increasing prosperity, had grown up in the men of New England. The Massachusetts men especially were proud of the progressive strength of their

I

State.   They coined silver money in 1652, 'stamped with the name of the colony and a tree, as an apt symbol of its progressive vigour.'[1]   Nine years earlier, Massachusetts and three of the other four New England colonies had taken the still more important and practical step of entering into a confederacy offensive and defensive.   The presence of Dutch settlers on the Hudson, of French settlers in Acadia (or Nova Scotia), and the frequency of hostilities with the Indian tribes, were the immediate cause of this league.   The Confederate States were to be called 'the United Colonies of New England.'   Two Commissioners from each colony were to assemble annually, 'or oftener, if need be,' to discuss and decide all matters that are 'the proper results or concomitants of a confederation.'   They were to determine on peace and war; and a proportionate rate was established, according to which each colony was to supply men to the confederate army in the ratio to its population.   But it was specially provided that each colony should remain separate and distinct, and have exclusive jurisdiction within its own territories.   The eight Commissioners exercised little practical authority; and probably for this reason the Confederacy of the United Colonies of New England did not excite any jealousy in the Long Parliament of the mother-country, and even survived for a con-

[1] Robertson's 'History of America,' book x.

siderable time the restoration of the Stuarts to the English throne.

I have sketched the early history of Virginia, the chief of the Southern colonies, and of Massachusetts, the chief of the Northern colonies, as far as Cromwell's time. To continue the narrative further, or to give details of even the early growth of the other colonies, would exceed the appointed limits and the proper scope of this book. I will now only mention generally the names of the other colonies, and the chief characteristics of their governments. I will also advert briefly to the main occurrences in the general history of British North America down to the time of the commencement of the first struggle between the French and the English races for ascendency in the New World. One topic I must deal with separately; that is, the introduction and the working of the navigation laws, those great instruments and supports of the once celebrated but now repudiated theory of THE COLONIAL SYSTEM.

Beginning with the Southern colonies, of which Virginia was the eldest and the principal, we shall find that before the end of the seventeenth century the large territory of Carolina to the south of Virginia had become a British colony. Afterwards, in 1719, this vast province was divided into North Carolina and South Carolina.

It has been mentioned already that it was in

Carolina that the first settlers, sent out by Sir Walter Raleigh, landed and perished; and that an equally unsuccessful attempt had been made by French Huguenots sent out by Coligni to found a permanent settlement in Carolina, which had received that name from the name of the then reigning King of France, Charles IX.[1]

The first Europeans who made an enduring settlement in Carolina came from Virginia; and, indeed, according to King James I.'s original patents, granted in 1607, the greater part of North Carolina was included in the South colony of Virginia. But in 1663 Charles II. granted to Lord Clarendon and seven others charters, which purported to make them proprietors of the province of Carolina, which was to include all the territory extending from the 36th degree of North latitude to the river San Matheo. An elaborate constitution for the government of this great region was drawn up by the celebrated statesman Shaftesbury and the still more celebrated philosopher John Locke. It was most comprehensive and minute, and it was lauded in Europe as a marvellous specimen of wisdom; but in the colony it was found utterly impracticable and useless. Like many other paper constitutions, it read well, but it would not work. Much confusion ensued, which resulted in the colonists practically ruling themselves by an elective assembly

[1] See note to p. 79, *supra*.

under a governor sent out by the proprietors. In 1719 the proprietary government was abolished, and a royal government established in each of the colonies of North and South Carolina, into which the old province was then subdivided.

As Carolina had been founded chiefly out of territories originally assigned to Virginia, so at a later period another colony, GEORGIA, was formed out of territories previously included in the early charters of Carolina. Georgia was founded in 1732 as a chartered colony by a private company; it became a royal government in 1752.

The foundation of Maryland, northward of Virginia, by Lord Baltimore, in 1616, has been already mentioned. The Constitution of Maryland was very peculiar. Lord Baltimore had authority like that which a feudal lord used to exercise over his domains in mediæval Europe; and his heirs retained considerable portion of this seigneurial authority down to the War of Independence. Maryland was thus originally one of the old Southern States; but in modern times it has been usually ranked among the Middle States, of which we shall have to speak a little farther on.

Among the Northern or New England colonies, New Plymouth and Massachusetts have already been described. Besides these, Rhode Island was founded in 1638, by Roger Williams and five companions,

who left Massachusetts with him to seek elsewhere
that liberty of conscience which the Massachusetts
men, when persecuted in England, had claimed for
themselves, but which, when established in the New
World, they systematically denied to others.   Rhode
Island and its founder deserve mention, for it was
the first civilised community, that avowed and
realised the principles of universal toleration.   The
historian Robertson says of Williams that ' his spirit
differed from that of the Puritans in Massachusetts;
it was mild and tolerating, and having ventured
himself to reject established opinions, he endeavoured to secure the same liberty to other men, by
maintaining that the exercise of private judgment is
a natural and sacred right; that the civil magistrate
has no compulsive jurisdiction in the concerns of
religion; that the punishment of any person on account of his religious opinions was an encroachment
on conscience and an act of persecution.   These
humane principles he instilled into his followers ;
and all who felt or dreaded oppression in other
settlements, resorted to a community, in which universal toleration was known to be a fundamental
maxim.   In the plantations of Providence [1] and
Rhode Island political union was established by

---

[1] One of Williams' first settlements, named by him ' Providence,'
was on the mainland.   Rhode Island, strictly speaking, was an
island in Narragansett Bay to which Williams and some of his followers proceeded.

voluntary association, and the equality of condition among the members as well as their religious opinions; their form of government was purely democratical, the supreme power being lodged in the freemen personally assembled. In this state they remained until they were incorporated by charter.' [1]

The very liberal character of this charter is remarkable, considering that Charles II. was the King who granted it, and that Clarendon was the minister by whose exertions on behalf of the colonists it was obtained. It is an act of justice to both sovereign and statesman to cite its principal provisions. It gave the rule of the colony to a governor, a deputy-governor, ten assistants, afterwards called senators, and to deputies elected by the townships. The laws were not to be contrary to the laws of England; but it was wisely added that the laws were to be made with regard to 'the constitution of the place and the nature of the people.' The charter further ordains that 'No person within the said colony, at any time hereafter, shall be anywise molested, punished, disquieted, or called in question, for any difference in opinion in matters of religion; every person may at all times freely and fully enjoy his own judgment and conscience in matters of religious concernments.'

Connecticut, like Rhode Island, was an offshoot

[1] Robertson's 'History of America,' book x.

colony from Massachusetts. It was founded in 1635.
Another colony (also emanating from Massachusetts) maintained itself for some time as a separate
colony at Newhaven, but ultimately was blended
with Connecticut. A charter was granted to Connecticut in 1662 of a most democratic nature. The
colonists were empowered to elect their own officers
and to make their own laws without restriction.

The fourth and largest portion of the New England colonies, as we now see them on the map, lies to
the north of Massachusetts, and is now divided into
Vermont, New Hampshire, and Maine. The two
last are the old names. Cabot had discovered the
eastern coast in 1497; and afterwards French adventurers had visited it and given it the name of ' Maine,'
from the old French county which was so called.
About 1635 some English · settlers fixed themselves
in the south-eastern region, and a proprietary charter
of Maine was granted in 1639 to Sir Frederick
George. In 1652 it was united to Massachusetts,
and continued to form part of that large state until
after the War of Independence. The region now
divided into New Hampshire and Vermont (both of
which were formerly included under the name of
New Hampshire) was irregularly settled by immigrants from various quarters between 1635 and
1677, when it was organised as a colony and received a royal charter. This recognised a repre-

sentative assembly, with the reservation to the King and his officers of a veto on its proceedings.

The liberality with which the weaker colonies of New England were treated by Charles II. and his ministers is the more remarkable, when contrasted with the very different conduct adopted by the Home Government towards the one powerful New England colony, Massachusetts. It was probably the comparative strength of Massachusetts, that made her suspected at home, especially as she assumed and maintained a tone of almost turbulent independence, whenever she considered herself to be injuriously interfered with by the British authorities. In the time of the Long Parliament she had by her agent in England publicly denied the right of the English Parliament to bind her by its legislation. The Massachusetts men protested that, 'If the Parliament of England should impose laws upon us, having no burgesses in the House of Commons, nor capable of a summons by reason of the vast distance, we should lose the liberties and freedom of English indeed.' They also protested against the Parliament modifying their charter or allowing appeals from their courts. The English Parliament replied to them, 'We encourage no appeals from your justice. We leave you with all the freedom and latitude that may, in every respect, be duly claimed by you.'

Indulgently treated by the Parliamentary Government, and afterwards by the Protector, Massachusetts, unlike the Southern colonies, showed little joy at Charles II.'s Restoration.   Before the Massachusetts men acknowledged him as king, they published a bold declaration of their natural and chartered rights. Charles confirmed their charter, but insisted on his royal right of interposition in their proceedings. Bickerings with the King and the King's Commissioners followed; and at last, in 1684, proceedings were taken in the English courts, by which the Massachusetts charter was declared to have been forfeited. Lord Macaulay, in his 'History of England,'[1] alludes to the 'remarkable scene' which occurred in one of the last councils held by Charles II. 'The charter of Massachusetts had been forfeited, and a question arose how, for the future, the colony should be governed.   The general opinion of the Board was that the whole power, legislative as well as executive, should abide in the Crown.   Halifax took the opposite side, and argued with great energy against absolute monarchy, and in favour of representative government.   It was vain, he said, to think that a population sprung from the English stock and animated by English feelings would long bear to be deprived of English institutions.   Life, he exclaimed, would not be worth having in a country where

---

[1] Vol. i., p. 272.

liberty and property were at the mercy of one despotic master.'

During the short reign of James II., which commenced soon after the holding of this council, the King was too much occupied with his innovations and troubles at home to be able to apply his principles of absolute government to his American dominions. Massachusetts was, though nominally disfranchised, left to rule herself; and the Revolution of 1688 put an end to attacks on behalf of the Crown upon popular rights on the western side of the Atlantic, as well as in the Britannic Islands.

One cause of the animosity shown by the Massachusetts men against the Home Government in Charles II.'s time, and which in Virginia caused actual insurrection, was the restriction of the colonists' freedom of trade by the Navigation Act. This restrictive policy is generally said to have been instituted by the statesmen of the Long Parliament, but it was not really until Charles II.'s reign that it was made to press with any severity on the North American settlers.

In 1650, after the execution of Charles I., and when the abolition of monarchy had been proclaimed in England, Virginia adhered for a time to the cause of royalty, as did also some of our colonies in the West Indies. At that time the carrying trade of Europe and of the European colonies in North

America and the West Indies was almost entirely in the hands of the Dutch. The English Parliament enacted first a law which prohibited all ships of foreign nations from trading with any English plantations without license from the Council of State. In the following year, 1651, the Parliament passed another law, which ordained that no productions of Asia, Africa, or America should be imported into any of the dominions of the commonwealth, except in vessels belonging to English owners, or to the people of the colonies settled there, or in the ships of that European nation of which the merchandise imported was the genuine growth or manufacture. This law was passed with the design to reduce the maritime power of Holland; a country against which the leaders of the English Parliament were at that time vehemently exasperated.[1] It did in fact do much injury to the Dutch, and it led to war between the two commonwealths. It did not affect the trade or shipping of the colonies so as to create any discontent there.[2] But the first Parliament of Charles II. re-enacted the restrictive laws of the commonwealth with very severe additions. The new Navigation Act gave the English shipowners and the English merchants a complete monopoly of the trade with the colonies. It enacted that no commodities should

---

[1] See Davies' 'Holland,' vol. ii., p. 709.
[2] See Bancroft's 'History of the United States,' vol. i., p. 381.

be imported into any settlement in Asia, Africa, America, or exported from there, except in vessels of English or plantation build, whereof the master and three-fourths of the mariners should be English subjects, under pain of forfeiting ship and goods; and that none but natural-born subjects, or such as should have been naturalised, should exercise the occupation of merchant or factor in any English settlement. The next object was to compel the colonists to send to England all the most valuable articles of colonial produce. These, at the time of Charles' Navigation Act, were sugar, tobacco, ginger, indigo, cotton, fustic, and woods used in dyeing. These accordingly were the *enumerated articles* which the colonists were forbidden to ship to any other country but England; and as from time to time new valuable articles were produced in the colonies, they were added by the English Legislature to the list of '*enumerated articles.*' In 1663 a new law prohibited absolutely the importation of any European commodity into the colonies unless it was laden in England, and conveyed thence in ships built and manned as the Act of Navigation required. Thus the colonists were compelled to buy in England, and in England only, all the manufactured and other European commodities which they required; and to send to England, and to England only, for sale all the commodities of any value which they (the colonists)

produced. The English legislators openly avowed
the policy on which they acted, by a declaration that,
'as the plantations beyond seas are inhabited and
peopled by subjects of England, they may be kept
in a firmer dependence upon it, and rendered yet
more beneficial and advantageous unto it, in the
further employment and increase of English shipping
and seamen, as well as in the vent of English
woollen and other manufactures and commodities;
and in making England a staple not only of the
commodities of those plantations, but also of the commodities of other countries and places for the supplying of them; it being the usage of other nations to
keep the trade of their plantations to themselves.'

The policy thus avowed, that the mother-country
should keep the trade of her colonies to herself, and
strengthen her maritime power by a monopoly of the
shipping of all commodities, forms part, and the
main part, of what is well known in the writings of
the two last centuries as THE COLONIAL SYSTEM.
But, as all the benefits, or seeming benefits, of this
part of the system accrue to the mother-country, and
all the burden falls on the colony, it has been found
necessary by all countries that have practised it (and
all European countries possessing colonies have more
or less practised it) to sustain the burdened colony
by some countervailing advantage at the cost of the
mother-country. This has been usually done by

giving the produce of the colony an artificial preference in the mother ·country's markets. Thus
the English Legislature sought very early to give
the tobacco of Virginia an advantage by forbidding the growth of tobacco in England or Ireland.
But in general the produce of a colony is not so
likely to be competed with by similar produce grown
in the European mother-country, as by similar produce grown in the colonies of other European
Powers. The home-country protected its own colony
against these sometimes by entirely prohibiting
their importation; sometimes by imposing *differential* duties; that is, by admitting the produce of
its own colony duty free, or on payment of a light
duty, but by exacting a heavy duty on the importation of similar produce from elsewhere.[1]

[1] Five different classes of restrictions contributed to make up the
entire Commercial System, which most European nations have
thought it advisable to adopt towards their colonies, and which England endeavoured to establish by her Navigation Acts :—

1. Restrictions on the exportation of produce from the colony.
elsewhere than to the mother-country.

2. Restrictions on the importation of goods into the colony from
foreign countries.

3. Restrictions on the importation of colonial produce into the
mother-country from foreign countries or colonies.

4. Restrictions on the carriage of goods to and from the colonies
in other shipping than that of the mother-country.

5. Restrictions on the manufacture of their own raw produce by
the colonists.—*Merivale on Colonisation*, p. 193.

In his seventh and eighth lectures, Mr. Merivale deals with these
restrictions *seriatim*, and demonstrates their uselessness or worse than
uselessness.

THE COLONIAL SYSTEM has, during the last fifty years, been gradually abandoned by England; and is now regarded by almost all statesmen in this country, and by the ablest foreign writers on political economy, as a monstrous and mischievous delusion; but it is still maintained to a considerable extent by France, and Spain, and Holland; and, within the recollection of most of the present generation of Englishmen, our political and scientific writers of all parties (with some illustrious exceptions) concurred in upholding it, and in lauding the patriotic wisdom of the framers of our Navigation Laws, which were considered to make up the corner-stone of the colonial system in the British Empire. I must now return to the Virginian colonists of Charles II.'s time, who regarded these laws as an intolerable oppression at their first introduction. I have in the last few pages deviated far from chronological order in sketching the progress of the Colonial System, and the revolution in Englishmen's opinions concerning it. But without doing so it was hardly possible to explain the nature and effect of the Navigation Laws; and the subject is so important that it was better to explain it at once, even at the risk of repetition hereafter.

As we have seen, the Virginians were eminently loyal to the Stuarts. Virginia was the last part of the dominions of England that submitted to the

Commonwealth, and nowhere was the proclamation of Charles II. as king more warmly welcomed than in this colony. Yet, during the rule of the Commonwealth, and during the rule of Cromwell, Virginia had enjoyed self-government, and almost complete liberty of commerce. When Virginia capitulated to the Commonwealth's forces in 1652, one of the terms of her surrender was, that the people of Virginia should 'have as free trade as the people of England.' The English Government had respected that stipulation, and no attempt was made to enforce with respect to Virginia the Navigation Acts of 1650 and 1651.[1] But, after the restoration of Royalty, the restrictions on colonial commerce, which Charles II.'s Parliament enacted, were brought into full and unsparing operation in Virginia and elsewhere. Severe distress to the colonists, who were thus deprived of their lucrative trade in tobacco with the Dutch and others, was the result; and this, together with a combination of local grievances, brought about in 1676 an insurrection in the most loyal of colonies. Headed by a remarkable man, named Nathaniel Bacon, the great mass of the Virginians took up arms against the Royalist Governor and his Council, and at one time the 'Grand Rebellion in Virginia' appeared to be certain of success.

[1] See Bancroft's 'History of the United States,' vol. i., p. 174.

While on the march to complete the revolution by bringing over to it the inhabitants of a small district, that had taken no part in the movement, Nathaniel Bacon was suddenly fever-stricken and died. Had he lived a little longer, he would have probably antici-pated George Washington's achievement by a century. But with the death of its leader the insurrection collapsed. His followers submitted to the Royalist Governor. A rule more severe and strict than that, which the colonists had risen against, ensued. A law was passed which visited with heavy punishment disrespectful speech respecting the Governor, or fault-finding with the admini. tration of the colony. Though retaining nominally her free constitution, Virginia was, in fact, under arbitrary government from the close of Bacon's insurrection until the English Revolution of 1688.

We have traced the origin and early progress of Virginia and her sister colonies of the southern group; we have traced also the growth of Massachusetts, and the other New English settlements towards the north. Between these two groups we see on the map the provinces of New York, New Jersey, Pensylvania, and Delaware. These were in existence as colonies belonging to England before the end of the seventeenth century; and it will be fitting now to examine how England acquired them.

The magnificent bay at the entrance of the Hudson River into the Atlantic, near which the great city of New York now spreads its wharves, its dockyards, its warehouses, and its mansions, had attracted Dutch traders and settlers, before it was frequented by the English. Hudson, who sailed up the river and gave it his name, was an Englishman; but when he made that voyage he was in the Dutch service; and the vessels which he then commanded came from the ports of Holland. The Dutch West India Company, in 1621, obtained from their Government authority to take possession of the territories adjacent to both the bay and the river. English traders fixed their posts in some parts of this district, and there were frequent disputes there between mariners and adventurers from the two nations; but the Dutch had the ascendency; and the country was generally known by the name of the New Netherlands, which the Dutch had given to it. In 1664, an English expedition, under Sir Robert Holmes, attacked and captured it; and the treaty of Breda, in 1667, confirmed the English in possession of a region which was valuable in itself, and peculiarly valuable to them inasmuch as it established a complete communication and compactness of dominion between their colonies along the coast of the Atlantic. King Charles II. made a grant of the conquered country to his brother, the Duke of York; and the territory and the chief city

then received the name of 'New York.' The city of
New York was retaken by the Dutch Admiral Evert-
son in 1673, and was called for a short time 'New
Orange,' but it was ceded back to England by the
Treaty of Peace of the following year, and was again
called 'New York'—the name which it has continued to bear.

By King Charles II.'s charter, the Duke was to
hold New York of the Crown, according to the regulation in the letters patent, part of which secured
to the settlers a legislative assembly. Many of the
Dutch inhabitants remained. The similarity between
them and the English as to race, creed, manners,
and language, caused the populations to blend speedily
and effectually, the English element having the predominance, more probably by reason of the English
being most numerous, than because they were the
victorious party. The Duke of York made many
grants of portions of his North American province.
Its south-western portion acquired the name of
'New Jersey,' but it was not definitely separated
from New York as a distinct colonial government
until 1736.

In 1681, King Charles, by charter, granted the
country westward of the river Delaware to the celebrated Quaker William Penn. Penn is honourably
conspicuous among European founders of colonies by
the justice, the humanity, and the sound good sense

of his conduct towards the native tribes. His regulations for the internal government of his settlement were wise and liberal. The large and fertile province in which he founded his settlement and in which he built his city of Philadelphia, took from him the name of Pensylvania. The little territory of DELAWARE, which juts out southward from the south-eastern corner of Pensylvania, became a separate settlement, under the name of ' Delaware.'

But of all the numerous grants of huge segments of the American continent made by Charles II., none was so gigantic, with respect to its titular comprehension of territory, as the grant made by that Sovereign in 1670 to the HUDSON'S BAY COMPANY.

Henry Hudson, the same English mariner whom we have mentioned as the discoverer of the Hudson River in behalf of the Dutch, had in 1610, in a voyage made by him in the service of his own country in search of a north-west passage to India, explored the straits called Hudson's Straits, and also many coasts of the great sea called Hudson's Bay, into which those straits lead out of the Atlantic. Hudson perished in his enterprise; but the results of his discoveries were not lost, and other English mariners from time to time followed in his track; and, though no north-west passage was discovered, it was found that a very lucrative trade for valuable furs might be carried on with the native tribes that wandered along

the coasts of the Straits, and the coasts of the vast inland sea that stretches southward from the Straits'
western extremity. After the Restoration, Prince Rupert (whose scientific fame ought to stand higher than
his military) took an interest in the narratives of these
voyages, and in the description given of the regions
and the races that were visited in the prosecution of.
them. He fitted out, in 1668, a vessel which was
designed to explore the country, and to ascertain if
trading settlements could be advantageously maintained there. The report brought back was favourable; and in 1670 the Hudson's Bay Company, with
Prince Rupert at its head, was formed for traffic in
these regions, and for occupying these territories; or
at least for so far appropriating them that no others
than the Company's members should be allowed to
trade or to settle there.

A charter was obtained from Charles II. incorporating the Company and giving to the Governor
and Company ' all the lands and territories upon the
countries, coasts, and confines of the seas, bays,
lakes, rivers, creeks, and sounds, in whatsoever latitude they shall be, that lie within the entrance of
the Straits, commonly called Hudson's Straits, that
are not already actually possessed by, or granted to,
any of our subjects, or possessed by the subjects of
any other Christian Prince or State.' The charter
also granted to the said Governor and Company and

their successors the 'sole trade and commerce of all those seas, straits, bays, lakes, rivers, creeks, and sounds, in whatsoever latitude they shall be, that lie within the entrance of the Straits commonly called Hudson's Straits, together with all the lands and territories upon the countries, coasts, and confines of the seas, bays, lakes, rivers, creeks, and sounds aforesaid, that are not already possessed by or granted to any of our subjects, or possessed by the subjects of any other Christian Prince or State,' with the fishing of all sorts of fish, whales, and sturgeons, and all other royal fishes, in the seas, bays, &c.; and the territory was to be holden of the Crown ' as of our manor of East Greenwich, in our county of Kent, in free and common socage, and not in capite, or by knight's service, yielding and paying yearly to us, our heirs and successors, for the same, two elks and two black beavers wheresoever and as often as we, our heirs and successors, shall happen to enter into the said counties, territories, and regions hereby granted.[1] '

[1] The right of the Crown to grant by its prerogative exclusive rights of trade is now regarded very differently from the theory and the practice, which prevailed respecting it in the sixteenth century. There is a valuable note on the subject to the fifteenth chapter of Mr. Forsyth's Cases, &c., on Constitutional Law, part of which I transcribe:—' The rights of the Crown to grant to a subject an exclusive right of trading with foreigners was upheld in the East India Company v. Sandys (10 " State Trials," 371). In that case the defendant pleaded the statute, 18 Edw. III., sess. 2, c. 3, but the judges held that this was limited to the trade in wool, which was the

It is impossible not to observe the vagueness of this grant as to territorial limits. It gives no bounds of mountains, rivers, seas, or of degrees of latitude or longitude. Under it the Company might claim (and they did claim) the sole possession of land and the sole exercise of trade from Labrador to the Pacific, from the frozen regions of the Arctic circle to the settlements which the French then had made in Canada or Louisiana, and to those of the Spaniards in Mexico. In our own time we have known formidable disputes and grievous risk of war arise out of the vagueness of this old donation. Soon

subject-matter of the Act. They agreed, however, that the clauses in the charter of the Company imposing penalties and forfeitures on persons invading their privileges were invalid. The judges in the same case also decided that the Statute of Monopolies (21 Jac. i. c. 3) did not extend to the case of trade with foreigners.' But it seems certain that such a grant would at the present day be held to be invalid at common law, if not by statute; and Lord Campbell, in his life of Lord Jeffreys ('Lives of the Chancellors,' vol. iii. p. 581), says that to maintain its validity 'is contrary to our notions on the subject.' Formerly, however, a different opinion certainly prevailed, and charters granting an exclusive right of trade have at various periods been granted by the Crown. Amongst these, the most notable were the charters granted to the Russian Company by Philip and Mary; to the East India Company by Elizabeth in 1600, and to the Hudson's Bay Company, by Charles II., in 1670. But in 1693 the House of Commons resolved that 'it is the right of all Englishmen to trade in the East Indies or any part of the world, unless prohibited by Act of Parliament; and since that period there does not appear to have been any exercise of the assumed power of the Crown to grant a monopoly of foreign trade. When such grant has been made it has been by authority of an Act of Parliament.' See further on this subject, p. 203, *infra*.

after its date it led to hostilities between the settlers, whom the Company sent out, and French adventurers from Quebec and other parts of Canada, who claimed to have occupied portions of the region to which the English then gave the name of 'Prince Rupert's Land,' but which was afterwards better known as 'THE HUDSON'S BAY TERRITORIES.' Part of the land so disputed was given up to the French by the Treaty of Ryswick in 1697; but it was restored to the English by the Treaty of Utrecht in 1713.

Another part of our North American territories was restored to us by the last-mentioned treaty. This was Nova Scotia, called by the French 'Acadia.' French settlers and English settlers had disputed with each other for its possession for several years before 1654, when a strong force, sent by Cromwell, completely established the English in the mastery. But in 1667 Charles II. ceded it to France by the Treaty of Breda. It was given back to England by the Treaty of Utrecht, which closed the war of the Spanish Succession, but the French retained the adjacent island of Cape Breton until the Seven Years' War.

There had been hostilities between the French and English settlers in America during the war of the Austrian Succession, which was ended by the Treaty of Aix-la-Chapelle in 1748; but no important change was made in their relative positions ; and the Treaty of Aix-la-Chapelle did nothing to determine the numerous disputes as to boundaries.

On the contrary, the results of the next great contest between the Powers of Europe, the Seven Years' War, were as important for the New World as for the Old. That was an era fertile in great spirits. It was the era of Pitt, Wolfe, Clive, Montcalm, and Frederick II. It gave us our Indian Empire ; and, if it did not give us North America as a permanent British dominion, it at any rate ensured that the Anglo-Saxon, and not the Franco-Gallic race and language should be predominant from the Atlantic to the Pacific, and from the Polar regions to the Isthmus of Darien.

A hundred and twenty years ago, France seemed far more likely than England to become the ascendant European power in North America. The Canadas and Cape Breton belonged to her. Southward she possessed Louisiana; and she claimed also the lands near the chain of lakes, that belt round the old thirteen British colonies as far as the neighbourhood of the Mississippi,—of the great river that rolls its waters from the precincts of Lake Superior for two thousand four hundred miles from north to south, till, flowing through Louisiana, they fall into the Gulf of Mexico. France claimed as her own, and acually had began to colonise the whole of the territories, which form the basin of the St. Lawrence and the magnificent valley of the Mississippi. The feeble and profligate Court of Louis XV. had, indeed, neglected the wise and vigorous policy recommended by the best French colonial statesmen of the age; according to which a complete chain of fortifications was to be formed throughout the regions between Canada and Louisiana, and ten thousand French peasants were to be sent out to form settlements under the shelter of these fortifications, along the shores of · the most southern of the great lakes, along the banks of the Mississippi, and those of its western affluents. But, though this project was slighted by the Home Government at Versailles, the bold and able men who commanded for France in Canada did much for its realisation. French agents penetrated these vast North American wildernesses, endeavouring to win for France the goodwill of the native tribes, or at least to direct their animosity against the English. Fortified posts were built wherever there seemed to be the faintest hope of maintaining them; and the fearless zeal of the French Roman Catholic missionaries was employed, together with the unequalled physical energy and daring of the Canadian hunters, for the purpose of laying the seeds of French influence throughout the upper half of the New World, so that a hostile crescent of French provinces should be drawn round the flanks and rear of the thirteen British colonies that were scattered along the Atlantic coast. The Anglo-American possessions then consisted of the very scantily populated region of Newfoundland, Prince Edward Island, Nova Scotia, and New Brunswick; and of the northern group of the four New England colonies—New Hampshire, Massachusetts, Rhode Island, and Connecticut; of the central middle group of the five colonies of New York, New Jersey, Pensylvania, with Delaware and Maryland; and of the southern group of the four colonies of Virginia, North Carolina, South Carolina, and Georgia. The population of the whole thirteen comprised about one million one hundred and sixty-five thousand white inhabitants, and about two hundred and sixty thousand negroes. The French dominions in the New World were far more ample and splendid, than those which were held by men of Anglo-Saxon race a century ago; and if we were to apportion our admiration of the various European settlers in America according to the highest standards of energy and ability to which individual great men attained, there is no nation that would have a higher claim to our praise than the nation which produced Cartier, Charleroix, Champlain, De Salles, De Courcelles, Frontenac, La Gallissonière, and finally, 'the wise and chivalrous' Montcalm. But though France never wanted heroes in the West—and the best and sagest of them all was there in time to guide her final struggle there with the rival race; though all this appeared to give her the fairest prospects of triumph over England in their competition for ' the magnificent prize of supremacy in America,' there was an essential difference between the systems on which the colonies of these two great European States had been founded and ruled, which both materially favoured the predominance of New England over New France, and made that predominance desirable for the general interests of human civilisation. In the government of the French Transatlantic possessions, the spirit of centralisation prevailed in its fullest intensity; while among the English settlers on the eastern coast of North America, the spirit of local self-government was more vigorously developed than in any other region of the world. The recent historian of American independence justly states, after paying full homage to the brilliant qualities of the leaders of French enterprise, of French discoverers, travellers, missionaries, hunters, and soldiers, that ' New France was governed exclusively by the monarchs of its metropolis, and was shut against the intellectual daring of its philosophers, the liberality of its political economists, the movements of its industrial genius, its legal skill, and its infusion of Protestant freedom. Nothing representing the new activity of thought in modern France went to America; nothing had leave to go there but what was old and worn out. The French Government thought only to transmit to its American Empire the exhausted policy of the Middle Ages—the castes of feudal Europe, its monarchy, its hierarchy, its nobility, and its dependent peasantry; whilst commerce was enfeebled by protection, stifled under the weight of inconvenient regulations, and fettered by exclusive grants. The land was parcelled out in seignories; and, while quit-rents were moderate, transfers and sales of leases were burdened with restrictions and heavy fines. The men who held the plough were tenants and vassals, of whom few could either read or write. No village school was open for their instruction, nor was there one printing-press in either Canada or Louisiana. The central will of the administration, though checked by concessions of monopolies, was neither guided by local legislature nor restrained by parliaments or courts of law. But France was reserved for a nobler influence in the New World than that of propagating institutions which in the Old World were giving up the ghost; nor had Providence set apart America for the reconstruction " of the decaying framework of feudal tyranny." [1]

The Victory of Quebec (September 13, 1759) in which both the contending Generals, Wolfe and Montcalm, received their death-wounds, decided the

[1] Bancroft, 'History of American Revolution,' vol. i., p. 522.

strife in America. By the Peace of Paris, Feb. 10, 1763, which closed the Seven Years' War, France ceded to England the Canadas and Cape Breton, and renounced all claim to Nova Scotia. The Mississippi was to form the boundary between the British colonies and Louisiana.[1]

This is the epoch of England's palmary dominion in North America. Yet even at this time, when the empire of England there appeared to be established so broadly and so brilliantly, sagacious statesmen foresaw and foretold its speedy disruption.[2]

---

[1] It may be well to remind students that the old French province of Louisiana comprised far more than is included in the State of that name, which is now one of the United States of America. French Louisiana was considered by the French to embrace all the immense tract of country that lies between the Mississippi and the Rocky Mountains, to the north-west of the frontier of the old Spanish possessions. It is to be remembered that the source of the Mississippi is as far north as latitude 47° 10'.

The French ceded Louisiana to Spain in 1762, but it was ceded back to France in 1800; and in 1803 Napoleon the First sold it to the United States for 60,000,000 francs.

Spain by the Treaty of Paris ceded the Floridas to England; but as they only remained in our possession for twenty years, and were ceded back to Spain in 1783, it has not been thought necessary to notice them in the text.

[2] Reasoning men in New York, as early as 1748, foresaw and announced that the conquest of Canada, by relieving the Northern Colonies from danger, would hasten their emancipation. An attentive Swedish traveller in that year heard the opinion, and published it to Sweden and to Europe; the early dreams of John Adams made the removal of 'the turbulent Gallics' a preliminary to the coming glories of his country. During the negotiations for peace, the kinsman and bosom friend of Edmund Burke employed the British

It is not a necessary part of this book to recount in detail the outbreak, the vicissitudes, or the closing scenes of the American War of Independence; and they certainly are subjects which no Englishman would go out of his way to contemplate. The war began by a skirmish at Lexington between the King's troops and the provincial Militia on April 19, 1775. Its turning-point was the capitulation of the British army under Burgoyne at Saratoga on October 16, 1777. The final catastrophe was the surrender of

press to unfold the danger to England from retaining Canada; and the French Minister for Foreign Affairs frankly warned the British envoy that the cession of Canada would lead to the independence of America. Unintimidated by the prophecy, and obeying a higher and wiser instinct, England happily persisted. 'We have caught them at last,' said Choiseul to those around him on the definitive surrender of New France; and at the transfer of Louisiana to Spain, his eager hopes anticipated the speedy struggle of America for separate existence. So soon as the sagacious and experienced Vergennes, the French ambassador at Constantinople—a grave, laborious man, remarkable for a calm temper and moderation of character—heard the conditions of peace, he also said to his friends, and even openly to a British traveller, 'The consequences of the entire cession of Canada are obvious. I am persuaded,' and afterwards he himself recalled his prediction to the notice of the British Ministry, 'England will ere long repent of having removed the only check that could keep her colonies in awe. They stand no longer in need of her protection; she will call on them to contribute towards supporting the burdens they have helped to bring on her, and they will answer by striking off all dependence.' Lord Mansfield also used often to declare that he too, 'ever since the peace of Paris, always thought the northern colonies were meditating a state of independency of Great Britain.'—Bancroft, *History of American Revolution*, vol. i., p. 524.

Lord Cornwallis at York Town on October 19, 1781. By the Peace of Versailles, which was concluded on September 3, 1783, the thirteen colonies of New Hampshire, Massachusetts, Rhode Island, Connecticut, New York, New Jersey, Pensylvania, Delaware, Maryland, Virginia, North Carolina, South Carolina, and Georgia (which had declared themselves independent on July 4, 1776), were solemnly acknowledged by Great Britain as the Free and Independent United States of America.

Though we here pass briefly over the events of the War of Independence, the causes of it require our attention. There had been many heart-burnings in many of the colonies produced by the conduct and demeanour of Governors and other officials sent out from England; there was a general and a growing discontent caused by the restraint which the English Navigation Laws and the Colonial system placed on American trade and commerce.[1] But the main and

---

1 'The colonial system, being founded on injustice, was at war with itself. The principle which confined the commerce of each colony to its own metropolis was not only introduced by England into domestic legislation, but was accepted as the law of nations in its treaties with other Powers; so that while it wantonly restrained its colonists, it was jealously and, on its own theory, rightfully excluded from the rich possessions of France and Spain. Those regions could be thrown open to British traders only by the general abrogation of the mercantile monopoly, which would extend the benefit to universal commerce, or by British conquest, which would close them once more against all the world but the victors;

instant cause of the great Transatlantic uprising was that, which the French statesman Vergennes had predicted after the British conquest of Canada. The Seven Years' War had greatly increased the national debt of England. In order to support that burden the more easily, England endeavoured to raise a revenue by taxing the North American colonists, for whose sake (in part) that increase of debt had been incurred. They resisted taxation as tyranny; and the War of Independence ensued.

England, until this period, had acted differently from all other Imperial States in modern[1] times

even against the nations which had discovered and planted them. Leaving the nobler policy of liberty to its defenders where it could, and wilfully, and as it were fatally blind to what would follow, England chose the policy of conquest and exclusion, and had already acquired much of the empire of Spain in America, and nearly the whole of that of France in both hemispheres.'—Bancroft's *History of American Revolution*, vol. i., p. 526.

[1] This observation is frequently extended to a contrast between England and the mother countries of ancient as well as of modern times; but, I think, not quite accurately. The Greek colonies certainly did not *as colonies* pay any tribute to their parent States. No doubt some Athenian colonies were included in the system of the 'subject-allies' of Athens, from whom she, when she had the power, levied very heavy tributes; but she treated other States and the colonies of other States in the same way.

The old Roman colonies were really garrisons planted by the Roman Commonwealth in favourable positions for securing her conquests. The old inhabitants of a Colonia were treated severely enough by the dominant Commonwealth, but that was not the case as to the Roman settlers themselves.

that have been possessed of colonies. The general rule and the general practice was that the Dominant State raised money from her dependencies either by taxation or by requisitions of tribute. But England, though she fettered the trade and commerce of her colonists with a view to her own benefit, raised all the vast sums necessary for her fleets and armies, and for paying the interest of her national debt and the other costs of her government, by taxes on the United Kingdom only. Adam Smith, writing in 1768, said with truth: ' The English colonists have never yet contributed anything towards the defence of the mother country, or towards the support of its civil government.'[1] The scheme of raising money by taxing the colonies had been more than once suggested to Ministers in time of financial difficulty, but they had had the prudence to decline it.[2] At last, in 1764, Mr. Grenville, the chief of the Treasury and Chancellor of the Exchequer, being determined to make America bear a share of the

---

[1] Smith's ' Wealth of Nations,' book iv. chap. 7.

[2] See instances referred to in Bancroft's ' History of American Revolution,' vol. i., pp. 68, 104.

Sir Erskine May (' Constitutional History of England,' vol. ii., p. 552) cites Coxe's ' Life of Walpole,' vol. i., p. 123, to show how the ' shrewd instinct of Walpole revolted against such an attempt.' It was suggested to him soon after he had been obliged to give way to the storm of unpopularity raised against him at home by his Excise Act. He answered, ' I have Old England set against me by the excise scheme; do you think I will have New England likewise? '

public burden of the empire, framed his fatal
Stamp Act. It was justly considered that, 'to
demand a revenue by instructions from the King,
and to enforce such a demand by stringent coercive
measures, was beyond the power of the prerogative
under the system established at the Revolution.'
But the omnipotence of the Imperial Parliament, of
the King, Lords, and Commons of Great Britain over
all the British dominions was regarded as indisputable by almost all the statesmen of the age. The
taxation of the colonies being resolved on, it was
therefore to be effected by Act of Parliament. There
was some discussion among Grenville and those
who co-operated with him as to what kind of tax
Parliament should first impose. ' All agreed that
the first object of taxation was foreign and inter-
colonial commerce. But that, under the Navigation
Acts, would not produce enough. A poll-tax was
common in America, but, applied by Parliament,
would fall unequally upon the colonies holding slaves.
The difficulty in collecting quit-rents proved that a
land-tax would meet with formidable obstacles. An
excise was thought of, but kept in reserve. An
issue of exchequer bills, to be kept in circulation as
the currency of the continent, was urged on the
Ministry, but conflicted with the policy of Acts of
Parliament against the use of paper-money in the
colonies. Everybody who reasoned on the subject

decided for a stamp-tax, as certain of collection; and in America, where law-suits were frequent, as likely to be very productive.'[1]

The American Stamp Act was brought into the Parliament of Great Britain early in the year 1765. The King's speech, at the commencement of the Session, drew attention to it as most important; and it is certain that George III. spoke his own feelings, as well as those of his Ministers, when he told the Lords and Commons of Great Britain that he presented to them the American question as one of ' obedience to the laws, and respect for the legislative authority of the Kingdom.' It is also certain that a large number, if not a majority, of educated Englishmen were at that time of the same way of thinking.[2]

---

[1] Bancroft's ' History of American Revolution,' vol. ii. p. 174.

[2] The most powerful reasoning in favour of American taxation that I have met with is in a pamphlet published by Soame Jenyns, in 1765. He was at that time senior member of the Board of Trade. Bancroft quotes largely from it. Part of it is as follows:—

' It is urged that, if the privilege of being taxed by the legislative power within itself alone is once given up, that liberty which every Englishman has a right to is torn from them; they are all slaves, and all is lost. But the liberty of an Englishman cannot mean an exemption from taxes imposed by the authority of the Parliament of Great Britain. No charters grant such a privilege to any colony in America; and had they granted it, the grant could have had no force; no charter derived from the Crown can possibly supersede the right of the whole Legislature. The charters of the colonies are no more than those of all corporations. They can no more

The Stamp Act was carried through both the Houses by large majorities. As Franklin (who was then in London) said, ' The nation was provoked by American claims of independence ; and all parties joined in resolving by this Act to settle the point.' Colonel Barré stood almost alone in spirited, and indeed violent resistance to the measure. Pitt was then kept away from Parliament by illness, and

plead an exemption from Parliamentary authority than any other corporation in England.

' If it be said that though Parliament may have power to impose taxes on the colonies, it has no right to use it, I shall only make this short reply : that if Parliament can impose no taxes but what are equitable, and the persons taxed are to be the judges of that equity, Parliament will in effect have no power to lay any tax at all.

' And can any time be more proper to require some assistance from our colonies than when this country is almost undone by procuring their present safety ? Can any time be more proper to impose some tax on their trade than when they are enabled to rival us in their manufactories by the protection we have given them ? Can any time be more proper to oblige them to settle handsome incomes on their Governors, than when we find those Governors unable to procure a subsistence on any other terms than those of weakening all their instructions ? Can there be a more proper time to compel them to fix certain salaries on their judges, than when we see them so dependent on the humours of their assemblies that they can obtain a livelihood no longer than during their bad behaviour ? Can there be a more proper time to force them to maintain an army at their expense than when that army is necessary for their own protection, and we are utterly unable to support it ? Lastly, can there be a more proper time for this mother country to leave off feeding out of her own vitals these children whom she has nursed up, than when they are arrived at such strength and maturity as to be well able to provide of themselves, and ought rather with filial duty to give some assistance to her distress ? '

Burke had not at that time a seat. It was fully expected in England that the Americans would submit to the Act, when carried in this high-handed manner; and its authors were confident of its success. But the tidings of its introduction and of its passing were received in the colonies with vehement and general indignation; and there were also some signs that American indignation would not limit itself to complaints and protests. Some very able pamphlets on the colonial side appeared, written and printed in the colony; and which, for clearness of argument and boldness of political views, may be ranked with the splendid orations afterwards pronounced on the same side in the British Senate.[1]

---

[1] As I have quoted part of Soame Jenyns's tract in favour of American taxation, I will quote part of one written on the other side, and extensively circulated in New York and the other colonies. The author's name is uncertain. 'It is not the tax, it is the unconstitutional manner of imposing it that is the great subject of uneasiness to the colonies. The Minister admitted in Parliament that they had in the fullest sense the right to be taxed only by their own consent, given by their representatives; and he grounds his pretence of the right to tax them entirely upon this—that they are virtually represented in Parliament. It is said that they are in the same situation as the inhabitants of Leeds, Halifax, Birmingham, Manchester, and several other corporate towns, and that the right of electing does not comprehend above one-tenth part of the people of England. And in this land of liberty—for so it was our glory to call it—are there really men so insensible to shame as before the awful tribunal of reason to mention the hardships which, through their practices, some places in England are obliged to bear without redress, as precedents for imposing still greater hardships and

The menacing symptoms in America, and the feuds
of parties and of rival courtiers at home caused the

wrongs upon America? The fundamental principle of the English
Constitution is reason and natural right. It has within itself the
principle of self-preservation, correction, and improvement. That
there are several towns, corporations, and bodies of people in England in similar circumstances as the colonies shows that some of the
people in England, as well as those in America, are injured and
oppressed, but shows no sort of right for the oppression. These
places ought to join with the Americans in remonstrances to obtain
redress of grievances. Our adherence to the English Constitution
is on account of its real excellence. It is not the mere name of
English rights that can satisfy us. It is the reality that we claim as
our inheritance, and would defend with our lives. Can any man be
represented without his own consent? Where is the advantage of
it, if persons are appointed to represent us without our choice?
Would not our greatest enemies be the most likely to endeavour to
be chosen for that office? Could such a right of representation be
ever desired by any reasonable man? Is English liberty such a
chimera as this? The great fundamental principles of a Government should be common to all its parts and members, else the whole
will be endangered. *If, then, the interest of the mother country and
the colonies cannot be made to coincide; if the same constitution may
not take place in both; if the welfare of the mother country necessarily requires a sacrifice of the most valuable natural rights of the
colonies, of their making their own laws and disposing of their own
property by representatives of their own choosing; if such is really
the case between Great Britain and her colonies, then the connection
between them ought to cease; and sooner or later it must inevitably
cease.* The English Government cannot long act towards a part of
its dominions upon principles diametrically opposed to its own,
without losing itself in the slavery it would impose upon the
colonies, or leaving them to throw it off and assert their freedom.
There never can be a disposition in the colonies to break off their
connection with the mother country so long as they are permitted
to have the full enjoyment of those rights to which the English
Constitution entitles them. They desire no more, nor can they be
satisfied with less.'—See Bancroft, vol. ii., p. 319.

Stamp Act to be repealed in 1766. Pitt returned to the House of Commons in the debates on the repeal; and he delivered one of the noblest of his speeches against taxing America. He avowed his joy that Americans had resisted. But the repeal was accompanied by a Declaratory Act, which stated, without reservation, the right of England to make laws for the colonies; and in 1767, Charles Townshend, who had become Chancellor of the Exchequer, repeated the calamitous experiment of taxation. He imposed a number of small import duties. The Americans resisted them, as they had resisted the imposition of stamps; and the Ministers withdrew all but a duty on tea, insignificant in amount, but maintained as a badge of Imperial domination. This combination of timidity and offensiveness produced increased agitation and violence among the colonists. Troops were sent out to coerce them, and civil war followed. Pitt had now become Lord Chatham. He and Lord Camden in the House of Lords, and Burke and Fox in the Commons, nobly exerted their eloquence first to avert, and afterwards to close by conciliatory measures the fatal conflict. The attempt to coerce and subjugate was continued until closed by the disasters and dishonours of the British arms, which have already been mentioned.

It is essential to our subject to pause and review some of the theories advanced during this controversy—I mean that portion of the controversy which was carried on by words and pens.

Not only in New England, but in the middle and Southern States also, the old spirit of stubborn independence, which had made Massachusetts in the time of the Commonwealth deny that the English Parliament had any power over her at all, was revived; and the general animosity of the colonists against the Navigation Laws made many of them join in asserting this bold and defiant proposition. Others, more moderate, were willing to admit that a general power of legislation for the whole Empire was vested in the Imperial Parliament; but they maintained that it was subject to the important exception that Parliament had no authority to tax colonies which were not represented in it. In support of this they appealed to Magna Charta, and the great fundamental laws of the Constitution connected with it, the statute ' *De Tallagio non Concedendo*,' and the statute entitled ' *Confirmatio Cartarum.*' The theory was boldly advanced that an Act of Parliament which contravenes the principles of the Great Charter has absolutely no validity at all. This doctrine found some supporters on the British as well as on the American side of the Atlantic; and it is not without the apparent sanction of some venerable legal authorities.

But such a doctrine would prove too much. If it were admitted, the consequence would be that every statute suspending the Habeas Corpus Act, every Act of Attainder, every Bill of Pains and Penalties, and every statute for summary trial and conviction before justices of the peace, was and is totally void. It would prove that Parliament has no power, under any circumstances and in any emergency, to pass any law of the kind; and that everything done in pursuance of such statutes was incurably illegal and wrongful. For it is certain that such statutes as I have been enumerating, contravene the parts of Magna Charta, which require that no man shall be imprisoned or in any way punished except after a lawful trial by his peers, quite as much as a statute for the taxation of an unrepresented colony contravenes the clauses in the Charter about scutages, aids, and prizes, and the clauses about tallages, aids, and prizes in the statute *De Tallagio non Concedendo*, and the *Confirmatio Cartarum*. The fact that a new statute, either for a new tax or for a new penal proceeding, is at variance with long usage and ancient Constitutional Principles, is a very good and weighty reason for pausing carefully, and for requiring proof of strong practical need for it before it is entertained. But, when once passed, it becomes part of the law, and is as binding as any other part of the law.

This principle extends to the whole of every POLITICAL SOCIETY; and an assemblage of colonies and other dependencies, with their parent or chief State, constitute a POLITICAL SOCIETY. There must exist in every political society a sovereign power—that is to say, ' a power the acts of which are not so subject to any other power, that they can be rendered void by the act of any other human will.' [1]   A very special part of this power is ' the *Dominium Eminens*, which the State has for public purposes over its citizens, and the property of its citizens.' [2]   And, as Lord Macaulay has most clearly shown,[3] there cannot be more than one supreme power in a society.   By the Imperial Constitution of the British Empire, as well as by the constitution of the United Kingdom, that sovereign supreme power is vested in the Imperial Parliament.

This was fully acknowledged during the American troubles by Burke and the greater body of the Whigs, who at the same time deprecated the taxation of America as unjust, and sought every opportunity to

---

[1] ' Summa autem illa [potestas civilis] dicitur, cujus actus alterius juri non subsunt, ita ut alterius voluntatis humanæ arbitrio irriti possunt reddi.'—Grotius, *De Jure Belli et Pacis*, lib. i., cap. vii., sec. 1.

[2] ' Dominium Eminens, quod civitas habet in cives, et res civium ad usum publicum.'—Grotius, Ibid., cap. vi., sec. 2.   See Sir George Bowyer, ' Constitutional Law,' p. 60; and see Mr. Merivale's ' Lectures on Colonisation,' p. 663, edit. 1861, as to the ' omnipotence of Parliament.'   See also Mr. Forsyth's ' Constitutional Cases,' p. 21.

[3] See his comment on the claims in the treatise of Molyneux, published in 1698, maintaining that the English Parliament had no authority over Ireland.   Lord Macaulay's refutation of this will be found in vol. v. of his History, p. 56.

check the attempts made by England to enforce her right of taxation in America by arms. Burke's definition of the authority of the Imperial Parliament, as contradistinguished from the local Parliament of the United Kingdom, has been already quoted;[1] but I will again draw attention here to some part of it. Burke describes the Parliament of Great Britain in her Imperial character as supreme over all the inferior legislatures. He expressly states that, 'her power must be boundless.' He says that they 'who think the powers of Parliament limited may please themselves to talk of requisitions. But suppose the requisitions are not obeyed? What! Shall there be no reserved power in the empire, to supply a deficiency which may weaken, divide, and dissipate the whole? We are engaged in war; the Secretary of State calls upon the colonies to contribute. Some would do it; I think most would cheerfully furnish whatever is demanded. One or two, suppose, hang back, and, easing themselves, let the stress of the draft lie on the others. Surely it is proper that some authority might legally say, " Tax yourselves for the common supply, or Parliament will do it for you." The case is to be provided for by a competent sovereign power; but then this ought to be no ordinary power—nor ever used in the first instance. This is what I meant when I have said at various times that

[1] P. 2, *supra*.

I consider the power of taxing in Parliament as an instrument of empire, and not as a means of supply.'

' Such, Sir, is my idea of the constitution of the British empire, as distinguished from the constitution of Britain; and on those grounds I think subordination and liberty may be sufficiently reconciled through the whole—whether to serve a fining speculatist or a factious demagogue I know not; but enough, surely, for the ease and happiness of man.'

I do not think it would be possible to give a better description of what the Imperial Parliament has the power to do, and of what the Imperial Parliament ought to do, than is given in this extract. Burke consistently spoke and voted on these principles. He was always the uncompromising opponent of American taxation, while at the same time he asserted with equal uniformity, and in language equally uncompromising, the full imperial supremacy of England over her colonies. Many have commented on what they call the inconsistency of these tenets; but, in truth, the inconsistency is only seeming; and the appearance of it is caused by the fallacious double meaning in which the same word is used in our language. I mean the word ' *right.'* Burke said that England had the *right* to legislate in all matters for America; and yet he said that England had not the *right* to pass a law imposing taxes on America. In the first assertion Burke meant the *right* arising out of the relation between mother country and colony, the municipal—or rather the imperial—*right*, which arises from the necessity of ultimate supreme power residing *somewhere* in a state-system of mother country and dependencies, and from the impossibility of that ultimate supreme power being placed anywhere except in the government of the mother country. In denying the *right* of England to tax America, Burke meant another sort of *right* than that which arises from the conventional laws either of particular nations or of particular assemblages of nations. He meant the *right* which arises from the eternal immutable laws of right and wrong—of ' the Just' and 'the Unjust.' Judging by these, he believed that the English Parliament, in which America was unrepresented, had no moral right to tax America. He believed the attempt to be a moral crime, which justified and sanctified resistance. But he no more thought that the colonists, who resisted such an attempt, necessarily ceased to be members of the English Empire, than that the Barons who resisted King John, ceased thereby to be members of the English nation.

During the American troubles a statute was passed by the English Legislature, and a judgment was given in the English Court of King's Bench, each of which, but especially the latter, deserves careful notice.

After the war had been raging for some time, the English Ministry passed a statute, which is commonly supposed to have renounced all taxation of colonies. The statute was really one, which, if it had been introduced a few years earlier, would probably have prevented the strife; but it came too late, when the Americans had proclaimed their independence, and had obtained such successes as made them reasonably sure of achieving it. The statute in question (18 George III., c. 12) is commonly known as the Declaratory Act. It begins with a recital:—' Taxation by the Parliament of Great Britain, for the purpose of raising a revenue in His Majesty's colonies, provinces, and plantations in North America, has been found by experience to produce great uneasiness and disorders among His Majesty's faithful subjects, who may nevertheless, be disposed to acknowledge the justice of contributing to the common defence of the empire, provided such contribution should be raised under the authority of the General Court or General Assembly of each respective colony, province, or plantation. And whereas, in order as well to remove the said uneasiness, and to quiet the minds of His Majesty's subjects who may be disposed to return to their allegiance, as to restore the peace and welfare of all His Majesty's dominions, it is expedient to declare that the King and Parliament of Great Britain will not impose any duty, tax, or assessment, for the purpose of raising a revenue, in any of the colonies, provinces, and plantations.' The Act then proceeds to declare, 'that from and after the passing of this Act the King and Parliament of Great Britain will not impose any duty, tax, or assessment whatever, payable in any of His Majesty's colonies, provinces, or plantations *in North America and the West Indies,* except only such duties as it may be expedient to impose for the regulation of commerce; the net produce of such duties to be always paid and applied to and for the use of the colony, province, or plantation in which the same shall be respectively levied, in such manner as other duties collected by the authority of the respective general courts or general assemblies of such colonies, provinces, or plantations are ordinarily paid and applied.'

This Act is sometimes referred to as having taken away permanently from the Imperial Parliament the power of taxing colonies. But it does not do so, nor could it do so. No Parliament can limit the authority of future Parliaments so as really to enact an irreversible law. As Blackstone has observed, with the repeal of the statute, which created the irreversibility, the law itself is at once made reversible. But in truth the Declaratory Act does not purport to abrogate its right of colonial taxation. Without pausing to observe that it only purports to

M

deal with the North American and West Indian colonies only, and only such of them as have Representative Assemblies, I will quote Sir George Bowyer's comment: ' In the debate in the House of Lords on the Colonial Slavery Bill, August 12, 1833, in which the extent of the power of the mother-country to legislate for the colonies was much discussed, Lord Chancellor Brougham remarked that the Declaratory Act contains " no abandonment of right " and " no declaration that the right is relinquished;" but a mere declaration that Parliament will not any longer tax the colonies. His lordship added, that even in the speeches and writings of Mr. Burke himself there is no single phrase, there is no single sentence, disputing the right of Parliament; he confines his doctrine entirely to the expediency of exercising the right of the mother-country as far as regarded the taxation of the colonies.'

Here, again, the same distinction occurs between moral and legal right which has been already noticed. It would be a moral wrong for the Imperial Parliament to tax a colony after having given a pledge or a promise, express or implied, that the Imperial Parliament would not do so. But a law imposing such a tax, if once passed by the Imperial Parliament, would be binding, and could not be legally disobeyed. ' *Fieri non debuit, factum valet.*'

The judgment, which I have referred to as so important, was delivered by Lord Mansfield in 1774, in the case of Campbell *v.* Hall—a case which deserves to be studied and remembered, as the leading case in constitutional colonial law. Nearly all the great principles of that law are stated by Lord Mansfield in his judgment in Campbell *v.* Hall fully, emphatically, and unmistakably; and some of them were then clearly enunciated on judicial authority for the first time. The case arose out of the affairs not of any American but of a West Indian settlement, Grenada, which was taken by us from the French during the Seven Years' War. But this judgment is of such general application as to almost all our colonies that I think it best to cite it as soon as I come to the year of its delivery.[1]

Grenada had capitulated, and one article of the capitulation was, that the island should continue to be governed by its then present laws until His Majesty's further pleasure should be known.

On October 7, 1763, the King, by proclamation under the Great Seal, gave express power and direction to the Governor of Grenada to summon and call a General Assembly in the manner usual in the colonies of America; and he empowered the Governor, with the consent of his council and the *representatives of the* people, to be summoned as aforesaid,

---

[1] I have already drawn largely on this judgment in chapter iii., when speaking of colonies acquired by conquest or cession; but it can hardly be read too often.

to *make, constitute, laws and ordinances* for the peace, welfare, and good government of the colony and its inhabitants thereof as may be agreeable to the laws of England, and under such regulations and restrictions as are used in other colonies.[1]

After this royal proclamation had authorised and directed the summoning a Representative Assembly in the colony, another royal proclamation, dated July 20, 1764, was issued, in which the King, *by virtue of his prerogative royal, imposed certain duties on exports from the island.*

James Campbell, who owned a plantation in the island, objected to pay these duties, and, on being forced to pay, brought an action against the Collector of Customs, William Hall, to recover back the money.

A special verdict, setting out the facts, was taken at the trial, and the case was ' very elaborately argued four several times ' before the Court of King's Bench, of which Lord Mansfield was the Chief Justice.

It was contended on behalf of the plaintiff:—

1. That the King, of his prerogative royal, had no right to legislate for the conquered colony even before the proclamation of October 7.

2. That, supposing such a power to have existed prior to that proclamation, the King could not of his prerogative royal legislate for the colony *after* he

---

[1] There were other proclamations, and they are adverted to in Lord Mansfield's judgment; but the material one was that of October 7, 1763.

had once granted to it a Representative Legislative Assembly.

Lord Mansfield delivered the unanimous judgment of the Court in favour of the plaintiff. It was sufficient, in order to entitle the plaintiff to judgment, that the Court held the second of the contentions on behalf of the plaintiff to be right; but Lord Mansfield, in a luminous and masterly judgment, went into the whole subject, and established a series of canons of constitutional law as to colonies, which have ever since been acknowledged and acted on. The case of Campbell and Hall, with a few notes, would form a text-book of constitutional colonial law.

Lord Mansfield affirmed certain propositions as quite clear. He treated them as fundamental axioms, as *data* from which it was safe to proceed to determine the particular case before the Court. It is right to give Lord Mansfield's opinions on such matters, so far as space will allow, in Lord Mansfield's own words. I cite part of the judgment from the first volume of 'Cowper's Reports.'

After setting out the facts, and mentioning the points made on behalf of the plaintiff, Lord Mansfield proceeded thus: 'A great deal has been said and many authorities cited relative to propositions on which both sides seem to be perfectly agreed, and which, indeed, are too clear to be controverted. The stating some of those propositions which we think quite clear will lead us to see with greater perspicuity what is the question upon the first point, and upon what hinge it turns. I will state the propositions at large, and the first is this:—

' " A country conquered by the *British* arms becomes a dominion of the King in the right of his Crown; and, therefore, necessarily subject to the Legislature and the Parliament of *Great Britain*."

' The 2nd is, " That the conquered inhabitants, once received under the King's protection, become subjects, and are to be universally considered in that light, not as enemies or aliens."

' The 3rd, " That the articles of capitulation upon which the country is surrendered, and the articles of peace by which it is ceded, are sacred and inviolable according to their true intent and meaning."

' The 4th, " That the law and legislative government of every dominion equally affects all persons and all property within the limits thereof, and is the rule of decision for all questions which arise there. Whoever purchases, lives, or sues there, puts himself under the law of the place. An *Englishman* in *Ireland*, *Minorca*, the *Isle of Man*, or the *Plantations*, has no privilege distinct from the natives."

' The 5th, " That the laws of a conquered country continue in force until they are altered by the conqueror. The absurd exceptions as to *Pagans*, mentioned in *Calvin's* case, shows the universality and antiquity of the maxim ; for that distinction could not exist before the Christian era, and in all probability arose from the mad enthusiasm of the *Croisades*. In the present case the capitulation expressly provides and agrees that they shall continue to be governed by their own laws until His Majesty's further pleasure be known."

' The 6th and last proposition is, " That if the King (and when I say the King I always mean the King without the concurrence of Parliament) has a power to alter the old and introduce the new laws in a conquered country, this legislation being subordinate —that is, subordinate to his own authority in Parliament—he cannot make any new change contrary to fundamental principles ; he cannot exempt an inhabitant from that particular dominion; as for instance, from the laws of trade, or from the power of Parliament, or give him privileges exclusive of his other subjects; and so in many other instances which might be put."

' But the present change, if it had been made *before* October 7, 1763, would have been made recently after the cession of *Grenada* by treaty, and is in itself most reasonable, equitable, and political.

' The only question, then, on this point is, whether the King had a power to make such change between February 10, 1763, the day the treaty of peace was signed, and October 7, 1763?

'Taking these propositions to be true which I have stated, the only question is, whether the *King* had of *himself* the power?

'It is left by the Constitution to the King's authority to grant or refuse a capitulation; if he refuses, and puts the inhabitants to the sword or exterminates them, all the lands belong to him. If he receives the inhabitants under his protection and grants them their property, he has a power to fix such terms and conditions as he thinks proper. He is intrusted with making the treaty of peace; he may yield up the conquest, or retain it upon what terms he pleases. These powers no man ever disputed, neither has it hitherto been controverted that the King might change part or the whole of the law or political form of government of a conquered dominion.'

Lord Mansfield then reviewed the legislation that had followed other conquests made by the Crown of England. He then noticed the absence of any express prior decision on the first point raised by the plaintiff's counsel, and added, 'It is not to be wondered at that an adjudged case in point has not been produced. No question was ever started before but that the King has a right to a legislative authority over a conquered country : it was never denied in Westminster Hall, it was never questioned in Parliament.' He then referred to the opinion of

the law officers of the Crown given in 1722 as to
the right of the King to levy taxes by prerogative
in Jamaica, as showing the distinction between a
settled colony (i.e. one of which English subjects
took possession by settlement) and a conquered
colony. The King alone may legislate for a conquered colony; but in a settled colony this cannot be
done except by an Assembly of the colonists or by
an Act of the British Parliament.

Lord Mansfield then proceeded to the second point
raised on behalf of the plaintiff, that although the
King had by the conquest of Grenada the power to
legislate for the island by virtue of his prerogative
royal, he ceased to have that power after he had
authorised and directed the summoning of a Representative Legislative Assembly. He stated that on
this point, after full consideration, the Court were of
opinion that the King, by granting a Representative
Assembly to the colony, precluded himself thenceforth from legislating for the colony by virtue of
royal prerogative; and that he had *irrevocably*
granted to all who were or should become inhabitants, or who had, or who should acquire, property
in the island of *Grenada*, or more generally *to all
whom it might concern*, that the *subordinate* legislation over the island should be exercised by an
Assembly, with the consent of the Governor and

Council, in like manner as the other islands belonging to the King.

Finally, the Court decided that the Royal Proclamation of July 20, 1764, imposing duties in the colony by virtue of the royal prerogative, was void, and that such legislation could now only be effected ' by the Assembly of the island, or *by an Act of the Parliament of Great Britain.*'

The careful student of this leading case in constitutional law (and it ought to be studied not merely in the epitome here given of it, but in the full reports given in ' Cowper's Reports,' vol. i., and ' State Trials,' vol. xx.) will see that it lays down many valuable rules besides the main proposition for which it is commonly cited as an authority.

The following rules are all to be found in that judgment :—

1. When a colony is acquired by conquest or cession, the Crown can legislate for it by sole royal prerogative.

2. This prerogative power of the Crown to legislate for a conquered or ceded colony is subordinate to the legislative power of the Imperial Parliament.

3. The Crown, in its prerogative legislation for a conquered or ceded colony, ' cannot make any new change contrary to fundamental principles.' Lord Mansfield illustrates this proposition, which appears at first rather vague, by adding that the King ' cannot

exempt an inhabitant from the laws of trade, or from the power of Parliament, or give him privileges exclusive of his other subjects.'

4. Articles of capitulation and articles of peace on which colonies are surrendered or ceded are inviolable.

5. All persons and all property within the territorial limit of a dominion are equally under its law and legislative government.   An Englishman who goes to a conquered or ceded colony has no privilege distinct from the natives.

6. In a colony, which is acquired by British settlers occupying it, the Crown has not the prerogative right of legislation which it has in a conquered or ceded colony. In a colony settled by occupation a Representative Assembly must participate in legislation.[1]

7. The Legislative power of the Assembly of such a colony is *subordinate* to the Imperial Parliament.

8. When the Crown has once granted to a conquered or ceded colony the right of having a Representative Legislative Assembly, the Crown cannot any longer legislate by prerogative royal for such colony. Such a grant of representative institutions is irrevocable *by the Crown*.

---

[1] As to what parts of the English law English settlers by occupation take with them, see *supra*, chapter iii.

9. The paramount authority of the Imperial Parliament over such a colony continues.

I now return to the general history of our North American possessions.

After the loss of the thirteen colonies, England retained in North America the Canadas, New Brunswick, Nova Scotia, Cape Breton, Prince Edward Island, Newfoundland, and the vast territories of the Hudson's Bay Company. In geographical extent the possessions which she still kept, far exceeded those which she had lost; but in population and in almost all natural resources the portion reft away from her was far the most valuable. Canada was the only remaining province that in 1783 had any considerable number of inhabitants. These at the beginning of the war with the thirteen colonies were almost all of French race, but they had proved loyal to England during the American War; and in consequence of the war large numbers of loyalists from the States had taken refuge in Canada under the British Crown. A wise statute called the Quebec Act had been passed in 1774, which confirmed the French Canadian *habitans* in their possessions, their laws and rights, on condition of taking an oath of allegiance, which was so worded as not to hurt the conscience of Roman Catholics. Nearly all the Canadians were Roman Catholics at the time of our acquiring the province, and a majority of them

continued to be so long afterwards. The Quebec
Bill guaranteed to them ' the free exercise of the religion of the Church of Rome, and confirmed to the
clergy of that Church their accustomed dues and
rights.'[1] But it gave the Canadians no share in the
Legislative Government, which was vested in a council of twenty-three appointed by the King.

The French settlers had chiefly located themselves
along the shores of the St. Lawrence, in the part of
Canada usually called Lower Canada, as being lowest
down the stream of that great river. It is sometimes
called Eastern Canada. North-eastern would be a
more correct description. The American loyalists,
who came to Canada during and at the close of the
American War, and the emigrants who afterwards
came out from Britain and Ireland, generally made
their settlements in Western or Upper Canada. In
1791 an Act of the Imperial Parliament divided
Canada into two provinces, styled respectively the
Upper and the Lower Provinces. A constitutional
government of the same form was granted by the
same statute to each of the provinces. It consisted
of a government appointed by the Crown, an Executive Council appointed by the Crown (which was
to exercise functions similar to those of the Privy

---

[1] The liberal provisions of the Quebec Act, and its recognition
of the Romish Church and its maintenance of that Church's endowments in Canada, form a strong contrast with the intolerance then
practised towards the Roman Catholics at home.

Council in England), a Legislative Council also appointed by the Crown, and a Representative Assembly, or third estate, elected for four years.

These constitutions did not ' work well.' Discontent (accompanied by occasional serious disorder) was especially rife in Lower Canada, though when invaded by the forces of the United States in the second American War (1812–1814) the Canadians again displayed steady loyalty to England.

But the discontents continued and grew worse and worse. Happily they have now ceased to exist; and the condition of things which aggravated (if it did not create) them, has now been so materially altered that there is little reason to dread their return. It, therefore, is needless to discuss them in detail; and some general remarks will be sufficient as to the state of Canada (and the same will apply to nearly all the North American colonies) in the interval between the introduction of REPRESENTATIVE GOVERNMENT and the new era in colonial history, which in the last few years has been commenced by the grant of RESPONSIBLE GOVERNMENT to Canada, and to other colonies of similar political and social conditions.

Mr. Merivale, in his work on ' Colonisation,' Lecture IV.,[1] has pointed out how much more the Home Government interfered with the Represen-

---

[1] P. 116, edition of 1861.

tative colonies after the American War than had been the case before that time. Speaking of Canada, Nova Scotia, New Brunswick, and the other North American provinces which we retained, he says: 'The greater degree of control which the mother-country has exercised, both in the formation of their constitutions and in the internal arrangements of the colonies, may be estimated from various circumstances; the reservation of land by the authority of the mother-State for the Church Establishment, the control exercised by the mother-State over the sale of all other waste lands, perhaps the most important functions of government in new countries, are altogether inconsistent with the principles of the founders of most of our old North American colonies. In some of these (the old colonies) the people had elected the governor himself; in some many of the executive functionaries. In some neither the Crown nor the governor had any negative on the laws passed by the Assemblies.'

Sir Erskine May remarks on the same subject[2] that, 'From the period of the American War, the Home Government, awakened to the importance of colonial administration, displayed greater activity and a more ostensible disposition to interfere in the affairs of the colonies. Until the commencement of the difficulties with America there had not even

---

[1] 'Constitutional History of England,' vol. ii., p. 566.

been a separate department for the government of
the colonies; but the Board of Trade exercised a
supervision, little more than nominal, over colonial
affairs. In 1768, however, a third Secretary of State
was appointed, to whose care the colonies were intrusted. In 1782, the office was discontinued by
Lord Rockingham after the loss of the American
provinces; but it was revived in 1794, and became
an active and important department of the State.
Its influence was felt throughout the British colonies.
However popular the form of their institutions,
they were steadily governed by British Ministers in
Downing Street.

'In Crown colonies—acquired by conquest or cession
—the dominion of the Crown was absolute; and the
authority of the Colonial Office was exercised directly,
by instructions to the governors. In free colonies it
was exercised, for the most part, indirectly, through
the influence of the governors and their councils.
Self-government was there the theory; but in practice, the governors, aided by dominant interests, in
the several colonies, contrived to govern according
to the policy dictated from Downing Street. Just as
at home the Crown, the nobles, and the ascendant
party were supreme in the national councils, so in the
colonies the governors and their official aristocracy
were generally able to command the adhesion of the
local legislatures.

'A more direct interference, however, was often exercised. Ministers had no hesitation in disallowing any colonial acts of which they disapproved, even when they concerned the internal affairs of the colony only. They dealt freely with the public lands as the property of the Crown; often making grants obnoxious to the colonists, and peremptorily insisting upon the conditions under which they should be sold and settled. Their interference was also frequent regarding church establishments and endowments, official salaries, and the colonial civil lists. Misunderstanding and disputes were constant; but the policy and the will of the Home Government usually prevailed.

'Another incident of colonial administration was that of patronage. The colonies offered a wide field of employment for the friends, connections, and political partisans of the Home Government. The offices in England available for securing parliamentary support fell short of the demand, and appointments were accordingly multiplied abroad.

. . . 'As colonial societies expanded, these appointments' from home further excited the jealousy of colonists, many of whom were better qualified for office than the strangers who came amongst them to enjoy power, wealth, and distinction, which were denied to themselves. This jealousy and the natural ambition of the colonists were among the principal

N

causes which led to demands for more complete self-government. As this feeling was increasing in colonial society, the Home Government was occupied with arrangements for ensuring the permanent maintenance of the civil establishments out of the colonial revenues. To continue to fill all the offices with Englishmen, and at the same time to call upon the jealous colonists to pay them, was not to be attempted. And accordingly the Home Government surrendered to the Governors all appointments under 200*l.* a year, and to the greater number of other offices appointed colonists recommended by the Governors. A colonial grievance was thus redressed and increased influence given to the colonist, while one of the advantages of the connection was renounced by the parent State.'

' While England was entering upon a new period of extended liberties after the Reform Act, circumstances materially affected her relations with the colonies, and *this may be termed the third and last period of colonial history.* First, the abolition of slavery, in 1833, loosened the ties by which the sugar colonies had been bound to the mother-country. This was followed by the gradual adoption of a new commercial policy, which overthrew the long-established protections and monopolies of colonial trade. The main purpose for which both parties had cherished the connection was lost. Colonists found their produce exposed to the competition of the world; and, in the sugar colonies, with restricted labour. The home consumer, independent of colonial supplies, was freer to choose his own market, whatever commodities were best and cheapest. The sugars of Jamaica [1] competed with the slave-grown sugars of Cuba; the woods of Canada with the timber of Norway and the Baltic.

' These new conditions of colonial policy seriously affected the political relations of the mother-country with her dependencies. Her interference in their internal affairs having generally been connected with commercial regulations, she had now less interest in continuing it; and they, having submitted to it for the sake of benefits with which it was associated, were less disposed to tolerate its exercise. Meanwhile the growing population, wealth, and intelligence of many of the colonies, closer communications with England, and the example of English liberties, were developing the political aspirations of colonial societies and their capacity for self-government.'

The most important event in the history of the

---

[1] It is by anticipation of the chapter relating to the West Indies that I cite here Sir Erskine May's remarks on Jamaica. But the subject of the introduction of Responsible Government is so very important that I am desirous to bring it at once clearly before the student.

introduction of Responsible Government is the mission of Lord Durham to Canada in 1838. He was
sent out by authority of an Act of Parliament as
Governor-General of all the provinces of British
North America, with special functions for the adjustment of certain important questions depending in
the provinces of East and West Canada respecting
the form and future government of the said provinces. In a Report drawn up by Lord Durham
(one of the most masterly and valuable State Papers
in existence) he showed fully the extent and the
causes of the existing evils, and entered both theoretically and practically on the nature of the changes
that were required. He recommended that the two
Canadian provinces should be reunited, with a single
legislative and administrative system, in which the
Governor should be aided by a Legislative Council
acting in harmony with a majority of the popular
Representatives in a House of Assembly. He also
recommended a union of all the British possessions in
North America under a similarly free Constitution.
He nobly insisted on our duty to secure the well-
being of our colonial fellow-countrymen. ' If,' he
said, ' in the hidden decrees of that wisdom by which
the world is ruled, it is written that these countries
are not for ever to remain portions of the Empire,
we owe to our honour to take good care that when
they separate from us they should not be the only

countries on the American Continent in which the Anglo-Saxon race shall be found unfit to govern itself.'

He added, ' The experiment of keeping colonies and governing them well ought at least to have a trial, ere we abandon for ever the vast dominion which might supply the wants of our surplus population, and raise up millions of fresh consumers of our manufacturers and producers of a supply for our wants. The warmest admirers and the strongest opponents of republican institutions admit or assert that the amazing prosperity of the United States is less owing to their form of government than to the unlimited supply of fertile land, which maintains succeeding generations in an undiminishing affluence of fertile soil. A region as large and as fertile is open to your Majesty's subjects in your Majesty's American dominions.'

The two Canadas were reunited by an Act of Parliament in 1840, and a system of government, such as Lord Durham had recommended, was established. Owing in great part to the remarkable ability of two successive Governors (Mr. Poulett Thompson, created Lord Sydenham, and Sir Charles Metcalf), the numerous real difficulties, which existed as to the introduction and working of the new system, were smoothed down or conquered; and a far greater number of worse difficulties which the opponents of the scheme had predicted, proved to be merely imaginary.

Responsible Government was fully conceded to Canada in 1847. As Mr. Merivale observes, no Act of Parliament was required to effect this most important change. The insertion and alteration of a few paragraphs in the Governor's commission and instructions were sufficient. But they are very significant. I quote again a few passages from the present rules and regulations for Her Majesty's Colonial Service, published by the Colonial Office :—

' Under Responsible Government the Executive Councillors are appointed by the Governor alone with reference to the exigencies of Representative Government, the other public officers by the Governor on the advice of the Executive Council. In no appointments is the concurrence of the Home Government requisite.

' The control of all public departments is thus practically placed in the hands of persons commanding the confidence of a Representative Legislature.' [1]

' In colonies possessing what is called Responsible Government the Governor is empowered by his instructions to appoint and remove members of the Executive Council, it being understood that Councillors who have lost the confidence of the local

---

[1] Rules and Regulations, chapter 1. Classification of Colonies, from ' The Colonial Office List ' for 1871, p. 152.

Legislature will tender their resignation to the Governor or discontinue the practical exercise of their functions, in analogy with the usage prevailing in the United Kingdom.' [1]

The last great measure recommended by Lord Durham—that of uniting all the British North American provinces into one dominion, with Representative and Responsible Government—was commenced indeed by the union of the two Canadas, but only during the last five years has it been placed in effective progress for full realisation.

An Act of the Imperial Parliament was passed in 1867, entitled the British North America Act, which almost deserves to be ranked with the Act of Union between England and Scotland, and that between Great Britain and Ireland.

By that statute (which came into force on July 1, 1867, by royal proclamation) the Canadian provinces of Ontario and Quebec, formerly called Upper and Lower Canada, were united, together with Nova Scotia and New Brunswick, into one dominion, called the Dominion of Canada.

Provision was made in the Act for the admission of Newfoundland, Prince Edward Island, British Colombia, and Rupert's Land (the Hudson's Bay Company territories) into the Union.

The Legislature of Newfoundland in 1869 passed a

1 Ibid., p. 155.

resolution in favour of union with the Dominion of Canada. In the same year the Hudson's Bay Company accepted a proposal of the British Government that they should cede all their territorial rights in North America to the Dominion of Canada. There can be no doubt but that all the British territories on that continent will soon be united in that great confederacy, and there will be then one organised state-system extending from the Atlantic to the Pacific, over the broadest part of North America.

The British North America Act orders that the Constitution of the Dominion shall be 'similar in principle to that of the United Kingdom;' that the executive authority shall be vested in the Sovereign of Great Britain and Ireland, and carried on in her name by a Governor-General and Privy Council; and that the legislative power shall be exercised by a Parliament consisting of the Queen (represented by the Governor-General appointed by her) and of two Houses, called the 'Senate' and the 'House of Commons.'

The members of the Dominion Senate are nominated for life by summons of the Governor-General under the Great Seal of Canada.

Twenty-four Senators are, according to the Act, to be appointed for Ontario, twenty-four for Quebec, and twenty-four for the Maritime Provinces, which term includes Nova Scotia and New Brunswick.

Ontario is to send eighty-two members to the Dominion House of Commons, Quebec is to send sixty-five, Nova Scotia nineteen, and New Brunswick fifteen.

The following clause of the Union Act is much more important than it may seem at first sight to be:—

'It shall not be lawful for the House of Commons to adopt or pass any vote, resolution, address, or bill for the appropriation of any part of the public revenue, or of any tax or impost, to any purpose that has not been first recommended to that House by message of the Governor-General in the session in which such vote, resolution, address, or bill is proposed.'

This enactment follows the rule of the British Constitution. It is calculated to prevent the extreme profusion, with which the pecuniary resources of other colonies possessing Responsible Government have been lavished. It is also calculated to prevent a majority in the House from paying with public money for the past services of their private partisans, and from bribing their partisans with public money to support them in future.

Provisions are made as to the number of Senators and Members of the House of Commons for the other provinces, and for their joining the Union.

The provinces forming the Dominion are to have

each a separate elective Legislative Assembly, a separate Legislative Council, and a Lieutenant-Governor. These provincial authorities are to have full power to regulate their own local affairs so that they do not oppose the General Government.

There are careful regulations as to the revenue and the military and naval forces of the Dominion.

The selection of the capital of the Dominion was vested in the Crown; and by royal appointment the city of Ottawa is the capital and the seat of Legislature of the Dominion of Canada and Confederate States of British North America.

The population of the Dominion—that is, of the four provinces included in it when the Act of Union was passed—is estimated to have amounted in 1870 to 4,250,000. Of this amount the population of Ontario (formerly Upper Canada) is reckoned at more than 2,000,000; that of Quebec province (formerly Lower Canada) at nearly 1,500,000; Nova Scotia at nearly 400,000; and New Brunswick at considerably more than 300,000.

The population of Newfoundland (as already mentioned) is estimated at about 130,000. That of Prince Edward Island may be reckoned at about 100,000. It is at present governed by a Lieutenant-Governor, an Executive Council appointed by the Crown, a Legislative Council of 13 members, and a House of Assembly of 30 members. Both these last bodies are elected by the people. The Colony has Responsible Government. The acquisition of the possessions of the Hudson's Bay Company, though it adds enormously to the territorial magnitude of the Dominion, does not at present contribute any large increase to its population. The Hudson's Bay Company formed no settlement (in the ordinary sense of the word) except at the Red River. At the Red River an agricultural settlement was established, the population of which amounts probably to about 10,000. The authorities of the Dominion of Canada have lately taken possession of it, though not without some difficulty. In the other parts of their vast territory the Company planted trading posts, .or factories, to carry on the traffic for furs with the Indian population that was scattered over those immense regions. The number of these trading establishments (all of which were fortified and armed so as to be secure from any attack by savages) about twenty years ago was estimated at 136. The number of the servants of the Company employed in them was about 1,400. The organisation and discipline of the Company's servants appear to have been excellent; and there are few cases, in which the native tribes of North America have been treated with so much justice and humanity as they have been by the Hudson's Bay Company.

The district of British Colombia, which lies between the Rocky Mountains and the Pacific Ocean, was considered until 1858 to form part of the territory of the Hudson's Bay Company. A little before that year considerable quantities of gold were found in the streams; and the discovery of gold, as usual, attracted to the scene large numbers of adventurers, so as to make it necessary for the imperial authorities to establish such an orderly government there as might give safety to life and property. The country was made a colony by an Act of Parliament; and Vancouver's Island was incorporated with it in 1866. The colony received at its first foundation a Constitution which has been twice modified; and in 1870 its Legislative Council was made such, as placed British Colombia and Vancouver's Island among colonies with Representative Assemblies. Of its present Legislative Assembly, nine members are elected by the people, and six nominated by the Governor. The settled white population of the colony is now estimated at between 10,000 and 16,000. The number of the Chinese and Indians is uncertain, but it can hardly be estimated as bringing up the entire population above 20,000.

Altogether the population of the British possessions in North America may be roughly calculated at about five millions.

To give the total area of territory of every kind

[1] British Columbia is now part of the Dominion of Canada.

would be difficult, and would be useless. Immense regions, over which the British Crown claims dominion, stretch northwards towards the Pole, which are uninhabitable by civilised man. The only useful estimate of area is to endeavour to judge approximately the extent of land in British North America, in which an European may be able not merely to wander for a time, but to live permanently, and to see children grow up who may also enjoy healthy existence.

An Englishman may live and thrive (so far as regards physical health), and the descendants of English-born settlers may live and thrive in the greater part of Newfoundland, in all Nova Scotia, all Prince Edward Island, all New Brunswick, and in all Canada, and in all British Colombia and Vancouver's Island. Of course there are some unhealthy districts, as there are in every European country and in almost every English county ; and the severe cold of the North American winter in many of the provinces, which I have mentioned, may be too much for enfeebled or naturally weak constitutions. But I speak of the general rule. Of the enormous region that lately belonged to the Hudson's Bay Company, a large part is, doubtless, utterly unsuited for Europeans. But except at the Red River the Company never attempted permanent colonisation ; and it is very probable that many districts fit for agriculture and for the permanent abode of settlers will be found and utilised, now that these territories have passed away from the hands of those who regarded them, and who wished them to be regarded by others as valuable only in respect of the furs of the wild animals, that lurked or wandered in their wildernesses.

We shall, on the whole, form no exaggerated estimate of the habitable and valuable area of our North American possessions, if we reckon it at about 700,000 square miles ; that is, at more than six times the area of the United Kingdoms of England, Ireland, and Scotland.

This great territory is rich in agricultural soil, in pastoral soil, in forests, in mines, in harbours, and in rivers which give natural lines of intercommunication. No prudent man will speculate boldly on its coming fortune. But we see here all the physical elements of power and prosperity ; and in the union of its provinces we discern political action on the part of the mother-country as rare as it is generous and wise. After tracing the chequered, and in one part calamitous history of British colonisation in North America, it is consolatory and cheering to find that our last scene is the prospect of the Dominion of Canada, of the Confederation of United British Provinces in that continent still under the British Crown.

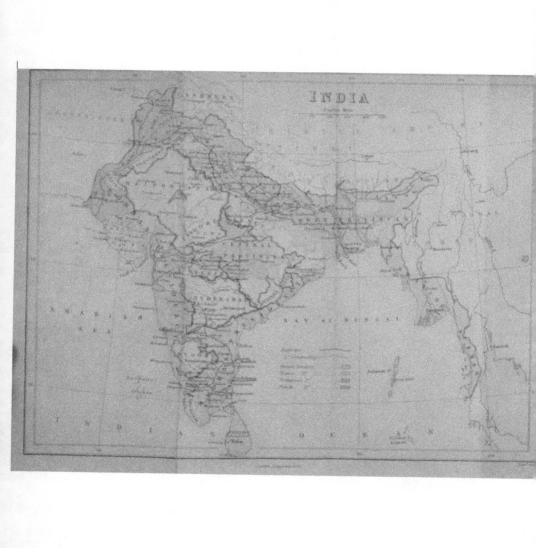

INDIA

CHAPTER V.

INDIA.

TURNING from North America, and looking eastward along the chart of the world, on which the British possessions are marked out, we see, a little northward of the equator, a large mass of territory called generally ' British India.' In size it is inferior to British America and to Australia ; but its population is four times the amount of the populations of the rest of the British Empire put together, including England, Scotland, and Ireland themselves. It is (with very few exceptions) all habitable country, and much of it is densely inhabited ; but its geographical position, within or close to the Tropic of Cancer, tells at once that it is not a land where European inhabitants can settle for life ; that is, for healthy vigorous life of the average duration for which

The Psalmist lotted out the years of man.

It is still more hopeless to attempt to rear consecutive generations of European race there. As a high Anglo-Indian medical authority has truly said, ' The little graves, with which every English burying-ground in India is studded, give fatal proofs of the vanity of such expectations.' The increased facilities for temporary return to Europe, or for temporary visits to the cooler regions of Australasia, may enable Englishmen to prolong their Indian careers beyond what was formerly, on the average, practicable; but the English occupants of India must always be more like a garrison kept up by successive reliefs from home, than an integral, self-supplying part of the population of the place itself.

These unalterable physical difficulties must always prevent Anglo-India from becoming a colony in any sense of the word, in which our possessions in North America or Australasia have been or are colonies. It is, indeed, generally felt that it is inappropriate and inconvenient to speak of India as a colony, and it is more usual to term it a *Dependency* of Great Britain; though the enormous bulk and populousness of the dependent object, compared with those of the upholding power, make the metaphor rather incongruous.

There are other peculiarities in our occupation of India, which have necessarily made it different from the general course of our colonisation. In North America, in Australia, in New Zealand, and most other places, where we have formed settlements, we found the country sparsely inhabited by rude tribes, of very various degrees of moral and social elevation if we compare them one with another, but all to be fairly classed as 'savages,' i.e. as 'wild men,' if compared with the peoples of European Christendom. But in India we found a dense population, highly civilised: it would not be erroneous to say that we found a dense population *over-civilised*; for everything, that depresses and diminishes the natural free-will and independence of Man, more than is necessary for making him live as an orderly member of a Political Society, is Over-Civilisation.

o

And the civilisation which we found in India, was emphatically Asiatic civilisation, as contradistinguished from European civilisation.[1]

It was a country, where (with some few local exceptions) there was no idea of internal liberty, and there was in the mass of the population no pride as to national independence. India had repeatedly been subjugated by foreign invaders. These invaders had generally blended to a considerable extent with the conquered races,[2] and had acquired their languid tranquillity, their spiritless refinement, and unventuresome acuteness. Still it was and is a population capable of being roused by fanaticism into temporary outbreaks of violence, such as

Furens quod fœmina possit.

I am not going to attempt to give in this chapter anything like an historical account of India. It would far exceed the space which I have at command. The students of the institutions of our empire ought to acquire it, and there are ample stores whence it may be collected;[3] but it is impossible to

---

[1] M. Guizot's 'Lectures on European Civilisation' describe best what European civilisation *is* and what Asiatic civilisation *is not*.

[2] See Kaye's 'History of East India Company,' p. 51.

[3] Professor Wilson's edition of Mill's 'History of British India' is the great magazine of information; but its bulk makes it formidable; and it is heavy reading. Wilson stops short of the very important events of the last twenty years. Thornton's history is more brief and more manageable.

The student who wishes to gain speedily a fair general knowledge

give any intelligible description of India as a dependent part of the British Empire without adverting

of the subject, would do well to read the chapters on India in Lord Mahon's (now Earl Stanhope) 'History of England from the Peace of Utrecht.' They are the thirty-ninth and fortieth chapters in the fourth volume; and the sixty-seventh, sixty-eighth, and sixty-ninth in the seventh volume. Take in conjunction with them Lord Macaulay's great essays on Clive and Warren Hastings.

To carry on the subject from 1783 take Thornton from that date; and on coming to 1797, read also the memoir of the Marquis of Wellesley in Lord Brougham's 'Historical Sketches.' It contains an able account of the state of India at the time when Lord Wellesley was appointed to the governorship, and it gives a clear statement of the policy which he pursued. Read also Kaye's 'Lives of Indian Officers.'

This will not give a complete knowledge of Anglo-Indian history; but it will make a very good first platform for it. It is nearly all attractive and interesting reading; and, as such, it is likely to be remembered.

The student of any part of any history ought always to use maps; but this is emphatically necessary when you are studying the progress of British Empire in India. A good mode of doing this may be copied from what we have of late seen so generally done to illustrate the progress of the Prussian army in France.

Take a common map of India and of the adjacent countries, and take some pins with sealing-waxed heads. As you read of a British settlement or conquest in any place, mark it on the map by sticking in one of these sealing-waxed pins. At first (or nearly at first) you will have three marked points, at Bombay, Madras, and Calcutta. From these three little specks on the edges of the great triangle of Hindostan you will find the marks of British conquest gradually extend over the whole peninsula, and far beyond its base towards Central Asia, and round eastward over Burmah.

Do this yourself. Do not be content with seeing it done. The action of your own hand in unison with your thoughts, whether by way of writing, of drawing, or of any other kind of manual co-operation, is a most effective 'memoria technica,' though you may never look at your handiwork again.

Besides the course of reading which I have recommended, the

to the peculiar characteristics of its native population, and the peculiar circumstances under which we came there, traded, conquered, and ruled.

In September, 1599, there was a meeting at Founder's Hall, in London, which was attended by the Lord Mayor, by several of the Aldermen, and many of the chief merchants of the city. The subject for consideration was, whether it was desirable to open a direct trade with India by sea round the Cape of Good Hope. An agent of the Turkey Company (incorporated in 1581) had made his way from Syria to Bengal, and had returned by the same route to England in 1591. Two voyages since then had been made by English mariners round the Cape to India. One of them had been calamitous, the other successful.

The city dignitaries and merchants at their meeting at Founder's Hall resolved·in favour of the project. A hundred and one of them formed themselves into an association for trading to the East Indies, and they subscribed 30,133*l.* as their capital. They petitioned Queen Elizabeth for a charter. In December, 1600, the first East India Company's charter was granted, incorporating ' The Governor and Company of Merchants of London trading to the East Indies.'

student should thoroughly get up Mr. Kaye's ' History of the Administration of the East India Company.' The same author's ' History of the Sepoy Rebellion ' should be read ; and, if read, will not be easily forgotten.

This charter gave the right of purchasing lands without limitation; and it also conferred for fifteen years the exclusive right of trading with all parts of Asia, Africa, and America, beyond the Cape of Good Hope, eastward of the Straits of Magellan. The Company was to be under the direction of a Governor and twenty-four persons elected annually. Four ships —the largest of 600 tons, the smallest 250 tons— were equipped, and laden with suitable merchandise, and manned with 480 seamen. Lancaster (who had made the first voyage in 1591), was invested with the command, under the title of admiral, and with the power of martial law. He sailed from Torbay in April, 1601, and arrived at Acheen, in Sumatra, early in the June of the following year. He returned to England a short time after the death of Queen Elizabeth.

In 1609, King James I. renewed the charter, and made it perpetual, but with a provision that it might be terminated on three years' notice, if any national detriment should at any time be found to ensue from it.

In 1613, the Company obtained from the Mogul Emperor a firman authorising them to erect factories on the Malabar coast. This potentate, the Great Mogul, has been familiar to us from childhood as a grotesque personage presiding over the covers of packs of cards; but in the beginning of the seventeenth century he was regarded by Europeans with admiring awe, such as, half a century earlier, had been felt for the Grand Turk. And the Sovereign who from his peacock-throne at Delhi then ruled over Hindostan (though the rule was not untroubled by revolt or unbroken by civil war) was a splendid realisation and realiser of power. By the lordly condescension of this great king, the English merchants and factors set up a trading post at Surat, which made the beginning of our establishment in India.

With regard to the law which the English in Surat were first under, the following account is given by Mr. Kaye:—'The laws under which our people lived at this time were necessarily two-sided. In regard to all our transactions with the native inhabitants of the place, we were subject to the judicial tribunals of the country. On the first establishment of our factory at Surat, Captain Best, in his treaty with the Viceroy, had stipulated that "in all questions, wrongs, and injuries that shall be offered to us and to our nation, we do receive from the judges, and those that be in authority, speedy justice, according to the quality of our complaints and wrongs done us, and that by delays we be not put off or wearied by time or change." But our people had no great liking for these native courts, and, when it could be done without manifest danger, took the law into their own hands. Among themselves justice was administered in criminal cases by virtue of a king's commission under the Great Seal, which empowered the Commissioners to punish and execute offenders by martial law. In civil cases, the will of the President, or Chief of the Factory, seems to have been absolute.' [1]

In 1638, the Company built Fort St. George, Madras; and in 1640 they obtained permission from the Mogul Emperor to erect a factory at Hooghly—this was near the village of Calcutta, which they afterwards had permission to purchase, and where they built Fort William. It will be convenient at once to speak of the primary Bengal settlement as Calcutta.

In 1661, King Charles II. granted the East India Company a charter authorising them to make peace or war with any prince not Christian, and purporting to authorise them to seize and send to England unlicensed traders.

In 1669, the island of Bombay, which King Charles II. had acquired from the Portuguese as part of the dowry of Catherine of Braganza, was granted by him

---

[1] Kaye's ' History of the East India Company,' p. 65. Mr. Kaye, in a note at p. 66, quotes from the MS. India House Records the proceedings in a case where, in February 1816, an Englishman was tried and put to death by martial law for a murder committed in the town of Surat. A sketch very valuable, historically as well as legally, of the early progress of English laws in India, is contained in a judgment of Lord Brougham's, part of which is cited in Appendix A.

to the Company. The principal seat of their trade on the western coast of India was soon transferred from Surat to Bombay; and we now may regard Bombay on the upper western coast of the Indian or Arabian sea, Madras on the lower eastern coast of the Bay of Bengal, and Calcutta on the Hooghly, near the upper part of that bay, as the three established primary bases of English power in India, whence it has extended itself over and far beyond the whole Mogul Empire.

The original merchants of the East India Company are to be held innocent of having sought, during the first century of their existence, for anything but gain. Honour and empire came to them uncalled for, and were scarcely welcome. But without guns and forts, without some civil and military establishments, and without revenues to maintain those establishments they could not have enlarged, or even protected their trade. They wished not only to strengthen themselves against the rapacity of Asiatic Viceroys and other officials, and against their Dutch competitors, but to possess the means of promptly suppressing the 'Interlopers,' as they termed the adventurers from England, who, tempted by the reported high gains of Indian traffic, fitted out ships and sent out cargoes of their own, in disregard of the Company's chartered privileges. A new Indian Company, in opposition to the old, was projected and soon set up in London. Each party brought their claims before Parliament. The validity of the Royal Charter of 1662, so far as regarded the grant of exclusive rights of trade, was boldly and explicitly denied. On the 19th of January, 1694 (old style 1693), it was solemnly resolved by the House of Commons that 'It is the right of all Englishmen to trade to the East Indies, or any part of the world, unless prohibited by an Act of Parliament.'

Lord Macaulay says of this:[1]—'This memorable vote settled the most important of the constitutional questions which had been left unsettled by the Bill of Rights. It has ever since been held to be the sound doctrine that no power but that of the whole Legislature can give to any person, or to any society, an exclusive privilege of trading to any part of the world.'

It cannot be admitted as a general principle that a resolution of the House of Commons can of itself establish a point of constitutional law or of any other kind of law. But it is an important fact that since the resolution in question there has been no exercise of the previously supposed power of the Crown to grant exclusive rights of foreign trade. Whenever any privileges of the kind have since been

[1] 'History of England,' vol. iv. p. 475.

given, it has been done by authority of an Act of Parliament.[1]

In 1702 the two companies agreed to a consolidation which was completed in 1709, and was confirmed by Act of Parliament. They became 'The United Company of Merchants trading to the East Indies.' The rights of the old Company were vested in the United Company; and its privileges were to be continued until three years' notice after 1726. In 1712 an extension of time until 1730 was granted by Act of Parliament. In 1730 the term was similarly prolonged to 1769, and in 1743 it was prolonged until 1783.

At the beginning of the eighteenth century Bombay was reckoned the chief of our Indian Establishments. It had been dignified by the title of a Regency in 1687, and its Governor was styled General-in-Chief of all our Indian settlements. Madras had then a corporation with a Mayor. The settlements in Bengal were made an independent Presidency in 1715. About ten years afterwards a Mayor's court was established at Calcutta, which had become the chief place of our trade in that part of the eastern world.

During the first hundred years after we obtained a lodgment in India the Dutch and Portuguese were

[1] See the observations of Mr. Forsyth on this subject in his 'Cases on Constitutional Law,' p. 434. His collection of the opinions of law officers of the Crown is very instructive, as showing the gradual decline of high prerogative doctrines.

our only European rivals there. They had ceased
to be formidable by the beginning of the eighteenth
century, but the French were then obtaining a powerful hold in the country; and during the middle twenty
years of the last century we had to maintain against
them in India, as in North America, a long and
arduous struggle for supremacy, and almost for
existence.

The French, like ourselves, at first only occupied
a few places on the coasts, or on the banks of the
great rivers at no great distance from the sea,
though their possession of Mauritius and of the Isle
of Bourbon was of great value to them, as giving
a basis for operations in Hindustan. In Bengal
their chief post was Chandernagore, the neighbour
and the rival of Calcutta. On the Coromandel coast,
at no great distance from our Madras, they held
Pondicherry, which formed the head-quarters of the
French power in the East. But the French, though
their position in India was originally the same as
ours, were beforehand with us in three great essen-
tials for the formation of an European empire in
that country. Mill, the historian of British India,
justly observes that 'the important discoveries for
conquering India were, first, the weakness of the
native armies against European discipline; secondly,
the facility of imparting that discipline to natives in
an European service. Both discoveries were made

by the French.' And both were made by them
under the guidance of Dupleix, one of the most remarkable men that Europe ever sent to the East.
For more than a century before the time of Dupleix
no European nation had gained a decisive advantage
in war against the officers of the Great Mogul. The
experience of former unsuccessful conflicts, and the
scantiness of military ability which prevailed in all
the colonies through a long disuse of arms, had
persuaded them that the Moors (so at that time the
Moslems in India were generally called) were a brave
and formidable enemy. But Dupleix, when attacked
near Madras by the Mogul Governor of the province,
at the head of a numerous army, boldly sent against
him a single battalion of French infantry. The
Europeans dismayed the Indians by the deadly
rapidity and accuracy of their fire, by the celerity
and precision of their movements, and by the un-
flinching boldness of their advance. The Orientals
fell back and fled; and thus was first broken the
spell which had held the Europeans in awe of the
native prowess; though the contrary belief and im-
plicit faith in the enormous superiority of the white
men to the natives cannot be said to have been established before Clive's marvellous exploit at Plassy.

Under Dupleix, also, the French began to train
Indians to the use of European weapons and to the
European discipline; while we, though we employed

native soldiers, and sometimes placed English muskets in their hands, suffered them to remain chiefly armed with sword and target, after the fashion of their country, and made no attempt to teach them the discipline of our own troops. The word Sipahi (which seems originally to have meant a bowman) has become a common term among Oriental nations for a soldier, though with some modification of sense. Among the Ottoman Turks it gradually became appropriated to the horse-soldiers; and then, after acquiring the military meaning of cavalier, it, in consequence of the Turkish feudal system, acquired a territorial meaning like that which our word 'Knight' bore in mediæval times when used with reference to the tenure of land, as in the words 'Knight-service,' 'Knights-fee.' In India the word 'Sipahi,' contracted into 'Sepoy,' was used in a special sense as meaning a native soldier in European pay; and was afterwards more strictly appropriated to the natives who were in European pay, and who were also armed and trained on the European system. We soon followed the example of the French in thus equipping and disciplining the natives of India.

The third great discovery requisite for the setting up an European empire in the East was the art of using the dissensions and the intrigues of the native powers one with another for the aggrandisement of foreign intruders at the expense of them all. Lord .

Macaulay, in his splendid picture of the career and character of Clive, has vividly sketched the state of decrepitude and anarchy, into which the once imposing empire of the Moguls had crumbled. He concurs with Mill in naming Dupleix as the first who saw that amid this chaos of Orientalism a powerful dominion for an ascendant European nation might be founded in India. Dupleix determined to obtain this for the French. He mixed with eagerness in the contests of Indian princes, first under the semblance of an humble but useful ally, but ever on the watch to acquire and secure substantial power ; and he was mindful also of the effect which the display of power produces upon Oriental minds. At one time his policy seemed triumphant. In 1744, he ruled, either in his own name or in the names of Oriental Nabobs and Rajahs, who were his mere instruments, over nearly the whole region then called the Deccan ; that is to say, the southern part of the Peninsula of Hindustan. He was more dreaded both by Asiatics and Europeans than any other potentate in the East. The English rivals of his nation were themselves dispirited by bad success, and were despised by the natives as far inferior to the countrymen of Dupleix.

The disorder and weakness of the Mogul Indian Empire in the eighteenth century (especially after the devastating inroad of Nadir Shah in 1739) are

to be noticed, not only as accounting for the rapid
growth of a superior Indian Empire in the hands of
Europeans, but as proving and explaining the extreme misery of the mass of the native population at
the period of the decline of the Mogul power. It
has, indeed, been justly questioned whether the
common accounts of the prosperity of Hindustan
under the best and strongest of her Mogul rulers
have not been greatly exaggerated. 'Neither life
nor property was secure under their rule. The
Mahomedan conquerors took what they wanted, and
executed whom they would. If a merchant possessed
gold or jewels, he was careful to hide his wealth. If
an artisan was more than commonly ingenious in his
craft, he concealed the extent of his skill. It was
dangerous to be rich. It was dangerous to be clever.
It was dangerous in any way to be a marked man.
If the sovereign was accessible to his subjects, so
was the executioner. Justice was administered with
such extraordinary promptitude that offenders were
hurried into the presence of their Maker almost
before they knew that they had committed any
offence.

'Nor was the personal clemency of the sovereign
himself any defence against such gross abuse of
arbitrary power. He had no means of communi-
cating his mild nature to the provincial viceroys
and governors, who ruled over remote parts of his

empire, or even to the ministers of his own immediate cabinet. His delegated authority was often cruelly abused. Old travellers tell of barbarous acts committed even in the presence of European gentlemen, at the recital of which humanity shudders and credulity is well-nigh staggered. There is hardly a native of India in the present day who does not hug to himself the precious thought that there is no longer any power in the State that can order, under the influence of a gust of passion or a spasm of caprice, even the meanest labourer to be trampled to death by elephants or disembowelled with a sharp knife. The poorest cooly is entitled to all the solemn formalities of a judicial trial ; and the punishment of death, by whomsoever administered and on whomsoever inflicted, without the express decree of the law, is a murder, for which the highest functionary in the Company's territories is as much accountable as a sweeper would be for the assassination of the Governor-General in Durbar.' [1]

The state of the country under the other Mogul Emperors, whom the Mahometan writers themselves acknowledge to have been either weak or wicked, or both, was of course more miserable than under the good emperors. But

> The most infernal of all evils here,
> The sway of petty tyrants in a State

---

[1] Kaye, p 41.

pressed still more heavily than the tyranny of the supreme despot on the inhabitants of the land. There was almost incessant local warfare and pillaging and outrage. Even under the more orderly governments which occasionally were maintained in some provinces, the peasant, the artizan, and the trader were plundered by official harpies, whom the reigning Prince was unable to check, and of whose depredations on those below them he was often entirely ignorant. Take, for instance, the account given of the mode in which the inhabitants of Mysore were compelled to bear their share of a war-contribution which the ill-success of their Sultan had occasioned. This occurred late in the eighteenth century; but it is a fair sample of what had long been repeatedly occurring under similar circumstances in India. The great officers of state were to contribute a portion of the necessary sum, and another portion was to be raised by a general assessment from the community. 'The mode of distributing this last share of the burden was left to the heads of the civil departments, who prudently endeavoured to relieve themselves as far as possible from its pressure. The accounts, however, were made up with all the strictness which was due to public decorum, and to the characters of the responsible parties who exercised control over them. Each civil officer was debited with the sum which in fairness he might be called upon to pay, and a corresponding entry of the discharge of the claim was made with due precision. Had the Sultan condescended to examine those records, he must have been delighted, not only by the accuracy with which they were made up, but by the severe exactness maintained by those who prepared them in regard to their own contributions. But the books were false witnesses, and those by whom they were compiled paid nothing.

'Their shares were paid by an extra levy upon the inhabitants of each district beyond the amount of the nominal assessment. There was one inconvenience attending this ingenious operation. The great men with whom it originated could not conceal the process from their official inferiors; the latter were not to be persuaded that those above them possessed any exclusive claim to the exercise of fraud and extortion; and it followed that, to secure impunity to themselves, the higher officers were obliged to connive at conduct similar to their own in every person engaged in the collection. It is not difficult to conceive what was the situation of a country thus plundered at the discretion of every revenue officer, from the chief who stood in the royal presence to the lowest runner who conveyed to the miserable inhabitants the unwelcome order to deliver their cherished hoards. Under such a system, it is obviously impossible to ascertain how much was

extorted from the suffering people; but it was generally believed that the sum far exceeded the whole
amount which, according to the allotment made by
the Sultan, they were called upon to pay. Yet, at
the end of several years, a balance of sixty lacs
still stood on the books of the treasury against the
country. Torture in its most horrible form was
resorted to; but from utter destitution even torture
could extort nothing; and that obstinate determina-
tion, which in the East so often accompanies and
fortifies the love of money, not unfrequently defied
the infliction.

' Such are the ordinary incidents of native governments; and it must be remembered that of such
governments that of Tippoo was by no means the
worst.'[1]

There is truth in the common saying that a
conquered people becomes always more or less a false
and cowardly people. It is not, indeed, universally
true. The case of the Anglo-Saxons under their
Norman conquerors is an honourable exception. But
it may be taken as generally true; and we may also
admit as generally true the proposition that the
moral guilt of this degradation of a conquered people
rests mainly with the conquerors who have caused
it. But this does not prove that the English rulers
of India are responsible for the present abasement of

[1] Thornton, p. 216.

P 2

the native population. 'We *found* the people of India abject, degraded, false to the very core. Mussulman domination had called into full activity all the bad qualities which Hindooism has in itself a fatal tendency to generate. Their faithlessness, if not engendered, aggravated, and perpetuated by Mussulman despotism, is now the great stumbling-block of British legislation. There is hardly an hour of his official existence in which it does not present itself in the path of the Christian functionary to impede his advance and embarrass his movements.'[1]

There was one remarkable case of successful rebellion by Hindoos against Mahometans, which for more than a century before the commencement of the great English conquests under Clive, had given to men of the old population of Hindustan military dominion over many of its cities and provinces. These native rulers were the Mahrattas, originally a confederacy of mountain tribes, who as early as the reign of the renowned Mogul Emperor Aurungzebe (1658–1707) acquired practical independence, and baffled all the efforts of the vast armies of that sovereign to suppress them. The Mahratta forces consisted chiefly of cavalry, and almost every portion of the Mogul Empire felt the scourge of their predatory warfare. But the Mahrattas could besiege and take cities as well as devastate open countries.

[1] Kaye, p. 51.

They were able also, in general, to retain their conquests, although there were many fluctuations of fortune in their struggles against Aurungzebe and Aurungzebe's successors. As rulers, the Mahrattas were no whit better than the Mahometan oppressors of the land. The usual features of Oriental despotism appear in their history. The founder of their power, Sevajee, a man of very great valour, genius, and energy, was succeeded by degenerate princes; and these were deprived of all real power by ambitious officers, who misgoverned the people in their names. One of these great Mahratta officers was called the Peishwa, and he was the real ruler of a large kingdom, the capital of which was Poonah, near the western coast. Another Mahratta sovereign, with the title of Guicowar, fixed his seat of government more to the north at Baroda, and ruled over the large part of the province of Guzerat. Another Mahratta prince reigned almost in the centre of Hindustan, at Nagpoor, over very extensive territories. Other Mahratta chieftains became petty sovereigns on a smaller scale; and with all of them, and with the military retainers of all of them, war was the favourite occupation, and plunder was the great object of existence.

Among the numerous Mahometan chiefs in India, who in the middle of the eighteenth century were really independent sovereigns—though most of them professed to be Mogul officers, and to take their authority from the Emperor at Delhi — the most important were—1st, the ruler of Bengal, who generally bore the title of Soubahadar, or lieutenant; 2ndly, the ruler of the greater part of the Deccan, or Southern Hindustan, who bore the sounding title of Nizam-ool-Moola; that is, of ' Regulator of the State.' The Nizam's capital was Hyderabad. The Governor of Oudh also had thrown off almost all reality of subjection to the Mogul Emperor. Any clever adventurer who could collect a force of irregular troops or even a gang of robbers (and the difference between the two was little more than nominal), and who could combine good luck with daring, treachery, and cruelty, might hope in those days to found a sovereignty more or less extensive. Hyder Ali, the ablest of the adventurers of this class, and in whom, and in whose son, as sovereigns of Mysore, the English afterwards found their most formidable adversaries, was now in the early stages of his career from robber-chiefdom up to royalty.

When the war of the Austrian succession had broken out in 1741, and France and England were arrayed in their usual opposition to each other in Europe, the French in India made vigorous efforts for the destruction of their rivals in the East. They took Madras in 1746. The terms of the capitulation were ill-kept by the conquerors; and the

English residents, who had been paraded as prisoners through the streets of Pondicherry, felt themselves justified in escaping from captivity. Among these was a young Englishman, a merchant's clerk, who, disguised in a heavy turban and loose Moorish trowsers and vest, succeeded in making his way from Pondicherry to the English Fort of St. David's. That heavy-turbaned English clerk was Robert Clive.

In the next year the English failed in an attack on Pondicherry. Intelligence came that peace had now been made in Europe, and Madras was restored to the English. There were, for a time, no direct hostilities between the English of Madras and the French of Pondicherry, but each party sided with some one or other of the Asiatic rulers, who were in perpetual conflict in that part of India, so that the war, in fact, continued.

This was the period when Clive, who had left a mercantile for a military career, performed the marvellous exploits at Arcot with which Lord Macaulay's Essay has made all familiar. Clive stemmed the tide of French success, and restored the faded reputation of Englishmen as men of valour and as men of victory in the East. A real pacification between the French and English in India was effected in 1754. But it was speedily terminated by the outbreak of the Seven Years' War in 1756; and the rival French and English nations resumed their warfare with each other in every quarter of the world.

Before, but only a little before the recommencement of war between France and England was known in India, an ignorant, arrogant, brutal Asiatic potentate, named Surajah Dowlah, who 'did not believe there were 10,000 men in all Europe,' had attacked and taken Calcutta, and his English captives there had died in agony in the Black Hole. Clive avenged this on June 23, 1757, at Plassy, where 3,000 soldiers (one-third only European) routed Surajah Dowlah's army, 50,000 in number, though aided by French artillerymen.

Large territorial cessions to the Company were among the immediate results of this victory. Calcutta (which had been re-occupied by the English before Plassy was fought) was now fortified, and an English Mint was established there; and in 1765 the Mogul Emperor, Shah Allum, granted to the East India Company, not only possessors' rights, but the right of fiscal and judicial administration—the Dewannee is the Oriental term—over the large and wealthy provinces of Bengal, Behar, and Orissa.

The direct contest between the English and French arms was fought out in another part of India, in our modern Presidency of Madras. A brave and skilful, but impetuous general, Count de Lally Tolendal, was sent out by the French Court as King Louis' Governor-General in India. In 1758, Lally captured and destroyed Fort St. David; but he was repulsed from Madras, and he was finally defeated by General Coote at the battle of Wandewash (22nd January, 1760), which may be regarded as the decisive battle between the French and English in India. Pondicherry soon surrendered to the conquerors. It was restored to the French at the following Peace of Paris (1763), and, though retaken in subsequent wars, has always been restored again. But the French power in India utterly collapsed at Wandewash. Their East India Company was dissolved soon afterwards; and though some French aid was afterwards given to Tippoo of Mysore and other enemies of the English in India, no attempt has ever been made to restore French dominion there. The Government of the second French Empire, in our own time, certainly accomplished much to found new French possessions in the East; but that has been done at Saigon, in Cochin China, and not in Hindustan, or its immediate vicinity.

In 1772, the affairs of India, and of the great English provinces which had been created there, attracted the serious attention of the British Parliament. A Regulating Act for India was passed. A Governor and a Council of four members were appointed for Bengal, with supreme authority over all the Presidencies of India; and a Supreme Court of

Judicature was established at Calcutta. Warren Hastings was the first Governor-General under this Act. This is not the place to discuss the merits or demerits of particular acts of his administration; but it certainly made a period during which the power prosperity of British India increased greatly.

It has been mentioned that the Regulating Act authorised the appointment of a Supreme Court of Judicature. The administration of justice had been found to be a subject of growing difficulty in India. It has been mentioned how the primary factory at Surat was governed by martial law, and how courts called 'Mayors Courts' were afterwards erected at the seats of government of the three Presidencies, at Bombay, Madras, and Calcutta.

These Mayors Courts (consisting each of the Mayor of the place and nine Aldermen) appear to have administered justice, civil and criminal, to the Company's servants and 'the hangers-on of the factories' on a very rough-and-ready system. But as the Company acquired territories, and large numbers of the natives came, practically, under the rule of its officials, the need of some better system of judicature became apparent. This was still more urgent after the English Government in Bengal assumed the 'Dewannee;' that is, the administration of government over the provinces. As all the dominions held by the Company were acquired by British subjects, they came necessarily under the authority of the English Crown, though a century and a half passed away before the Crown took them under its own direct rule.[1]   These territories were not desert lands, or lands merely roved over by a few savages.   The consequence was, that when possessed by the English they could not be considered as lands acquired by *occupation*, like the colonies in North America and elsewhere.[2]   These Indian lands had dense civilised populations, living under well-known and long-established laws.   According to *general* rule (as recognised and declared afterwards by Lord Mansfield in his judgment in the case of Campbell and Hall[3]), the old laws would have continued in force, and would have applied to all who came to live in these new acquisitions of the Crown, until the Crown used its power of legislation by introducing new laws.   But a distinction was made in practice, and has been confirmed on principle by high authority.   In a recent judgment of the Judicial Committee of the Privy Council, the legal position of the first English merchants, and other residents in their factories on the Indian coasts, is thus spoken of.   'If the settlement had been made in a Christian country of Europe, the settlers would have become subject to the laws of the

---

[1] The statute 53 G. III. c. 155, sec. 95, declared the undoubted sovereignty of the Crown over the territorial acquisitions of the East India Company.

[2] See supra, p. 60, and p. 165.   [3] See p. 165, supra.

country in which they settled. It is true that in India they retained their own laws for their own government within the factories which they were permitted by the ruling powers of India to establish; but this was not on the ground of general international law, or because the power of England or the laws of England had any proper authority in India, but upon the principles explained by Lord Stowell in a very celebrated and beautiful passage of his judgment in the case of "*The Indian Chief*," 3 Rob. Adm. 29.'

The passage here referred to is the following:— 'In the East, from the oldest times, an immiscible character has been kept up; foreigners are not admitted into the general body and among the society of the nation; they continue strangers and sojourners, as all their fathers were—*Doris amara suam non intermiscuit undam.* Not acquiring any national character under the general sovereignty of the country, and not trading under any recognised authority of their own original country, they have been held to derive their present character from that of the association or factory under whose protection they live and carry on their trade.'[1]

But if it was neither expedient nor just that the

---

[1] See Forsyth, p. 20. At the end of this volume (appendix A) will be found portions of the judgment delivered by Lord Brougham in 'Mayor of Lyons v. East India Company.' (Moore's P. C. Reports, vol. i. p. 175.) They give a very valuable sketch of the establishment and limits of English law in India.

Anglo-Indian resident should be placed under Hindoo or Mahometan law, so it was found harsh and iniquitous to deal with nations according to the requirements and the penal sanctions of English law, of which the natives had not been forewarned, and which they could not understand even when they had to suffer under them. Hastings understood his position as a ruler and an ordainer. He saw that English law was in many respects inapplicable to the usages of Asiatic society. He felt that ' A great and solemn duty was now spreading itself out before us—the duty of infusing the principles of English justice into the administration of the Mahometan law—of regulating and purifying the dispensations of that law, and improving existing institutions, rather than demolishing them. During the years intervening between the grant of the Dewannee and our open assumption of the duties of Dewan, the Company's servants had acquired some knowledge and experience which might be turned to profitable account. But they were not then competent to take into their own hands the entire management of the Courts of Justice. The experiment at the early period would have been a dangerous one.' [1] Hastings established in each district two Courts of Judicature —a Civil and a Criminal Court. The Company's European Collector of Customs presided in the Civil

[1] Kaye, 'History of the East India Company,' p. 326.

Court, attended by the provincial native Dewan as assessor. The old Mogul officers presided in the Criminal Courts, with Mahometan doctors to expound the law. 'The Company's European servants had no immediate connexion with the business of these Criminal Courts. But the Collector was ordered to exercise a sort of general superintendence over their procedure, so as to see that all necessary evidences are summoned and examined, that due weight is allowed to their testimony, and that the decision passed is fair and impartial, according to the proofs exhibited in the course of the trial.' [1]

Hastings appointed two superior Courts of Appeal from these local tribunals. The Civil Court of Appeal was to be presided over by the President and two members of the Council. The Criminal Court of Appeal was to be composed of Mahometan law officers; the European chief officers exercising a general control of it, so as to insure that the main principles of justice were upheld.

In 1774 the Crown, as empowered by the Regulating Act, issued letters patent constituting a Supreme Court of civil and criminal, of admiralty and ecclesiastical, jurisdiction. The English judges appointed under these letters patent sought to administer law in India according to the strict rules and technicalities of Westminster Hall. The result was general dis-

[1] Kaye, p. 327.

content and confusion; and in 1781 an Act was passed defining and limiting their powers. Since that time, according to Mr. Kaye, the Company's Courts and the Crown Courts co-existed without scandalous collisions.

Warren Hastings left India in 1785, and was succeeded by Lord Cornwallis, an English nobleman of high principle, benevolent heart, and of considerable abilities, both as a statesman and a general.

It is as a civil reformer and legislator that he is most illustrious; though great gratitude and honour are due to him for his successful conduct of the first Mysore war with Tippoo Saib. But the 'Cornwallis Regulations' are the title-deeds of his rank in Anglo-Indian history. Aided by Shore, Barlow, and Sir William Jones, he drew up and published a code of judicial and administrative rules 'which have since then been the basis of our civil administration in India.' These regulations were translated into the native languages, printed, and widely circulated. Lord Cornwallis provided for perfect religious liberty, so that the followers of each creed exercised its rites and worship without disturbance to the public peace, and without molestation to the religious liberty of others. He made the judicial officers distinct from the revenue-collectors, and the judgeships were to be considered appointments, 'the first in importance in the civil service.' He retained for the natives their old laws,[1] but he abolished mutilation and other barbarous punishments. He anxiously provided means of redress for the native inhabitants against all arbitrary exactions and illegal usurpation of authority.

[1] 'Great misunderstandings,' wrote Sir George Barlow, 'have prevailed with regard to the new constitution for the civil government of the British possessions in India established by the Marquis Cornwallis in 1793, and completed by his successor Marquis Wellesley. The change did not consist in alterations of the ancient customs and usages of the country affecting the rights of person and property. It related chiefly to the giving security to those rights, by affording to our native subjects the means of obtaining redress against any infringement of them, either by the Government itself, its officers, or individuals of any character or description. . . . . Lord Cornwallis made no innovations on the ancient laws and customs of the people. On the contrary, the main object of the constitution which he established was to secure to them the enjoyment of those laws and customs, with such improvement as times and circumstances might suggest. When he arrived in the country the Government was, in fact, a pure despotism, with no other check but that which resulted from the character of those by whom the Government was administered. The Governor-General not only was the sole power for making all laws, but he exercised the power of administering the laws in the last resort, and also all the functions of the executive authority. The abuses to which such a system of government is liable, from corruption, negligence, and want of information, are too well known to require being particularised. It is, in fact, from the want of a proper distribution of these authorities in different hands that all abuses in government principally proceed. His lordship's first step was to make it a fundamental law (1793) that all laws framed by the Government should be printed and published in the form prescribed by Regulation 43, and that the Courts of Judicature should be guided by the laws so printed and published, and no other. It had before been the practice to carry on the affairs of the Government and those of individuals by a correspondence by letter with all the subordinate officers.'—Kaye's ' Memoir of Lord Cornwallis,' p. 154.

One of the most celebrated measures of Lord Cornwallis's administration relates to the land revenue of Bengal. The merits and demerits of this, the 'Permanent Zemindary Settlement,' as it is called, have been and still are warmly debated by historical writers and political economists, and it would lead me far beyond my limits if I were to enter on the subject here.[1]

[1] The policy or impolicy of Lord Cornwallis's Zemindary Settlement appears even now (May 1871) to be the subject of enquiry and discussion before the House of Commons Committee on Indian Finance. The following extract from Thornton (who is unfavourable to the Cornwallis policy) will explain its main features :—' At the threshold of the enquiry lay the question—To whom did the property of the soil belong? On this point different opinions have ever been maintained, and all of them in some degree of plausibility. By some it has been held that in India the land has always been regarded as the property of the sovereign; by others, that in most parts of the country the persons called Zemindars are the rightful proprietors; while by a third party it has been contended that the great majority of cultivators have a permanent interest in the soil, and that the Zemindar was only the officer through whom, in many cases, the claims of Government were settled. These theoretical differences of opinion have given rise to others of a practical character, as to the parties to be recognised by Government in levying its claims upon the land; whether a settlement should be effected with a person called a Zemindar, who is responsible for the whole assessment upon a given district, generally of considerable extent; with an association of persons occupying lands within a particular locality termed a village, the inhabitants of which are connected by peculiar institutions; or with the individual cultivators, known in the language of the country by the name Ryots. These three modes of settlement are respectively described as the Zemindary, the Village, and the Ryotwar systems; and the presumed advantages of each have been maintained with great zeal. But no difference on this point embarrassed the Government of Lord Cornwallis. All the influential servants of the

Q

But it does appear certain that all done by Lord Cornwallis was done by him after earnest and impartial enquiry, and with an honest desire to promote the welfare of those whom he had been sent out to govern.

Lord Cornwallis had gone out to India as Governor-General, and also as Commander-in-Chief. He was the first Governor who went out under the new system for ordering the affairs of India which William Pitt had instituted in 1784, and which was continued for nearly half a century. Before then

Presidency appear to have agreed with the Governor-General in the preference expressed by the Home authorities for the Zemindary system of settlement. On the right in the soil the same unanimity did not prevail; but the Governor-General cut short all enquiry by determining, certainly with great precipitancy, to recognise the right as residing exclusively in the Zemindars. He not only affirmed his belief that it actually belonged to them, but declared that, if it did not, it would be necessary to confer it upon them, or upon some other persons; as nothing, in his judgment, would be more pernicious than to regard the right as appertaining to the State. Lord Cornwallis either entirely overlooked, or chose to appear ignorant of, the possibility of other rights existing in connection with the land besides those of the Government and the Zemindar. Mr. Shore, an able civil servant, afterwards Lord Teignmouth, recommended caution and further enquiry; but the Governor-General seemed to think that his duty was not to enquire, but to act. The sanction of the Home authorities for declaring perpetual and decennial settlements which had recently been made was asked and obtained; and on the 22nd of March, 1793, the assessments made under that settlement were authoritatively proclaimed to be fixed for ever.'—Thornton, p. 219. Mr. Kaye ('History of the East India Company's Administration,' p. 123) speaks more favourably of Lord Cornwallis.

the Proprietors of East India Stock and their Court of Directors had been, through the Governors whom they appointed, the absolute masters of British India. Lord North and his fellow-Ministers of the Crown had endeavoured in 1782 to remove Warren Hastings. But though Lord North could command majorities in Parliament, a majority of the Proprietors of East India Stock differed from him, and it was found that without their consent the Governor of India was, as the law then stood, irremovable. In 1783 Mr. Fox and Lord North, who had formed their Coalition, brought in their celebrated India Bill, and thereby caused the overthrow of the Coalition Ministry. Mr. Fox proposed to vest the supreme power of ruling India in a Board of seven Commissioners, appointed in the first instance by Parliament, and afterwards by the Crown. They were to have eight assistant-managers, appointed first by Parliament, and afterwards by the Crown. This was denounced as an attempt to aggrandise the power of the Coalition party at the expense both of the Crown and the Company. It failed in the House of Lords ; and Mr. Pitt (who succeeded Mr. Fox in office) in the following year framed a new scheme on the principle of Double Government.

Mr. Pitt left the Company in possession of their large powers, but subject to a Board of Control representing the Crown.

This Board was originally composed of six Privy Councillors, nominated by the King; and besides these the Chancellor of the Exchequer and the principal Secretaries of State were, by virtue of their offices, members of the Board.

'By an Act passed in 1793 it became no longer necessary to select the members from among Privy Councillors. In practice the senior member, or president, ordinarily conducted the business, and on rare occasions only called upon his colleagues for assistance. It was the duty of this Board to superintend the territorial or political concerns of the Company; to inspect all letters passing to and from India between the Directors and their servants or agents which had any connection with territorial management or political relations; to alter or amend, or to keep back, the despatches prepared by the Directors, and, in urgent cases, to transmit orders to the functionaries in India without the concurrence of the Directors. In all cases where the proceedings of the Directors had the concurrence of the Board of Control, the Court of Proprietors had no longer the right of interference. The salaries of the president and other officers of the Board, as well as the general expenses of the establishment, were defrayed by the East India Company.

' The Court of Directors consisted of twenty-four proprietors elected out of the general body. The qualification for a seat in the direction was the possession of 2,000*l.* stock. Six of the Directors went out of office every year; they retired in rotation, so that the term of office for each was four years from the time of election. The Directors who vacated their seats might be re-elected, and generally were so, after being out of office for one year. The chairman and deputy chairman were elected from among their own body by the Directors, thirteen of whom must have been present to form a court.

'The power of the Directors was great: they appointed the Governor-General of India and the Governors of the several Presidencies; but as the appointments were all subject to the approval of the Crown, they might be said to rest virtually with the Government. The Directors had the absolute and uncontrolled power of recalling any of these functionaries; and in 1844 they exercised this power by recalling Lord Ellenborough, the Governor-General. All subordinate appointments were made by the Directors, but, as a matter of courtesy, a certain portion of this patronage was placed at the disposal of the President of the Board of Control.'[1]

This system of Double Government was said to be cumbrous, and to be perplexing and perplexed. But it was long continued at each successive renewal by Parliament of the privileges of the Company.

[1] Political Cyclopædia, title 'East India Company.'

It has only been abolished after the Sepoy Mutiny, in 1857, showed 'the necessity of establishing a single and supreme authority,' though important changes were introduced in 1833 and 1853, which will be adverted to presently.

If the sagacity of the Home Proprietary Government, of the Timocracy of Indian rulers, and the Ministers of the Crown who have co-operated with them, were to be tested by the average abilities of the Governors-General whom they have sent to India, they would be entitled to very high praise indeed. Lord Cornwallis, the Marquis of Wellesley, Lord Hastings, Lord William Bentinck, Lord Ellenborough, Lord Hardinge, Lord Dalhousie, Lord Canning, Lord Elgin, and Lord Lawrence, are splendid examples of what the Company and Crown's proconsulate in India has been; and there is not a single name on the list, which England has, on the whole, cause to be ashamed of, or which India has reason to execrate. I cannot here sketch the series of their biographies or their Indian careers. I can only mention some under whom the most remarkable strides in advancement of empire were made, or the most important political and social regulations were introduced.

Lord Cornwallis has already occupied our attention in his capacity of a legislator for the British provinces of India. His external policy also is to be noticed, not so much in respect to the military advantages and conquests acquired under him (though these were considerable and important) as with regard to the introduction of the system of forming a set of subject-allies among the yet unconquered native states. Such a condition—the condition of subject-alliance — is the real position in which many of the native Indian states are placed relatively to the British Empire. They are usually called ' Subsidiary Allies.' The English keep up a military force in these states, and undertake the defence of the country. The native princes pay the expense of our military establishments there. The internal government is nominally left entirely in the native rulers' hands ; but an agent of the British Government resides in the capital of each subsidiary allied state, and exercises considerable influence over domestic government. The kingdom of Oudh became a subsidiary ally of this kind in Lord Cornwallis's time.

Lord Wellesley, who was appointed Governor-General of India in 1797, completed (by the army under General Harris) the conquest of Mysore ; and · the British power was then thoroughly established in Southern Hindustan. He made also great territorial acquisitions for the Company in Central and North-Western India. Lord Wellesley did much to carry out Lord Cornwallis's plans of administrative reform ; and he showed himself honourably anxious for the establishment of a system of education by which an efficient class of able and high-spirited men should be trained up for the Indian public service. He drew up an elaborate paper on the subject, entitled 'Notes by the Governor-General in Council.' Parts of it may be read with advantage even at the present time.

' The civil servants of the English East India Company,' he remarked, ' can no longer be considered as the agents of a commercial concern. They are, in fact, the ministers and officers of a powerful sovereign; they must now be viewed in that capacity, with reference, not to their nominal, but to their real occupations. They are required to discharge the functions of magistrates, judges, ambassadors, and governors of provinces, in all the complicated and extensive relations of those sacred trusts and exalted stations, and under peculiar circumstances, which greatly enhance the solemnity of every public obligation, and aggravate the difficulty of every public charge. Their duties are those of statesmen in every other part of the world, with no other characteristic difference than the obstacles opposed by an unfavourable climate. We cannot safely allow any precaution to be relaxed to furnish a sufficient supply of men qualified to fill the high offices of state with credit to themselves and with advantage to the public. . Without such a constant succession of men in the several branches and departments of this Government, the wisdom and benevolence of the law must prove vain and inefficient.'

Lord Wellesley's intended organ for providing this education was a college, or rather an university, to be founded in Calcutta. He hoped that it would not only educate English statesmen for India, but that it would soon be frequented by native students, who might there seek after knowledge in community with their European rulers, and feel that the bond of a common education united them in the service of one great empire.

Lord Wellesley was sanguine as to the success of his intended foundation, which he hoped would perpetuate his name in the East far more than any of the conquests which had been achieved under his sway. But he had created a feeling of alarm and surprise among the Directors on account of the ambitious rapidity (as it appeared) with which he made territorial conquests, and by which he exhausted their revenues, and brought the Company to the very verge of bankruptcy. He had alienated the Directors still more by the haughty and imperious tone, which he assumed in his correspondence with them and respecting them. Sir James Mackintosh used to illustrate the different effects which a residence in India produces on Englishmen of different temperaments by saying that 'some it *Sultanised*, and

some it *Brahminised.*' He used to refer to Lord
Wellesley as a perfect type of the *Sultanised* Anglo-
Indian. Lord Cornwallis (who was in England during
Lord Wellesley's Indian administration) pointed out,
in a letter to a friend, who was expected to be the
Marquess's successor, how much embarrassment had
been caused by the neglect and incivility of Lord
Wellesley towards his 'honourable masters.' He
told Barlow, ' Be civil with the Directors, and avoid
any direct attack on the authority of the Court, and
you may do everything which your zeal for the
public welfare would make you desire. Had Lord
Wellesley thought it worth while to use a little
management with the Court of Directors, he might
have settled his college on any plan within moderate
bounds which he thought fit.'

Unfortunately, Lord Wellesley could neither man-
age the Court of Directors nor his own temper,
when his imperial schemes were thwarted. His
university project was a costly one, especially considering the state to which the finances of the Company had ebbed during his administration. The
Directors hesitated and objected. Lord Wellesley
insisted more and more angrily on his favourite
measure being adopted, and the Directors (who
were no more *Brahminised* than he was) grew angry
in turn, and rejected it altogether.

An earnest admirer of Lord Wellesley (and there

is much, very much, on the whole, to admire in Lord Wellesley's career), his biographer, Mr. Pearce, after detailing these events, properly remarks that ' it is but justice to the Honourable East India Company to say that, after the heat of these discussions had passed away, they, in a magnanimous spirit, took up the plan of Lord Wellesley, and put it into execution with so much success, that many have doubted, and still doubt, whether the maintenance of Fort William College, as originally designed, would have been more useful to the servants of the Company than the College of Haileybury. This question is yet open ; but the experience of several years has shown that the education imparted at Haileybury has had a most important influence in elevating the general character of the servants of the East India Company, and has added an immense impetus to the cause of native education in India.'

This eulogium on Haileybury (now a thing of the past) was well deserved. Lord Wellesley must have watched its success with honourable pleasure, such as Lord Cornwallis also would have felt had his life been prolonged, as was that of the Marquis of Wellesley. And we may venture to believe that Wellesley and Cornwallis would have equally rejoiced, if they could have foreseen the present system by which the Indian service, with its numerous lucrative and splendid appointments, is thrown

open by competitive examination to the best-qualified
for it of all Her Majesty's subjects, whatever may
be their birth-place, their race, or their creed.

The territorial extent of the British Empire in
India continued to increase, not always by the wish
of the English rulers there, and almost always
against the wish of the Courts of Directors and Proprietors at home. To them the acquisition of territory meant war, and war meant drained revenues
and imperilled dividends. I believe also that many
of those, who were interested in India, grieved often
to see military armaments and operations absorb
the treasure, which otherwise might have been
utilised in pacific public undertakings, in improved
means of communication, in irrigation, and in other
beneficial works of sustenance. But nearly all (there
are some, but few marked exceptions) our Indian
wars during the present century have been on our
part unavoidable. Enemies, ignorant or disdainful
of the obligations of international law, have attacked
our frontiers; it has been necessary in self-defence
to quell them, and the only mode of effectually
quelling them has been not merely to defeat but
to thoroughly conquer them. I do not say that
ambition has been unknown to British viceroys or
to British generals in the East; but I believe
that by far the greater number of our Indian
wars have been forced upon us, and that we have

unwillingly realised the territorial gains that have followed them.

Conquests made in the East, the South, or the West of Hindustan naturally blended with the respective Presidencies of Bengal, Madras, or Bombay, as each conquered province lay nearest to each Presidency. But the extensive acquisitions made in the North-West received a system of their own, and were known as the North-Western Provinces. They were theoretically a portion of. the Presidency of Bengal; but they had their own Lieutenant-Governor, and for most practical purposes made a distinct district. Other territories became afterwards distinct portions of British India, as will be seen at the end of this chapter in the sketch of the eight local administrations (subordinate to the general control of the Governor-General and the Council-General) which now make up British India Proper.

The Burmese War (1823–1826) was forced upon us by the insults and aggressions of the haughty and warlike Burmese nation, which, after overthrowing all Asiatic powers with which it came in contact, advanced its frontier close upon the Eastern boundaries of British India, and not only threatened but actually invaded Bengal. The result of the war was the cession by the Burmese of Arracan and the Tennaserim provinces. I am anticipating in point of date; but this is the most convenient place for observing that war with the Burmese was recommenced in 1852, and ended in the annexation to British India of the province of Pegu, containing an area of 22,000 square miles, and including the whole of the Burmese coast and the delta of the great river Irrawaddi.

In 1833, when the question of renewing the East India Company's charter came before the first Reformed Parliament, an essential change was made in character of the great Eastern institution. It lost altogether its primary character, that of a trading corporation, and was permitted to continue its existence in its acquired character only, that of a political and governing body. This change had been foreshadowed by previous legislation. When the charter had been renewed in 1813, the trade to the whole of the Company's territories and to India had been thrown open to British subjects generally, but the Company retained its monopoly of the importation of tea into the British Islands. The Company proved unable to compete in trade with private merchants; and at the close of 1832 (the last year before the great change) the value of goods exported during the year by the Company was a little under 150,000*l.*, while the value of those exported by private traders during the same time exceeded 3,500,000*l.* In 1833 not only was the Company's monopoly of tea abolished, 'but the Company was restricted from carrying on any commercial operations whatever upon its own account, and was confined altogether to the territorial and political management of the vast empire which it had brought beneath its sway. The title of the Company became simply "The East India Company." Their warehouses and the greater part of the property which was required for commercial purposes were directed to be sold. The real capital of the Company in 1832 was estimated at 21,000,000*l.* The dividend guaranteed by the Act which abolished trading privileges was 630,000*l.*, being 10½ per cent. on a nominal capital of 6,000,000*l.* The dividends were made chargeable on the revenues of India, and were made redeemable by Parliament after 1874.'[1]

The appointments and the powers of the Governor-General and other officers remained unaltered. So did the authority of the Board of Control.

The constitution of the East India Company, in other respects, during the last stage of its existence, from 1833 to 1858, may be generally understood from the following brief analysis of portions of the Act of 1833 :—

The government of the British territories in India was continued in the hands of the Company until April 1854. The real and personal property of the

---

[1] Political Cyclopædia, title 'East India Company.'

Company to be held in trust for the Crown, for the service of India. (§ 1.)

The privileges and powers granted in 1813, and all other enactments concerning the Company not repugnant to this new Act, were to continue in force until April, 1854. (§ 2.)

From April 22, 1834, the China and tea trade of the Company was to cease. (§ 3.)

The Company was to close its commercial concerns and to sell all its property not required for purposes of government. (§ 4.)

The debts and liabilities of the Company were charged on the revenues of India. (§ 9.)

The Governor-General in Council was empowered to legislate for India and for all persons, whether British or native, foreigners or others. (§ 43.)

If the laws thus made by the Governor-General were disallowed by the authorities in England, they were to be annulled by the Governor-General. (44.)

Any natural-born subject of England might proceed by sea to any part or place within the limit of the Company's charter having a custom-house establishment, and might reside thereat, or pass through to other parts of the Company's territories to reside thereat. (§ 81.)

Lands within the Company's territories might be purchased and held by any persons where they are resident. (§ 86.)

No native nor any natural-born subject of His Majesty resident in India shall, by reason of his religion, place of birth, descent, or colour, be disabled from holding any office or employment under the Government of the Company. (§ 87.)

Slavery to be immediately mitigated, and abolished as soon as possible. (§ 88.)[1]

The two last paragraphs deserve marked attention. The abolition of slavery in the West Indies (which had been the strongholds of slavery in the British Empire) was contemporaneous with this Act. About the same time measures were taken for doing away with slavery in Ceylon, in Mauritius, and in other parts of our dominion where it existed. For very many years we have been able to say that there is not a slave beneath the British flag.

The other clause which I have designated for special notice, is that respecting the admission of the natives to office. This was nobly responded to by the Directors of the Company. In December 1854 they sent out the following 'admirable letter' to the government of India:—

'By Clause 87 of the Act it is provided that no person, by reason of his birth, creed, or colour, shall be disqualified from holding any service.

'It is fitting that this important enactment should be understood, in order that its full spirit and

[1] Political Cyclopædia, ut supra.

R

intention may be transfused through our whole system of administration.

'You will observe that its object is not to ascertain qualification, but to remove disqualification. It does not break down or derange the scheme of our Government, as conducted principally through the instrumentality of our regular servants, civil and military. To do this would be to abolish or impair the rules, which the Legislature has established for securing the fitness of the functionaries in whose hands the main duties of Indian administration are to be reposed; rules to which the present Act makes a material addition in the provisions relating to the College at Haileybury. But the meaning of the enactment we take to be, that there shall be no governing caste in British India; that, whatever other tests or qualifications may be adopted, distinctions of race or religion shall not be of the number; that no subject of the King, whether of Indian, or British, or mixed descent, shall be excluded either from the posts usually conferred on our uncovenanted servants in India, or from the covenanted service itself, provided he be otherwise eligible, consistently with the rules and agreeably to the conditions observed and exacted in the one case and in the other.

'In the application of this principle, that which will chiefly fall to your share will be the employment of natives, whether of the whole or the mixed blood, in official situations. So far as respects the former class—we mean natives of the whole blood—it is hardly necessary to say that the purposes of the Legislature have, in a considerable degree, been anticipated. You will know, and indeed have in some important respects carried into effect, our desire that natives should be admitted into places of trust as freely and extensively, as a regard for the due discharge of the functions attached to such places will permit. Even judicial duties of magnitude and importance are now confided to their hands, partly no doubt from considerations of economy, but partly also on principles of a liberal and comprehensive policy; still, a line of demarcation, to some extent in favour of the natives, to some extent in exclusion of them, has been maintained. Certain offices are appropriated to them; from certain others they are debarred, not because these latter belong to the covenanted service, and the former do not belong to it, but professedly on the ground that the average amount of native qualifications can be presumed only to rise to a certain limit. It is this line of demarcation which the present enactment obliterates, or rather for which it substitutes another, wholly irrespective of the distinction of races. Fitness is henceforth to be the criterion of eligibility.

‘ To this altered rule it will be necessary that

you should, both in your acts and your language,
conform. Practically, perhaps, no very marked difference of results will be occasioned. The distinctions between situations allotted to the covenanted
service and all other situations of an official or
public nature will remain generally as at present.

' Into a more particular consideration of the effects
that may result from the great principle which the
Legislature has now for the first time recognised and
established, we do not enter, because we would avoid
disquisition of a speculative nature. But there is
one practical lesson, which, often as we have on
former occasions inculcated it on you, the present
subject suggests to us once more to enforce. While,
on the one hand, it may be anticipated that the
range of public situations accessible to the native
and mixed races will gradually be enlarged, it is, on
the other hand, to be recollected that, as settlers
from Europe find their way into the country, this
class of persons will probably furnish candidates for
those very situations to which the natives and mixed
races will have admittance. Men of European enterprise and education will appear on the field, and it is
by the prospect of this event that we are led particularly to impress the lesson already alluded to on
your attention. In every view it is important that
the indigenous people of India, or those among them
who, by their habits, character, or position, may be

induced to aspire to office, should, as far as possible, be qualified to meet their European competitors. Hence there arises a powerful argument for the promotion of every design tending to the improvement of the natives, whether by conferring on them the advantages of education, or by diffusing among them the treasures of science, knowledge, and moral culture. For these desirable results we are well aware that you, like ourselves, are anxious ; and we doubt not that, in order to impel you to increased exertion for the promotion of them, you will need no stimulant beyond a simple reference to the considerations we have here suggested.

' While, however, we entertain these wishes and opinions, *we must guard against the supposition that it is chiefly by holding out means and opportunities of official distinction that we expect our Government to benefit the millions subjected to their authority.* We have repeatedly expressed to you a very different sentiment. *Facilities of official advancement can little affect the bulk of the people under any Government,* and perhaps least under a good Government. *It is not by holding out prizes to official ambition, but by repressing crime, by securing and guarding property, by creating confidence, by ensuring to industry the fruit of its labours, by protecting men in the undisturbed enjoyment of their rights, and in the unfettered exercise of their faculties, that Governments best minister to the*

public wealth and happiness. In effect, the free access
to office is chiefly valuable when it is a part of
general freedom.'

In 1838 came the great error, the great calamity,
and the great warning of the Afghan War. It was
an ambitious advance far beyond the natural limits of
Hindustan; and, if the gigantic schemes of aggrandisement, which our early successes in that war appeared to make practicable, had been realised, we
should, in all human probability, have been led to
similar extensions of dominion and to weakening of
effective power by conquests in Persia, Bokhara, and
Turkestan, and perhaps by unavoidable collision with
our ancient friends the Ottoman Turks themselves.
The strain upon the military and financial resources
of our empire would have been unendurable; and the
Sepoy Mutiny, which broke out eighteen years after
our Afghan expedition, would have found us with
our European forces hopelessly scattered, and unavail-
able for present action on the scene of deadly peril.

The Afghan War was the cause of the war in
Scinde in 1842. Scinde, an extensive and rich tract
of country along the lower half of the river Indus,
whence it takes its name, was under the misgovernment of a dominant class of nobles called the Ameers,
who kept up armed bands, recruited from among
the warlike mountain-tribes of Beloochistan. By

these mercenaries they oppressed the native peasantry, and carried on their frequent feuds among
themselves. The passage of our troops through
Scinde and the navigation of the Indus by our
flotillas had been found indispensable for the operation of the Afghan campaigns. This had created
jealousy and hostility towards the British in the
minds of the Ameers ; and they were collecting a
large army, with the design of making an attack upon
the British territories, when their intended assault
was anticipated by the daring of Sir Charles Napier,
who with a very scanty British force gained a rapid
series of brilliant victories over foes who fought
stubbornly and well. Scinde was annexed to the
British Empire, and its conqueror, Sir Charles
Napier, was appointed its Governor. He ruled it for
four years with administrative ability even surpass-
ing the military talent which he had displayed in its
conquest. A taint of the iniquity of our Afghan
war hangs about the origin of the war by which we
conquered Scinde. But it is consolatory to know
that the overthrow of the Ameers and the consequent change of masters has been an unspeakable
blessing to the great mass of the Scindian population, who had long groaned under the most rapa-
cious and insolent tyranny of a military aristocracy,
supported by lawless bands of foreign soldiery. The

historian of the war in Scinde [1] has said with truth that now ' the labourer cultivates in security his land; the handicraftsman, no longer dreading mutilation of his nose or ears for demanding remuneration for his work, is returning from the countries to which he had fled, allured back by good wages and employment. Young girls are no longer torn from their families to fill the zenanas of the great, or sold into distant slavery. The Hindoo merchant and Parsee trafficker pursue their vocation with safety and confidence; and even the proud Beloochee warrior, not incapable of noble sentiments, though harsh and savage, remains content with a government which has not meddled with his right of subsistence, but only changed his feudal ties into a peaceful and honourable dependence. He has, moreover, become personally attached to a conqueror, whose prowess he has felt in battle, and whose justice and generosity he has experienced in peace.' [1]

In viewing the last of our great Anglo-Indian conquests, the subjugation and the annexation of the Punjab, there is nothing to alloy the gratification which arises from contemplating the heroism which our armies displayed in two severe wars with a highly-disciplined and very brave enemy. They were on our part wars of self-defence, and wars for which we had given no provocation whatever. A

[1] Sir William Napier

remarkable military adventurer, Runjeet Singh, had formed in the country of the Five Rivers (the Punjab) a military State out of the nation or religious confederacy of the Sikhs. His large armies had been thoroughly disciplined by excellent French and Italian officers, who had taken service with him after the downfall of the first Napoleon. The Sikhs were in particular admirable gunners; and Runjeet Singh surpassed many European rulers in the number and equipment of his parks of artillery, and in the abundance and the organisation of munitions and military stores of every kind. He was throughout a long life the firm friend of the British; but when the 'Old Lion of the Punjab' (as Runjeet Singh was termed) died, the fierce soldiery, whom he had kept under stern rule, scorned the authority of a woman and a child, and they loudly demanded to be let loose to seek plunder and conquest in the adjacent British territories. Their chiefs, unable to restrain them, rather went with them than led them; and the British rulers of India were suddenly required to defend the country against these ferocious and formidable aggressors. After a series of hard-fought and sanguinary battles, the Sikh armies were broken and driven back across the Indus. The English advanced to the Sikh capital, Lahore; and its siege had commenced, when those who acted in the name of the titular sovereign of the Punjab, the young Maharajah, supplicated for peace, which was granted, and the Treaty of Lahore, signed on March 9, 1846, left the Punjab still an independent State. But the savage pride of the Sikh soldiery had not been thoroughly quelled. Outrages were committed on British envoys and officers; the war was renewed; and after two more great battles, at Chillianwalla and Gujerat, the Sikhs were again compelled to submit, and (as our safety imperiously required) the Punjab was made part of the British dominion (March 29, 1849). Since then the Sikh regiments have proved eminently loyal and brave in the British service.

Lord Hardinge had been Governor-General at the time of the first Sikh war. He had nobly placed his military talents at the disposal of the Commander-in-Chief, Sir Hugh Gough, afterwards Lord Gough. The presence in our camps of one of the ablest and most experienced of Wellington's generals was no slight accession of strength to the British arms; and our triumph in the first Sikh war may be truly said to have been achieved, not only under but in a great extent by Lord Hardinge.

Early in 1848 Lord Hardinge was succeeded in the Governorship of India by Lord Dalhousie, under whom the annexation of the Punjab was completed, and also that of Pegu, which has been already mentioned.

The British territories in India were also largely augmented during Lord Dalhousie's viceroyalty by the annexation of certain States, which were situate within the old circle of our dominion, but which had previously been left under native rulers, though all were, more or less, subject to the controlling supervision of Agents of the British Government, and all were bound to follow the Imperial leadership and mandates of the British as to forming treaties and alliances, and as to making and carrying on war.

Annexations of this kind had occurred, from time to time, long before Lord Dalhousie came to India. As might have been expected, some of the petty princes of the Native States in the condition of Subject Alliance were often found to be plotting against us, or withholding their stipulated tributes or contingents, or engaged in some other breach of that allegiance, which the great Paramount Anglo-Indian Government claimed as its due. The forfeitures thus incurred were sometimes, though not always, enforced; and, when they were enforced, the full penalty was not always exacted. There was indeed a great difference in the opinions of Anglo-Indian statesmen as to the merger of the Native Principalities being or not being advantageous for our interests. Some thought (to use expressions afterwards employed by Lord Dalhousie) that it was sound policy 'to take advantage of every just oppor-

tunity that offers itself for consolidating the territories which already belonged to us, by taking
possession of States that may lapse in the midst of
them ; for thus getting rid of these petty intervening
principalities, which may be made a means of annoy-
ance, but which never can be a source of strength ;
for adding to the resources of the public treasury;
and for extending the uniform application of our
system of government to those whose best interests
will be promoted thereby.'[1] Others (and among
them there were men whose names stand very high
in Anglo-Indian history) considered that the Native
States were a source to us of strength rather than
of weakness ; and that, though it was probable that, if
Great Britain retained her high position among the
States of Europe, the whole of India would in the
course of time become one British province, we
ought most carefully to abstain from accelerating
that great change.[2]

These last-mentioned opinions had generally been
held by our rulers in India in the interval between
the governments of Lord Wellesley and Lord Dalhousie. But even the most prudent and forbearing
of our Governors were sometimes goaded by the

[1] See Kaye's Sepoy War, vol. i. p. 74.
[2] Kaye's Sepoy War, vol. i. p. 80. In the note a minute by
Colonel Low is cited, in which Lord Hastings, Sir Thomas Munro,
Sir John Malcolm, the Hon. Mountstuart Elphinstone, and Lord
Metcalfe are named as holders of these opinions.

provocations and misdeeds of the native princes to measures of annexation. Thus, Lord William Bentinck, in 1834, dethroned the Rajah of Coorg, and incorporated his dominions with the territories of the East India Company. The same eminently mild and pacific Governor, in the same year, took the principality of Mysore under direct British rule, in consequence of the misgovernment that prevailed there, under its late native maharajah.[1]

But these were trifling aggrandisements compared with the acquisition of the kingdom of Oudh. Oudh is one of the finest provinces in India. 'Its area, about equal in extent to Holland and Belgium together, is estimated at 23,730 square miles, of which 12,885 square miles are returned as cultivated, 6,577 as culturable, and 4,168 as unculturable.' 'The population is about $11\frac{1}{4}$ millions, or 474 persons to the square mile, a density that is not equalled even in Belgium.'[2] A glance at the map will show the importance of its position relatively to communication between the Lower Provinces (or Presidency of Bengal) and the North-Western Provinces, and the Punjab. The misgovernment of the kings of

---

[1] His adopted son and intended successor is being educated under officers appointed by the British Government, in order to fit him for the administration of the province which is to be placed eventually in his hands. See Parl. Blue Book on India, Sept. 1871, no. 230, p. 18.

[2] Parl. Blue Book, p. 40.

Oudh had been so atrocious, warnings had been given and contemned so often, that the dethronement of these oppressors by the British was an act of humanity, as well as of justice. Indeed, as the kings of Oudh were bound by express treaty with us to establish 'an administration conducive to the prosperity of their subjects, and calculated to secure the lives and properties of the inhabitants,' no doubt was felt, in 1850, as to its being ' the paramount duty of the British Government to step in and arrest the atrocities which were converting one of the finest provinces in India into a moral pestilence.' Many, indeed, were convinced that we were bound to assume the government of the country, who yet wished that it should not be completely absorbed in our Indian Empire.[1] But by far the greater number, both in England and in India, of those who had authority, considered the complete annexation of Oudh to be expedient as well as just, and Oudh was annexed accordingly.

A little earlier in Lord Dalhousie's viceroyalty some annexations had been made of territories not, even collectively, so important as Oudh, but which were subjected to the process of Imperial absorption, under circumstances, which excited more alarm among the Asiatics, and which have occasioned more differences of opinion among Europeans respecting

[1] See Kaye's Sepoy War, vol. i. p. 136.

their propriety, than attended the confiscation of
Oudh. In 1849 the Rajah of Sattara died without
an heir of his body, but leaving an adopted heir. In
1853 the Rajah of Nagpoor and Berar died, without
an heir of his body, and not having adopted an heir;
but an adoption of a son by his eldest widow would,
according to Hindu law and usage, have had the
same effect as an adoption by the Rajah himself.
Both Sattara and Berar were Mahratta States, the
rulers of which had in former times been overthrown
in war. In each case the British Government had
resuscitated the fallen State, and had set up a native
prince, by whom and by whose heirs it was to be
ruled. Lord Dalhousie and his supporters pronounced that the provision in favour of heirs meant
heirs of the body only, and did not extend to heirs
by adoption. On the other side it was urged, that
the practice of adoption, in cases where a man was
likely to die or had died childless, was universal
among the Hindus, and was a religious necessity for
them, inasmuch as their creed teaches that unless a
son, either a son begotten or a son adopted, performs
a man's funeral rites, that man must remain in hell.
It would be improper here to give an opinion on
these much disputed cases ; nor, indeed, could the
materials for a sound opinion be easily here collected.
There can be no doubt as to the principle, on which
the promises of the English Government to recognise

these rajahs and their heirs in their royalties ought to be interpreted. It is the principle, by which all promises are to be interpreted, when the terms of the promise admit of more senses than one. The party making the promise is bound to keep it in the sense in which he, at the time of making it, had good reason to believe it to be understood by the other party. In order to apply this test, a complete knowledge of all the antecedent and surrounding circumstances of the cases is necessary, which it would be vain to strive after obtaining here. Rightly or wrongly, wisely or unwisely, Sattara and Berar were treated by our Government as fiefs, which had escheated to the Paramount Power for lack of heirs, and they were made to augment the Indian territory, over which we exercise immediate dominion.[1]

Lord Dalhousie's administration of India was signalised not only by great territorial aggrandisement, but by public works of the greatest utility and almost unparalleled grandeur. The Ganges Canal, which serves the double purpose of irrigation and navigation, is one of the foremost. The system

---

[1] See Kaye's Sepoy War, p. 93, for the sensible distinction taken by the Court of Directors between the Sattara case and that of Kerowlee, a Rajpoot State, the chief of which had died leaving an adopted heir only. The Directors refused to annex Kerowlee, an ancient State, which stood towards us in the relation of protected ally only; whereas the Sattara State, which they annexed, was 'of recent origin, derived altogether from the creation and gift of the British Government.'

of Indian railways was commenced, the electric telegraph was introduced, and an almost infinite number of local works were completed, each small in itself, and benefiting immediately a limited circle, but in the aggregate diffusing an incalculable amount of plenteousness and prosperity throughout the land. Much also was done by wise legislative and administrative improvement. The Governor-General was relieved from an overwhelming press of duties by the appointment of a Lieutenant-Governor for Bengal. A Legislative Council was organised distinct from the Supreme Council, the public having access to its deliberations, and its debates and papers being printed and issued to the world. The Indian Civil Service, by an Act passed in 1853, was thrown open to all who, being natural-born subjects of the British Sovereign, should offer themselves as candidates for examination and admission.

Great exertions were made also for the intellectual and moral improvement of the people; schools for the education of natives were established; the Hindoo College at Calcutta was revived and improved; a Presidency College was founded in the same city, to give a higher scale of education to the youth of Bengal; similar colleges were sanctioned at Madras and Bombay; grants-in-aid to all educational establishments were authorised, subject to government inspection of the schools

aided ; a committee was appointed to consider
the plans for establishing regular universities at
Calcutta, Bombay, and Madras ; a distinct educational department was formed at the seat of government, with directors-general of public instruction
in all the Presidencies and governments ; and the
East India Company, by a despatch framed in 1854,
sanctioned a most extensive educational scheme for
the whole of India, to be rendered available to all
the natives who might be willing and able to claim
its advantages.

All these things, and many more, were accomplished during Lord Dalhousie's administration of
India from March 1848 to March 1856. In a memoir
drawn up by Lord Dalhousie a little before he left
India, and addressed to the East India Company,
he recounted these things in no boastful spirit, but
with an undisguised feeling of honourable satisfaction.
He drew up a careful account of the condition and
prospects of our Anglo-Indian Power, such as they
then appeared to him and to other thoughtful and
experienced statesmen; and he expressed a hope,
which all at the time thought well founded, that
from the review of the state of India which he
presented to the Directors they would derive some
'degree of satisfaction with the past, and a still
larger measure of encouragement for the future.'
But this memoir contained one passage more sig-

nificant and more fraught with weighty truth, than was deemed at the time by either him who penned, or by those who perused it. It ought always to be present to the minds of those who have to rule India. Lord Dalhousie said, ' No prudent man, who has any knowledge of Eastern affairs, would ever venture to predict the maintenance of continued peace within our Eastern possessions. Experience, frequent, hard, and recent experience, has taught us that war from without or rebellion from within may at any time be raised against us in quarters where they were the least to be expected, and by the most feeble and unlikely instruments. No man, therefore, can ever prudently hold forth assurance of continued peace in India.'

This was written in March, 1856. On May 11, 1857, three native regiments that had murdered their European officers at Meerut entered Delhi, where the aged Mogul Prince, the descendant of Aurungzebe, of Akbar, and of Timour, was maintained as a pensioner by the British Government. Before sunset the native garrison of Delhi had joined the Meerut mutineers, there had been a massacre of Europeans, and a young man of the race of the ancient Mogul dynasty was set up by the rebels as King of Delhi and Lord of India. .

This is no place for a narrative of the rise, the

progress, or the suppression of the Sepoy Rebellion; a war of mutiny which, for atrocity and horror, can only be paralleled with the war of the Carthaginian mercenary troops against their masters, the ἄσπονδος πόλεμος of antiquity.

It is enough to note here that when the rebellion was thoroughly quelled, it was considered necessary to reörganise the general system by which India was ruled. The plan of Double Government which Pitt had inaugurated was, after seventy years' trial, abolished. The powers and territory of the East India Company were transferred to the Queen of England; and the administration (in England) of Indian affairs was intrusted to a Secretary of State and a Council of fifteen, of whom seven were elected by the Company's Board of Directors and eight nominated by the Crown.

An emphatic warning had been given before the Sepoy Mutiny that some change of this kind was probable. In 1853, when the term of renewal of the Company's charter granted in 1833 was coming to a close, a fresh lease of dominion for a long term of years was not again granted. The powers of the Company were merely continued until Parliament should otherwise provide; and there was a monitory declaration that the Company held their territories in trust for the Crown.

The following is an epitome of the chief provisions of the statute by which the great transfer of dominion was finally made. It received the royal assent on August 2, 1858 :—

TITLE OF ACT, 'AN ACT FOR THE BETTER GOVERNMENT OF INDIA.'

Preamble.

' Whereas by an Act of the session holden in the sixteenth and seventeenth years of Her Majesty, chapter ninety-five, " to provide for the government of India," the territories in the possession and under the government of the East India Company were continued under such government, in trust for Her Majesty, until Parliament should otherwise provide, subject to the provisions of that Act and of other Acts of Parliament, and the property and rights in the said Act referred to are held by the said Company in trust for Her Majesty, for the purposes of the said Government : and whereas it is expedient that the said territories should be governed by, and in the name of, Her Majesty : ' be it therefore enacted as follows ; that is to say,

Transfer of the Government of India to Her Majesty.

I. The government of the territories now in the possession or under the Government of the East India Company, and all powers in relation to government vested in or exercised by the said Company in trust for Her Majesty, shall cease to be vested in or exercised by the said Company, and all territories in the possession or under the government of the said Company, and all rights vested in, or which, if this Act had not been passed, might have been exercised by, the said Company, in relation to any territories, shall become vested in Her Majesty, and be exercised in her name ; and for the purposes of this Act India shall mean the territories vested in Her Majesty as aforesaid, and all territories which may become vested in Her Majesty by any such rights as aforesaid.

II. India shall be governed by, and in the name of, Her Majesty, and all rights in relation to any territories which might have been exercised by the said Company if this Act had not been passed shall and may be exercised by and in the name of Her

Majesty, as rights incidental to the Government of India; and all the territorial and other revenues of, or arising in, India, and all tributes and other payments in respect of any territories which would have been receivable by or in the name of the said Company, if this Act had not been passed, shall be received for and in the name of Her Majesty, and shall be applied and disposed of for the purposes of the Government of India alone, subject to the provisions of this Act.

III. A Secretary of State is to exercise all the governing powers heretofore exercised by Court of Directors, Court of Proprietors, and Board of Control.

IV. Provision concerning sitting of Secretary and Under-Secretary in House of Commons.

V. Concerning re-election of Secretaries to House of Commons.

VI. Secretary of State for India to receive salary equal to those of other Secretaries of State.

Council of India.

VII. A Council of India, of fifteen persons, to be formed, and to be styled ' The Council of India ; ' the Council of India now bearing that name to be styled henceforth ' The Council of the Governor-General of India.'

VIII. The Court of Directors of the East India Company to elect from among the Directors of the Company, or from among those who have been Directors, seven members of the Council of India, and the Crown to appoint the other eight.

IX. Vacancies among the Crown members to be filled up by Her Majesty, and among the other seven by the Council by election.

X. The major part of the Council, with certain exceptions, to be persons who shall have served or resided ten years in India.

XI. Members to hold office during good behaviour.

XII. Members not to sit in Parliament.

XIII. Annual salary of 1,200l. to each member.

XIV. Members may resign ; if after ten years' service, on a pension of 500l., subject to certain conditions.

XV. Secretaries and other officers of Company to become officers of Council of India, subject to any changes afterwards made by Privy Council and sanctioned by Parliament.

XVI. Secretary in Council to make all subsequent appointments in the Home establishment.

XVII. Compensation to such officers of the Company as are not retained permanently by the Council.

XVIII. Any officer of the Company, transferred to the service of the Council, to have a claim to the same pension or superannuation allowance as if the change of Government had not taken place.

Duties and Proceedings of the Council.

XIX. Council to conduct affairs of India in England; but all correspondence to be in the name of, and signed by, the Secretary of State.

XX. Secretary of State may divide the Council into Committees.

XXI. Secretary of State to sit and vote as president, and appoint vice-president.

XXII. Five to be a quorum; meetings convened by Secretary of State not fewer than one each week.

XXIII. Secretary of State to decide questions on which members differ. Any dissentient member may require his opinion to be placed upon record.

XXIV. Secretary's proceedings to be open to all the Council, except in 'secret service' despatches.

XXV. Secretary to give reasons for any exercise of his veto against the decision of the majority.

XXVI. Secretary allowed to dispense with the two preceding clauses in urgent cases.

XXVII. Functions of the 'Secret Committee' transferred to Secretary of State.

XXVIII. Despatches marked 'secret' not to be opened by members of Council.

Appointments and Patronage.

XXIX. The appointments of Governor-General of India, fourth ordinary member of the Council of the Governor-General of India, and Governors of Presidencies in India, now made by the Court of Directors, with the approbation of Her Majesty, and the appointments of Advocate-General for the several Presidencies, now made with the approbation of the Commissioners for the affairs of India, shall be made by Her Majesty by warrant under her royal sign manual; the appointments of the ordinary members of the Council of the Governor-General of India, except the fourth ordinary member, and the appointments of the members of Council of the several

Presidencies, shall be made by the Secretary of State in Council, with the concurrence of a majority of members present at a meeting; the appointments of the Lieutenant-Governors of provinces or territories shall be made by the Governor-General of India, subject to the approbation of Her Majesty; and all such appointments shall be subject to the qualifications now by law affecting such offices respectively.

XXX. Inferior appointments to be made in India as heretofore, except transference of regulating and appellate powers from Court of Directors to Council.

XXXI. Certain former enactments as to appointments, &c., to the Civil Service repealed.

XXXII. Secretary of State to make regulations for admitting all persons being natural-born subjects of Her Majesty (and of such age and qualification as may be prescribed in this behalf), who may be desirous of becoming candidates for appointment to the Civil Service of India, to be examined as candidates accordingly, and for prescribing the branches of knowledge in which such candidates shall be examined, and generally for regulating and conducting such examinations, under the superintendence of the said last-mentioned Commissioners, or of the persons, for the time being, entrusted with the carrying out of such regulations as may be from time to time established by Her Majesty for examination, certificate, or other test of fitness in relation to appointments to junior situations in the Civil Service of the Crown, and the candidates who may be certified by the said Commissioners or other persons as aforesaid to be entitled under such regulations, shall be recommended for appointment according to the order of their proficiency as shown by such examinations, and such persons only as shall have been so certified as aforesaid shall be appointed or admitted to the Civil Service of India by the Secretary of State in Council.

XXXIII. Appointments to naval and military cadetships to vest in the Crown.

XXXIV. Competitive examinations for engineers and artillery of the Indian army.

XXXV. A certain ratio of cadetships to be given to the sons of persons who have served in India.

XXXVI. All the other cadetships to be in the gift of the members of the Council, subject to approval; the Secretary of State to have twice as many nominations as an ordinary member.

XXXVII. In all unchanged rules concerning appointments, power of Court of Directors to be vested in Council.

XXXVIII. The same in reference to any dismissal from service.

Transfer of Property.

XXXIX. Company's property, credits, and debits, to vest in the Crown—except the *East India Stock* and the dividends thereon.

XL. Secretary in Council may buy, sell, or borrow, in the name of the Crown, for the service of India.

Revenues.

XLI. Expenditure of revenues in India to be subject to the control of the Secretary in Council.

XLII. Liabilities of Company and dividends on India stock to be borne by Secretary in Council out of revenues of India.

XLIII. Secretary in Council to keep a cash account with the Bank of England, and to be responsible for all payments in relation to India revenue.

XLIV. Transfer of cash balance from the Company to the Council.

XLV. A stock account to be opened at Bank of England.

XLVI. Transfer of stock accounts.

XLVII. Mode of managing Council's finances at the Bank.

XLVIII. Transfer of Exchequer bills, &c., from Company to Council.

XLIX. Power of issuing bonds, debentures, &c.

L. Provisions concerning forgery.

LI. Regulations of audit department.

LII. The Crown to appoint auditor of Indian accounts, to whom all needful papers are to be sent by Secretary in Council.

LIII. Annual accounts to be furnished to Parliament of the revenue and expenditure of India, accompanied by reports on the moral and material progress of the several Presidencies.

LIV. Order for war in India to be made known to Parliament within a specified period.

LV. Except for preventing or repelling actual invasion of Her Majesty's Indian possessions, or under other sudden and urgent necessity, the revenues of India shall not, without the consent of both Houses of Parliament, be applicable to defray the expenses of any military operation carried on beyond the external frontiers of such possessions by Her Majesty's forces charged upon such revenues.

Existing Establishments.

LVI. Company's army and navy transferred to the Crown, but with all existing contracts and engagements holding good.[1]

LVII. Future powers as to conditions of service.

LVIII. All commissions held under the Company to be valid as under the Crown.

LIX. Regulations of service to be subject to future change, if deemed necessary.

LX. Court of Directors and Court of Proprietors cease to hold power in reference to Government of India.

LXI. Board of Control abolished.

LXII. Records and archives of Company to be given up to Council—except stock and dividend books.

LXIII. Powers of Governor-General on assuming duties of that office.

LXIV. Existing enactments and provisions to remain in force, unless specially repealed.

Actions and Contracts.

LXV. Secretary in Council may sue and be sued as a body corporate.

LXVI. And may take the place of the Company in any still pending actions.

LXVII. Treaties and covenants made by the Company to remain binding.

LXVIII. Members not *personally* liable for such treaties or covenants.

LXIX. A Court of Directors still to exist, but in smaller number than before.

LXX. Quarterly courts not in future obligatory.

LXXI. Company's liability ceases on all matters now taken under the care of the Council.

---

[1] The Indian army was amalgamated with the Queen's army by the subsequent statutes 23 and 24 Vict. c. 100, and 24 and 25 Vict. c. 74.

Saving of Certain Rights of the Company.

LXXII. Secretary in Council to pay dividends on India stock out of India revenue.

LXXIII. Dividends to constitute a preferential charge.[1]

The change in the Government of India effected by this statute was made known by a proclamation of Her Majesty Queen Victoria to the princes, chiefs, and peoples of India, which was read in the principal cities of India on the first day of November 1858. Parts of that proclamation refer to the then recent mutiny. But there are portions of it which set forth the general principles on which Her Majesty's Government of India is to be administered, and those portions deserve respectful and grateful attention. Thus saith the Sovereign of the British Empire—

We hereby announce to the native princes of India that all treaties and engagements made with them by, or under the authority of, the Honourable East India Company are by us accepted, and will be scrupulously maintained; and we look for the like observance on their part.

We desire no extension of our present territorial possessions; and while we will permit no aggression upon our dominions or our rights to be attempted with impunity, we shall sanction no encroachment on those of others. We shall respect the rights, dignity, and honour of native princes as our own; and we desire that they, as well as our own subjects, should enjoy that prosperity and that social advancement which can only be secured by internal peace and good government.

We hold ourselves bound to the natives of our Indian territories by the same obligations of duty which bind us to all our other sub-

[1] An Act passed in 1861 made some changes in the numbers and composition of the Councils of India.

jects; and those obligations, by the blessing of Almighty God, we shall faithfully and conscientiously fulfil.

Firmly relying ourselves on the truth of Christianity, and acknowledging with gratitude the solace of religion, we disclaim alike the right and the desire to impose our convictions on any of our subjects. We declare it to be our royal will and pleasure that none be in anywise favoured, none molested or disquieted, by reason of their religious faith or observances, but that all shall alike enjoy the equal and impartial protection of the law; and we do strictly charge and enjoin all those who may be in authority under us that they abstain from all interference with the religious belief or worship of any of our subjects on pain of our highest displeasure.

And it is our further will that, so far as may be, our subjects, of whatever race or creed, be freely and impartially admitted to offices in our service, the duties of which they may be qualified, by their education, ability, and integrity, duly to discharge.

We know and respect the feelings of attachment with which the natives of India regard the lands inherited by them from their ancestors, and we desire to protect them in all rights connected therewith, subject to the equitable demands of the State; and we will that, generally in framing and administering the law, due regard be paid to the ancient rights, usages, and customs of India.

One passage in this proclamation should be very specially noticed. It is the passage in which Her Majesty announces that the Sovereign of the British Empire is bound to the natives of India by the same obligations of duty, which bind the Sovereign to all the other subjects of the Empire. This points out the right general principle on which India is to be ruled, and which is not identical with the principle now frequently paraded by popular speakers and writers as the true one.

For a very long time the British rulers of India avowedly considered that ' the two principal objects

which the Government ought to have in view in all
its arrangements are, to insure its political safety, and
to render the possession of the country as advantageous as possible to the East India Company and
the British nation.' They had regard also to 'the
happiness of the governed;' but their reason for
valuing it was because it tended to make the British
Government of India more secure, and more profitable to the British rulers.[1]

The erroneous selfishness of this old policy has
long been discerned and condemned. Many of our
present politicians now go into the opposite extreme,
and assert that 'India is to be governed for the sake
of the Indians,' meaning thereby not merely that
the immediate benefit of the natives is to be one
great object of Anglo-Indian Government, but that
it is to be the sole object; and that, in comparison
with it, all such considerations as the health and
happiness of European residents in India, or the
general maintenance and advancement of the power
and welfare of the British Empire, are to be utterly
disregarded and ignored.

I believe this new cry of 'India for the Indians'
to be as erroneous in theory (though not so fla-

[1] See in Mr. Kaye's first chapter of his 'History of the East
India Company' his very interesting narrative of the preparation
and correction of the Minutes, in 1793, on which the Cornwallis
Regulations were founded.

grantly mischievous in practice) as the old maxim of
' India for the British.' The true principle with
regard to India, as with regard to every other part
of the British Empire, is, that India ought to be
governed for the general good of the whole British
Empire, and of the whole inhabitants of that Empire, so far as they are affected by such government. As, of course, the natives of India itself are
far more closely affected than any others can be
by such government, their immediate interests are
to be constantly and anxiously regarded, especially
in local regulations; but Imperial rule is to be conducted upon Imperial principles, and is not to lose
its unity and its vigour by being subordinated to
provincial cupidities, or jealousies, or influences of
any description.

A general sketch of the present condition of India,
of its political and territorial divisions, of the systems
of government control, and provincial, now established
there, of the selection of rulers, and of the relations
of India-rule to Home-rule, will form the most useful
conclusion to the present chapter.[1]

---

[1] This sketch is taken to a great extent from the Parliamentary
Blue Book ' Statement of the moral and material progress of India
during the year 1869–70,' ordered by the House of Commons to
be printed May 15, 1871. I have also obtained great assistance
from a book on the system of Administration in India, entitled
' Indian Polity,' by Mr. George Chesney, Accountant-General to
the Government of India, published in 1868 by Longmans, Green,
& Co.

It is usual in modern maps of India to mark the provinces under British administration in red colour, and those under native administration in yellow. If the reader will turn to a map thus prepared, his first impression (unless he is familiar with Anglo-Indian statistics) will probably be that of surprise at seeing so large a portion of India beyond the bounds of our acquisitions. But all these large masses of territory, which are colourably the dominions of native princes, are in reality British dependencies. There is no such thing in India as an Independent political society, or an Independent sovereign nation, such as constitutes a Sovereign State in the eye of International Law. All the local rulers of the native so-called States in India *habitually obey the commands of a determinate human superior*, that is of the British Government. While in this condition they form *political societies, which are merely limbs of another larger society*, that is of the British Empire.[1] The term 'Subject-Allies'

[1] For this test, see Austin's Province of Jurisprudence, p. 201 to p. 208. In Phillimore's International Law, vol. i. p. 91, the following is given as the 'proper and strict test to apply' in order to ascertain whether a protected State has or has not lost its International existence as a Sovereign State :—We are directed to ascertain 'the capacity of the protected State to negotiate, to make peace or war with other States, irrespectively of the will of its protector.' . . . 'It must, however (in order to remain a member of the commonwealth of Sovereign States), retain this capacity *de facto* as well as *de jure*.'

Mr. Chesney (p. 213 of his Polity of India) correctly says that 'There is in truth no such thing as purely native rule in India,

best expresses the condition of the Indian States that are not under our direct administration, and I shall continue to speak of them by that term.

All India is under the authority of a Governor-General or Viceroy, appointed by the Crown, and removable by the Crown, and also bound to follow the instruction of Her Majesty's Secretary of State for India, who is aided in England by a Council which will be described presently. It is convenient first to consider our Government as exercised in India by the officials stationed there.

The Governor-General of India has the power of declaring war and making peace: and he has at his disposal an army, which in the Parliamentary statement published in 1871, was reckoned as follows:—

Military Forces in 1870–71.

British officers	6,545
British non-commissioned officers and men . .	60,425
Native soldiers	122,122
Field guns	484 [1]

But an order for war in India must be made known

Not to mention that every native State is more or less controlled by British authority, exercised through a Resident, or other agent of the British Government; every native ruler is, so to speak, constantly on his best behaviour; assured that any marked instance of mis-government will at once draw on him the interference of the paramount power; and having, until quite lately, the constant apprehension before him of deposition, and of the annexation of his dominions, should he allow the opportunity to occur.'

[1] It is not necessary to describe here the special armies of Bengal, Bombay, Madras, &c.

to the Imperial Parliament within a limited period ; and, except in cases of repelling or preventing invasion, or of other urgent necessity, the consent of both Houses of Parliament is requisite before the revenues of India can be applied for any military operation beyond the frontiers.

The Governor-General appoints the Resident Agents in the territories of each of our Indian Subject-Allies, through whom the native rulers are guided and controlled.

With regard to British India Proper, the Governor-General is invested with legislative as well as with executive powers of government. The subordinate powers of the minor governors will be spoken of presently. The general supreme power (supreme, that is, so far as regards officials and others resident in India) is in the Governor-General. He may make laws and regulations for all persons, whether British or native, foreigners or others, within the Indian territories under the dominion of Her Majesty, and for all servants of the Government of India within the dominions of princes and states in alliance with Her Majesty.

These vast powers of the Viceroy of India are exercised by him in co-operation with Councils; and it is very important to understand the meaning of ' Government by Council' (or rather ' Government *in* Council') as invented and practised by Anglo-

T

Indian statesmen. First, however, we will ascertain the composition of the chief Council, styled 'The Council of the Governor-General of India.'

The surest and best account of it may be chiefly taken from the Parliamentary Blue Book.

' The Supreme Government [that is to say, supreme in India, but subject to the control of the Crown, acting by the Secretary of State in England,] the Supreme Government, which passes in review the entire administration of India, consists of the Governor-General and his Council of five members [who are all appointed by the Secretary of State for India]; the Commander-in-Chief, whose duties frequently oblige him to be absent, being an "extra-ordinary" member. The business of the Government is conducted in five separate departments— Financial, Home, Foreign, Military, and Public Works; each department is under the charge of a secretary, and each is besides, the special care of a member of the Supreme Council, who has authority to deal with affairs of routine and minor importance, and to select what is worthy of the consideration of the Governor-General and his collective Council. Formerly all the business was dealt with by the Council collectively, and the present form of Cabinet Government was the necessary result of the enormous increase of territory, and consequent pressure of business which took place during Lord Dalhousie's administration. It has been usual for the Governor-General to superintend the political business of the Foreign Office; but Lord Mayo, since he entered on office, has, in addition, taken under his special charge the Department of Public Works, which at present has no recognised head in the Council, and is directing his attention to the introduction of a better organisation into this important branch of the administration. The Financial Department is concerned, not with revenue business, but with matters involving a permanent charge on the State. The Foreign Department corresponds directly with the political agents of Rajpootana and Central India, and the Commissioners of Mysore and the Assigned Districts. Formerly it took charge of business coming up from the Non-regulation Provinces, the Home Department exercising a similar supervision over the Regulation [1] Provinces; but since, of recent years, the principal differences that marked the two systems have been removed by the introduction of the penal and criminal procedure, and the work of the Home Department has been much increased in consequence, the telegraphs have been taken over by the Foreign Department, while the Post Office has been placed under the Financial Secretary.'

The decision of a majority is regarded as the de-

[1] An explanation of these terms will be found in a subsequent page of this book.

cision of the Governor and Council, the Governor
having a vote as a member of the Council, and also
a casting-vote if the numbers on a division are equal.
Besides this, the Governor has power to overrule the
decision of a majority of the Council, and to act on
his own judgment in opposition to them in matters
in which he considers it to be urgently important for
him to do so; but he is bound, in such a case, to
draw up a minute recording his reasons.

Mr. Mill, in a passage of his work on ' Representative Government,' quoted by Mr. Chesney in his work
on the ' Polity of India,' has thus eulogised this
system of Government by Council: ' These Councils[1]
are composed of persons who have professional
knowledge of Indian affairs, which the Governor-
General and Governors usually lack, and which it
would not be desirable to require of them.

' As a rule, every member of Council is expected to
give an opinion, which is of course very often a simple
acquiescence; but if there is a difference of sentiment, it is at the option of every member, and it is
the invariable practice, to record the reasons of his
opinion, the Governor-General or Governor doing the
same. In ordinary cases the decision is according to
the sense of the majority; the Council, therefore, has
a substantial part in the Government; but if the

---

[1] Mr. Mill is speaking of the Provincial Councils of Madras and
Bombay as well as of the Governor-General's Council.

Governor-General, or Governor, thinks fit, he may set aside even their unanimous opinion, recording his reasons. The result is that the chief is, individually and effectively, responsible for every act of the Government. The members of Council have only the responsibility of advisers; but it is always known, from documents capable of being produced, and which, if called for by Parliament or public opinion, always are produced, what each has advised, and what reasons he gave for his advice. From their dignified position, and ostensible participation in all acts of Government, they have nearly as strong motives to apply themselves to the public business, and to form and express a well-considered opinion on every part of it, as if the whole responsibility rested with themselves. This mode of conducting the highest class of administrative business is one of the most successful instances of the adaptation of means to ends, which political history, not hitherto very prolific in works of skill and contrivance, has yet to show. It is one of the acquisitions with which the art of politics has been enriched by the experience of the East India Company's rule.'

The Council above described (which is frequently spoken of as the Executive Council) used formerly to pass laws; but this is now done in the Legislative Council. The composition of the last-mentioned body is thus set forth in the Parliamentary

Blue Book already referred to. ' The Legal member takes charge of Government Bills in the Legislative Council. This Council consists of twelve members (besides the seven members of the Executive Council), of whom one-half must be unconnected with the public service. The six official members are civilians of experience, chosen from different parts of the country; as non-official members, two leading Calcutta merchants have hitherto been appointed, and four natives of rank, also chosen from different parts of the country. Bengal, Madras, and Bombay possess Councils of their own, and the Council of India therefore legislates for those provinces which are unprovided with Local Councils, or on matters of general importance. The debates are open to strangers, and the Governor-General has the power of veto over all measures passed.'

I will now proceed to sketch separately the sub-Governments into which India is divided; and I will first deal with those, which make up British India Proper, reserving the most important of our India subject-allies for subsequent consideration: but some of the Subject-Allied States are politically grouped with some of the sub-Governments of British India Proper, and will therefore be mentioned as we go through the list of our own directly governed territories.

British India Proper now consists of the following eight divisions :—

1st. The Lower Provinces, corresponding with part of the old Presidency of Bengal.

2nd. The Presidency of Madras.

3rd. The Presidency of Bombay.

4th. The North-Western Provinces.

Territories comprehended in these four divisions make up what are called the Regulation Provinces.[1] The remaining four are Non-Regulation Provinces. The difference between Regulation and Non-Regulation will be explained when we pass from the consideration of the 4th division to that of the

5th. Oudh.

6th. The Central Provinces.

7th. The Punjab.

8th. British Burmah.

We commence with the Government of the Lower Provinces. It is the largest and most important portion of the old Presidency of Bengal, which, before 1833, included also the North-West Provinces. The sub-division of British India, which we are now considering, has been further circumscribed in its limits since 1861, but its territory is still ' the largest, the most populous, and the richest of the eight

---

[1] Many large Non-Regulation Districts also are within these four Governments.

divisions which make up British India. It has an area of 240,000 square miles, about equal to that of France; its population numbers forty millions, and its revenue amounted in 1869-70 to 15,770,000*l.*, from which, after deducting the provincial charges against income, there remained a surplus of about nine millions sterling to be added to the smaller contributions of the other provinces, the united surplus forming the fund out of which is discharged the Imperial as distinguished from the provincial expenditure of India.'[1]

The immediate government of the Lower Provinces is administered by a Lieutenant-governor. He has the assistance of a Legislative Council, which, in 1870, comprised several non-official Europeans, and seven native members.

The following Subject-Allied States are politically connected with the Lower Provinces:—Cooch, Behar, the Cuttack districts, and the Naga Hills. These are now under British management. Kemjhar is ruled by its Rajah under the influence of a British Resident. None of these Subject-Allied States is important as to territory, population, or otherwise.

2. The Presidency of Madras stretches along about one-half of the coast line of peninsular India. It reaches (with very irregular width of territory) from its north-eastern boundary at Ganjam for 1,187

[1] Parl. Blue Book.

miles along the coast of the Bay of Bengal to Cape Comorin at the southern extremity of India. Its line of prolongation upwards along the western coast is interrupted by the Subject-Allied Territories of Travancore and Cochin; but northward of them it stretches to the point near Honawar, where it meets the southern frontier of the Bombay Presidency. The territorial area of the Madras Presidency exceeds that of the British Islands collectively; and its population is estimated at twenty-seven millions.

The Governor of Madras is appointed by the Crown. He has a Council of three members, one being the commander-in-chief of the forces that make up the Madras army, the other two being members of the Civil Service. For legislative functions the Council is augmented by nine additional members, four of whom are non-officials. Laws passed by the Madras Legislative Council require the assent of the Governor-General.

The Subject-Allied States of Travancore and Cochin are under the political supervision of the Governor of Madras. Travancore has an area of 4,700 miles, and a population of a million and a half. It is prosperous; and so is the adjoining State of Cochin, which adjoins Travancore on the north, and which is 'about the size of Bedfordshire.'

The Presidency of Bombay includes a number

of British territories that lie along the western coast of the Indian peninsula from the southern limits, where they abut on the Madras Presidency, and on the Subject-Allied State of Mysore, up northwards to some extent inland from the end of the Gulf of Cambay. These territories make up the division of the Presidency called Bombay Proper. To the north-west lies the large province of Scinde, which was conquered and made British territory in 1844. The collective area of Bombay Proper and Scinde is 134,135 square miles. Their collective population is about fourteen millions. Between Sindh and Bombay Proper lie a number of Subject-Allied States, which (with some others) are politically connected with the Government of Bombay. The collective population of these Subject-Allies is about six millions; the collective area of their territories is about 71,320 square miles.

The Governor of Bombay is appointed by the Crown. He is assisted for purposes of general administration by a Council of three members ; for legislative purposes nine other members are added. The acts of this Legislative Council of Bombay require the assent of the Governor-General.

There are so many Subject-Allies under the supervision of the Governor of Bombay, that I cannot here particularise and describe them all. The coloured map is the best teacher on such matters.

The reports of their recent progress and condition are generally favourable.[1] I cite some passages which show the frequency of British interference with their administrations, and also the salutary effects of such interference.

'No less than four of the independent princes of Kattywar died during the year under review. Three of them, the chiefs of Durraungdra, Moorvee, and Bhownugger, had won the confidence of all classes of their subjects, and were honoured for the ability and justice with which they governed their states. The Rajah of Durraungdra was succeeded by his son, but the administration of the other two, and of Gondul, has been temporarily assumed by the British Government during the minority of the young chiefs.'

'Two out of the collection of independent native states, forming Rewa Kanta, are under British management during the minority of their Rajahs, who are being educated at Ahmedabad. In these two, Barrea and Loonawarra, the revenues are yearly increasing.'

'Nothing eventful occurred in the Jagheer States, in the southern Mahratta country, which are under the management of their own chiefs. Education made good progress, and public works received a fair share of attention. In Meeruj and Moodhul,

[1] See Blue Book, pp. 80, 81.

which are temporarily under British management during the minority of their chiefs, a great advance has been made.

'The little district of Alkalkote, which has recently been taken under British management in consequence of the misrule which prevailed there, has a population of 66,000. The new rates of assessment, which were introduced experimentally, were well received, and produced a considerable increase to the Land Revenue. The people are manly and independent, and seem anxious to have their children educated.

'The affairs of Sawunt Waree continued to be satisfactorily administered. In Jinjeera, the jurisdiction in criminal matters has been taken from the chief, and vested in a British officer. This measure was carried out in the interests of the people, and after repeated warnings to the chief.'

Few, probably, of the numerous European travellers along the Red Sea who land for a few hours at Aden, are aware that this strong military post and great coasting depôt for steamers is part of the Indian Presidency of Bombay. Such is the fact. The chief political ruler there, called the Resident, is a Bombay official. The great increase of the Red Sea traffic between Europe and the East, caused by the opening of the Suez Canal, must rapidly and greatly augment the value of this important Indo-Arabian possession of the British Crown.

The North-Western Provinces (which are now far from being the North-Western parts of British India) acquired their name from their position relatively to the Lower Provinces of Bengal, with which they were formerly connected. They used all to be included in the Presidency of Bengal, or (to speak more accurately) in the Presidency of Fort William in Bengal. These North-Western Provinces were separated from the Lower Provinces of Bengal in 1833. They are under the jurisdiction of a Lieutenant-Governor, appointed by the Governor-General, who has no Council either Executive or Legislative. The Lieutenant-Governor is always an old Indian official; and as these Provinces (unlike Bengal, Madras, and Bombay) have no maritime cities, no great centres of European commerce, and only a very small number of European settlers, it is thought that they are best governed under a single sub-ruler thoroughly acquainted ' with the language and customs of the people, the Indian regulations, and the different tenures of land.'[1] In point of fact these Provinces ' are in all material respects in advance of the rest of India.' Their collective territories have ' an area of 83,687 square miles, and a population numbering more than thirty millions of inhabitants, or about 361 persons to the square mile. The Province is, therefore, nearly equal in extent to

[1] Chesney, p. 125.

England, Wales, and Ireland together, and more thickly peopled than Great Britain alone.'[1]

The North-Western Provinces have a Board of Revenue, and a High Court of Jurisdiction. The North-Western Provinces comprehended politically as well as locally the little Subject-Allied State of Rampoor, which is well governed by its native prince on the British system of administration.

All our old Indian dominions, that is to say, all parts of India which have been British possessions for more than half a century, are comprised within the four Governments which we have been describing, the Government of the Lower Provinces, the Presidencies of Madras and Bombay, and the Government of the North-Western Provinces. Nearly, but not quite, all our old Indian dominions have been and are administered as to their revenues and as to judicial matters by members of a regularly organised body of officials, called the Covenanted Service.[2] I am not speaking of Governor-Generals, governors, chief justices, and other high ministers appointed

[1] Blue Book, p. 34.

[2] 'So termed because each member of the service, before leaving England, enters into a covenant with the East India Company [now with the Secretary of State], wherein his privileges are recited, and he binds himself not to trade, or receive presents, &c. The practice of binding the Company's servants by covenants not to accept irregular perquisites was introduced by Lord Clive in 1765, and who set the example by executing such a covenant himself.'— *Chesney*, p. 209, note.

from England, but of the officials who perform the great bulk of administrative duties. These covenanted civil servants conduct the business of Government in these old British Indian dominions according to fixed and elaborate systems of ' Regulations,' which first were issued from the Council Chamber for the government of the Bengal territories in Lord Cornwallis's time.[1] Before him there were no definite rules of Government promulgated with authority. The Regulations were afterwards introduced, with slight modifications, into the Madras and Bombay Presidencies, and also into great part of the territories, which make up what are now called the North-Western Provinces.

The old British India territories brought within the pale of the Regulations, are called the ' Regulation Provinces ' in contradistinction to the territories, to which the ' Regulations ' have not been applied, and which are called the Non-Regulation Provinces. Fifty years ago the bulk of British India was under the Regulations. For a territory to be British but Non-Regulation was an exceptional state of things. But none of the vast additions made to our Indian Empire during the last half century have been made subject to the Regulations. The proportion between Regulation India and non-Regulation India is now reversed as to area; but the old Regulation Pro-

[1] See supra, p. 242, note.

vinces still are pre-eminent in wealth, in density of population,[1] and in commercial and political importance.

These old provinces received, and they received with advantage, the very complex and elaborate code of the Regulations, which provide for almost every possible detail in the procedure of both fiscal and judicial courts. But it was felt from the very first that such an artificial and intricate system was unsuited for wilder populations; and, accordingly, some of the frontier districts of Bengal itself were excluded from the pale of the Regulations ; and, as a general rule, the great masses of conquered territory, which have been the rapid gains of the nineteenth century, were placed under simpler and easier, though ruder methods of administration. Our rule in Assam, in British Burmah, in Scinde, in the Punjab and other new provinces, was more like military, than civil rule ; and was, in fact, principally carried on by military men, who fulfilled the political and judicial duties imposed on them with the invariable uprightness and general good sense, which are the characteristics of English gentlemen, but not without an unavoidable amount of confusion and wrong-doing, where titles to property had to be investigated, and the details of tenure and of State claims

---

[1] Except in contrast with the Non-Regulation districts of Oudh, where the population is 474 to the mile.

required adjustment. The rule, however, was not altogether martial. Some civilians of the covenanted civil service took part in the administration. Many Europeans also obtained special employment, who were neither in the army nor in the covenanted civil service. The number of these last has by degrees greatly increased. They make up what is termed the Uncovenanted Service,—a very heterogeneous body, which it would be difficult to describe in detail with any approach to accuracy either as to appointment, organisation, or status.

The broad substantial difference, which originally existed between Regulation and Non-Regulation Government, is now greatly diminished. It formerly was the difference between a very carefully organised and, therefore, complicated system of administration on the one side, and a rough and ready action of authority on the other. But by degrees the method of ruling the Non-Regulation Provinces has become more and more systematic and definite. All are now prescribed and controlled by powers superior to the local officials. The action also of the Governor-General's Supreme Legislative Council in passing measures of finance and law, which apply to all British India Proper, has, since 1860, been important in effacing the practical distinction between Regulation and Non-Regulation Provinces.

We will now resume our enumeration of the eight divisions of British India. Four of them, that is to say, the Lower Provinces, Madras, Bombay, and the Northern Provinces, have been mentioned. We come now to

5th. Oudh.—This rich and densely-populated province was annexed to our dominions in 1853, during the Viceroyalty of Lord Dalhousie, as mentioned in a previous page,[1] when also its area and population were stated. Oudh is under the 'care of a Chief Commissioner. It is divided into four commissionerships, comprising twelve districts, each under its deputy commissioner.'[2]

6th. The Central Provinces bear a name that is nearly correct. They were formed into a separate administration in 1861, after our Indian Empire had attained its present frontiers. They 'form a territory not much smaller in extent than Great Britain and Ireland, with one-third of the population.'[3] They are under the authority of a Chief Commissioner. The British India portions of them are divided into four commissionerships and nineteen districts. Their collective area is 82,860 square miles, and their population is a little over nine millions. Politically connected with them, and under the supervision of their Chief Commissioner, are a number of not very important Subject-Allied

[1] See p. 253, supra.   [2] Blue Book, p. 40.   [3] Ibid., p. 41.

States. The total area of them is 28,261 square miles; their population amounts to 1,100,000.

7th. The Punjab.—The territories within the Government of the Punjab and its dependencies include far more than we were accustomed to understand as being parts of the Punjab, at the time when the Sikh wars made that name so well known in England. According to the Parliamentary Blue Book, the Punjab Government includes all British India that lies between the river Jumna on the east, and the Sulleima mountains on the west, and which lies northward of the provinces of Scinde, Rajpootana, and the North-Western Provinces. Its northern frontiers touch Affghanistan, Thibet, and the Chinese Empire. It will be observed, on looking at the map, that the Punjab Government extends so far southward as to comprise the important province of Delhi, and the ancient capital of the Mogul sovereigns of India.

According to the same authority, the total area of the territories under the Government of the Punjab and its dependencies 'is as large as France, that is to say, it is over 200,000 square miles in extent, more than half of which is the territory of feudatories. The British possessions in the province are about as large as the kingdom of Italy. Their area is returned as 102,001 square miles, of which 31,513 square miles, or less than one-third, are cultivated ; 25,333 square miles, or about one-fourth, are culturable, and the remainder is unculturable waste.'

'The Punjab and its dependencies were constituted a Lieutenant-Governorship in January 1859. It is divided for administrative purposes into 10 divisions, with an average area of 10,200 square miles; these comprise 32 districts, with an average area of 3,188 square miles, which are again subdivided into 132 tahsils, or revenue and judicial subdivisions, with an average area of 772 square miles.

'The Native States with which the Government of the Punjab has political relations, are of two classes: 1st. *Dependent and Feudatory States.* 2nd. *Independent States,* including frontier tribes. The Feudatory States attached to the Punjab are 34 in number, and their area amounts approximately to 104,000 square miles; their population to about five millions; their revenues to about 1,600,000*l.* per annum; their military forces (exclusive of mere armed retainers) to about 50,000 men, and the total tribute received from them to 28,000*l* per annum. The chiefs are guaranteed full and unreserved possession of their territories, and in return are bound to execute justice, and promote the welfare of their subjects; to prevent suttee, slavery, and female infanticide; to co-operate with the British Government against an enemy ; to furnish supplies, and to grant, free of expense, land required for railroads and imperial lines of road. The chiefs of Kashmír, Patiála, Bháwalpore, Jínd, and Nabha have full power of life and death over their subjects, and are exempt from inquiry into complaints made against them, privileges that are not extended to the remaining feudatories. The same five States, with Kapúrthulla, have between them more than 48,000 troops.

'Three of the States, Bháwalpore, Chamba, and Pataodi, are under the management of British officers. The first State was taken over in 1866, at the request of the leading men, owing to the anarchy that followed the death of the late chief, and the minority of his successor. The country has prospered, and the people are contented.'

'Chamba is managed by a British officer at the chief's own request. The income of the State (17,300l.) has nearly doubled since its first superintendent was appointed.'

'Of the Feudatory States not under the management of British officers, by far the most important is Kashmír. The present ruler is the Maharajah Ranbír Singh, son of Golab Singh, who commenced his career as a horseman in the service of Maharajah Runjít Singh, the energetic ruler of the Punjab. His dominions may be described as the Hill country, and its dependencies between the Indus and the

Ravi, excluding Chamba and Lahoul. The area of country is 25,000 square miles. The population is estimated at a million and a half; the gross revenue of the State is supposed to be 640,000*l.*, and the organised military force is believed to amount to about 31,383 men.'[1]

8th. British Burmah.—Mention has already been made[2] of the wars with the Burmese in 1824 and 1852. By the first of those wars we acquired the maritime provinces of Arracan and Tenasserim, which will be seen in the map stretching in long narrow strips of territory along the eastern shores of the Bay of Bengal. The block of territory between them, called Pegu, was conquered and retained in 1852. It includes the very important harbour and city of Rangoon.

These make up the Province of British Burmah, which has an area of 98,881 square miles (being nearly three times the size of Scotland), with a population of about two millions and a half. The total length of sea-board is nearly nine hundred miles.

[1] The fact that Kashmír is included in this Parliamentary paper shows that it is regarded as part of our Indian Empire, and that it would be practically treated so if occasion required. I should, otherwise, have doubted its being part of our dominion. It does not appear that the native ruler of Kashmír 'habitually obeys the commands of a determinate human superior' (see p. 271, supra). It is hard to say whether he would find himself at liberty to carry on hostilities with his Thibetian or Chinese neighbours without the consent of the British Government.

[2] See p. 237, supra.

British Burmah, at the northern extremity of Arracan, abuts on the British Indian Lower Provinces, and it has been politically connected with India. But there is little in common with the Burmese and the Hindoos. British Burmah is governed by a Chief Commissioner. The sub-officials are chiefly military men, but the chief judge (styled Recorder) of Rangoon is usually an English barrister. The Burmese appointments are in general permanent; and the service there has little connection with that of India generally.

I will now mention some of our principal Subject-Allied Indian States, which have not been already incidentally noticed as political appendages of some one of the sub-governments of British India Proper. Beginning from the north, we see, yellow-coloured on the map, the large territory of Rajpootana. It derived its name from the rule of Rajpoot princes over the greater part of it. They were never thoroughly subjected by the Mohammedan sovereigns of India; and during the last half of the eighteenth century, they were completely independent. The desolating attacks of the Mahrattas compelled them to seek British alliance and protection.

There are eighteen principalities of Rajpootana, varying much as to size and population. Their collective area is reckoned at 80,000 square miles, with an aggregate population of about nine millions.

'The eighteen principalities of Rajpootana are supervised by the Governor-General's Agent, with a staff of political agents and assistants, amounting in all to 20 officers. Their united salaries and the other purely executive charges of the agency amount to nearly 37,000*l.* The chiefs exercise supreme, civil, and criminal jurisdiction within the limits of their respective States. They are restrained by no check save the moral influence and fear of the British Government. Disputes among themselves are adjudicated by the courts of Vakeels, consisting of one upper court and four lower courts, at which, when British interests are concerned, or at the request of the members, or in cases of importance, the agent of the Governor-General or one of his subordinate officers takes his seat as president, and has a casting vote.'[1] It is to be added that 'Rajpootana is garrisoned by British brigades stationed at Nusseerabad and Neermuch, and the main lines of road throughout the country are constructed by British officers at the charge of the Imperial Treasury.'[2]

Another group of Subject-Allied States will be seen to the south-west of Rajpootana. They are marked on the map as the Indian Agency. This is sometimes called the Central Agency. These States are supervised by an Agent appointed by the Governor-General. Their collective territories are estimated at nearly

[1] Parl. Blue Book, p. 15.   [2] Chesney, p. 54.

80,000 square miles, with an aggregate population of eight millions. Strong brigades of British troops are stationed at Mhow and Gwalior.[1]

Further south we see the large and important district of Hyderabad. This, and the district of Berar on the north (coloured red), represent the territory of the Nizam, the successor of the Mohammedan Viceroy of the Deccan.[2]

Berar is part of certain districts which were assigned by the Nizam in 1853 to be administered on the British system by the British Resident Agent at the Nizam Court in Hyderabad. 'By a later treaty in 1861, the British Government, actuated mainly by a desire to reward the Nizam for his loyal bearing during the Mutiny, restored a considerable portion of the original assignment to his own direct management; and the Hyderabad Assigned Districts in their present form are composed entirely of the Valley of Berar, which extends from the confines of the Central Provinces on the east, to those of the Bombay Presidency on the west; with the Sautpoora range of mountains as its northern, and the Ajunta range and the Paeen-Gunja river as its southern boundaries. The area thus circumscribed is a little less than 18,000 square miles, and has a population estimated at three millions.

'The whole province is divided, for purposes of

---

[1] Chesney, p. 8.   [2] See p. 214, supra.

administration, into East and West Berar, each having its own Commissioner, who is subordinate only to the Resident. Five deputy commissioners, fifteen assistants, and eight extra residents, complete what may be called the upper and middle portions of the administrative structure proper. Apart from fortuitous circumstances, such as the American War, which made cotton the absorbing product, the history of this province during the ten years it has been in our hands deserves the consideration of all who have any doubt with respect to the comparative superiority of British or native rule.

' The gross provincial revenue has gradually risen from 420,905*l.* in 1862–63 to 704,500*l.* in 1869–1870. Cheap and prompt justice has been brought within the reach of all. A settlement of the land revenue, the basis of all sound agricultural prosperity in India, is approaching completion. A scientific system of forestry is being introduced. Police establishments have gradually been organised, and the old-fashioned gaols have been replaced by new ones. Last, but not least, education has been offered to all classes of the people, and is more widely appreciated every year.' [1]

The British Resident in Hyderabad, besides exercising administrative powers over these assigned districts, exercises political functions over that portion of

[1] Blue Book, p. 8.

the Hyderabad country which is immediately under the Native Government.

The area of this last-mentioned territory is 80,000 square miles. The recent improvement in the condition of its people is reported to be 'marvellous.'

'The public treasury is full; the Hyderabad Contingent has not fired a hostile shot since the suppression of the Mutiny; the police have been placed on a satisfactory footing; the once dangerous mob of the capital is thoroughly under restraint; and it is not too much to say that all this, and more, has been accomplished by Sir Salar Jung, the able Minister of the Nizam, who, in the face of opposition on the part of his sovereign and the nobles, has persevered in his course of sound political and financial administration, receiving throughout the support of the British Government, and winning their respect and admiration.' [1]

More to the south lies the Principality of Mysore, once the dominion of our bitterest Indian enemies, Hyder Ali and Tippoo Saib. It has an area of 27,000 square miles, about equalling that of Bavaria. The population is estimated at rather more than four millions. Its present political condition is reported to be as follows:

'This principality was taken under British protection in 1834, in consequence of the misrule that prevailed under the late Maharajah, and will so continue

[1] Blue Book, p. 14.

during the minority of his adopted son and successor. The chief authority in the province is the Commissioner, who corresponds directly with the Governor-General in Council. The administrative divisions of the province are Nandidroog, Ashtagram, and Nagar; the little State of Coorg also forms part of the Commisioner's charge; and these are subdivided into eight districts. To fit him for the future duties and responsibilities of his position, the young Maharajah is being carefully educated under the care of Colonel Malleson.'[1]

I have now gone through (with some unimportant exceptions) all the territories of our Subject-Allies, as well as the districts of British India Proper, which make up our Indian Empire.[2]

The total area of British India Proper amounts to 880,000 square miles. The population was estimated in 1868 at rather more than 140,000,000. The total area of the territories of the Subject-Allies is 597,000 square miles, with a collective population estimated at about 45,400,000. Thus, the grand total area of our Indian Empire approaches the amount of one mil-

---

[1] Blue Book, p. 19.

[2] The French still retain in India, Pondicherry, Chandernagore, Karical, Mahé, and Yanam; and the Portuguese still possess Goa, Damam, and Dia. But the collective population of all these possessions of European Powers, other than the British, in India, does not amount to 200,000.

lion and a half square miles, and the grand total population exceeds one hundred and eighty-five millions.[1]

Among these 186,000,000 of human beings, there are about 130,000 British, men, women and children, included; but the proportion of children, for reasons above explained, is very small.[2]

More than half the British in India are soldiers.

The manner and extent of English home-rule over India, that is of the rule exercised over India by the ministers of the Crown and other residents in England, have been already incidentally dealt with. We have seen[3] that after the Sepoy Rebellion, an end was put to the old plan of a double English government for India, consisting partly of a Board of Control appointed by the English Ministry, and

[1] I take the figures from Mr. Chesney, who observes that 'the whole country is slightly less in extent and population than the continent of Europe without Russia.'

[2] See p. 192, supra. I have taken the number of British in India with an allowance for probable increase during ten years, on account of the great increase in public works and other causes, from 'The Statesman's Year Book for 1871,' which further states that according to the returns made in 1861, '22,536 of the Europeans then in India were men and boys in civil life, including the civilians in the public service; the remaining 19,306 being females, of whom 9,773 were over 20 years of age. When the census was taken, the number of females of English origin in India above the age of 15 was 11,636, including 8,356 wives and 1,146 widows. Of the officers and men of the Royal army 93 per cent. of all ages were unmarried, while the proportion of civilians above the age of 20 unmarried amounted to 50 per cent.'

[3] See p. 254, supra.

partly of a Court of Directors chosen by East Indian
stockholders. A Secretary of State for India (always
a member of the Ministry for the time being) is now
the main organ of the Queen's rule over the Indian
Empire. He is assisted by a permanent Under-
Secretary of State, not in Parliament, and by a political Under-Secretary of State, who, if the Chief
Secretary is a Peer, is required to be a member of
the House of Commons, and who usually goes out of
office on a change of Ministry. The Secretary acts
also in co-operation with an Indian Council in
England, consisting of fifteen members who may not
sit in Parliament. They hold their seats in the
Indian Council during good behaviour. [1]

Practically the most important change as to the
actual workers of the machinery of Government
in India has been the general alteration in the mode
of appointing new members of the Indian Civil Service. Formerly these appointments formed part,
and not the least valued part, of the patronage
enjoyed by the East India Company's Directors.
Their nominees, and their nominees only, filled up
(after a short period of study at Haileybury College)
the vacancies that occurred from time to time in
India. But all this has been done away with. The

---

[1] An epitome of the chief clauses of the 'Act for the Better
Government of India' has been given at p. 255, supra. Clauses 7
to 28 inclusive relate to this Council.

Imperial Parliament, by the Act for the Better Government of India (21 and 22 Victoria, cap. 106, section xxxii.), required that appointments to the Indian Civil Service should be thrown open to all natural-born subjects of Her Majesty, and that candidates should be appointed according to the order of their proficiency as shown by the results of competitive examination.

This system has ever since been maintained; nor is it likely to be departed from. I do not think that it has had the effect, which some predicted, of bringing into the Indian Service a number of men inferior to the old writers as to social position, as to refinement, and as to high feeling. The nominees of the Directors were generally youths who came from the higher sections of the English middle classes. So do most of the successful candidates in the new examinations. The expense of the early education, and of the subsequent cramming, which are almost indispensable for success, is too heavy to be defrayed by those who are low down in worldly circumstances.

It is said, with far more truth, that the new system does not send up a supply of men of the very highest order of intellect. There are two reasons for this. One is that men of first-rate intellect and energy will generally prefer an English to an Indian career. The other reason is that, as a rule, competitive examinations bring to the front not the men who know their subjects most profoundly and comprehensively, but the men who can put upon paper in a limited time the greatest display of knowledge, so as to get most marks.

However, this seeming evil of the competitive examination system is not without countervailing advantages. This last-mentioned class of men—men who can promptly, lucidly, and artistically utilise their mental resources (which they cannot do without a fair share of self-confidence)—are likely to make better men of business, to face difficulties more boldly, and to find solutions of them more readily, than men, who are more profound in thought and who are laden with more learning, but who are somewhat slow and irresolute in action.[1]   Of course, it is best

---

[1] I can best illustrate this by an example from real Anglo-Indian life.   In Mr. Kaye's History of the East India Company, p. 452, there is a sketch of a gentleman who was appointed one of the Board for administering the Punjab soon after its conquest, and who proved unfit for the task.   'He was a man of a thoughtful nature ; and, I am inclined to think, of an original turn of mind : but he was not one to put his ideas with much promptitude into action.   He was somewhat wanting, indeed, in energy and activity ; and his abilities, though of a very high order, found more congenial employment in a settled than in a new country.   He was not quick enough, and enthusiastic enough for the work that lay before him.'

This gentleman would hardly have succeeded in a competitive examination.   On the other hand, the 'Competition Wallahs,' even if they have not very high intellect, or any original turn of mind, are likely to exhibit the faculties which the conquering Romans are said to have admired most in statesmen, the faculty of being first-to have, if possible, a combination of profound knowledge and of versatile readiness; but that can hardly be expected of the whole, or of the majority of a numerous body. And, for the general duties of Indian administration, the readiest men, if also fairly well-informed, will generally be found to be the most effective.

rate men of business, and the faculty of combining Daring with Discretion :—Πραγματικώτατοι καὶ σὺν νῷ τολμηρότατοι.

CHAPTER VI.

THE AUSTRALASIAN COLONIES.

Extent of Australasia—Climate—Population—List of Colonies—
New South Wales: its early History—Sheep Farming—Convict
Labour — Transportation abolished—Representative and Respon-
sible Government—Present Constitution—Population—Trade —
Gold Fields—Coal Mines—Probable Future—Victoria: its origin
as Port Phillip District — It becomes a separate Colony — Rapid
Progress—Area — Climate — Population—Gold Fields—Constitu-
tion—South Australia: its Extent, &c., and Natural Resources—Its
Constitution — Western Australia: its Extent, its Ill-fortune, its
recent Representative Institutions — Queensland: its Extent,
Climate, Capabilities, Constitution—Tasmania: its Discovery, Con-
vict Settlements, Constitution, Area, &c.—Its backward Condition.
—New Zealand: its great Natural Advantages—Infested by Euro-
pean Adventurers and Outlaws — Interference of the English
Government—High Capabilities of the Natives—Colony founded—
Rapid Progress of European and Decline of Maori Population—
New Zealand Wars—Present Constitution.

SOUTH-EASTWARD of our Indian possessions we see
conspicuous on the map the huge land of Australia,
called by some an island, because the sea surrounds it, but termed by others, more justly, a continent, on account of its magnitude; inasmuch as its
area comprises more than 2,500,000 square miles.
Near its south-eastern extremity lies Tasmania or
Van Diemen's Land, an island of 26,215 square
miles in area. To the east of Tasmania lie the three
islands which are known collectively by the name

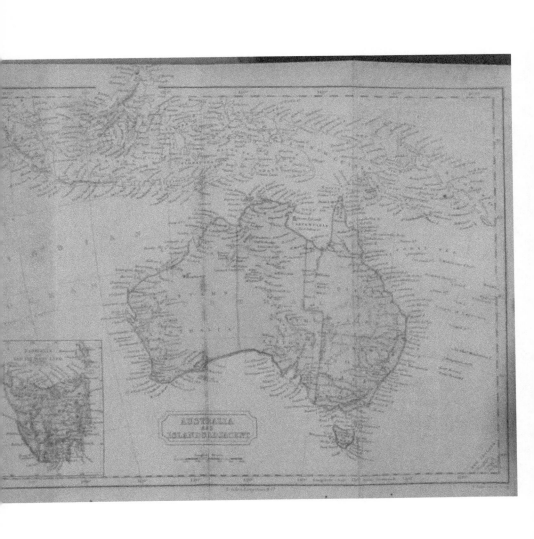

AUSTRALIA
AND
ISLANDS ADJACENT

of New Zealand. Of these the northern island contains about 44,000 square miles, the middle about 55,000, and the south island 1,500. This last, the south island, is sometimes called Stewart's Island. It is at present uninhabited, and has been only partially explored.

Australia, Tasmania, and New Zealand together make up Australasia. This word would, in etymological strictness, apply to all Southern Asia; but it is practically used to denote only the three countries which have been mentioned. As the map shows us, the northern third of Australia lies within the Tropic of Capricorn, but its southern extremity extends to the thirty-ninth degree of south latitude. There are, consequently, great differences of climate in its various regions. But much the greater part of Australia (so far as it has hitherto been explored) is perfectly habitable by Europeans, who may retain there undiminished physical activity and strength; and it may be inhabited by the children and by the children's children of Europeans. Some parts of it (New South Wales, for instance) are reckoned among the best climates in the world ' for the health and comfort of man and beast.' Tasmania is similarly healthy; and New Zealand appears to be the special part of the earth, in which men, women, and children of Anglo-Saxon race enjoy the fullest immunity from disease, and attain the maximum of active vigour.

There are seven Australasian Colonies : five in Australia—that is to say, West Australia, South Australia, Victoria, New South Wales, and Queensland: Tasmania and New Zealand make up the seven. All seven are agricultural colonies, taking the word 'agriculture' to include (as before explained[1]) settlements where the colonists obtain wealth from the land by means of flocks and herds, and not merely those where the colonists live by tillage.

All seven are colonies with representative institutions, and all except Western Australia have responsible governments.[2]

The great majority of the inhabitants of all seven colonies are of European race. The whole number of colonists in them must now be nearly two millions, and is increasing rapidly.

In the third chapter of this book, when speaking of the various classification of colonies, we had occasion to speak of *penal* colonisation, and of the motives which induced English statesmen near the end of the last century to choose Australia as a receptacle of British convicts.[3] New South Wales was the site of the earliest penal settlement; and in now proceeding to sketch the Australasian colonies separately, I will

---

[1] See p. 48, supra.   [2] See p. 69, supra.
[3] See chapter iii., supra, p. 54.

begin with New South Wales, as the first in point of antiquity—if antiquity can be properly predicated of colonies, the oldest of which has come into existence during the last hundred years.

New South Wales was formerly named New Holland by the Dutch mariners who first visited that part of Australia. But the Dutch made no attempts to form any settlement there; and no part of Australia can be said to have been explored before the voyage of Captain Cook in 1769. Cook landed in a bay, to which he and his scientific companion, Sir Joseph Banks, gave the name of Botany Bay, from the abundance of new plants and herbs found in its vicinity. Cook sailed along the whole eastern coast of Australia, making careful observations of its outline. The popularity which the published narrative of Cook's voyages rapidly acquired in England, drew much attention to these regions, which now became known by the name of New South Wales—a name which originally comprised much more than the territory which now bears that appellation. The neighbouring colonies of Victoria and of Queensland have both been formed out of districts which formerly made portions of New South Wales.

The first ships that reached the Australian coast with Englishmen intended for residence in Australia arrived there in 1787. The 'Sirius' frigate brought out Captain Archer Phillip as the Governor, and six transports brought the new colonists. They were numerous; but more than eight hundred of them were to reside in Australia as convicts; and two hundred more of them were soldiers, who were to reside in charge of the convicts.

This formation of the first penal settlement at Sydney has been mentioned already.[1] The first years of the colony were unpromising. The natives were found to be unfriendly, and almost incapable of European civilisation, while they had little or no civilisation of their own. Indeed, the native tribes of Australia, the aborigines,[2] as they are commonly termed, appear to be among the most degraded specimens of the human race that have ever been discovered. By degrees the prospects of the colony brightened. Corn was sown, and profitably reaped. Horses and cattle, brought out from England, began to thrive and multiply; and one of the free colonists, John Macarthur, laid the foundation of Australia's prosperity, by importing sheep from India and the Cape, and by devoting skill and toil to sheep-rearing, and to the improvement of the breed by continued importations of the best merinos from England and Spain. In 1803, Macarthur took to England the first specimen of Australian wool. He exhibited it with just

---

[1] Chapter iii., supra, p. 55.

[2] I somewhat dislike using this word, as it seems to imply a disbelief in the unity of the human race, an unity in which I believe very firmly.

pride, and ventured to prophesy that 'the quantity and quality of Australian wool would so increase and improve as at no distant time to render England altogether independent, not only of Spain, but of all the nations of the Continent, for its supply.' His prophecy was received with laughter, but he lived to see it realised. Before his death, in 1834, the number of pounds of wool exported from Australia amounted to two millions and a quarter. It was found that there was something in the soil and climate of Australia that 'made bad fleeces good, and good ones better.' Wool became, and continues to be, the great staple production of the colony; and the number of pounds exported from the present province of New South Wales alone (after Victoria and Queensland had been dismembered from it) had increased in 1864 to nearly twenty-five millions.

Much of the rapid progress of sheep-farming in Australia was due to Sir Richard Bourke, who was Governor there from 1831 to 1838. Instead of restraining settlers as much as possible from diverging from the neighbourhood of Sydney (which had been the policy previously followed), he encouraged them to form 'out stations' in the distant pasturages. The colonists, who thus advanced into the interior, and who obtained large allotments of land on easy terms from the Colonial Government, were called 'squatters,'[1] a word of very different import in Australia, from what it bears elsewhere. Many of these became owners of flocks and herds rivalling those of the old patriarchs in number. Convict-labour was cheap,[2] and easily procured. In 1837 no fewer than 8,000 convicts were 'assigned' to the squatters, and 'were serving as shepherds and neatherds in New South Wales.' Large numbers also of convicts were employed on public works, and especially on roads, which were of very great value to the colonists.

The system of transportation to New South Wales

---

[1] '"A squatter" is a term first applied to the early emigrants in America, who settled or squatted down upon a small piece of land in the forest there, cleared it of the native timber, and grew wheat or other grain and vegetables upon it, sufficient for the maintenance of his own family. The surplus he disposed of at any market convenient to the spot on which he squatted. The American squatters, as a class, are generally persons of mean repute and small means, who have taken unauthorised possession of these patches of land. The squatters of New South Wales form a very different class of persons. They are amongst the wealthiest of the land, occupying, by the tenure of Crown leases or annual licences, thousands and tens of thousands of acres. Young men of good family and connection in England, retired officers of the army and navy, graduates of Oxford and Cambridge, are all amongst them.'—*Reminiscences of New South Wales, &c.*, p. 210, cited by Mr. Bourne, p. 251.

[2] That is, 'cheap' so far as regarded the master who hired it. On its general costliness Mr. Merivale remarks:—'The labour of convicts is probably the dearest of all labour; that is, it costs more to some portion or other of society. The master himself obtains it cheaper than the services of a free labourer; but this is only because the State has already expended a much greater sum than the difference on the maintenance and restraint of the convict.'— P 353.

(to 'Botany Bay,' as it was commonly called among the classes in England which furnished most of its recruits), as practised from the time of its first institution, had many serious defects and evils, besides the main evil of its constantly contaminating the colonial population. Transportation as a punishment was uncertain and unequal. Many transported convicts were (even during the term of their sentence) much better off than they ever had been, or ever would have been in England. Others suffered great and unwarrantable hardships, and in many instances were exposed to cruelty and to abomination. The attention of English statesmen was directed to this painful but important topic through the efforts mainly of Archbishop Whately and Sir William Molesworth. A Parliamentary Committee, in 1838, reported strongly against the system. Punishment by transportation was not forthwith abolished, but it was conducted on different principles. Convicts were no longer 'assigned' as labourers to individual colonists. They were kept either for the whole, or for a considerable part, of their sentence at penal labour on the Government works; and those, who obtained a release from this labour before their term was ended, were not made 'assigned servants,' but became 'ticket-of-leave' men, not bound to any particular master. The 'squatter' in the colony had now no longer any immediate interest in upholding transportation; and it had long been odious to the other classes of colonists. This was especially the case among the poorer free immigrants from England, who looked with jealous hatred on convict-labour as lowering the wages of their own.[1]   A general agitation arose in the colony, and was maintained with increasing vehemence for several years. It met with great sympathy in England. The iniquity of pouring our moral sewage into the flourishing young communities of Australasia was denounced as strongly here as on the other side of the equator; and in 1855 the transportation of convicts to Australasia was entirely abandoned, excepting to Western Australia. It was continued to that colony for peculiar reasons, which will be mentioned when Western Australia is particularly considered.

A Representative Government was given to New South Wales in 1841. Its present constitution was established by Act of Parliament in 1855, since modified in some respects by local Acts, which have received the sanction of the Imperial authorities. New South Wales possesses all the privileges of responsible government.[2]

The Governor of New South Wales is appointed by the Crown. The Crown nominates also the members of the Legislative Council, who are not less than

[1] See Merivale, p. 371.

[2] For an explanation of 'Responsible Government' and the causes which led to it, see the chapter on our North American possessions, p. 180, supra.

twenty-one in number; and four-fifths of them must consist of persons not holding office under the Crown, except officers in the Royal army or navy. They are appointed for life.

The Legislative Assembly consists of seventy-two members. The electors are of two classes. The first class is of resident electors. For these no property qualification whatever is required. Every male of the full age of twenty-one, being a ' natural-born subject, or who, being a naturalised subject, has resided in the colony for three years, is entitled to vote as a resident elector for the electoral district in which he resides at the time of making out the annual electoral register, if he has resided for six months previously in the same district.

The second class is of non-resident electors. Every such male subject as above described is entitled to be registered as a voter for an electoral district, if he has had a freehold or leasehold estate within the district for six months preceding the time of making the register, or has been in receipt of rents or profits of any such estate; and if such estate is of the total value of 100l.; or if its rents or profits amount to 10l. a year; or if such subject occupies a house, shop, or office of the annual value of 10l.

The voting is by ballot.

Any person properly qualified and registered as a voter is eligible as a member of Assembly.

No one who is a member of the Legislative Council can be also a member of the Legislative Assembly.

English law is the law of the colony.

The population of New South Wales amounts to nearly half a million. It is increasing steadily and rapidly, both by the natural increase of the number of births over deaths in a healthy climate, where the necessaries of life are abundant, and by immigration from Great Britain. The rate, however, of immigration is now diminished, in consequence of the colony having ceased to give aid to immigrants from the mother-country by assistance from the colonial funds. This used to be administered by the co-operation of the Emigration Commissioners in England. At one period the amount of ' Assisted Immigration' into New South Wales was very considerable. In the ten years ending with 1862, sixty-nine thousand immigrants came from the United Kingdom to the colony at the colony's expense, either wholly or principally. During the same period ninety-five thousand came at their own cost.

The trade of New South Wales has increased five-fold in the last twenty years. This rapid augmentation is due in a great extent to the discovery of the gold-fields in the Bathurst district in 1851. But New South Wales possesses a far more valuable natural store of wealth and power than any gold-fields can supply. She has coal in abundance, and it lies close to navigable waters. So long as steam continues to rule sea and land, a coal-producing maritime country has and will have incalculable advantages over others, especially if iron and copper are to be found in the vicinity of the coal, as is the case in New South Wales. The natural political future of Australia appears to be a confederation of her present provinces, and of other provinces to be formed out of her yet unsettled territories. That may be (and it is to be hoped that it will be) a confederation like that of our North American provinces, under the supremacy of the British Crown. The Dominion of Australia would be a fitting peer to the Dominion of Canada. It may, perhaps, eventually become a confederation of the Independent States of Australia. But if the Australian provinces continue to be separate from each other, either as colonies or as provinces or as states, it seems very certain that the most powerful of them will be New South Wales.

The colony of Victoria is separated by the river Murray from that of New South Wales, of which it formerly made a portion under the name of the Port Phillip District. That name (the name of the first Governor of New South Wales) was given to it in 1802, by Lieutenant Morton of the ship 'Lady Nelson,' which was the first European vessel that entered the then desert harbour, at the northern extremity of which the city of Melbourne now flourishes. Con-

victs and soldiers were sent out from England in
1803, with the intention of founding a new penal
colony at Port Phillip, like that already in existence
at Sydney.   But the commander of the expedition
left Port Phillip after a brief sojourn there, and
took his convicts and military to Tasmania, in Van·
Diemen's Land, where they formed the settlement
of Hobart Town.   Some small colonising expeditions were made twenty years afterwards from Van
Diemen's Land to Port Phillip; and in 1834 and
the two subsequent years inland expeditions from
Sydney advanced to the southern shore.   The beauty
and fertility of the land became celebrated.   Immigration thither from Sydney increased rapidly; and
in March 1837, Sir Richard Bourke, the Governor
of New South Wales, visited Port Phillip, and founded
the towns of Melbourne and Geelong.   The new
district was claimed as a province of New South
Wales, and was ruled by a chief magistrate sent
thither by the Government at Sydney.   In 1842
the Port Phillip district was permitted to send
six representatives to the Legislative Council then
lately established for New South Wales.

In 1851 the district of Port Phillip was erected
by an Act of the Imperial Parliament into a separate
colony, and received its present name of Victoria.
It has an area of 86,831 square miles.   It comprises the south-eastern corner of Australia, and

forms the part where Australia projects furthest into the southern latitudes. In consequence of its greater distance from the equator, Victoria has a climate more enjoyable by Europeans than the climate of any other Australian colony. The population, which in 1836 was only 177, had increased in 1869 to 690,000. Melbourne, the capital city, which has not been in existence for half a century, contains 130,000 inhabitants. There is a considerable number of Chinese in the colony. The number of Chinese males in 1861, according to the census then taken, was 24,724. They had with them only seven Chinese women. It is probable that not only Victoria, but many others of our colonies and possessions in the south-east, will before long make great use of Chinese labour.

A large number of Germans also, and of colonists from other parts of the European continent, are to be found in Victoria. This is the case in our other Australasian settlements. But still by far the larger part of the population consists of those who have been born of British parents in the colony, or who have themselves immigrated thither from the British Islands. Victoria has for many years past largely aided, and continues to aid migration thither from the home-country.

The gold-fields discovered in Victoria are far more extensive and productive than any that have been found in other parts of Australia, or, as we might truly say, in any other part of the world. According to the 'Colonisation Circular' for 1869: [1]

'About one-third of the colony, or an area of nearly 30,000 square miles, is supposed to have gold under its surface ; but of this area only a tenth has, as yet, been laid open to miners, and less than one three hundredth has been actually opened up. The whole colony, with the exception of the immediate vicinity of Melbourne, is divided, for mining purposes, into seven principal districts. "Miners' Rights," or licences, are granted for any number of years not exceeding fifteen, at the rate of 5l. a year, and about 600,000 have hitherto been issued. In each of the seven mining districts there is a legislative body, termed a Mining Board. These boards are empowered to make bye-laws, applicable to the district generally, with respect to mining affairs and occupation under business licences. Each of these boards consists of ten members, four of whom retire from each board annually by rotation, when their places are supplied by the election of four others to fill the vacancies, or by the re-election of the retiring members. The members of the mining boards are elected by ballot, and each male holder of a " Miner's Rights " is entitled to a vote. Each district has its separate Court of Mines,

[1] Cited by Mr. Bourne, p. 396.

which is a Court of Record, and is presided over by a district Judge. One of the Judges of the Supreme Court is appointed to act as Chief Judge of the Court of Mines. The Courts of Mines have jurisdiction to hear and determine all suits cognisable by a court of law or by a court of equity which may arise concerning any Crown land claimed under " Miners' Rights," leases, or licences, mining partnerships, boundaries, contribution to calls, and generally all questions and disputations which may arise between miners in relation to mining upon Crown lands. The duties of the wardens, of whom one is in each division, are mostly of a judicial character, and they generally act as police magistrates. As wardens they hear and determine all suits cognisable by a court of law which the Courts of Mines are empowered to hear, and they may proceed summarily to settle any dispute concerning any Crown land, share, or interest in any claim. The mines of the colony are placed under a Mining Department, whose head has a seat in the Legislative Assembly and in the Cabinet.'

The produce of the Victoria gold-fields during the eighteen years from 1851 to 1868 amounted in value to 143,000,000*l.* The colony derives a large revenue from its gold, partly in the form of export duty, partly in the form of mining licences and leases.

The aggregate of the gold revenue for 1865 was nearly 130,000*l.*

According to its present constitution, Victoria has a Governor appointed by the Crown, aided by an Executive Council of ten, who in fact are a Cabinet, administering the affairs of the Colony on the princi- ples of ' Responsible Government.' It has a Parlia- ment of two Chambers, both elective.

' There is a Legislative Council of 30 members elected for 6 Provinces, and an Assembly of 78 mem- bers returned by the 49 Electoral Districts: this Constitution was established by an Act passed by the Legislature of Victoria, 1854, to which Her Majesty assented, in pursuance of the power granted by Act of Parliament 18 & 19 Vict. cap. 55. One of the Members of Council returned for each of the Electo- ral Provinces retires in rotation at the expiration of every two years. The qualification of Members is possession of freehold property worth 2,500*l.* or annual value of 250*l.* The qualification of Electors of Members of Council is possession of freehold worth 1,000*l.* or annually 100*l.* outside of Munici- pal districts : but within such districts freehold or leasehold property rated at 50*l.* a-year is sufficient. Graduates of Universities within the British domi- nions, barristers and solicitors, legally qualified medical practitioners, officiating ministers of religion, certificated schoolmasters, and officers of the army and navy when not on active service, also have votes for the Legislative Council. The functions of the Upper House differ very slightly from those of the House of Lords. Money Bills may be either accepted or rejected, but they may not be altered.

'An Act was passed in 1857 to abolish the property qualification required of Members of the Legislative Assembly, and manhood suffrage exists so far as the election of that body is concerned. The duration of the Assembly is three years, and vote by ballot has been in operation for a number of years.' [1]

Westward of Victoria and of New South Wales lies the colony of South Australia; not quite accurately named, inasmuch as the epithet 'South' seems to imply that it includes the southernmost regions of Australia; but, in fact, no part of South Australia trends so far southward as some districts of Victoria extend. The term 'Central Australia' would describe it more correctly; for, by Royal Letters Patent granted in 1863, this colony now extends northward so far as to include all the Australian territories from the southern to the northern sea, that lie between the 129th and 138th degrees of east longitude. Its total territorial area is computed at upwards of 380,000 square miles.

South Australia was first colonised in 1836, by emigrants from Great Britain, sent out by a company

---

[1] From the account in the 'Colonial Office List for 1871.'

called the South Australian Colonisation Company,
which, in 1835, obtained a grant from the Imperial
Government of the lands of this colony: the conditions were that the revenue arising from the
sale of land—1*l*. per acre being the minimum price
fixed—should be appropriated to the immigration
of agricultural labourers, and that the control of the
Company's affairs should be vested in a Commissioner
approved by the Colonial Secretary, and a Governor
of the colony appointed by the Crown. The first
settlers went out in a large and (as was supposed)
thoroughly organised body, which was at once to
form a new community, containing members of every
necessary or ornamental occupation, trade, and pro-
fession. They landed in December 1836 in St. Vincent's Gulf, at the mouth of the river Glenelg, and laid
the foundation of Adelaide, the capital of the colony,
about seven miles higher up that river. This experiment at colonisation was at first unsuccessful, and
the colony was only rescued from total ruin by a
loan from the Imperial Government. The management of South Australia then passed entirely from
the hands of the Company into those of the Crown.
Its natural wealth as a corn-producing as well as a
sheep-feeding country began to give it prosperity,
which was rapidly augmented by the discovery of
abundant ores of copper between 1842 and 1850.
In 1856 the colony received its present constitution.

The Executive now consists of a Governor appointed by the Crown, and an Executive Council of five officials, who constitute the Responsible Ministry, and who must be members of one or other of the Houses of Parliament. The Parliament consists of two Houses, both of which are elected by the people. One House is called 'The Legislative Council;' and is composed of eighteen members, six of whom retire every four years, their successors being then elected for twelve years. The Executive has no power to dissolve this body. It is elected by the whole colony voting as one district. The qualifications of an elector to the Legislative Council are, that he must be twenty-one years of age, a natural-born or naturalised subject of Her Majesty, and have been on the electoral roll six months, besides having a freehold of 50l. value, or a leasehold of 20l. annual value, or occupying a dwelling-house of 25l. annual value. The qualification for a member of Council is, that he must be thirty years of age, a natural-born or naturalised subject, and a resident in the province for three years. The President of the Council is elected by the members.

The other House of the South Australian Parliament is called the House of Assembly. It consists of thirty-six members, elected respectively by the inhabitants of the several districts. The term for which the Assembly is elected is three years, but the Governor has the power of dissolving it. It is practically elected by manhood suffrage; for the sole qualification of an elector is that of having been on the electoral roll for six months, and of having arrived at twenty-one years of age; and the qualification for a member is the same. The Speaker of the House of Assembly is chosen by the members of a new House on its first meeting. Judges and ministers of religion are ineligible for election as members, as are aliens who have not resided five years in the colony. The elections of members of both Houses take place by ballot.

Besides the riches of South Australia in corn, wool, and copper, it has of late years been found to possess a soil and climate well adapted for the growth of the vine; and wine-making has become an important branch of its industry and commerce. The population is now probably about 200,000. The number of natives is very small, and is rapidly diminishing.

The position of Western Australia is denoted by its name. It used, at one time, to be often spoken of as the Swan River Settlement. This colony was established in 1829; and, according to Royal Commission, it includes all Australia (or New Holland, as formerly called) west of the 139th degree of east longitude.

Only a very small portion of this enormous territory has ever been occupied. The occupied portion (and it is only very sparsely peopled) is reckoned to extend about 600 miles in length from north to south, by about 150 miles in average depth.

This has been the least prosperous of all the Australian colonies. Its natural capabilities are great; the climate is especially healthy, and large sums of capital were invested in its first settlement. But partly through the rapacity of the emigrants of the upper class, who appropriated vast allotments of the best lands, and partly through the equally unfair folly of the labouring emigrants, who deserted from their employers, and sought to make themselves instantly independent land-proprietors, the new settlement became a scene of misery and desolation. Some survivors struggled on; but the population, after the colony had been thirty years in existence, did not exceed 6,000. Its present amount is computed at about 22,000. When the other Australian colonies were vehemently refusing to receive more convicts from England, West Australia petitioned for them; and the advantage of convict-labour in making roads and other public works is said to have been greatly valued by this very feeble member of the Australian sisterhood.

Representative Government was given to Western Australia in June 1870. It is the only Australasian colony that has not yet received Responsible Government. The colony is now to have a council of eighteen members; twelve to be elected, six to be nominated by the Crown. The colony is divided into ten electoral districts. Voting is to be by signed voting papers, and not by secret ballot. The Chief Justice is to try election petitions.

The colony of QUEENSLAND comprises the north-eastern portion of Australia. It was formerly part of New South Wales, but was made a distinct colony in 1859.

The first exploration of its territory with a view to settlement was made in 1824 by Mr. Oxley, then Surveyor-General of New South Wales. He in that year entered the river Brisbane, and chose the site of the then future city which now bears that name, and is the capital of the colony, about twenty miles above Moreton Bay, where that river falls into the sea.

The total area of Queensland is estimated at nearly 680,000 square miles; and of these the portions already occupied by pastural stations amount to 195,000 square miles.

As will be seen on the map, a large part of Queensland lies within the Tropics; but the climate is said to be far less unfavourable to Europeans, than is usually the case in inter-tropical regions. This is caused by the elevation of the land above the sea-level. The ground from the coast of a great part at least of Queensland rises rapidly in a succession of terraces, so that nearly all the customary productions of both tropical and temperate regions can be cultivated successfully in the province. It is said, for example, that apples and plantains may be seen growing on various parts of the same estate.

Queensland is governed by a Governor and by two Houses, called the Legislative Council and the House of Assembly. It has Responsible Government. The Legislative Council is nominated by the Governor. The Assembly is elective. There are twenty-two electoral districts, and the House consists of thirty-two members elected for five years. Every natural-born or naturalised subject of Her Majesty possesses the elective franchise if he have a freehold estate in possession, situate in the district for which his vote is to be given, of the clear value of 100*l.*, or if a householder, or occupier of a house, warehouse, or shop of the clear annual value of 10*l.*, or if having a leasehold estate of the value of 10*l.*, which, at the time of registration, has not less than three years to run, or if having a salary of 100*l.* a year, or if being the occupant of a lodging, and paying for board and lodging 40*l.* a year, or for lodging only at the rate of 10*l.* a year. The population of Queensland is now probably about 120,000 of European birth or origin. The number of natives is uncertain.

TASMANIA.

Off the southern extremity of Australia lies an island containing 26,215 square miles of territory. It was discovered in 1642 by Tasman, a Dutch navigator sailing under the orders of Van Diemen, a Governor of the Dutch East Indies. From these two it acquired its names of Tasmania and Van Diemen's Land, which were long used indiscriminately; but 'Tasmania' has now become the prevalent and recognised appellation. Tasmania was long considered to form part of New Holland or Australia, but in 1797 and 1798 a young navy surgeon named Bass, of the King's ship 'Reliance,' then stationed at Sydney, employed his leave of absence in exploring the southern Australian coasts. He sailed through the straits since called by his name, and round the whole coast of Tasmania, which was thus proved to be an island. It was soon used both by the authorities at home and by the Governors at Sydney as a place, whither such convicts might be sent as Sydney could not conveniently receive. The foundation of Hobart Town in 1804 by a party of soldiers and convicts, which had been designed to form a settlement at Port Phillip, has been already narrated. George Town on the river Tamar, in the north of Tasmania, was founded about the same time. The chief occupation of the Tasmanian settlers for many years was the carrying on a destructive war with the native tribes. These grew weaker and weaker, and the number of the Europeans in the island was gradually increased by the arrival of free settlers as well as of convicts. But the convicts long formed a very large proportion of the English population. In 1824 there were nearly 6,000 of them. The number of free residents, exclusive of the military force, amounted to very few more.

In that year Tasmania (which had previously been treated as an appendage of New South Wales) was made a separate colony with a government of its own. The new colony made gradual progress in commerce and agriculture, but its advance for a long time was slow. The island was infested with formidable gangs of runaway convicts or 'bush-rangers;' and the struggle with the natives (who were more ferocious, though not more civilised, than the native Australians) was still continued savagely on both sides. By degrees both bushrangers and natives were subdued or destroyed, destruction being the general process. But the excessive indrain of convicts (that is to say, excessive in proportion to the number of free inhabitants) produced perni-cious effects, until and for some time after the year 1853, when transportation to Tasmania was finally abolished.

The colony's present constitution was settled in

1855. The executive power is vested in the Governor, who is aided by a Council of Responsible Ministers. The 'Parliament of Van Diemen's Land' consists of a Legislative Council and a House of Assembly. Both Houses are elected by the people. The Legislative Council is composed of fifteen members, chosen for twelve electoral districts. Each member holds his seat for six years from the day of his election, at the expiration of which time his seat becomes vacant. The competency of the Council is not affected by vacancies so long as seven members remain. No judge of the Supreme Court can be a member of the Legislative Council. The qualification of members is to be thirty years of age, and to be a natural-born or naturalised subject. The qualification for electors is the possession of a freehold estate of 50*l.* annual value, or being a barrister, a graduate in an university, or a minister of religion, or an officer of the army or navy.

The House of Assembly consists of thirty members, and there are twenty-four electoral districts. Any natural-born or naturalised subject can be elected, provided that he is not a judge of the Supreme Court or minister of religion. The duration of the Assembly is five years. The qualification of an elector for the Assembly is property of the value of 100*l.* in the district for which he votes, or household property of the annual value of 10*l.*, or being a barrister or solicitor on the roll of the Supreme Court, or legally qualified medical practitioner, or minister of religion, resident for twelve months before election in the district. The voting is by ballot.

The population of Tasmania is about 100,000. The native tribes may be said to have become extinct. The sole survivors in 1867 were four native women.

The climate of Tasmania is cool and equable, and the island is not afflicted by the long droughts which from time to time prevail in Australia. The soil is favourable for both agriculture and pasturage ; excellent timber trees are abundant, and the soil is believed to be rich in minerals. But very little has been done to develope and utilise the natural resources of the land ; and, with the exception of Western Australia, Tasmania is of all our Australian colonies the most backward in condition.

NEW ZEALAND.

Almost the last of our colonies in date of colonial existence, but almost the first in promise, is New Zealand—as we style collectively the islands that lie about six hundred miles eastward of Australia, between the 34th and 48th degrees of southern latitude, and between the 126th and 179th degrees of east longitude. The area of the whole group exceeds the area of Great Britain; and two-thirds of this large surface are very favourable for tillage and for pasturage. The forests are abundant; and ship-building has already become an important branch of New Zealand trade. Gold, copper, iron, and coal are found in various portions of the soil. The climate is pure and bracing; and immigrants from Europe enjoy in New Zealand more health and longevity than in any other part of the world. The only drawback is the frequent prevalence of strong and boisterous winds. The islands have a very ample proportion of sea-board, and there are many excellent harbours. With these natural advantages in itself, and with the benefit of an excellent commercial position relatively to other countries, New Zealand, when once thoroughly possessed by a vigorous, an intelligent, and an enterprising civilised race, seems certain to be the seat of a flourishing community, and perhaps at some period of a powerful nation.

Like Tasmania and Australia, New Zealand was first discovered, and was first named, by Dutch navigators, in the middle of the seventeenth century. About a hundred and thirty years afterwards it was visited, and to some slight extent explored, by Captain Cook. Its native tribes were found to be of a character very different from that of the tribes of Australia. The Maoris (as the natives of New Zealand are called) are physically strong, well-formed, and athletic. They are brave and intelligent, and have a natural aptitude for discipline and organisation. On the other hand, they were cruel and vindictive beyond the average ferocity of barbarians. Cannibalism was almost universally practised, when the materials for it could be procured; and it was at once the cause and the effect of almost incessant warfare between tribe and tribe. European adventurers (including outlaws and pirates), without settled rule or subordination, landing on the coasts and mingling with the Maoris, gave them the vices and diseases of corrupt European civilisation without mitigating their barbarism. The evil thus done more than balanced the good, which resulted from the often successful efforts of European missionaries to convert and to reclaim the New Zealand natives.

For a long time no European State formed any settlement in New Zealand. But in 1831 the enormities perpetrated there by fugitive convicts from New South Wales and Van Diemen's Land, and too often, also, by the masters and crews of British vessels, attracted the indignant notice of Lord Goderich, who was then English Secretary of State for the Colonies. The Governor of New South Wales was directed to interpose and to check these practices as far as possible; and in 1839 the Governor of New South Wales was authorised by the English Ministers to 'regard all British residents in New Zealand as subject to his authority;' and to treat with the natives of New Zealand for the purchase of land by British settlers, having regard to the just interests of both parties. He was to be the native ' official protector.' [1]

A little before this time a company had been formed in England, called ' The New Zealand Company,' for the purpose of promoting British colonisation in New Zealand. It was not supported or recognised by the English Government; but it sent out large numbers of settlers, and it purchased large tracts of land from New Zealand chiefs. The Company proved ultimately a failure, from causes as to which there is much dispute, and which would require too much space in this volume for their discussion. In January, 1840, an English Lieutenant-Governor was sent to New Zealand; and in the November of that year a Colony of New Zealand was constituted by Royal Charter. Immigration thither has gone on with rapid though not uniform rate of progress. The number of Europeans in New Zealand in 1851 was a little under 28,000. In 1858 it exceeded 59,000. In 1861 it had reached 99,000. In 1864 it was over 172,000. At the last enumeration, in December, 1867, the New Zealand population of European birth or origin, exclusive of the military, amounted to 218,637.

[1] Parliamentary Papers for 1840. Cited by Mr. Bourne, p. 340.

Unhappily the numbers of the native population have decreased at nearly an equal ratio; and it seems too certain that a gallant race of 'noble savages,' men of high physical and intellectual capabilities, and whose preservation and amalgamation with the English race has been an object sought by statesmen of every class of politics, will before the expiration of many more years have vanished from the face of the earth. In the middle, sometimes called the Southern Island,[1] the number of the Maoris has dwindled from 15,000—its estimated amount in 1848—to 2,000 in 1868, and 'most of these are old people.' In the Northern Island the number of the natives was reckoned at 105,000 in 1848; in twenty years they had decreased to 36,000.[2] Warfare between the two races may account to some extent for this decline of the Maori nation, but it by no means accounts for such a sweeping depopulation of the land so far as regards its ancient inhabitants.

Disputes about land caused, between 1843 and 1847, a series of sanguinary conflicts between the colonists and the Maoris, which were renewed on a larger and more formidable scale between 1862 and 1864. The natives have been the unsuccessful party; but the advantages gained by the European settlers, with the aid of regular troops from England, have often been very dearly bought; and the Maoris have

[1] See p. 307, supra.   [2] Bourne, p. 353.

Z

shown valour and skill sufficient to command the respect and regret of their conquerors. Many of them are now in sincere alliance with the English; others have retained a spirit of sullen hatred towards the intrusive white men, which is too sure to break out again and again in hostilities, which will only precipitate the destruction of the Maori race. In conformity with the resolution voted by the Imperial Parliament in 1862 that colonies which enjoy self-government should undertake the responsibility and cost of their own military defence, the last English regiment has lately been withdrawn from New Zealand. But the European colonists now so much outnumber the Maoris, and their superiority in equipment and organisation is so far superior, that there can be no doubt about the issue of any new war, that may break out in New Zealand, though the insurgents may at first obtain slight temporary advantages, and may inflict some amount of havoc and slaughter on outlying and exposed stations.

The colony is now, for purposes of local district government, subdivided into nine provinces—Auckland, Wellington, New Plymouth or Taranaki, Nelson, Otago, Canterbury, Hawke's Bay, Southland, and Marlborough. Each province is governed by a provincial council, and an elected superintendent.

The general government of the whole colony consists of a Governor appointed by the Crown, a

Legislative Council, and a House of Representatives. The Legislative Council consists at present of forty members, nominated by the Crown for life, and the House of Representatives of seventy-six members, elected by the people for five years. Every owner of a freehold worth 50*l.*, or tenant householder, in the country at 5*l.*, in the towns at 10*l.* a year rent, is qualified both to vote for or to be a member of the House of Representatives. The House of Representatives includes four Maori members, representing the natives.

CHAPTER VII.

THE OTHER COLONIES AND DEPENDENCIES.

African Colonies—The Cape—Settlement by the Dutch—Capture by the British—Kaffir Wars—Abandonment of the Orange River Territory—Annexation of British Kaffraria—Area of the Colony—Constitution—Climate, &c.—NATAL—The West African Settlements — ASIATIC COLONIES — CEYLON: its Area, Former and Present Occupants, Climate, Population, Government, &c.—The Straits Settlement—Labuan—Hong Kong—Mauritius—THE WEST INDIES—Their Institutions — Slavery—Slave Trade abolished—Slavery abolished—Jamaica—Antigua — Barbadoes—Dominica — Grenada—Montserrat—Nevis—St. Lucia—St. Vincent—Tobago—Trinidad—Turk's—The Virgin Islands — Bahamas — Bermudas—Guiana—The Falkland Islands—Honduras—St. Helena—Gibraltar—Malta—Heligoland.

WE have now contemplated and considered the three great masses of the transmarine portions of the Britannic Empire. We have given our attention to British North America, to India, and to Australasia. A great number of other colonies and dependencies yet remain to be noticed; not equalling any one of the three great phalanxes of colonial power already reviewed, but constituting in their aggregate a curtilage of dominion, such as no Power in the world, save England, possesses.

It will be convenient to group these remaining colonies and dependencies according to the com-

CAPE of GOOD HOPE
COLONY
AND NATAL

monly-recognised quarters of the globe in which they are situate. I will take first our

COLONIAL POSSESSIONS IN AFRICA.

I give Africa the precedence, not on account of the aggregate population, or amount of exports and imports of our possessions there, but because Africa contains the colonised territories in which alone (after those of North America and Australasia) there is any reasonable probability of Europeans thriving and multiplying, so as to form in process of time a community equal to those of old Europe physically and intellectually, socially, politically, and morally.

THE CAPE COLONY.

The small promontory at the south-western extremity of the continent of Africa, called the Cape of Good Hope, was discovered by the Portuguese Commander Bartholomew de Dias in 1486. Eleven years afterwards Vasco da Gama (whose name is generally associated with its discovery) sailed round it and reached the East Indies. Mariners of all nations that traded eastward, found the Cape a convenient place to resort to for obtaining water and provisions, and for some slight amount of traffic with the Hottentot tribes which inhabited its vicinity.

In 1620 two English East India commanders, by a proclamation dated from Saldanha Bay, took possession of the Cape in the name of Great Britain; but no settlement was formed. In 1652 the colony was colonised by the Dutch East India Company, under Van Riebeek.

The British took possession of it in 1795, but ceded it at the Peace of Amiens to its former possessors. It was again taken in 1806 by the English, to whom it was confirmed at the general peace in 1815, and has since continued a British colony. The native tribes found by the Dutch were Hottentots, savages of very feeble frame and spirit, and very low in the scale of humanity. The Dutch treated these wretched beings with great cruelty, taking their lands away, and making domestic slaves of them. The English, after they took the Cape, endeavoured to ameliorate the condition of the Hottentots. The capture of more slaves was forbidden; and laws were passed to give those already in slavery some protection from barbarity on the part of their masters. The Boors (as the Dutch settlers are called) resented this as an interference with their vested rights, and a strong spirit of disaffection towards the English Government long prevailed among them.

During the first years of British rule at the Cape the Kaffirs began to appear on the frontiers of the colony. They were a conquering race, pressing hard on the Hottentots and other inferior tribes. The first war between them and the British broke out in 1811, under circumstances little creditable to the colonial authorities. There were other Kaffir wars in 1818, 1834, and 1846. These wars were carried on with great bitterness and cruelty on both sides. Their results were large augmentations of the British territory. This was considerably reduced in 1853, when we voluntarily abandoned a large district called the Orange River Territory. It has become an independent Republic, in which the dominant body consists of descendants of the old Dutch settlers.

The abandonment of the Orange River Territory was effected by a Royal Order in Council and proclamation, whereby Her Majesty did 'declare and make known the abandonment and renunciation of our dominion and sovereignty over the said territory and the inhabitants thereof.'

There has been much question as to the Crown being able by its mere prerogative power to cede and abandon any territory, which has once become British, and thereby to take away the character of British dominion from such territory, and the *status* of British subjects from its inhabitants. There is no doubt but that the Crown can do this by treaty following a war; but the question is, whether the

Crown can do so when there has been no war, and consequently no such treaty. The matter is discussed by Mr. Forsyth in his volume of ‘Cases and Opinions on Constitutional Law.’[1] Probably the distinction there indicated is a true one: that a difference exists between territory acquired by the Crown by conquest or cession, which has not been the subject of parliamentary legislation, and territory, to which Acts of Parliament have been applied: and it has been thought that the Crown may by its prerogative cede the former but not the latter to a foreign Power.

It seems to me that there would also be good grounds for arguing that a distinction as to this liability to be abandoned and dis-Britished by prerogative must exist between mere Crown colonies, the laws of which can be annulled or varied by Royal prerogative, and colonies which have received representative institutions, and in which the power of the Crown to legislate by mere prerogative has thereby terminated.[2]

This diminution of the territory of the Cape Colony was more than made up for by the annexation of the province now called British Kaffraria. The present boundaries of the colony are: the Orange River on the north and north-east, which divides it from Great Namaqualand, Griqualand, and the Free

[1] Page 183, et seq.   [2] See p. 169, supra.

State Republic; on the east and north-east, the 'Tees, a small tributary of the Orange River, to its source, thence along the Stormbergen mountains, the Indwe and Great Kei Rivers, which divide it from the Basuto territory and Kaffirland. On the south, it is bounded by the Indian Ocean; on the west by the Atlantic. The total area is about 201,000 square miles, with a population of 560,000. 'It enjoys a climate which may perhaps be called without exaggeration the most salubrious known; that is, the most adapted to the human constitution in general without distinction of race, and one of the most delightful.'[1] The vines, silk, fruits, and corn of Southern Europe flourish in this colony. It is rich in flocks and herds, besides the more doubtful advantage that gold and diamonds have been found in some parts of its soil.

The Cape is an agricultural colony;[2] and it is a representative colony, having received a charter in 1853, which established Representative Government. Responsible Government has not yet been introduced there. According to the present constitution of the colony[3] the Governor is now assisted by an Executive Council, composed of certain office-holders appointed by the Crown. There is a Legislative Council of twenty-one elected members,

---

[1] Merivale, p. 116.   [2] See this term explained, p. 48, supra.
[3] 'Colonial Office List' for 1871.

presided over, *ex-officio*, by the Chief Justice, and a House of Assembly of sixty-six elected members, representing the country districts and towns of the colony. The Colonial Secretary, the Attorney-General, the Treasurer-General, and the Auditor-General, who are members of the Executive Council, can take part in the debates of the Legislative Council and House of Assembly; they cannot vote in either House; but in the House of Assembly they are allowed to introduce measures. There is an election at the end of every five years for the Council, when eight and seven members are elected alternately. The qualification for members is possession of immovable property of 2,000*l.*, or movable property worth 4,000*l.* With the exception of paid office-holders and others specified in the Order in Council, any person may be elected a member of Assembly. Members of both Houses are elected by the same voters, who are qualified by possession of property, or receipt of salary or wages, of not less than 50*l.* per annum or not less than 25*l.* with board and lodging.

NATAL.

This young and promising colony was at first (1843) an offshoot and subordinate member of the Cape Colony, from which it is distant about 600 miles. The territory received its name of 'Natal' from having been discovered by Vasco da Gama on Christmas Day 1497.

In 1856 Natal was erected into a distinct and separate colony.[1] It is within the second of the three classes in which British Colonies are officially arranged according to their modes of government. Its affairs are administered by a Lieutenant-Governor, assisted by an Executive Council, composed of the chief justice, the senior officer in command of the troops, the colonial secretary, the treasurer, the attorney-general, and the secretary for native affairs; and a Legislative Council, composed of four official members, viz., the colonial secretary, the treasurer, the attorney-general, and the secretary for native affairs, and twelve members elected by the counties and boroughs.

The elected members of Council hold their seats for four years from date of election, unless the Council is dissolved by the Governor. There are eight electoral districts, and possession of property to the value of 50l., or rents from property of an annual value of 10l., entitle a man to a vote; the usual provisions respecting the disqualification of aliens and others hold good. No person can be elected a member of Council unless he is a duly qualified and registered elector, nor unless he shall have been invited to become a candidate for election

[1] See p. 69, supra.

by at least ten electors of the county or borough which it is proposed he shall represent; nor unless such requisition shall have been transmitted to the resident magistrate at least fourteen days before the election.[1]

Natal has an area of about 16,145 square miles. Its sea-board is 170 miles extent. The coast region, extending about twenty-five miles inland, is very fertile, and has a climate perfectly healthy. Sugar, coffee, tobacco, and cotton, and other products of tropical countries, thrive abundantly. The midland district is well adapted for cereals and other usual European crops. Coal, copper ore, iron, and other minerals, are found in several places, and there is little doubt that when the great mountain range is properly explored it will be found very rich in mineral wealth. Large forests of valuable timber abound along the mountain slopes.

The population of Natal was estimated in 1866 at nearly 200,000, of whom 20,000 were of European race, and 170,000 were Zulu Kaffirs.

SIERRA LEONE, GAMBIA, CAPE COAST CASTLE, AND LAGOS.

Our other African possessions, the names of which are given above, are small and unimportant.

---

[1] 'Colonial Office List' for 1871.

They are all Crown colonies, and all are situate along the West coast of Africa. All are unhealthy for Europeans. Sierra Leone is the chief of these West African colonies.

ASIATIC COLONIES.

The principal British possession in Asia (not included in India) is the island of CEYLON, a Crown colony.[1] Ceylon has an area of 25,742 square miles, being less than Ireland by about one-sixth. The soil is generally poor; and the climate of five-sixths of the island is unfavourable for Europeans who reside there for any long consecutive period of years. But there is a mountain zone (which has an area of about 4,212 miles) with a climate remarkably healthy for Europeans. The children of English parents thrive there in ruddy health and strength, such as we see among the peasant children in the best parts of England.

The greater number of the Europeans in Ceylon (exclusive of the military) are engaged in coffee-planting; and Ceylon may be regarded as a plantation colony. The labour for the coffee-estates is almost entirely supplied by Tamil coolies from

[1] A Crown colony is officially defined as being one in which the Crown has the entire control of legislation, while the administration is carried on by public officers under the control of the Home Government.

the Indian coast, who usually, but not invariably, return to their own country with their earnings, after having worked for two or three seasons. The Singhalese natives form the bulk of the non-European inhabitants, but there is also a large permanent population of Tamil origin · speaking the Tamil language.

The maritime districts of the island were occupied by the Portuguese and the Dutch successively, before the island came into the power of the British. In these districts, and especially in the towns, there is a large number of inhabitants of mixed race; that is to say, partly of native and partly of European origin. These 'Eurasians' (which is the name generally given to those sprung from unions between Europeans and Asiatics) are in Ceylon termed 'Burghers.'

The English conquered and took possession of the Dutch settlements in Ceylon in 1795 and 1796. By royal proclamation, dated September 23, 1799, it was ordered 'that, for the present and during His Majesty's will and pleasure, the temporary administration of justice and police in the settlements of the island of Ceylon, now in His Majesty's dominion, and in the territories and dependencies thereof, should, as nearly as circumstances will permit, be exercised by the British Governor in conformity to the laws and institutions, that subsisted under the ancient Government of the United Provinces, subject to such deviations, in consequence of sudden and unforeseen emergencies, or to such expedients and useful alterations, as may render a departure therefrom either absolutely necessary and unavoidable, or evidently beneficial and desirable.' The same proclamation directed that the practice of torture in criminal trials should cease, and also the practice of punishing by mutilation, and other barbarous modes of punishment. The proclamation commanded that all criminal proceedings should thenceforth be public and held in open court. It contained further the following important clause as to liberty of conscience :—' We do hereby allow liberty of conscience and the free exercise of religious worship to all persons who inhabit and frequent the said settlements of the Island of Ceylon, provided always that they quietly and peaceably enjoy the same without offence or scandal to government.'

Ceylon was for a short time made, for purposes of government, part of the Indian Presidency of Madras; but in 1801 it was made a separate colony.

The territories of the Kandyan kings in the interior of Ceylon had remained under native rulers during the Portuguese and Dutch times, though the warfare between Europeans and Kandyans was almost incessant. In 1815 the outrages and insults of the then Kandyan king brought on a war between him and the British, in which Kandy was conquered, and the whole island was thus brought under British dominion.. A rebellion of the Kandyans broke out in 1817, which led to their more complete subjugation. The Governor's proclamation, which was issued after the suppression of this rebellion, declared ' that every Kandyan, be he of the highest or lowest class, is secured in his life, liberty, and property from encroachment of any kind or by any person, and is only subject to the laws, which will be administered according to the ancient and established usages of the country, and in such manner and by such authorities and persons as in the name and on behalf of His Majesty is therein declared.'

The proclamation also announced that, ' As well the priests as all the ceremonies and processions of the Budhoo religion shall receive the respect which in former times was shown them; at the same time, it is in no wise to be understood that the protection of Government is to be denied to the peaceable exercise by all other persons of the religion which they respectively profess, or to the erection under due license from His Excellency of places of worship in proper situations.'

It would be improper to speculate on any attempt of the Crown to withdraw the concessions and promises thus given, when first the maritime provinces(i. e. all Ceylon except the Kandyan territories), and afterwards when the Kandyan territories were acquired by the Crown by means of conquest.[1] Within those self-imposed restrictions the Crown can introduce any law or laws in the colony, and can alter as it pleases the local, political, and military administration by which the colony is managed.

The legislative power of the Crown has frequently been exercised in Ceylon. At one time the Crown's legislative authority was delegated to the Governor alone, then to the Governor and a Council; and the composition and functions of this Council have been from time to time changed.[2] The Crown has also always retained its power of legislating and governing by Royal Charter, and by Orders in Council, that is, by orders issued in Her Majesty's Council at home.

The Roman-Dutch law, as it prevailed in the colony at the time of the conquest of the maritime provinces, is still substantially the law of Ceylon. English law, however, has been introduced as to important matters, including the laws of shipping,

[1] These pledges have been more than once ratified and repeated. Thus the ordinance 5, 1835 (confirmed by the Crown), declares that the laws and institutions which subsisted under the ancient Government of the United Provinces, shall continue to be administered, subject nevertheless to such alterations as have been or shall be hereafter by lawful authority ordained. The same ordinance repeats the pledge to allow liberty of conscience and free exercise of religious worship to all persons quietly and peaceably enjoying the same without offence to Government.

[2] See Thomson's 'Institutes of the Laws of Ceylon,' vol. i. p. 3.

A A

of bills of exchange and promissory notes, and of evidence generally. Trial by jury in serious criminal cases has been long established. The Kandyans retain mainly their old laws and customs. In the numerous matters which now arise for adjudication in the Kandyan provinces, on which there was no native law, the same law as that which exists in the rest of the island is now in force.

The Moors also have their own Mohammedan law as to sacrifice, marriage, and other matters ; and there is a special code of Indian law in similar matters in force for the Tamils.

In trials by jury the jurors are thirteen in number, and the verdict of a majority is sufficient.

A Council of Government was established by Royal Letters Patent in 1831. It was modified in 1833, and the Government was then made nearly the same as it is at present.

The Government is administered by a Governor, aided by an Executive Council of five members, viz., the Officer commanding the Troops, the Colonial Secretary, the Queen's Advocate, the Treasurer, and the Auditor-General ; and a Legislative Council of fifteen members, including the members of the Executive Council, four other officeholders, and six unofficial members nominated by the Governor.

The Executive Council has the general duty of assisting the Governor by its advice. In various cases by local enactments he is required to act with this advice.

In the Legislative Council no vote or resolution can be passed, and no question be admitted to debate there, when the object of such ordinance, resolution, or question is to dispose of or charge any part of the revenue of the island, unless the Governor shall have first proposed such legislation.

Ceylon costs England nothing. The colony pays 160,000*l.* per annum to the Imperial Government for the expense of military protection.

The value of imports into the island, in 1869, was 4,635,023*l.* The value of its exports in the same year was 3,631,065*l.* The exports consist chiefly of coffee, cocoa-nut oil, cinnamon, and plumbago.

The revenue of the colony has increased, without any fresh item of taxation, from 476,273*l.* in 1855, to 1,091,606*l.* in 1870.

A census has been taken in Ceylon during the present year (1871). Its details are not yet known, but the total population of the whole island is announced to amount to 2,405,287.

STRAITS SETTLEMENTS.

Proceeding eastward from Ceylon, we come to the Straits Settlements of Singapore, Penang, and Malacca. They were formed under the Indian Government, but were transferred to the control of the Colonial Secretary in 1867, by an order in Council, made pursuant to the Statute 29 and 30 Vict. c. 115.

The seat of government for the collective colony is at Singapore. Penang and Malacca have each their Lieutenant-Governor.

The general governing body of the colony consists of a Governor, aided by an Executive and Legislative Council: the latter body comprises eleven official members and five unofficial members, appointed by the Governor. It is a Crown colony.

The population, estimated at about 275,000, is very mixed. There are Malays, Chinese, Bengalese, Arabs, Burmese, Siamese, and numerous mixed breeds. The number of Europeans is small; and from the nature of the climate is never likely to be considerable. The commercial exports and imports are very large.

Malacca was first occupied by the Portuguese, then by the Dutch, and then by the English. After being in our temporary possession more than once, it was finally ceded to us by treaty in 1824.

Penang was ceded by a native prince to the Indian Government in 1786.

Singapore was occupied by the British in 1819.

To the north-east of the Straits lies the island of LABUAN, near the north-west coast of Borneo. Labuan was ceded to Great Britain by the Sultan of

Bruni in 1846. It abounds in coals, and has a good harbour.

This little Crown colony has a population of about 4,000. It has an area of 45 square miles. It is ruled by a Governor and a Legislative Council of three members.

HONG KONG.

Northward of Labuan lies the Crown colony of Hong Kong. It is one of a number of islands lying off the south-eastern coast of China, near the mouth of the Canton river. It was ceded to Great Britain by treaty in 1841. Its colonial charter was granted in 1842. It is little more than a factory for British commerce, and a military and naval station for the protection of the British engaged in trade with China.

The Governor is aided by an Executive Council of the chief official personages, and by a Legislative Council composed of four official and four non-official members nominated by the Crown.

MAURITIUS.

The island of Mauritius, in the Indian Ocean, is usually reckoned among Asiatic colonies. It was taken from the French in 1810, and ceded to the British, by the Treaty of Paris, in 1814. It is a

Crown colony, and it is a plantation colony. Its population on December 31, 1869, was 322,924, of whom 206,771 were Indian coolies imported for the sugar estates. It comprises an area of 708 square miles, without the Seychelles group, Roderigues, and a number of other small dependencies, about sixty in number.

Mauritius is governed by a Governor, assisted by an Executive Council of three members; that is, of the Colonial Secretary, of the Procureur or Advocate-General, and of the officer in command of the troops. There is also a Legislative Council, consisting of seven official and ten non-official members; the former comprising the three Executive members above spoken of, and the Collector of Customs, Auditor-General, Treasurer, and Collector of Internal Revenues; the latter ten non-official members are chosen from the landed proprietors of the island, and submitted to her Majesty in Council for approval and confirmation.

THE WEST INDIES.

The British possessions in the West Indies were long regarded as much more important to this country than they are considered to be at present. So long as the colonial system [1] flourished—that is to

---

[1] See p. 126 and 146, supra.

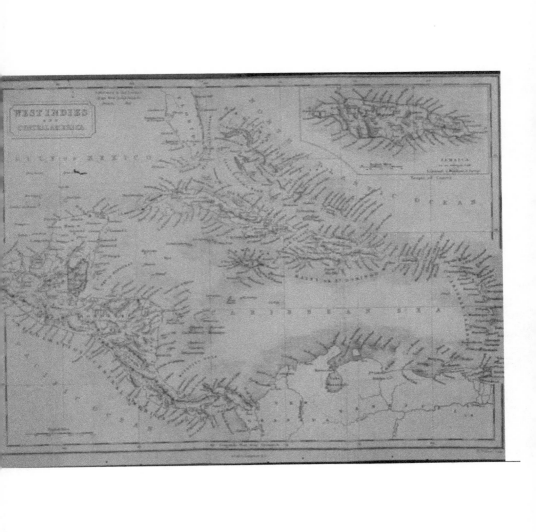

say, until about half a century ago—we looked to
these islands exclusively for our supplies of sugar,
rum, and other articles, and we protected them jealously against the competition of foreign rivals.

All this is now changed, and a still greater change
in the condition of these islands and their inhabitants was made by our abolition of slavery in 1833.
All these islands had been plantation colonies, and
the raising articles of tropical produce in them for
consumption here had been almost entirely carried on
by the labour of negro slaves.

They are now regarded with little interest by
Englishmen, excepting those who, by inheritance or
otherwise, have property there. But they deserve,
and will probably before long receive much more
attention from British statesmen, and from the
British public. This is especially the case with regard to Jamaica, which is in all respects of more
value than the rest of the British West Indies put
together. I have lately heard it said on very high
authority that 'Jamaica has a future;' and I hope to
show cause for expecting that future to be a bright
one. I shall take Jamaica first, and deal with it
somewhat at large. With regard to the other West
Indian colonies much briefer notices will be sufficient.

In the chapter on the North American colonies
we had occasion to mark the introduction of negro
slavery into the plantations, the institution and the

long prevalence and the final demolition of the Navigation Laws and of the old colonial system of trade.[1] These things all apply to the West Indies as well as to the colonies on the North American continent, and it would be superfluous to repeat the narrative here.

The abolition of slavery throughout the British Empire has also been incidentally mentioned; but this affected the West Indies so specially, that the subject must be now again adverted to.

Previously, however, to doing so, it should be stated that nearly all our West Indian possessions (excepting some of the smaller and most recently acquired) had, almost as soon as they became British Colonies, received constitutions, which were intended to imitate those of the mother country. ' The Governor was the viceroy of the Crown; the Legislative Council, or Upper Chamber, appointed by the Governor, assumed the place of the House of Peers; and the Lower House insisted on the privileges of the Commons, especially that of originating all taxes and grants of money for the public service. The elections were also conducted after the fashion of the mother country.'[2]

These institutions were theoretically excellent, but, unfortunately, in the West Indies, the necessary

<hr>

[1] See pp. 124, 179, supra.
[2] Sir Erskine May, ' Constitutional History,' vol. ii. p. 549.

materials for their salutary practical operation were deficient. The very great majority of the inhabitants were slaves; and there was in none of these islands a middle-class population numerous enough and influential enough to supply sound elements for a popular second chamber. Representative institutions very rarely worked well in the West Indian islands. In the most important island, Jamaica, they worked specially ill.

For a very long time England, while considering itself to be highly enlightened and civilised, looked (as other enlightened and civilised European States looked) complacently and approvingly on the existence of slavery in the West Indian colonies, and on the vigorous practice of the slave-trade, by which these colonies received fresh supplies of servile negro population. It was even thought laudable policy to become slave-carriers for other nations. Statesmen of all parties, in the early part of the last century, thought it patriotic to obtain for England the 'Assiento,' as it was termed, that is the lucrative monopoly of bringing negroes from West Africa to the Spanish American Dominions.

Towards, however, the end of the century, men were found who thought and spoke differently; and they were men whose words were weighty. Dr. Johnson was one of the first of them. Wilberforce and other statesmen also came forward who gave a practical co-operation in Parliament to the strong efforts which Clarkson, Zachary Macaulay, Stephen, and others, were making against the maintenance of the slave trade. An Act prohibiting British subjects from engaging in any way in the slave trade was passed in 1807. Then the struggle was continued for the overthrow of slavery itself, which was effected in 1833. In that year an Act was passed by the Imperial Parliament, by which slavery was abolished in all British colonies ; and twenty millions sterling were voted as compensation to the slave-holders.[1]

This abolition of slavery was emphatically an Imperial act. The local authorities struggled against it almost to the last. And when it is urged (as it sometimes is still urged) by advocates of the old West India Proprietary interest, that the change was too sudden and too violent, it is to be remembered that the Home Government had, both long before and a little before the Slavery Abolition Act, attempted measures, which would have led to the amelioration of the condition of the slaves and to their ultimate emancipation, but these measures were obstructed by the local authorities. In 1823 the Imperial House of Commons, on the motion of Mr. Canning, passed a series of Resolutions respecting the negro slaves in the West Indies, the effect of which, if carried out,

---

[1] I have not space to describe the attempted intermediate state of Negro-apprenticeship, which was speedily abandoned.

would have resulted in abolishing the use of the lash in the field, or its application, under any circumstances, to females; regulating the punishment of refractory slaves; preventing the separation, by sale, of husband, wife, and children; protecting the property of slaves; admitting their evidence in courts of justice, facilitating their manumission, and providing for their religious instruction by a regular ecclesiastical establishment, with two bishops at its head, one presiding over Jamaica, the other over the Leeward Islands. The resolutions of the House of Commons were laid before the King; and Royal Orders in council were issued ordaining their observance. The local legislatures of the Colonies met these directions by angry resolutions against the attempt made to coerce their constitutional rights by votes of one of the Houses of Parliament, and by the prerogative of the Crown. On the point of Constitutional Law the colonists were right; but on the moral merits of the controversy it now seems marvellous that there could have been any difference of opinion.

Eight years afterwards, the English Ministry (Lord Grey's Reform Bill Ministry) caused Orders in Council to be issued, which limited and fixed the hours during which the slaves were to be required to work, appointed officers called 'Protectors of the Slaves,' who were to watch against abuse of power by the masters, and which also contained ' other regulations calculated to prepare the slaves gradually for enfranchisement '[1] Certain commercial and fiscal privileges were offered to such of the Representative colonies as might adopt these Orders. There was no readiness among the colonists to do so; and a rumour spread among the slave population that the King of England had granted their freedom, but that it was wrongfully withheld from them by their masters. A negro insurrection in Jamaica (perhaps the worst of the numerous servile outbreaks of which that island has been the scene) was the result of this rumour; and, when the insurrection was quelled, the West Indian proprietors were more and more vehement in their protests against the attempts of the British Government to interfere with their private property, meaning thereby their negro slaves.

But on the other hand, an uncompromising anti-slavery feeling had now become general and vehement among the British public; and one of the earliest results of the passing of the Reform Bill was the abolition of slavery by the Imperial Parliament, as already mentioned.

Large as the sum of twenty millions was, which was voted by way of compensation to the slave-holders, it proved inadequate to save the owners of West Indian property generally from calamitous re-

[1] Alison's 'History of Europe,' vol v. p. 418.

verses of fortune. All the colonists did not suffer equally. Barbadoes and Antigua declined less than any of the other islands in material prosperity. Mr. Merivale, at pages 314 to 341 of his work on Colonisation, has pointed out the causes of the exceptional condition of these two colonies after the abolition of slavery.

I will now deal with the West Indian colonies separately, beginning with

JAMAICA.

This beautiful island is the largest, and by far the most valuable, of the British West Indies. Cromwell's conquest of it from the Spaniards in 1655 has been already mentioned. It had a Representative Constitution, which came to an end in 1866; after it had lasted for nearly 200 years. The Jamaica Legislature voted the abolition of their constitution, and this was confirmed by an Act of the Imperial Parliament.

At present there is in Jamaica a Legislative Council, consisting of official and unofficial members. The official members are the senior military officer, the Colonial Secretary, the Attorney-General, together with such other officers or persons as Her Majesty may think fit, and certain unofficial members, not exceeding six in number.

There is also established a Privy Council.

The members of the Privy Council are, the Lieutenant-Governor, or senior military officer in command, the Colonial Secretary, the Attorney-General, and such other persons, not to exceed eight in number, who may be named by the Queen, or provisionally appointed by the Governor, subject to the approval of Her Majesty.

The area of Jamaica is 4,256 square miles. It has a coast-line of more than 500 miles, and numerous harbours, five of which are excellent. Scarcely any part of the island is more than thirty miles from the sea.

The climate is hot, and unhealthy for Europeans in the lower plains along the southern coast; it is less so on the northern coast. But by far the greater part of the island is of considerable height above the sea-level. The surface varies. There are numerous ranges of hills, which in the eastern part rise to the dignity of mountains. There are also numerous plateaux and table-lands, of considerable extent and of great fertility. The hill-sides and the valleys have a rich soil, and are well wooded; and nearly all the districts of the interior have the benefit of numerous rivers, streams, and springs. Europeans can enjoy permanent health and strength in many of these regions. We are apt to talk and to think of Jamaica as a mere sugar-island;

but it also produces Indian corn abundantly, two, and sometimes three crops being raised within the year. It supplies also arrowroot, pimento, coffee, tobacco, and many other valuable products of its rich and easily cultivated soil. Its wealth in timber is very great. Horned cattle, sheep, goats, swine, and nearly all kinds of poultry thrive and multiply.[1]

Yet with all these natural resources, Jamaica has never ranked higher than a mere plantation colony. The reasons of this have been, first, the pernicious effect of the extensive introduction of slave-labour; and, next, the gross mismanagement of the vast tracts of unoccupied land which existed in the island when it became a British possession.

Our misgovernment in this respect began early. The greater part of the island was recklessly granted away by the Crown, as lord of the manor, to various members and dependents of the great English families. The grants were made on the condition of paying a trifling annual quit-rent. Many of the recipients of these grants (the Patentees as they were called) never took possession under them. The descendants and representatives of other patentees abandoned their properties in the island when its affairs became unprosperous.

[1] It is satisfactory to read in one of the present Governor, Sir John Grant's despatches, ' that the old Jamaica planters' prejudice, which treated as baneful to the colony all attempts to turn attention to anything but sugar-cultivation, is fast expiring.'

During the slavery times little attention was paid
to the existence of these large territories in Jamaica
without occupants or managers, but not without
owners, though the particular owners of each district
were generally unknown. But negro emancipation
created in the island a large free peasant population.
These free blacks were eager to acquire land; they
were willing and anxious to pay purchase-money, if
a vendor with a title could be found, so as to give
them security of tenure. They naturally applied to
the local Governments to sell them the waste lands.
But the title to almost every block of land was
known to be outstanding in some indeterminate
absentee; and the Government could neither transfer
the land to desirous and desirable purchasers, nor
prevent the land from being occupied by squatters.
Ever and anon a reappearing owner, or some one
pretending to act by an owner's authority, would
assert an owner's rights by evicting the squatters,
sometimes under circumstances of very great hardship.

A wise attempt was made at one time by the
Legislature of Jamaica to recover some of the waste
lands for the Crown, by a law that land granted on
quit-rents should be forfeited, if the quit-rents were
left unpaid for a certain number of years. A particular officer was appointed in Jamaica for the
receipt of these quit-rents, and it was ordained that

unless the books of the officer showed payment of quit-rent within the prescribed time, the land should be held forfeit to the Crown. But this salutary system was soon neglected; and when the lately-appointed Government directed search to be made at the Receiver-General's, in order to ascertain what lands might be made available for State purposes, it was found that the quit-rents' books had not been kept up, so as to supply the necessary legal evidences.

Considerable improvement in these matters has been made of late; but the land-question is still Jamaica's great difficulty. Its present Governor, when speaking in December 1867, of the prospects of an advance in the material wealth and prosperity of the colony, observed, ' If only some reasonable settlement of the land-question were effected, I am convinced that the advance would be astonishing.'[1]

In the latest Parliamentary Report[2] the official statement as to land is as follows:—

' The area of the island is about 2,720,000 acres: of these 492,246 acres are ascertained to be cultivated, leaving 2,227,754 acres set down as uncultivated.

' Of the uncultivated land quit-rent was paid on 1,138,205 acres: leaving upwards of a million of

[1] Reports on Colonial Possessions, Part I., West Indies, p. 8.
[2] Report for 1869, presented to Parliament 1871.

acres, including unpatented lands as well as abandoned properties, on which quit-rent has not been collected.'

The other source of the difficulties of Jamaica, that arising from long-continued negro slavery and from the immediate effects of emancipation, is fast disappearing. Since Jamaica has been under her present government, as a Crown colony, there have been no disturbances of any kind. All the despatches speak of all classes of the community being peaceable and tranquil. The financial documents also show clearly the return of prosperity, or rather the dawn of a new prosperity far better than the old. The year 1867-68 showed a small surplus, 'being the first year in the history of the colony for an indefinite period in which there was not a deficit.' The year 1868-69 gave a surplus of 58,896l.

The population of Jamaica at the last-mentioned date is stated [1] to have been

White.	Mixed Race.	Black.	Total.
13,816	81,074	346,374	441,264

The most cheering sign in the state of Jamaica is the improved and improving condition of the free negroes. They are orderly, industrious, intelligent, and contented. The common idea respecting the Negro race is that, if not under compulsion, they will work just enough to procure a few yams or some

[1] Colonial Office List, 1871.

other easily-reared vegetable, that perhaps they will undertake a little more work for the sake of some spirits or a little finery, and that then they will give themselves up to torpor, varied only by childish pastime or brutish drunkenness. But the Jamaican Black has the wants of a higher civilisation; and he works to supply those wants. His wife and his children, as well as himself, must be well-fed, and also what he thinks well-clad. His house must have comforts, and even some ornaments. At present, though he will hoe and dig, and do other agricultural work for himself, he is very reluctant to do for others the field work which was formerly the special department of slaves. The existence of this feeling is at present a great impediment in the way of employers, but it is not to be wondered at, and in process of time it may be expected to disappear.

Above all, the Jamaican Black appreciates education, and is willing to pay a tax to enable the State to educate his children. Can we say as much of all our countrymen in England ?[1]

[1] These statements as to the present state and the prospects of Jamaica, and as to the Free Blacks there, are partly based on recent Parliamentary Blue Books; but I have made very great use of valuable information supplied to me by Mr. H. Irving, who is now Colonial Secretary in Ceylon, and was lately Colonial Secretary in Jamaica.

ANTIGUA

is the most important of the Leeward Islands, and the residence of the Governor-in-Chief of the British portion. It lies in 17° 6′ N. lat. and in 61° 45′ W. long., and is about 54 miles in circumference, its area being about 108 square miles, of which half are under cultivation. The population at the last census in 1861 was 37,125. Antigua was discovered by Columbus in 1493, who named it after a church in Seville, Sta. Maria la Antigua. It was first inhabited by a few English in 1632. Subsequently, in 1663, a grant of it was made by Charles II. to Lord Willoughby, who sent out a large number of colonists. After an interval of French occupation, it was declared a British possession by the treaty of Breda in 1666. It is a Representative colony. According to the 'Colonial Register' for 1871, it is proposed to establish a Federation of the British Leeward Islands under one Government—namely, Antigua, St. Christopher, Nevis, Dominica, Montserrat, and the Virgin Islands; and the following resolutions, embodying the terms of the Federation, passed the Legislature of Antigua by unanimous vote in June 1870:—

Whereas it is expedient, for the more efficient and economical government of the Leeward Islands, to restore the ancient union of the said islands under one Government in such a simplified form as may be

adapted to the circumstances of the present time:
Be it therefore Resolved:

1. There shall be established a General Legislative Council for the Leeward Islands.

2. The said Council shall consist of twenty members—namely, a President appointed by the Governor from one of the Local Legislatures, and three *ex-officio* members, six nominated members, and ten members elected by the several Legislatures of Antigua, St. Kitts, Dominica, and Nevis.

3. Five of such members shall represent this island.

4. The representative members for this island shall be selected for the purpose from the Legislative Council thereof.

5. For this island one of such members shall be nominated by the Crown, four of the members shall be chosen by the elected members of the Council; in both cases the members may be chosen from the elected, nominated, and official members indifferently.

6. Questions arising in the General Legislative Council shall be decided by a majority of voices, and the President shall in all cases have a vote; and when the voices are equal the decision shall be deemed to be in the negative.

7. The duration of the Council shall be three years. The Crown to have power to prorogue and dissolve.

BARBADOES.

A Representative colony. It is the most eastward of the Caribbean Islands, and is situated in 13° 4′ N. lat. and 59° 37′ W. long. It is nearly 21 English miles long and 14 in breadth, and comprises an area of 166 square miles. It is supposed to have been first visited by the Portuguese. It has been occupied and held successively by various British owners, under grants from the Crown; but after the restoration of Charles II. the Proprietary Government was dissolved, and the sovereignty of Barbadoes annexed to the British Crown. Population in 1861, 152,127. Barbadoes and Antigua suffered less than any other West India colony in their financial state after Negro Emancipation.

DOMINICA.

A Representative colony, conquered by the English in 1756. A partly Representative House of Assembly granted in 1775. Dominica is about to join the general Federation of the Leeward Islands. (See the notice of Antigua.)

GRENADA.

A Representative colony. After several changes of masters in the wars between the English and French, it was finally assigned to the British in 1783.

MONTSERRAT

is a Representative colony, settled by the English in 1632. It had a Legislative Council and Assembly as early as 1668. It is about to join the Federation of the Leeward Isles. (See Antigua.)

NEVIS, ST. CHRISTOPHER, AND ANGUILLE

have long been united for purposes of Government, and are about to be included in the Leeward Federation.

The form of government of this colony has been Representative. They were occupied by the English in 1623.

ST. LUCIA

is one of the windward division of the Caribbees, situate in 13° 50′ N. lat., and 60° 58′ W. long., at a distance of about 30 miles to the south-east of Martinique, and 21 to the north-east of St. Vincent. It is 42 miles in length and 21 at its greatest breadth; it comprises an area of 250 square miles, and a population in 1866 of 29,519. At the period of its discovery by Columbus, in 1502, it was inhabited by the Caribs, and so continued until taken possession of by the King of France in 1635. In 1639 the English formed their first settlement, but

were all murdered in the following year by the
Caribs. In 1642, the King of France, still claiming
the right of sovereignty, ceded it to the French West
India Company. No island has ever been the scene
of such numerous hostilities and contentions for possession and conquest from the year 1663 to 1803,
when it surrendered on capitulation to General
Greenfield, since which period it has continued
without interruption under British rule. It has Representative Government.

ST. VINCENT.

The island of St. Vincent was discovered by Columbus on January 22, 1498. It is situated in
13° 10′ N. latitude, and 60° 57′ W. longitude, at a
distance of 21 miles to the south-west of St. Lucia.
It is 18 miles in length and 11 in breadth, and contains about 85,000 acres of land. Some of the
Grenadines, a chain of small islands lying between
Grenada and St. Vincent, are comprised within the
government of the latter island. The possession of
St. Vincent was long disputed by the English and
the French. It was finally assigned to England by
the Treaty of Versailles in 1783. It has Representative Government.

TOBAGO

is the most southerly of the Windward group, 11° 9′ N. lat., and 60° 12′ W. long., about 70 miles to the south-east of Grenada, 18½ miles to the north-east of Trinidad, and 120 miles distant from Barbadoes ; it is 32 miles long and from 6 to 12 broad, and has an area of 97 square miles, and a population in 1861 of 15,410. The island was discovered by Columbus in 1498, and by him named ' Assumption ;' it was then occupied by the Caribs. The British flag was first planted here in 1580, and the sovereignty claimed by James I. in 1608. This, like the other West India islands, has been subjected to the various alternations of possession and other vicissitudes of war and conquest; ultimately, in 1803, it was taken possession of by Commodore Hood and General Greenfield, and finally, in 1815, ceded in perpetuity to the British Crown. It is a Representative colony.

TRINIDAD

is the most southerly of the West India islands, lying to the eastward of the continent of South America, between 10° 3′—10° 50′ N. lat., and 61°—62° 4′ W. long.; its length is about 60 miles, its breadth varying from 35 to 44. It is separated from the peninsula of Venezuela by the Gulf of Paria.

It was discovered by Columbus in July, 1498, and thus named by him from the three mountain summits first perceived from the masthead when discovered; but no permanent settlement was made there until 1588. In 1676 the French took possession of it, but soon after ceded it to Spain. In February, 1797, an expedition, under the command of Admiral Harvey and Sir Ralph Abercrombie, was sent out to effect the reduction of Trinidad, which resulted in the surrender of the island. In March 1802, by a definitive treaty, it was ceded to the British. It is a Crown colony.

TURK'S AND CAICOS (Cayos or Keys).

These islands were formerly included among the Bahama group, from which they were separated in 1848; they lie between 21°—22° N. lat., and 71°—72° 30′ W. long. The population in 1861 was 4,372. This also is a Crown colony.

THE VIRGIN ISLANDS.

A group of islands in the West Indies, partly belonging to Denmark, partly to Great Britain, forming a connecting link between the Greater and Lesser Antilles. They consist chiefly of a cluster of rocks. The largest in the group belonging to Great Britain is Tortola, situate in 18° 27′ N. lat., and 64° 40′ W.

long. Such of the islands as are British became so in 1666. This also is a Crown colony.

Besides the colonies already mentioned we possess in or near to America the

BAHAMAS,

a chain of islands lying between 21° 42'—27° 34' N. lat., and 72° 42'—79° 5' W. long. The group consists of about twenty which are inhabited, and of a vast congeries of about 3,000 islets and rocks, comprising an area of 3,021 square miles, and a population of about 40,000. The principal islands are New Providence (containing the capital, Nassau), St. Salvador, Harbour Island, Great Bahama, Long Island, Eleuthera, and Berry Islands. St. Salvador was the first land discovered by Columbus on his voyage in 1492. New Providence was settled by the English in 1629, and held by them till expelled by the Spaniards in 1641, who, however, made no attempt to settle there. It was again colonised by the English in 1657, but fell into the hands of the French and Spaniards in 1703, after which it became a rendezvous for pirates, who were eventually extirpated in 1718, and a regular colonial administration was established. In 1781 the Bahamas were surrendered to the Spaniards, but at the conclusion of the war were once more annexed, and finally confirmed to Great Britain by the Peace of Versailles in 1783. The colony has a Representative House of Assembly.

THE BERMUDAS,

or Somers Islands, are a cluster of about 300 small islands, on the western side of the Atlantic Ocean, in lat. 32° 15′ N. and long. 64° 51′ W., at a distance of about 580 miles from the nearest land, in North Carolina.

Fifteen or sixteen of these islands are inhabited; the rest are of inconsiderable size, the largest, or Bermuda proper, containing less than 20 square miles of land, and nowhere exceeding three miles in breadth.

The climate is remarkably mild and healthy. They were first colonised by the English under Admiral Sir George Somers, who was shipwrecked here in 1609, on his way to Virginia. On his report, the Virginia Company claimed them, and obtained a charter for them from James I. in 1612. This company sold their right for 2,000l. to an association of 120 persons, who obtained a new charter in 1616, incorporating them as the Bermuda Company, and granting them very extensive powers and privileges.

Representative Government was introduced in 1620.

BRITISH GUIANA,

sometimes called Demerara, is part of the continent of South America. It includes the settlements of Demerara, Essequibo, and Berbice. It was first partially settled by the Dutch West India Company in 1580. It was from time to time held by Holland, France, and England. It was restored to the Dutch in 1802, but in the following year retaken by Great Britain, to whom it was finally ceded in 1814. It is of great extent, and has much natural wealth; but the climate is unfavourable to Europeans. It has a Representative Government of a very complicated character.

THE FALKLAND ISLANDS

lie far to the South in the Atlantic Ocean. Their total area is about 7,000 square miles. Their climate is remarkably healthy, and European animals and vegetables thrive in them. They were occupied for brief periods by French and Spaniards in the last century; but in 1771 the sovereignty of them was given up to the British. We made no settlement there until 1833, when we took effective possession of them for the sake of protecting the whale fishery. They form a Crown colony.

HONDURAS.

British Honduras is a province on the east coast of Central America. It is very rich in logwood and mahogany, which induced many adventurers from Jamaica and other British colonies to frequent it. In 1861 it was made a colony subordinate to Jamaica; but in 1870 it was made a colony of itself. It has no representative institutions.

Far out in the ocean, between South America and Africa, lies the island of St. Helena. St. Helena was transferred from the East India Company to the direct government of the British Crown in 1833. It is rather a naval station than a colony. Its total population is under 7,000.

It is enough merely to mention the naval and military stations of Gibraltar and Malta, in Europe; and also the little island of Heligoland, in the North Sea. Heligoland is the only one of the three that can be called a colony, and it is on a very small scale; its population when last reckoned, was under 2,000. It thrives chiefly as a bathing-place for visitors in summer.

CHAPTER VIII.

CONCLUSION.

General Bonds of Union between the Colonies and the Imperial Government—Through what Officers the Crown regulates Colonial Affairs—Secretaries of State for the Colonies—Colonial Appointments, how made—Governors and other Officials—Troops in Colonies, how commanded—Competitive Examinations, how far applied to Colonial Appointments.

We have now gone through a long list of colonies and other transmarine possessions, showing great dissimilarities in their institutions when merely compared with each other, or when tested with reference to the closeness of their relations with the Imperial State. Some of these—that is to say, the important colonies, which have Responsible Governments—may appear at first sight to have very little practical subordination to the British dominion; but it will be found that there are certain links, and very important links, which bind *all* the outlying portions of our empire together.

1. There is the indisputable omnipotence of the Imperial Parliament over the whole empire, and over every part thereof, whether colony, dependency, province, or outpost.

2. Every law made by a colonial Legislature is

liable to be disallowed and rendered null by the British Crown.

3. The Crown appoints all the Governors.

4. It depends on the Crown and the Imperial Parliament whether the whole empire, and each and every part of the empire, shall be at peace or at war with any foreign Power. The limited right of commencing hostilities, which is delegated to the Governor-General of India, is the only exception to this rule.

5. The Crown is the supreme fountain of justice, to which ultimate appeals from all the judicatures of the colonies and other dependencies are preferred.

These powers of the Crown are chiefly exercised through two of Her Majesty's five principal Secretaries of State, through the Secretary of State for the Colonies,[1] and the Secretary of State for India.

---

[1] Formerly there used to be only two Secretaries of State. The Board of Trade then took direct cognisance of colonial affairs, but was obliged to refer to one of the Secretaries of State if executive action on the part of the Home Government was thought necessary. Mr. Bancroft (Hist. American Revolution, vol. i. p. 17) thus describes how badly that system worked :—' The method adopted in England for superintending American affairs, by means of a Board of Commissioners for Trade and Plantations, who had neither a voice in the deliberation of the Cabinet, nor access to the King, tended to involve the colonies in ever-increasing confusion. The Board framed instructions without power to enforce them, or to propose measures for their efficiency. It took cognisance of all events, and might investigate, give information, or advise ; but it had no authority to form an ultimate decision on any political questions whatever. In those days there were two Secretaries of State charged

The functions of the Secretary of State for India have already been described in the chapter on our Indian possessions. The Secretary of State for the Colonies is (like the other principal Secretaries of State) a member of the Cabinet; and is liable to quit office on a change of Ministry. He is assisted

with the management of the foreign relations of Great Britain. The executive power, with regard to the colonies, was reserved to the Secretary of State, who had the care of what was called the Southern Departments, which included the conduct of all relations with the Spanish peninsula and France. The Board of Trade, framed originally to restore the commerce and encourage the fisheries of the metropolis, was compelled to hear complaints from the executive officers in America, to issue instructions to them, and to receive and consider all acts of the colonial legislatures; but it had no final responsibility for the system of American policy that might be adopted. Hence, from their very feebleness, the Lords of Trade were ever ready to express their impatience at contradiction; easily grew vexed at disobedience to their orders, and much inclined to suggest the harshest methods of coercion, knowing that their petulance would exhale itself in official papers, unless it should touch the pride or waken the resentment of the Responsible Minister, the Crown, and Parliament.'

In 1782, when the disturbances in North America were growing very serious, a third Secretary of State, a Secretary for the American or Colonial Department, was appointed. But at the end of the American War in 1783 the new office was abolished; and there remained only the chief Secretaries of State, as before. Their duties were now divided into those of the Home and those of the Foreign Secretary, the Colonial Department being assigned to the share of the Home Secretary.

In 1794 a principal Secretary for War was appointed; and the affairs of the colonies were transferred to the War Secretariate in 1801. In 1854 a principal Secretary of State for the express and sole department for the Colonies was appointed. The fifth principal Secretary of State, the Secretary for India, was added, as already mentioned, in 1858.

C C

by a permanent Under-Secretary of State, not in Parliament, and by another Secretary of State who is usually selected from among the members of that House of Parliament of which his chief is not a member, so that there is always present in each House a colonial minister. The Parliamentary Under-Secretary for the Colonies usually, like his chief, quits office on a change of ministry.

With regard to the appointments to office in the Colonies, it has been already mentioned that the Governor is invariably appointed by the Crown. He also holds office during Her Majesty's pleasure. In practice, 'his tenure of office is, as a rule, confined to a period of six years from the assumption of his duties.'[1] The following official description of his most important general powers is taken from the Rules and Regulations issued by the Colonial Office:—

General Powers of an Officer appointed to conduct a Colonial Government.

22. The powers of every Officer, administering a Colonial Government, are conferred, and his duties for the most part defined in Her Majesty's Commission and the Instructions with which he is furnished. The following is a general outline of the nature of the powers with which he is invested, subject to the special law of each Colony:—

23. He is empowered to grant a pardon or respite to any criminal convicted in the Colonial Courts of justice.

---

[1] Colonial Office List. Rules and Regulations, p. 153.

24. He may pardon persons imprisoned in Colonial Gaols under sentence of a Court-martial; but this is not to be done without consulting the Officer in command of the Forces.

25. He has in general the power of remitting any fines, penalties, or forfeitures, which may accrué to the Queen, but if the fine exceeds 50*l.*, he is in some Colonies only at liberty to suspend the payment of it until Her Majesty's pleasure can be known.

26. The monies to be expended for the Public Service are issued under his warrant, as the law may in each particular case direct.

27. The Governor of a Colony has usually the power of granting licences for marriages, letters of administration, and probate of wills, unless other provision be made by Charter of justice or local law. He has also, in many cases, the presentation to benefices of the Church of England in the Colony, subject to rules hereinafter laid down.

28. He has the power, in the Queen's name, of issuing writs for the election of Representative Assemblies and Councils, of convoking and proroguing Legislative Bodies, and of dissolving those which are liable to dissolution.

29. He confers appointments to Offices within the Colony, either absolute, where warranted by local laws, or temporary and provisional, until a reference has been made to Her Majesty's Government.

30. In Colonies possessing responsible Government he has, with his Council, the entire power of suspending or dismissing public servants who hold during pleasure. In other Colonies he has the power of suspending them from the exercise of their functions under certain regulations, which must be strictly observed, and a limited power of dismissal.

31. He is empowered to administer the appointed oaths to all persons, in Office or not, whenever he may think fit, and particularly the Oath of Allegiance provided by 21 & 22 Vict. c. 48, s. 1.

32. He has the power of granting or withholding his assent to any Bills which may be passed by the Legislative Bodies.

33. But he is required, in various cases, by his Instructions, to reserve such Bills for the Royal Assent, or to assent to them only with a clause suspending their operation until they are confirmed by the Crown. These cases are not defined alike in all Instructions; but they comprise, generally speaking, matters touching the Currency, the Army and Navy, Differential Duties, the effect of

Foreign Treaties, and any enactments of an unusual nature touchng the Prerogative or the rights of Her Majesty's Subjects not resident in the Colony.

34. If anything should happen which may be for the advantage or security of the Colony, and is not provided for in the Governor's Commission and Instructions, he may take order for the present therein.

35. He is not to declare or make war against any foreign State, or against the subjects of any foreign State. Aggression he must at all times repel to the best of his ability; and he is to use his best endeavours for the suppression of piracy.

36. His attention is at all times to be directed to the state of discipline and equipment of Militia and Volunteers in the Colony, and when either Force may be embodied, he should send home monthly Returns, with a particular account of their arms and accoutrements.[1]

When there are any of Her Majesty's troops stationed in a colony, the Governor is titular commander-in-chief of them; but they are under the management and immediate control of the military officer in command; and, if the colony is invaded or assailed, the officer in command assumes the entire military authority over the troops. At other times the Governor determines the objects for which the troops are to be employed, and their distribution; but he is bound to consult, as far as possible, with the officer in command.[2]

Latterly it has been the policy of the Imperial Government to withdraw the Queen's troops from colonies possessing Responsible Government, and to require such colonies to find the means for self-

[1] Colonial Office List Rules and Regulations, p. 153.
[2] See Rules and Regulations, Section 11.

protection against revolts of native tribes, or others, within their boundaries, and against sudden attacks on their frontiers.[1]

With regard to civil appointments in colonies, the rules already cited as to the general powers of Governors show that there is a wide distinction between colonies with Responsible Government, and colonies which are Crown colonies, or representative colonies without Responsible Government. In the Responsible-government colonies, that is to say, in far the greater part of our North American dominions, and in all our Australian dominions, except Western Australia, the control of all public departments is practically placed in the hands of persons commanding the confidence of the local representative legislature. The Governor in such colonies selects the Executive Councillors with reference to the exigencies of representative government, that is to say, with reference to the exigency of being supported by local parliamentary majorities. He appoints to the other public offices on the advice of his executive council, that is to say, of his ministry. 'In no

---

[1] In 1865 an Act of the Imperial Parliament (28 Vict. c. xiv.), called the Colonial Naval Defence Act, authorised the proper Legislative authority in every colony, with the approval of Her Majesty in Council, to provide vessels of war and to raise and maintain seamen and naval volunteers at the expense of the colony.

The colony of Victoria is, I believe, the only one hitherto that has provided itself with a naval force of its own.

appointment is the concurrence of the Home Government requisite."[1]

In other colonies the general scheme of appointment is thus set forth in the Rules and Regulations
in the Colonial Office List:—

In other Colonies Public Offices are generally granted in the
name of Her Majesty, and holden during Her Majesty's pleasure.
In some cases, however, it is specially provided by law that they
shall be granted by the Governor or by the Governor in Council
or by some judicial authority, and in some few cases they are
holden during good behaviour.

The general rule is, that Public Offices of considerable rank,
trust, and emolument, should be granted by an instrument under
the Public Seal of the Colony in Her Majesty's name. The appointment may be made either provisionally, when the instrument
is issued under authority of Her Majesty's General Instructions and
subject to the Royal approval, or absolutely, when the instrument
is issued in pursuance of Her Majesty's Special Instructions, which
Special Instructions are conveyed to the Governor generally in the
form of Warrants under the Royal Sign Manual and Signet.

The distinction between Offices which are, and Offices which are
not, of considerable rank, trust, and emolument, being in itself
vague and indefinite, has been rendered as precise as the nature of
the case admits, by the following distinction. Offices are classed
under three heads:—1, those of which the emoluments do not
exceed one hundred pounds per annum; 2, those of which the
emoluments exceed one hundred and do not exceed two hundred
pounds per annum; 3, and those of which the emoluments exceed
two hundred pounds per annum.

When a vacancy occurs in the first or lowest of the three classes
last mentioned, the Governor, as a general rule, has the absolute
disposal of the appointment, subject only to the condition of reporting every such appointment by the first opportunity.

When a vacancy occurs in the second or middle class, the Gover-

---

[1] Rules and Regulations, p. 152.

nor reports it to the Secretary of State, together with the name and qualifications of the person whom he has appointed to fill it provisionally and intends to fill it finally, which recommendation is almost uniformly followed.

When a vacancy occurs in the third or highest class, the Governor follows the same course as to reporting the vacancy and provisional appointment; but he is distinctly to apprise the object of his choice that he holds the Office in the strictest sense of the word provisionally only until his appointment is confirmed or superseded by Her Majesty. He is at liberty also to recommend a candidate for the final appointment, but it must be distinctly understood that the Secretary of State has the power of recommending another instead. In these cases the confirmation or other final appointment takes place in the form already mentioned, of a warrant under the Royal Sign Manual and Signet.

It is of course impossible to lay down any general rule for deciding in what cases the recommendation of a Governor will, or will not, be ultimately sanctioned and confirmed by the Queen; but in general it may be stated, that Her Majesty will be advised to regard more favourably appointments which are in the nature of promotions of meritorious Public Servants, than appointments made in favour of persons new to the Public Service; and that when any new Office has been created the Governor's recommendation for filling it up will carry with it less weight than in the case of offices which the Governor may have found already established. In the cases of such new Offices there will always be more than usual reason to anticipate that an appointment will be made directly from this country.

In several of the colonies there is an organised Civil Service, resembling the Covenanted Service in India. Members of it usually commence their official career in the lowest grade as 'writers' or 'cadets.' In three of the colonies, these primary appointments are determined by the results of competitive examinations, but not by open competition.

Writers for the Civil Service of Ceylon are selected

after a competitive examination by the Civil Service Commissioners from among candidates, part of whom are nominated by the Secretary of State for the Colonies, and part by the Governor of Ceylon.

Cadets for the Civil Service in Hong Kong are appointed after a competitive examination by the Civil Service Commissioners, from among candidates nominated by the Secretary of State for the Colonies.

The same mode of nomination and examination has been introduced for the appointment of cadets to supply the Civil Service in the Straits Settlements.

Finally, the system of competitive examination has lately been announced as applicable to the appointment to clerkships in the Imperial Colonial Office itself.[1]

[1] See Colonial Office List 1871, p. 204.

APPENDIX

———◆———

THE following extracts from the judgment delivered by Lord Brougham in the Judicial Committee of the Privy Council in the case of '*The Mayor of Lyons* v. *East India Company*,' give valuable instruction as to colonies acquired by cession, and colonies acquired by occupancy, and as to the character in which the East India Company made its entry on the soil of India.

The whole judgment, and the arguments in the case (which also are well worthy of attention), will be found in the first volume of Moore's 'Privy Council Reports,' pp. 175–299.

'It is agreed, on all hands, that a foreign settlement obtained in an inhabited country, by conquest or by cession from a foreign Power, stands in a different relation to the present question, from a settlement made by colonizing, that is, peopling an uninhabited country. In the latter case it is said, that the subjects of the Crown carry with them the laws of England, there being, of course, no *lex loci*; in the former case it is allowed, that the law of the country continues until the Crown or the Legislature changes it. This distinction, to this extent, is taken in all the books. It is one of the six propositions stated in *Campbell* v. *Hall* as quite clear, and no matter of controversy in the case; and it had been laid down in *Calvin's* case, in *Dutton* v.

Howell, in *Blanbrun* v. *Jadd-Salk*, by Lord Holt, delivering the judgment of the Court; and nowhere more distinctly and accurately than in the decision of this Court. Two limitations of this proposition are added, to which it may be material that we should attend. One of these refers to conquests or cessions. In *Calvin's* case an exception is made of infidel countries; for which it is said, in *Dutton* v. *Howell*, that though Lord Coke gives no authority, yet it must be admitted as being consonant to reason. But this is treated in terms as an "*absurdity*" by the Court in *Campbell* v. *Hall*. The other limitation refers to new plantations. Mr. Justice Blackstone says, that only so much of the English law is carried into them by the settlers as is applicable to their situation and to the condition of an infant colony. And Sir William Grant, in *Attorney-General* v. *Stuart*, applies the same exception even to the case of conquered or ceded territories, into which the English law of property has been generally introduced. Upon this ground he held that the Statute of Mortmain does not extend to the colonies governed by the English law, unless it has been expressly introduced there, because it had its origin in a policy peculiarly adapted to the mother country.

'Then, is Calcutta to be considered an uninhabited district, settled by English subjects, or as an inhabited district, obtained by conquest or cession? If it falls within the latter description, has the English law incapacitating aliens ever been introduced? If that law has never been introduced, has there been such an introduction of the English law generally, that those parts which have been introduced draw along with them the law touching aliens? An answer to these three questions, if it do not exhaust the argument, seems to carry us sufficiently near to the conclusion at which we seek to arrive, and it will include a consideration of the only reason for the proposition upon which the judgment below is mainly rested, viz., that the royal prerogative extends necessarily and immediately to all acquisitions, however made, and that the forfeiture of aliens' real estate is parcel of that prerogative.

'I. The district on which Calcutta is built was obtained by purchase from the Nabob of Bengal, the Emperor of Hindostan's lieutenant, at the very end of the seventeenth century. The Company had been struggling for nearly one hundred years to obtain a footing in Bengal, and till 1696 they never had more than a factory here and there, as the French, Danes, and Dutch also had. Till 1678 their whole object was to obtain the power of trading, and it was only then that they secured it by a firman from the Emperor. From that year till 1696 they in vain applied to the Native Government for leave to fortify their factory on the Hoogly; and it was only then that they made a fortification, acting upon a kind of half consent, given in an equivocal answer of the Nabob. Encouraged by the protection which they were thus enabled to afford the natives, many of them built houses, as well as the English subjects; and when the Nabob on this account was about to send a 'cady or judge, to administer justice to these natives, the Company's servants bribed him to abstain from this proceeding. Some years afterwards the Company obtained a grant of more land and villages from the Emperor, with a renewed permission to fortify their factories. During all this period tribute was paid to the Emperor, or his officer the Nabob, first for leave to trade, afterwards as "Zemindars" under the Emperor; and in 1757, the year memorable for the battle of Plassey, the treaty with Jaffeir Ally, indemnifying them for their losses, ceding the French possessions, and securing their rights, and binding them to pay

their revenues like other " Zemindars." Eight years later
they received, likewise from the Native Government, a
grant of the Dewanny or Receivership of Bengal, Bahar,
and Orissa; and of their subsequent progress in power it
is unnecessary to speak.   Enough has been said to show
that the settlement of the Company in Bengal was effected
by leave of a regularly established Government in possession of the country, invested with the rights of sovereignty
and exercising its powers; that by permission of that
Government, Calcutta was founded and the factory fortified, in a district purchased by the owners of the soil, by
permission of that Government, and held under it by the
Company as subjects owing obedience, as tenants rendering
rent, and even as officers exercising by delegation a part
of its administrative authority.   At what precise time,
and by what steps, they exchanged the character of subject for that of sovereign, or rather acquired by themselves,
or with the help of the Crown, and for the Crown, the
rights of sovereignty, cannot be ascertained.   The sovereignty has long since been vested in the Crown, and,
though it was not at first recognised in terms by the
Legislature in 1813, the Act 53 Geo. III. c. 155, s. 95, is
declaratory, and refers to the sovereignty as " undoubted,"
and as residing in the Crown.   But it is equally certain
that, for a long time after the first acquisition, no such
rights were claimed, nor any of the acts of sovereignty
exercised, and that during all that time no English authority existed there, which could affect the land, or bind any
but English subjects.   The Company and its servants were
then in the position of the Smyrna or the Lisbon factories
at the present time.'

INDEX.

power over, 203–217; engages attention of English Parliament, 217; Regulating Act, 217; introduction of English law in, 218–223; the Cornwallis Regulations for, 224; double Government of, 227; native princes become subject-allies, 231; war in generally forced on the English, 236; the North-Western Provinces, 237; changes made in the Company's privileges in 1833; extension of British power in, and in neighbouring countries, 247–250; great public works and legislative and educational improvements, 251; tranquillity always precarious, 253; placed under the immediate dominion of the Crown, 260; present Government of, 261; true principles on which it should be governed, 270; sketch of present political and territorial divisions and Governments, 270; all India is now really within the British Empire, 271; the Governor-General there, 272; his powers, *ibid.*; his Councils, 273; British India Proper, how composed, 279; Regulation and non-Regulation provinces, 286; general area and population of India, 300; present English rule over, 301; civil-servants in, how chosen, 302; probable effects of the Competitive Examinations, 304

Indian History, how to be studied, 194, *note*
— Army, 266, 272
Imperial Parliament, its power, 2, 5; its composition, 34
Ireland, early constitutional state of, 23; its state before the Union, 25; the Union, 27; Catholic Emancipation, 29; how affected by the 1832 Reform Bill, 30; how by the 1868 Reform Bill, 34

JAMAICA conquered by Cromwell, 113; its past and present Constitution, 365; importance formerly attached to it, 359; now unduly slighted, *ibid.*; its area, climate, &c., 366; ill effect of wasteful Crown grants of lands in, 367; its present financial prosperity, 370; good condition of its Free Negroes, 570
James I.'s charters for North and South Virginia, 89, 102; for East Indian Company, 197

James River, 94
Jamestown, 94
Jersey. *See* Channel Islands

LABUAN, a Crown Colony, 356; its area, &c., *ibid.*
Lally-Tolendal, his career in India, 216
Laws in Crown Colonies, 60; in Occupancy Colonies, 66
Lower Provinces of India, their extent and importance, 279

MADRAS, fort built at by East India Company, 199; a corporation there, 202; taken by the French, 214; restored to English, 215
— Presidency, its present area and government, 280
Mahrattas, origin and power of, 212
Maine, whence named, 120
Malta, 57
Mansfield, Lord, his exposition of the Law of Colonies, 163
Martial Law in Virginia, established in James I.'s reign, 96; Lord Bacon's approbation of, 96; abolished in Virginia, 97
Maryland, its colonisation and government, 117
Massachussets, first explored by Capt. Gosnold, 88; settled in 1628, 109; bold liberalism of its early colonists, 110; their religious intolerance, 110; peril under Charles I., 112; favoured by Long Parliament and Cromwell, 113; peril under Charles II., 122
Mauritius, 357
Military force in Colonies, how far under Governor's authority, 388; present policy of withdrawing Imperial military forces from Colonies having Responsible Government, 338
Mogul, emperor, his powers, 198; permits the English to erect factory at Surat, *ibid.*; and at Hooghly, near Calcutta, 199; decay of his power, 206; grants Bengal, Behar, and Orissa to the English East India Company, 216
Montserrat, West Indian Colony, 375
Mysore, present state of, 299

NAPIER, SIR CHARLES, his conquest and administration of Scinde, 247

LONDON: PRINTED BY
SPOTTISWOODE AND CO., NEW-STREET SQUARE
AND PARLIAMENT STREET

CPSIA information can be obtained
at www.ICGtesting.com
Printed in the USA
LVHW101231230223
740172LV00006B/398